WAR WITH THE NEWTS

Karel Čapek

WAR WITH THE NEWTS

Introduction by Ivan Klíma

Northwestern University Press
Evanston, IL

Northwestern University Press
Evanston, Illinois 60208-4210

Originally published in Czech under the title *Valka s mloky* in 1936 by
Fr. Borový, Prague. English translation by M. and R. Weatherall first
published in 1937 by George Allen and Unwin Ltd., London.
Introduction copyright © 1985 by Ivan Klíma. Published 1985 by
Northwestern University Press.

Second printing 1990
First European Classics printing 1996

Printed in the United States of America

ISBN 0-8101-1468-2

Library of Congress Catalog Card Number 88-136681

The paper used in this publication meets the minimum
requirements of the American National Standard for Information
Sciences—Permanence of Paper for Printed Library Materials,
ANSI Z39.48-1984.

Čapek's Modern Apocalypse
by Ivan Klíma

In a span of less than seven years the bit of land that constitutes Bohemia witnessed the births of three writers who were to achieve worldwide renown. Jaroslav Hašek was born in April, 1883, Franz Kafka not quite three months later, and Karel Čapek on January 9, 1890. Although all three came from similar middle-class backgrounds and to a great extent shared a common personal and generational experience, one would be hard put to find three more distinct human and literary types. Kafka was a quiet, orderly, and introverted recluse who seldom ventured beyond his circle of Jewish friends; his terse, often unfinished but always imaginative stories related for the most part to the special reality of his inner world and were written in perfect Prague-style German. Hašek was an eccentric, irresponsible Bohemian anarchist and carouser surrounded by a bunch of equally irresponsible boon companions and drunkards; he cranked out hundreds of carelessly written humoresques that caricatured the contemporary world. Only in *The Good Soldier Schweik* did he step out of the shadows somewhat. Here his language, too, was transformed into brilliant renditions of the vulgar speech of the people. Finally, there was Karel Čapek. At a very early age—he was just 28 in 1918 when the Czechoslovak Republic came into being—he resolved to take partial responsibility for the intellectual and moral level of the new state and brought together the country's intellectual elite (even President of the Republic T. G. Masaryk attended the regular Friday gatherings held in Čapek's home). His works of fantasy and philosophical prose, like his regular newspaper columns, were written in a Czech that was simple and precise, yet so rich that it influenced a significant part of the next generation of writers and journalists.

When I look for something these three men had in common, I find only an unusual frailty, which kept them not only from living out a full lifetime but also from spending their adult years at the side of a woman or in the bosom of a family. It was this genuinely painful condition that inspired most of Kafka's great prose, drove Jaroslav Hašek to join his pals in the beer halls of Prague or to wander off for days, and probably accounted in part for Karel Čapek's consuming interest in public affairs and the fate of mankind.

At the turn of the century Bohemia, and Prague in particular, witnessed the development of a rich cultural life. Not long before, the prevailing atmosphere had been rather narrowly provincial. After a protracted period in which Czech culture and even the Czech language had barely remained alive, it took the better part of the nineteenth century merely to ensure their right to exist. Everything—the Czech Museum, Czech theater, Czech politics, the Academy, Czech publishers—was just getting established, often in a tenacious struggle with authorities. The patriotic public had to have been inspired by these active manifestations of national identity. But the days of this sort of uncritical patriotism were slowly drawing to an end. A new generation of the Czech intelligentsia vowed to judge its efforts not by domestic but by European standards. Czech-German Prague gradually became a cultural center in which Czechs, too, could play an important role. A number of outstanding people came to the university; there was a tremendous rush of publishing activity (literary and artistic journals alone numbered several dozen); and presses vied in the release of new publications in both original and translated form. In those days there was not a single important foreign writer whose latest work could not soon be found in Czech translation.

This activity, however, was still viewed as extraordinary, as something fought for and earned, and thus inspiring. The stimulating atmosphere in which the two languages and cultures met—and, most often, contended—certainly contributed to the development of artists who, after a long hiatus, were once again ready to address the world.

Karel Čapek did not arrive in Prague until the end of his studies at the *gymnasium*. He had spent his childhood in Úpice, a small town in the hills of eastern Bohemia, where his father was a doctor. Čapek often remembered his country childhood in his feuilletons, tales, and other short prose. The world of his longer novels and plays seems to be altogether different. But alongside the philosopher and intellectual who sees all the way to civilization's tragic end, one readily senses in these works a man of the country who watches, in anguish and amazement, the collapse of age-old values and established ways of life, finding danger and portents of destruction in modern man's estrangement from the natural order.

At the age of nineteen, Čapek enrolled in the Philosophy Faculty at Charles University (in subsequent years he studied at the Philosophy Faculty in Berlin and pursued German and English philology at the Sorbonne). It was at this time that he began to publish his first short works of prose. Like his first plays, he wrote these together with his older brother Josef. The early prose certainly bespeaks a scintillating spirit and literary and linguistic gifts, but we do not find in it what was later to become so characteristic of Čapek's work. There is none of his philosophical reflection, none of his splendid storytelling, none of his fantastic and anxious vision. The most powerful experience for Karel Čapek and his generation, as well as their greatest shock, still lay ahead—the First World War.

The suddenness and scope of the war had a searing effect on Europe's young generation. Artists whose works had often shone with admiration for the human spirit and its technical achievements suddenly stood face to face with rampant destruction. Like Franz Kafka, Karel Čapek never experienced combat firsthand. For once, his physical infirmity (rheumatism and a painful gout of the vertebrae which plagued him all his life) brought him some good: he was excused from joining the ranks. However, unlike the totally self-absorbed Kafka and the easy-going Hašek, Čapek experienced the catastrophe of the war with the greatest sense of urgency.

The conclusion of the war and its outcome appeared to make up for all the hardships that had been suffered. After three centuries of domination, the Czechs had once again gained their own independent state. For a while, euphoria overwhelmed all other emotions. Two completely different experiences strongly influenced Čapek's work, the tragedy of the war and the nation's restored independence. A comparison of his prewar and postwar work shows that he now felt much more concern for "what is really happening to the world."[1] This concern, however, shifted between two distant poles. On the one hand, Čapek strove in his journalistic and shorter prose work to help form the spiritual climate of the new republic (there were practically no important events that failed to arouse his interest or impel him to state an opinion). On the other hand, in his novels and dramas he created apocalyptic images and moved his plots toward calamities that threatened mankind's existence.

Of course, there were numerous writers who addressed society prophetically and urged it to follow the "correct" path. Perhaps never had so many manifestoes been written, so many political banalities set to verse, so many topical, politicizing pamphlets published to assert claims of great and engaged activity as in those postwar years. Many of Čapek's literary friends adopted socialist slogans, at least for the time being, in the form in which they arrived from revolutionary Russia, slogans promising that the revolution would be followed by a new, more just and classless society which would put an end to violence and even to the state.

Čapek was too sensitive and responsible to accept the notion that, after all the recent violence, new violence, though now revolutionary, could resolve any human problems. He adopted Masaryk's conception of democracy, which stressed democracy's ethical and simultaneously activist content: "All political striving . . . derives from moral judgments; democracy is a striving against tyranny, against violence . . . . Democratism is founded on work . . . . Modern man acknowledges evolution; a democrat also believes in work, in fine work . . . ."

Čapek accepted as his share of this "fine work" his painstaking journalistic activity. "I consider it a matter of immense importance

---

[1]Later, just after the publication of *War with the Newts*, Čapek himself described his type of creative work in these terms: " . . . literature that does not care about reality or about what is really happening to the world, literature that is reluctant to react as strongly as word and thought allow, is not for me."

to a people how newspapers are produced," he wrote in 1934, "whether well and responsibly, or badly and using means that are culturally and morally debased . . . ." He continued working as a journalist until his death more than twenty years later. Thanks mainly to his efforts, *Lidové noviny* [*The People's Gazette*], the paper for which he worked, gained a unique place when it succeeded in combining the qualities of a serious daily paper and an exacting literary review.

In January, 1921, the National Theater in Prague, the foremost theater in the country, performed a Karel Čapek play with the strange title *R.U.R.* The author was known to be a talented young writer who had already written several plays together with his brother and one on his own, a moderately successful if rather traditional piece. The theme of his new play, however, astounded first Czech and then foreign audiences, for it dealt with synthetic people—"robots"—and their revolt against the human race. The play was a hit around the globe and soon brought its thirty-one-year-old author international acclaim (its nonhuman heroes held such fascination for the contemporary world that the word "robot," coined by Čapek, has been assimilated by numerous languages). With his drama about the robots Čapek inaugurated a series of fantastic and utopian[2] works. He continued in this vein with a novel, *The Factory of the Absolute*, and a comedy, *The Makropulos Affair*, on the Shavian theme of longevity, both of which appeared in 1922, and the 1924 novel *Krakatite*. After a long hiatus he returned to utopian themes with the famous novel *War with the Newts* (1936) and, a year before his death, the drama *The White Plague* (1937).

Three of the works I have mentioned develop a fantastic motif in striking detail; even their denouements are almost identical. What impelled Karel Čapek to rework his apocalyptic vision so persistently? Many saw in his work instant utopias that presaged technological discoveries with potentially dangerous consequences; others

---

[2] I am using the term Čapek himself chose to describe his work, although in view of the content a more appropriate designation might be "anti-utopian"—which is equally applicable to the later works of Huxley, Zamyatin, Boye, Orwell, and Bradbury.

saw a brilliant satire on contemporary political conditions both at home and abroad.

But Čapek's creative work in science fiction had a different purpose: it attempted to provide a philosophical explanation for the antagonisms that were repeatedly plunging the world into crisis.

I am a writer myself. I know that a work of literature cannot be reduced to some message, argument, or philosophy which can be expressed both concisely and in universal concepts. If I am about to consider Čapek's philosophy in his fundamental works, I am risking this oversimplification only because Čapek himself sets out the same way—almost all his works are accompanied by some kind of theoretical commentary. Although he preferred to conceal the didactic and philosophical element in his work by employing rich and fantastic plots, a wealth of brilliantly observed technical and everyday detail, and a vital, even colloquial language, Čapek was certainly the type of artist who wrote à la thèse.

Čapek made a thorough study of philosophy. Among contemporary schools of thought, he was most strongly influenced by Anglo-American pragmatism. Opponents have charged the adherents of pragmatism with intellectual shallowness, inconsistency, and failure to mold a genuine philosophical system—although they could not very well have done so, given their resistance to conventional truths and "great" ideas. It was precisely the pragmatists' unwillingness to generalize (something the political ideologies of the day did readily), their interest in everyday human activity, and the respect they showed every individual's truth that appealed to Čapek.

Čapek had already become familiar with the philosophy of James, Dewey, and Schiller during the war. In the same period he had also written a dedicated and sympathetic study on the subject. In the course of the next few years he published several additional detailed articles in which he attempted to define his philosophical views—especially in the area of noetics—as precisely as possible.

Like other pragmatists, Čapek was a relativist and took a skeptical view of the power of understanding, particularly the speculative understanding which attempts to establish universally valid systems. Even the most universal discoveries about reality will become personal to each individual mind and therefore partial and premature. Accordingly, Čapek considered the predilection for generalizations (especially in the area of social relations) to be one of the least propitious tendencies of human thought. "Please, for a moment, approach 'socialism' and other words now in world currency as moral and personal values, not as party or political values," he wrote shortly after the war. "A great number of people who went into the war as the new generation have come out of it with a terrible, gnawing hyper-consciousness of these values, and with their former certainty about them shaken just as terribly. This uncertainty could not be called disillusionment or skepticism or indifference; rather, it is a dismay which finds good and evil on both sides and rejects viewpoints based on principle . . . ."

Čapek's skepticism was the basis for his humanistic demand that no prejudice, no conventional truth or its concerns, be placed above the value of human life. The function of this skepticism was to remove artificial idea-obstacles between people and to stimulate conciliation, tolerance, and active participation in life. "You don't see two bales of hay, but thousands of straws. Straw by straw you gather what is good and useful in the human world; straw by straw you discard the chaff and the weeds. You don't cry out because of the oppression of thousands but because of the oppression of any individual; you've had to destroy the one truth in order to find thousands of them . . . . Ultimately, for want of anything more perfect, you simply believe in people."

In Čapek's works revolutionaries find themselves side by side with dreamers and explorers, demagogues with people's tribunes and redeemers. All these characters, no matter how different or apparently antagonistic their motives, contemplate changing or improving the world by some momentous act. With their absolute visions and judgments about the world, they run afoul of temperate and usually less interesting conservatives—simple folk or people of learning, but always tolerant, willing to help others, and ready to do anything, even to perform the most insignificant task. They know their own limits and the limits of the reality in which they live. They understand that everything has its season and its tempo

and that the world cannot be changed for the better by upheaval, no
matter how well intentioned. This is why they enjoy Čapek's sympathy.

Čapek doubted that anything posed a greater threat to mankind
than uncontrolled Faustian desire. A man who feels equal to the
creator labors under the delusion that he can and should make the
world conform to his own idea. In reality, he simply ceases to perceive its complexity, disturbs one of its subtle, imperceptible struc-
tures, and triggers calamity.

In *The Factory of the Absolute* everyone believes he has found the
true god and that he will save others by bringing them his god and
inculcating his own faith and concept of love. People are filled with
messianic idealism, but their ideals are contradictory and lead to
disputes; the disputes grow into wars. While professing lofty intentions, they overlook other people and justify their own intolerance.
At the end of the book one of the heroes confesses, "A person might
think that another belief is the wrong belief, but he musn't think
that the fellow who holds it is bad, or common, or stupid." And later, "You know, the greater the thing somebody believes in, the
more passionately he despises those who don't believe in it. But the
greatest belief would be to believe in people. . . . Everybody's just
great at thinking about mankind, but about one single person—no.
I'll kill you, but I'll save mankind. . . . It'll be a bad world until
people believe in people . . . ."

An equally messianic desire and undisciplined need to transform
the world brings on the calamity that befalls mankind in the famous
play about the robots. "Alquist, it wasn't a bad dream to want to
end the slavery of work," says Domin, the director of the robot factory, shortly before his death. "I didn't want a single soul to have to
do idiotic work at someone else's machines, I didn't want any of
this damn social mess! Oh, the humiliation, the pain are making
me sick, the emptiness is horrible! We wanted a new generation!"

In the play Domin's dream of creation is opposed by the engineer Alquist: "I think it would be better to lay one brick than make
too grandiose plans." Elsewhere, he implores, "O God, shed your
light on Domin and on all those who err; destroy their creation and
help people return to their cares and their work; keep the human

race from annihilation . . . . the whole world, entire continents, all humanity, everything is one crazy, brutish orgy. They won't even lift a hand for food; it's stuffed right into their mouths so they don't even have to get up . . . ."

In *R.U.R.* we see the first confrontation—at least on a spiritual level—between the "man of the coming times," the revolutionary, the realizer of momentous plans, and the person who believes that man should, in the interest of preserving his own race, continue slowly on the path of his forebears, preferring what is perhaps a harder and poorer existence to the risk of unleashing demons no one will be able to control. The Domins lead the world to ruin. The Alquists warn against following them.

People need no saviors or redeemers, no robots, miracle drugs, or inexhaustible energy sources, and they need not look for grand designs or earth-shaking solutions. On the contrary, they should learn to live in harmony with the world into which they were born and take personal responsibility for it. This sense of responsibility is born of service and participation in everyday human affairs. Only "straw by straw" can the world and human attitudes be improved.

The standards by which Čapek judged human action as positive or negative were so unusual that many readers missed the point of his works. Others were angered. Radical in their own thinking, they showered Čapek with reproach for idealizing the little man, the average person, and even outright provincialism. They claimed that in denying a person's right to generalization and universal truth, Čapek was also stripping him of the right to action that would bring an end to social injustice. They offered their own, revolutionary solutions, which in that time of protracted economic and political crisis seemed to be the only promising alternatives.

This debate has raged to the present day, some believing that it is appropriate to rectify the state of human affairs by force if necessary, others contending that man must try to influence conditions by changing himself first. The events that have transpired in the very country in which Čapek lived and where I, too, live, a country where, in the half-century since Čapek's death, life has deteriorated into a succession of violent upheavals, support, in my opinion, the side of Čapek's truth in this life-and-death controversy.

The skepticism with which Čapek contemplated mankind's future reflected only one side of his personality. There was also something harmonious, even playful in him that managed to endure from the time of his childhood. He took a child's pleasure in thinking up stories. He placed no limits on his imagination and delighted in the unexpected situations he was creating, the new territory he was entering, as well as in the spiteful scoffing that permeated even the works auguring catastrophe. There was also real wonder in his observation of objects and human craftsmanship. With a boy's fascination he would watch a skilled laborer and then tell about his work in the same amusing way one might talk about an avocation or a hobby. (Čapek himself was a passionate gardener, raised dogs and cats, collected oriental carpets and folk music from around the world, took excellent photographs, and made skillful drawings for a number of his books.) He manages to reveal unexpected forms and qualities, the "soul" of objects that are encountered every day—a vacuum cleaner, a camera, a doorknob, a stove. Thus it was that alongside his apocalyptic visions and work in science fiction, perhaps as a counterbalance, he produced travel sketches, newspaper columns, and short prose fiction (his *Stories from One Pocket* and *Stories from the Other Pocket*, which appeared in 1929, enjoyed extraordinary popularity). In these works Čapek granted to people and things what he did not grant them in his longer science fiction— that they might approach each other in the custom of past centuries rather than in the ways of the present.

Čapek himself tells about the origin of his novel *War with the Newts* (1936): "It was last spring, when the world was looking rather bleak economically, and even worse politically—Apropos of I don't know what, I had written the sentence, 'You mustn't think that the evolution that gave rise to us was the only evolutionary possibility on this planet.' And that was it. That sentence was the reason I wrote *War with the Newts*." "It is quite thinkable," Čapek reasons, "that cultural development could be shaped through the mediation of another animal species. If the biological conditions were favorable, some civilization not inferior to our own could arise in the depths of the sea . . . . If some species other than man were to attain that level we call civilization, what do you think—would it do the same stupid things mankind has done? Would it fight the same wars? Would it invite the same historical calamities? What would we say if some animal other than man declared that its education and its numbers gave it the sole right to occupy the entire world and hold sway over all of creation? It was this confrontation with human history, and with the most pressing topical history, that forced me to sit down and write *War with the Newts*."

A multitude of political allusions (the figure of the Chief Salamander, whose name was "actually Andreas Schultze" and who "had served someplace during the World War as a line soldier" certainly calls to mind the leader of the Nazi Reich, Adolf Hitler, and the chapter on the book of the royal philosopher paraphrases the Nazi theories of the time) led some contemporary critics to conclude that Čapek had abandoned his relativism to write an anti-Fascist pamphlet. This view, incidentally, has been supported to the present day by official Czech and Soviet literary historiography.

The thinking of many of Čapek's contemporaries was rooted in uncompromising and aggressive ideologies which sought to reduce even the most complex problems and conflicts to the simplistic language of slogans. The world was witnessing increasing confrontations between classes, nations, and systems—communism and capitalism, bourgeoisie and proletariat, democracy and dictatorship (the black-and-white ideological thinking which continues to dominate the world). Ostensibly, everything could be grasped and explained in such language. Its chief effect, however, was to obscure the human side of every problem; conflicts and issues were elevated to an impersonal level governed by power, strength, and abstract interests, where man was not responsible for his behavior or actions, and even less for the fate of society.

A writer can make no more fatal mistake than to adopt the simplistic view and language of ideology. Čapek was undoubtedly among the most resolute opponents of Fascism, Nazism, and communism, but now, as before, he sought the causes of modern crises in areas that could be defined by the experience and capabilities of the individual. He found that his contemporaries were becoming estranged from the values that had guided them for centuries and were adopting false values foisted upon them by technology and a consumerist pseudoculture. They were making gods of achievement, success, and quantity.[3]

> Isn't our admiration for machines, that is, for mechanical civilization, such that it suppresses our awareness of man's truly creative abilities? We all believe in human progress; but we seem predisposed to imagine this progress in the form of gasoline engines, electricity, and other technical contrivances . . . . We have made machines, not people, our standard for the human order . . . . There is no conflict between man and machine . . . . But it's another matter entirely when we ask ourselves whether the organization and perfection of human beings is proceeding as surely as the organization and perfection of machines . . . . If we wish to talk about progress, let's not rave about the number of cars or telephones but point instead to the value that we and our civilization attach to human life.
>
> > —from the article
> > "Rule by Machines"

By forcing individuality into the background, technological civilization makes room for mediocrity and a stifling collectivism.

In a critical commentary on Ortega y Gasset's essay *Revolt of the Masses*, Čapek observes: "Our age is distinguished by the fact that the ordinary spirit, aware of its own ordinariness, is bold enough to defend its right to ordinariness, and asserts it everywhere . . . . The mass . . . imposes on the world its own standards and its own taste and strives to give its barroom opinions the force of law . . . .

---

[3]As early as 1926, Čapek criticized these false values of "the American way of life" in a letter to the *New York Sunday Times*. He contrasted them to the values of old Europe: "Do you recall how Homer depicts Achilles' shield? It took one song of the *Iliad* for the blind poet to describe how that shield was made; in America you would have made a casting and produced tens of thousands per day; granted, shields might be made cheaply and successfully this way, but Iliads could not . . . . In Europe, to this very day things come about slowly; perhaps an American tailor could make three coats in the time one of our people could make one, and it's equally possible the American tailor could produce three times as many as ours; but one may well ask whether the American will also spend three times as much of his life in the process . . . . To my knowledge, American efficiency concerns itself with multiplying output, not life. It's true that man works in order to live; but it is evident that he lives also while he is working. One could say that European Man is a very poor industrial machine; but this is because he is not a machine at all."

The masses . . . have been imbued with the power and glory of their modern surroundings, but not with spirit." Čapek, however, differs with the Spanish philosopher by stressing that the fortunes of mankind are threatened not so much by the mediocrity of the masses as by wholesale failure among individuals, particularly those responsible for maintaining our cultural values and the level of thought—i.e., the intellectuals.

Culture means "above all, continuity with every human endeavor that has gone before"; its significance lies in the fact that it supports the awareness of values already established by mankind and thus helps us "not to lose them and not to sink below them."

Betrayal by the intellectuals was the worst betrayal Čapek could imagine, for its consequences were immeasurable. "A culturally leveled intelligentsia ceases to fulfill certain obligations on which most higher values depend . . . . If culture breaks down, the 'average' person—the simple, ordinary man, the farmer, the factory worker, the tradesman, with his normal thoughts and moral code—will not be heard, and will go off in search of something that is far beneath him, a barbaric and violent element . . . . Destroy the hierarchical supremacy of the spirit, and you pave the way for the return of savagery. The abdication of the intelligentsia will make barbarians of us all."

Culture which drops below its own level and loses what it had attained breaks down. Since this is what had just taken place throughout much of Europe, Čapek was convinced that we were witnessing "one of the greatest cultural debacles in world history . . . . What happened was nothing less than a colossal betrayal by the intelligentsia . . . ."

Where ideologues spoke of the crisis of the system, Čapek was more consistent, more skeptical, more personal; he found a crisis in man, his values, his sense of responsibility. The fall of the intelligentsia marked the beginning of the fall of the entire civilization, the beginning of tremendous calamities.

As he always did when he resolved to pursue a great theme, Čapek turned to the sphere of science fiction. Not only did it suit his storytelling preferences, but a fictional world in fictional time gave him more room for movement and enabled him to shape that world and order the action with maximum focus on the factors which, in his view, were leading to ruin.

At the same time, Čapek wanted to evoke a sense of verisimilitude and topicality. He therefore patterned his narrative on the events of the time, the catchwords, the diplomatic maneuvers, and the advertising slogans, and he made allusions to living people and their work. He also reinforced the feeling of real life by including exact imitations of the most diverse genres of nonfiction, from reminiscences and news stories to interviews and statements by famous personalities.

Such efforts to make his science fiction more lifelike and closer to a documentary record of actual events were characteristic of Čapek's "anti-utopias" and set them off sharply from the majority öf works in that genre. Zamyatin, Boye, Orwell, and Bradbury thought through to their absurd end the destructive (generally totalitarian) tendencies they saw in contemporary society. They created worlds that were terrifying in their alienation or totalitarian violence, but at the same time so artificial as to be remote from everyday human experience. Čapek depicted those same disastrous social tendencies in more realistic (and usually ironic) terms. He did not invent new world empires—the United State, Oceania, or the World State, the Bureau of Guardians or the Ministry of Love; he did not describe television eyes that would follow a person's every movement, or Kallocain and other drugs that would deprive him of his will. Čapek's Vaduz conference resembles any diplomatic meeting of the time, just as the board meeting of the Pacific Export Company resembles a board meeting of any contemporary enterprise. His people experience the joys and worries of life in the age of the newts much as they did in Čapek's own day. The fantastical newts appear to exist in everyday life. But this everyday life is moving toward disaster, precisely because its everyday quality has taken it in that direction. Čapek's fiction is less horrifying (at the beginning, it is even humorous), but all too reminiscent of the world we all live in; and this lends urgency to its admonitions about where that world may be headed.

However lifelike Čapek's utopia may appear, it remains a fiction, an artistic image that cannot be reduced (as some critics have tried to do) to a mere allegory in which the newts are substituted for one of the forces in the contemporary world conflict. No poetic symbol or allegory can be neatly translated back into reality.

The newts have emerged on the scene, and thus entered history, as an independent factor. Of course, they are not loaded down with prejudices or their own history and culture, and in this they resemble children. Eager learners, they strive to emulate everything they perceive to be more developed or more advanced. Like a mirror, they reflect the image of human values and the contemporary state of culture.

What kind of world is encountered by these creatures whose main strength lies in their being average and in their "successful, even triumphal inferiority"? What does modern civilization offer the huge masses of creatures untouched by culture? As Čapek develops his story of the newts and their history, he also refines his answer, and it is a depressing one. Human civilization is racing blindly in pursuit of profits, success, and material progress. Wealth, amusement, and pleasure have become its ideals, and it deifies everything that helps realize those ideals—industry, technology, science, entrepreneurism. En route to its goals, it has not even noticed the loss of what gave it life: human personality, culture, spirit, soul. Inquiry and reflection have been replaced with journalistic jabber, personal involvement in social affairs with a passive craving for sensation, ideas with slogans and empty phrases. "Your work is your success. He who doesn't work doesn't eat! . . . " All this has led to the world's becoming inundated with masses of people dangerous in their mediocrity and their readiness to accept any belief and adopt any goal. Yes, the masses resemble the newts; and the newts have become assimilated by the masses. "Of course, they don't have their own music or literature, but they'll get along without them just fine; and people are beginning to find that this is terribly modern of those Salamanders . . . . They've learned to use machines and numbers, and that's turned out to be enough to make them masters of their world. They left out of human civilization everything that was inexpedient, playful, imaginative, or old-fashioned, and so they eliminated from it all that had been human . . . ."

Everything that happens to the human race in this "Age of Newts" looks like a natural disaster, not because the newts are a natural phenomenon but because no one anywhere in the world can be found who feels personal responsibility for his creations, his actions, his behavior, and the social enterprise that is civilization. Or, more accurately, there is just one person, a doorkeeper, who meets his responsibility; he is that insignificant "little man." Among the powerful, the chosen, no thought has been given to the long-term consequences of the trend civilization is following. Culture has been leveled, art has been displaced by kitsch, philosophy has declined and taken to celebrating destruction, everything has been overcome by petty, local, and mainly nationalistic considerations.

Human civilization has indeed spread throughout the planet, but people show no evidence of being able to treat anything other than particularized concerns; thus, they have no means of *considering*, let alone *controlling* the consequences of their own actions. Modern civilization is so destructive that no being could come into contact with it and escape unscathed. Even the newts are marked by their encounter with people and their "culture." This is why, with no precautions, they begin to destroy dry land as soon as they find it to be in their interests to do so. People committed to "higher" and "suprapersonal" concerns, people who have long since given up the right to share actively in determining their own future, even when threatened with the extinction of not just one people or state but of mankind, work together with the newts to bring about their own destruction. "All the factories" cooperate, "All the banks. All nations."

In the face of this predicament, what people undertake for their salvation could only be viewed as half-hearted and panoptical. The human race has nothing left with which to fight for its existence. These are people who are about to destroy their own planet.[4]

---

[4]Relatively little attention has been given to Čapek's contribution to the Soviet anthology *Den mira* [*Day of Peace*], edited by Maxim Gorky and published in Moscow in 1937. People from around the globe described how they had spent the day on September 27, 1935. In the section "The Writer's Day" Čapek wrote, among other things, "Today I completed the last chapter of my utopian novel. The main charac-

Čapek was a writer of great metaphors, brilliant fantasies, and apocalyptic visions. He was an author who appeared to focus on the events of the external world, on competing ideas, conflicts between nations, the shortcomings of civilization—in sum, conflicts of an entirely impersonal nature. But can real literature develop from impersonal motives, solely from an intellectual need to address a problem, even a very important one? I doubt it.

An argument between Čapek's typical heroes was not merely an argument intended to shed light on a philosophical problem. It was first and foremost Čapek's personal argument. He had an innate, almost prophetic consciousness of sharing responsibility for the fate of human society. He, too, needed to dream of mankind's happiness, of a more peaceful, more secure world. His need was to think up plans, to bring people a good message. At the same time, he realized that all dreams of lofty spirits, all prophetic visions, change into their opposites, and it is precisely these that lead people into fatal conflicts. So he set himself limits. He was Domin in *The Factory of the Absolute*, Prokop in *Krakatite*, Captain van Toch and the entrepreneurial genius Bondy in *War with the Newts*. In these figures he wanted to "smash [himself] with [his] very power," the transgression of which Prokop stands accused in *Krakatite*. But time and again he offered repentance, calling himself to order in the words of Alquist or the unknown X. He was punishing himself for the damage he could have done.

Čapek's entire work testifies to the contradiction faced by a seeing, knowing creative spirit, a spirit that longs to purify and enlighten the world but fears its own imperfection and limitations, fears what people will do with its visions. This dilemma will undoubtedly haunt mankind forever. Čapek's work illuminates it with the power of personal experience.

Translated by Robert Streit

---

ter of this chapter is nationalism. The content is quite simple: the destruction of the world and its people. It's a loathsome chapter based solely on logic. Yes, it has to end this way: what destroys us will not be a cosmic catastrophe but mere reasons of state, economics, prestige, and so on."

Contents

CONTENTS

Third Book
War with the Newts

First Book

Andrias Scheuchzeri

mind your own business, sir. And he would curse vehemently and freely as is in keeping with an elderly but still for his age an active captain of a boat.

But if instead of asking impertinent questions you let Captain J. van Toch growl and curse away to himself, you might discover more. Doesn't his manner show that he wants to get something off his chest? Let him be, his temper will work itself off. "Well, look here, sir," bursts out the captain. "Those fellers of ours there in Amsterdam, those damned Jews up there will get it into their heads, pearls, they say, man, keep your eyes open for pearls. People are like mad for pearls, they say, and all that." Here the captain expectorates indignantly. "Just so, to put money into pearls! That comes from people like you always wanting to have wars, or whatnot. Flight from gold, that's all it is. And that's called the crisis, sir." Captain van Toch hesitates a little, wondering if he oughtn't to begin a discussion with you about problems of economics; for in these days people don't talk about anything else. Here, however, in front of Tanah Masa it's too hot and enervating for that; and Captain van Toch waves his hand and mumbles: "You say pearls! In Ceylon, sir, they cleared up the whole lot five years ago; in Formosa you're not allowed to fish for them. And so here we are, Captain van Toch, on the look-out for new fishing-grounds. Sail to those damned little islands; maybe you'll find whole banks of shells there." The captain blows contemptuously into a sky-blue handkerchief. "Those rats in Europe imagine that there's something to be found here that nobody knows about yet! Jesus Christ, what mugs they are! It's a wonder they don't ask us to look into these Bataks' snouts to see if they're not snivelling pearls. New fishing places! There's a new brothel in Padang, yes, but new fishing places? Sir, I know all these islands here like the palm of my hand—from Ceylon as far as that damned Clipperton Island. . . . If anybody thinks that he can still find something that he can make money out of, then good luck to him, sir! For thirty years I've been around in these parts of the world, and now these fellers want me to discover something here!" Captain van Toch nearly chokes with this defiant statement. "Let them send some greenhorn here, he'll find things that'll make them blink their eyes; to ask someone who knows the place like Captain van Toch. . . . You'll grant that, sir. In Europe, there you might still come across some odd thing; but here—don't people come here just to sniff and nose out what can be devoured? and not even devoured, what can be bought and sold? Sir, if in the whole of the damned tropics there was anything left worth a brass farthing, three agents would be trying to get something out of it and signal with dirty handkerchiefs to boats of seven nationalities to stop. That's it, sir. I know what it's like here better than the Colonial Office of Her Majesty the Queen. I beg your pardon." Captain van Toch with all his might tries to master his righteous indignation, in which after more blasphemy he succeeds. "Do you see those miserable sluggards over there? They're pearl fishers from Ceylon, may God not punish me, Sinhalese as the Lord created them; but why he did it I don't know. That's what I'm shipping with me now, sir; and when I find a stretch of shore somewhere on which there's no Agency or Bat'a or Custom Office posted up, I let them loose into the water to look for shells. That smaller rascal can dive as much as forty fathoms deep; over there on Princes Island he fished up from a depth of forty-five fathoms the handle of a cinema contraption, sir, but pearls—no, not a oner! Hopeless paralytics, these Sinhalese. Well, this is the sort of damned job I have, sir: make out as if I were buying palm olive, and at the same time look for new fishing places for pearl-oysters. Perhaps they'll want me to discover a virgin continent yet, eh? Surely that's no job for a decent mercantile captain, sir. J. van Toch isn't a damned adventurer, sir. No, sir." And so on; the sea is big, and the ocean of time has no limits; spit into it, man, and it won't give; curse your fate, and you won't move it. And so, after much preparation and fussing, at last we have reached that J. van Toch, the captain of a Dutch ship *Kandong Bandoeng*, who sighing and cursing climbs down into a boat to get across to the kampong on Tanah Masa and have a parley with the drunken cross between a Cuban and a Portuguese about some business affairs.

"Sorry, Captain," said the cross between a Cuban and a Portuguese at last, "but there aren't any shells growing here on Tanah Masa. These dirty Bataks," he said, with infinite disgust, "eat even jelly-fish; they live more in the water than on land; the women here stink like fish, you can't imagine—what did I want to say? Aha, you were asking about the women."

"And isn't there a strip of coast here," inquired the captain, "where these Bataks don't crawl into the water?"

The cross between the Cuban and the Portuguese shook his head. "There isn't. Unless it's Devil Bay, but that's no good for you."

"Why?"

"Because . . . nobody must go there, sir. Will you have another one, Captain?"

"Thanks. Are there any sharks there?"

"Sharks, and all the rest," the half-breed mumbled. "A nasty place, sir. The Bataks wouldn't like anybody to stick his nose in there."

"Why?"

". . . There are devils there, sir. Sea devils."

"What is a sea devil like? Is it a fish?"

"No, not a fish," the half-breed objected evasively. "Just a devil, sir. A deep-sea devil. The Bataks call it 'tapa.' Tapa. They have their town there, they say, those devils. Will you have another one?"

"And what does it look like . . . that sea devil?"

The cross between a Cuban and a Portuguese shrugged his shoulders.

"Like a devil, sir. I saw one once . . . that is, only its head. I was coming back in a boat from Cape Haarlem . . . and suddenly it stuck out such a mug from the water in front of me."

"Well, and what does it look like?"

"It has a muzzle. . . . Like a Batak, sir, but absolutely bald."

"Wasn't it really a Batak?"

"No, sir, it wasn't. In that place no Batak would ever crawl into the water, you know! And then . . . it blinked at me with its *bottom eyelids*, sir." The half-breed shivered with terror. "With its bottom eyelids which come up right over its eyes. That's a tapa."

Captain J. van Toch toyed with the glass of palm wine in his fat fingers. "And you hadn't had a drop too much? You weren't drunk?"

"I was, sir. Otherwise I shouldn't have rowed that way. The Bataks don't like it when somebody upsets those devils."

Captain van Toch shook his head. "Man, there aren't any devils. And if there were, they would look like Europeans. That thing must have been some kind of fish or something."

"A fish," stammered the cross between a Cuban and a Portuguese. "A fish hasn't got any hands, sir. I'm not a Batak, sir. I went to school in Badjoeng . . . maybe I still know the Ten Commandments and other scientific doctrines; an educated man would know what a devil is like and what is a beast, wouldn't he? You ask the Bataks, sir."

"These are just negro superstitions," explained the captain with the breezy superiority of an educated man. "Scientifically it's pure nonsense. A devil can't live in water, can he? What would he do there? You mustn't believe the natives' tales, my lad. Somebody called that bay Devil Bay, and ever since then the Bataks have been scared of it. That's it," said the captain, hitting the table with the fat palm of his hand.

"There's nothing there, my lad, it's scientifically clear, isn't it?"

"It is, sir," the half-breed consented, who went to school in Badjoeng. "But no sensible man has any business in Devil Bay."

Captain J. van Toch turned crimson. "What?" he bawled. "You dirty Cuban, you think that I shall be frightened of your devils? We'll see about that," he cried, rising with all the greatness of his honest fourteen stones. "I'm not going to waste my time here with you when I have my business to look after. But remember there aren't any devils in Dutch colonies; if there are any anywhere, then they're in the French ones. There might be some there. And now fetch me the mayor of this damned kampong here."

It was no trouble to find the above-mentioned dignitary: he was squatting beside the half-breed's shop chewing a stick of sugar-cane. He was an elderly gentleman and naked, but far thinner than mayors are in Europe. A bit further behind him, and keeping at a respectful distance, the whole village was crouching together, women and children and all, clearly expecting to be filmed.

"Well, listen, my lad," said Captain van Toch, addressing him in Malay (he might just as well have spoken to him in Dutch or English, for the venerable old Batak didn't know a single word of Malay, and the cross between a Cuban and a Portuguese had to translate all the captain's speech into Batavian; but for some reason the captain felt that Malay was more suitable). "Well, listen, my boy, I shall need a few big strong brave boys to go hunting with me."

The half-breed translated, and the mayor nodded his head to signify that he almost understood; then he turned to the wider auditory and delivered an oration that was an obvious success.

"The chief says," the half-breed interpreted, "that the whole village will go hunting with the tuan captain wherever tuan would like to go."

"So you see. Then tell them that we are going fishing for shells in Devil Bay."

A quarter of an hour of excited discussion followed in which the whole village took part, especially the old women. Finally the half-breed turned to the captain. "They say, sir, that you can't go to Devil Bay."

The captain grew red in the face. "And why not?"

The half-breed shrugged his shoulders. "Because there are tapa-tapa there. Devils, sir."

The captain began to turn purple. "So tell them that if they don't go . . . that I shall knock all their teeth out . . . that I shall slit their ears . . . that I shall hang them . . . and that I shall burn their lousy kampong—do you understand?"

The half-breed translated it faithfully, whereupon again a somewhat lengthy and lively debate ensued. At last the half-breed turned to the captain. "They say, sir, that they will go to complain to the police at Padang that tuan threatened them. There are regulations about it. The mayor won't leave it at that."

Captain J. van Toch began to turn blue. "Well, tell

18

him," he roared, "that he is . . ." And he kept on talking without giving himself time to take breath for at least eleven minutes.

The half-breed translated as much as his stock of words would permit; and after a fresh, long, but meaty conference of the Bataks he interpreted to the captain: "They say, sir, that they would be willing to refrain from legal proceedings if tuan captain deposits a fee at the local offices. They say," he hesitated, "two hundred rupees; but that's a bit too much, sir. Offer them five."

Captain van Toch's face began to break into russet blotches. First he threatened to massacre all the Bataks in the world, then he made a reduction to three hundred kicks, finally he would have been satisfied if he could have stuffed the mayor for the museum in Amsterdam; on the other side the Bataks went down from two hundred rupees to an iron pump with a wheel, and at last stood firm at the captain's giving the mayor by way of a fee a smart petrol lighter. "Let them have it, sir?" pleaded the cross between a Cuban and a Portuguese ("I've got three lighters in my store, but they haven't got a wick"). Thus peace was re-established on Tanah Masa; but Captain J. van Toch knew that now the prestige of the white race was at stake.

●   ●   ●   ●   ●

In the afternoon a boat put off from the Dutch ship *Kandong Bandoeng*, in which among others were present Captain van Toch, a Swede called Jensen, an Icelander called Gudmundson, a Finn named Gillemainen, and two Sinhalese pearl fishers. The boat headed straight for Devil Bay.

By three o'clock when the ebb was just at the turn the captain was standing on the shore, the boat hovered about a hundred yards away to look out for sharks, and both the Sinhalese divers were waiting with knives in their hands for the signal to jump into the water.

"And now you," the captain commanded the taller naked one. The Sinhalese slipped into the water, waded a few steps, and then sank below. The captain glanced at his watch.

After four minutes and twenty seconds about sixty yards to the left a brown head emerged; with strange, desperate, and yet paralysed haste the diver scrambled up on the boulders with the knife for cutting off the shells in one hand and in the other the shell of a pearl oyster.

The captain frowned. "Well, what's wrong?" he demanded sharply.

The Sinhalese was still clambering over the boulders gasping loudly with terror.

"What's happened?" the captain shouted.

"Sahib, sahib," the diver managed to groan, and sank down on the shore gasping out raucously. "Sahib . . . sahib . . ."

"Sharks?"

"Djins," moaned the diver. "Devils, sir. Thousands, thousands of devils!" He dug his fists into his eyes. "All devils, sir!"

"Let me see that shell," the captain commanded,

and then opened it with the knife. In it there was a small clear pearl. "And that was all you found?"

The Sinhalese took three more shells out of the bag which he had slung round his neck. "There are plenty of shells, sir, but those devils keep guard over them. . . . They watched me while I was cutting them off . . ." His shaggy hair stood up on end with horror. "Sahib, not here!"

The captain opened the shells; two were empty, and in the third there was a pearl like a pea, as round as a drop of quicksilver. Captain van Toch looked alternately at the pearl and at the Sinhalese in a heap on the ground.

"You," he faltered, "would you dive down there again?"

The diver shook his head without saying a word.

Captain van Toch felt a strong itch on his tongue to curse; but to his surprise he found that he was talking in a low voice and almost softly: "Don't get frightened, boy. And what do they look like, those . . . devils?"

"Like little children," the diver gasped out. "They have a tail, sir, and they are about as big as this." He held his hand about a yard from the ground. "They stood round me, and watched what I was doing there . . . there was such a ring of them . . ." The Sinhalese began to shudder. "Sahib, sahib, not here!"

Captain van Toch thought it over. "And what, do they blink with the lower eyelids, or what do they do?"

"I don't know, sir," cried the diver hoarsely. "There are thousands of them."

The captain looked round for the other Sinhalese; he was standing about a hundred and fifty yards away, waiting indifferently with his arms folded over the shoulders; after all, when you're naked you've nowhere to put your hands except on your own shoulders. The captain nodded to him silently, and the tiny man dived into the water. In three minutes and fifty seconds he emerged, scrambling up to the boulders with slippery hands.

"Well, get out," shouted the captain, but then he peered with more attention at those desperately groping hands; and he started off over the rocks; you'd never believe that such a bulk could have been so active. Only just in time he caught hold of one hand, and with much panting he dragged the diver out of the water. Then he let him lie on a boulder, and wiped the sweat away. The Sinhalese lay quite motionless; one of his legs was cut through to the bone, apparently by a rock, but otherwise he was unhurt. The captain lifted up one of his eyelids; only the white of the eyes was visible. He had no shells and no knife.

Just then the boat with the rest of the crew drew nearer to the shore. "Sir," the Swede Jensen shouted, "there are sharks here. Shall you keep on fishing?"

"No," said the captain. "Come here and pick up these two."

"Look, sir," observed Jensen, when they were returning to the boat, "how it suddenly goes shallow here. It's cut straight across here right to the shore." He pointed, poking with his oar in the water. "As if there was some kind of a dam below the water."

•   •   •   •   •

It was not till he was on the boat that the little diver came round; he sat with his knees under his chin, trembling all over his body. The captain sent the men away, and sat down with his legs apart.

"Well, out with it," he said. "What did you see there?"

"Djins, sahib," whispered the small Sinhalese; then his eyelids also began to quiver, and little specks of goose-flesh broke out all over his body. Captain van Toch cleared his throat. "And what do they look like?"

"Like . . . like . . ." A thin strip of the white began to appear in the man's eyes. With unexpected agility Captain van Toch slapped both his cheeks with the palm and back of his hand to bring him round.

"Thanks, sahib," sighed the small diver, and the pupils swam out again in the white of his eyes.

"Are you all right now?"

"Yes, sahib."

"Were there any shells there?"

"Yes, sahib."

Captain J. van Toch went on with the cross-examination with no small amount of patience and thoroughness. Yes, there are devils there. How many? Thousands and thousands. They are about as big as a ten-years-old boy, sir, and almost black. They swim in the water like you or me, but they sway their bodies as well from side to side, like this, like this, always like

23

this, like this, from side to side. . . . Yes, sir, they've got hands too, like human beings; no, they haven't any horns or hair. Yes, they have a tail a little bit like a fish, but without the tail-fin. And a big head, round like the Bataks'. No, they didn't say anything, sir; it was only as if they were smacking their lips. While the Sinhalese was picking up the shells about thirty fathoms deep he felt something touch him on his back like little cold fingers. He turned round, and there were hundreds and hundreds of them. Hundreds and hundreds of them, sir; some were swimming, and some were standing on the bottom, and they all were watching what the man was doing there. Then he dropped the knife and the shells, and tried to come to the top. While he was doing that he struck at some of the devils who were swimming above him, and what happened then, that he didn't know, sir.

Captain J. van Toch gazed throughtfully at the trembling little diver. That boy won't be any good for anything any more, he said to himself; I shall send him from Padang back to Ceylon. Grumbling and snorting he went into his cabin. There he shook out from the paper bag two pearls on to the table. One was as tiny as a grain of sand, and the other like a shining silver pea turning to pink. And the captain of the Dutch boat gasped and took out from the cupboard his Irish whisky.

●　　　●　　　●　　　●　　　●

Towards six o'clock he again had himself taken in the boat to the kampong, and straight to that cross between a Cuban and a Portuguese. "Toddy," he said, and that was the only word he spoke; he sat on the corrugated iron verandah, he held the thick glass in his fat fingers, and drank and spat and peered from underneath his shaggy eyebrows at the scraggy yellow hens which, God knows, were pecking in the little dirty yard between the palms. The half-breed didn't dare to say anything; he only filled up the glass. Slowly the captain's eyes became bloodshot, and his fingers grew stiff. It was nearly dusk when he rose and hitched his trousers up.

"Are you going to turn in, Captain?" the cross between the deuce and the devil inquired politely.

The captain stuck his finger into the air. "And I should like to come across," he said, "any devils that there may be in the world that I haven't met yet. You, which way is it here to that damned north-west?"

"This way," panted the half-breed. "Where are you going, sir?"

"To hell," grunted Captain J. van Toch. "To have a look at Devil Bay."

•   •   •·   •   •

This was the evening that the strange behaviour of Captain J. van Toch first began. He didn't return to the kampong till dawn; he didn't utter a word, and had himself taken to the boat, where he locked himself in his cabin till nightfall. So far that didn't surprise anyone, for *Kandong Bandoeng* had enough to do taking in the blessings of the island Tanah Masa (copra, pepper, camphor, gutta-percha, palm olive, tobacco, and labour); but when at dusk he was informed that all the cargo was stowed away he only snorted, and said: "Boat for kampong." And again he never came back till dawn. The Swede Jensen, who helped him on board, inquired merely out of politeness: "So we sail to-day, Captain?" The captain spun round as if he had been struck on his backside. "It's nothing to do with you," he snapped. "Mind your own damned business!" For a whole day the *Kandong Bandoeng* lay at anchor a cable's length from the shore of Tanah Masa, and did nothing. Towards sunset the captain rolled out from his cabin, and commanded: "Boat for kampong." The Greek Zapatis peered after him with one blind and the other squinting eye. "My lads," he crowed, "either our old man has got a girl there, or else he's gone completely dotty." The Swede Jensen frowned. "It's nothing to do with you," he snapped at Zapatis. "Mind your own damned business!" Afterwards he took the Icelander Gudmundson with him in a small boat, and rowed towards Devil Bay. They waited with the boat behind the rocks, and watched for what would come next. In the bay the captain was walking up and down, and it seemed as if he was waiting for somebody; at times he halted, and shouted something like ts, ts, ts. "Look," said Gudmundson, pointing out to the sea, now dazzlingly scarlet and gold with the sunset. Jensen counted two, three, four, six fins as sharp as a blade that moved towards Devil Bay. "Godfathers," mumbled Jensen. "There's a lot of sharks here." Every few seconds a blade dipped under, a tail swished through the water, and there was a violent commotion. Captain J. van Toch began to jump about madly on the shore, poured out curses, and threatened the sharks with his fists. Then a short tropical twilight faded, and the moon swam out over the island; Jensen pulled at the oars and drew the boat near to the shore, until they were only two hundred yards away. The captain was now sitting on a rock, and making ts, ts, ts. Some creatures were moving round him, but what they were they couldn't make out very well. They look like seals, thought Jensen, but seals don't crawl like that. They emerged from the water between the rocks and waded along the shore waddling like penguins. Jensen silently rowed a bit further, and stopped two hundred yards from the captain. Yes, the captain was saying something, but what it was only the devil could understand; most likely something in Malay or Tamil. He was gesticulating as if he were throwing something to those seals (but these aren't seals, Jensen assured himself), and all the time he was jabbering Chinese or Malay. Just then the raised oar slipped from Jensen's hand and splashed into the water. The captain looked up, raised himself, and ran about thirty yards towards the water; suddenly it began to lighten and crackle; the captain was firing his Browning in the direction of the boat. Almost simultaneously there was a hissing, swirling, and splashing in the bay as if a thousand seals were dashing into the water; but by then Jensen and Gudmundson had pulled on their oars and rushed their boat behind the nearest promontory so fast that it fairly whizzed. When they got back to the ship they didn't say a word

27

2

Mr. Golombek and
Mr. Valenta [1]

IT was a newspaper man's dog-days when nothing,
absolutely nothing happens, when there are no politics,
and not even a European crisis; and yet even at this
time of the year newspaper readers lying in the coma
of boredom on the banks of rivers, or in the rare shade
of trees, demoralized by the heat, nature, country
peace, and as a whole by the healthy and simple life
of the holidays, hope with daily disappointment that
at least in the papers there will be something new and
refreshing, some murder, war, an earthquake—in short,
something; and if there isn't, they crumple up the
papers and peevishly declare that there's nothing in
the papers, just Nothing at all, and on the whole
they're not worth reading, and they won't take them
any longer.

And in the meantime five or six forlorn people were
sitting in the editorial offices, for the other colleagues
were also on leave, and they peevishly crumpled up
the papers and complained that in the papers there
was nothing, just Nothing at all. And from the com-
posing-room the type-setter emerged, and said reproach-

[1] See *The Quest for Polar Treasures*, by Jan Welzl (George
Allen & Unwin).

fully: "Gentlemen, gentlemen, we haven't got a leader for to-morrow yet."

"Well, perhaps print . . . that article . . . on the economic situation in Bulgaria," one of the forlorn gentlemen opined.

The type-setter sighed heavily: "But who would read it, Mr. Editor? Again in the whole paper there won't be Anything to Read."

Six forlorn gentlemen raised their eyes to the ceiling as if they might find there Something to Read.

"If only something happened," suggested one of them vaguely.

"Or to have . . . some . . . interesting report," hinted another.

"About what?"

"That I don't know."

"Or to think out . . . some new vitamin," mumbled the third.

"What now, in summer?" objected the fourth. "Man, vitamins, they're intellectual things that suit the autumn better . . ."

"My Gosh, it's hot," yawned the fifth. "There ought to be something from the Polar regions."

"But what?"

"Well. Something like that Eskimo Welzl was. Frozen fingers, eternal ice, and such-like things."

"It's easy to say that," remarked the sixth. "But where to get it?"

A hopeless silence spread through the editorial office.

"I was in Jevičko on Sunday . . ." the type-setter faltered, breaking the silence.

"Well, what about that?"

"They say there's a Captain Vantoch on leave there. He was born there in Jevičko."

"What Vantoch?"

"Oh, a fat one. He's supposed to be a sea captain, that Vantoch. They say that he's fished for pearls somewhere out there."

Mr. Golombek looked at Mr. Valenta.

"And where did he fish for them?"

"On Sumatra . . . and on the Celebes . . . well, somewhere there. He's been living there for thirty years, they say."

"Man, that's an idea," said Mr. Valenta. "That might make a first-class article, Golombek; are we going?"

"Well! we can see," thought Mr. Golombek, and slipped down from the table on which he was sitting.

•   •   •   •   •

"That's the gentleman there," said the landlord at Jevičko.

Straddling widely at a table in the garden there was a fat gentleman in a white cap, drinking beer and thoughtfully scribbling with a fat finger on the table. Both gentlemen made a beeline for him.

"Mr. Valenta."

"Mr. Golombek."

The fat gentleman raised his eyes. "What? What do you say?"

"I am Mr. Valenta, an editor."

"And I am Mr. Golombek, an editor."

The fat gentleman raised himself with dignity. "Captain van Toch. Very glad to meet you. Sit down, boys."

Both gentlemen were very willing to sit down beside him, and they put out their writing-pads in front of them.

"And what will you have to drink, boys?"

"Raspberry juice," said Mr. Valenta.

"Raspberry juice?" the captain repeated distrustingly. "And why? Landlord, fetch some beer. Well, what is it you're after?" he inquired, leaning with his elbows on the table.

"Is it true, Mr. van Toch, that you were born here?"

"Yes, I was."

"Please tell me, how did you get to the sea?"

"Well, via Hamburg."

"And how long have you been a captain?"

"Twenty years, my boy. I've got the papers here," he said emphatically tapping his breast pocket. "I can show you."

Mr. Golombek had a desire to have a look to see what a captain's papers are like, but he suppressed it. "And so, Mr. Captain, in those twenty years you have seen a good deal of the world, haven't you?"

"Yah. Well, a good deal. Yah."

"And what particularly?"

"Java, Borneo, Philippines, Fiji Islands, Solomon Islands, Carolines, Samoa, Damned Clipperton Island. A lot of damned islands, my boy. Why?"

"Well, only because it's interesting. We should like you to tell us more, you know."

"Yah. Well, only so, isn't it?" The captain fixed on them his pale blue eyes. "So you're from the police, from the police, aren't you?"

"No, we're not, Mr. Captain. We're from the newspapers."

"Oho, from the newspapers. Reporters, eh? Well, write down: Captain J. van Toch, captain of the ship *Kandong Bandoeng*——"

"What?"

"*Kandong Bandoeng*, of Surabaya. Object of the journey: vacances—what do you call it?"

"Leave."

"Yah, the Deuce, leave. Well, put it into your papers like this, so-and-so has arrived. And now put away that note-book, chaps. Good health."

"Mr. van Toch, we have come to see you so that you could tell us something about your life."

"And why?"

"We shall put it in the papers. It's very interesting for the people to read of distant islands, and what their countryman, a Czech, a native of Jevičko, has seen and what experiences he's had."

The captain nodded his head. "That's true. My boy, I'm the only captain from the whole of Jevičko. Well, that is so. They say that there's also a captain of the swing boats, but I think," he added confidentially, "that he's not a real captain. It's measured by the tonnage, do you know?"

"And how big was your boat?"

"Twelve thousand tons, young man."

"Then you were a big captain, weren't you?"

"Yah, a big one," said the captain with dignity. "Boys, have you got any money?"

The two gentlemen looked at each other a bit doubtfully. "Yes, we've got some, but not much. Perhaps you're in need of some, Captain?"

"Well, I might need some."

"So you see. If you tell us a lot, we shall put it in the newspapers, and you'll get some money for it."

"How much?"

"Well, perhaps . . . one or two thousand," said Mr. Golombek generously.

"In pounds sterling!"

"No, only in crowns."

Captain van Toch shook his head. "Well then, no. I've got that myself, young man." He fished out from his trousers pocket a fat wad of paper notes. "See?" Then he leaned with his elbows on the table, bent towards them both. "Gentlemen, I could let you in for a big Geschäft. How do you call it?"

"A big business."

"Yah. A big business. But then you'll have to give me fifteen . . . well, wait a bit, fifteen, sixteen million crowns. How about that?"

Again the two gentlemen looked at each other uncertainly. For editors have their experiences with the most peculiar kinds of madmen, crooks, and inventors.

"Wait," said the captain. "I can show you something." With his fat fingers he fished in the small pocket of his waistcoat, pulled out something, and laid it on the table. It was five pink pearls the size of cherry-stones. "Do you know anything about pearls?"

"How much are they worth?" gasped Mr. Valenta.

"Yah, lots of money, my boy. But I only carry them . . . o appro. as an sample. Well then, would you like to join in?" he inquired, offering his broad palm across the table.

Mr. Golombek sighed. "Mr. van Toch, as much as that——"

"Stop," interrupted the captain. "I know you don't know me; but ask about Captain van Toch in Surabaya, Batavia, in Padang, or wherever you like. Go and inquire, and everybody will tell you, 'Yah, Captain van Toch, he's as good as his word.'"

"Mr. van Toch, we believe you," Mr. Golombek protested. "But——"

"Wait," declared the captain. "I know you don't want just to throw your good money away; I praise you for that, my boy. But you'd put it in a boat, eh? You'd buy that boat, you'd be the owner of that ship, and you could go with it, yah, you could do that so that you'd know what I'm up to. But the profit we shall make there, that will be fifty-fifty. It's a straight deal, isn't it?"

"But, Mr. van Toch," groaned Mr. Golombek at last, rather uneasily, "but we haven't got as much money as that!"

"Yah, then that makes a difference," said the captain. "Sorry. Then I don't know, gentlemen, why you came to see me."

"For you to tell us your story, captain. Surely you must have had so many adventures——"

"Yah, that I have. Damned adventures, I have."

"Have you ever experienced a shipwreck?"

"What? A shipwreck? Ah, not that. What do you think! If you give me a good boat, nothing can happen to it. But you can ask in Amsterdam for my references. Go and ask."

"And what about the natives? Did you get to know the natives there?"

Captain van Toch shook his head. "That's nothing for civilized people. That I won't tell you."

"Tell us something else instead."

"Yah, tell," mumbled the captain distrustfully. "And you will sell it then to a company, and then it will send its boats there. I'll tell you, my lad, men are great thieves. And the greatest thieves are those bankers in Colombo."

"Have you often been to Colombo?"

"Yah, many times. And in Bangkok too, and Manila. Young men," he said suddenly, "I know of a boat. A nice handy boat, and cheap for the money. She's lying at Rotterdam. Go and have a look at her. Well, Rotterdam, it's right over here," he pointed with his thumb over his shoulder. "Just now boats are dirt cheap, boys. Like old iron. She's only six years old, and has a Diesel engine. Would you like to have a look at her?"

"We can't, Mr. van Toch."

"Well then, you're strange people," sighed the captain, as he blew his nose loudly into the sky-blue handkerchief. "And don't you know of anyone here who would like to buy a boat?"

"Here in Jevičko?"

"Yah, here, or somewhere round about here. I should like that big Geschäft to be here in my country."

"That's very nice of you, captain."

"Yah. Those others are too great thieves. And they have no money. Since you come from the papers, you must know the big pots here, such as bankers and shipowners, what do you call them, financiers, eh?"

"Financiers. We don't know anything about them, Mr. van Toch."

"Ah, that's a pity." The captain grew gloomy.

Mr. Golombek remembered something. "Perhaps you know Mr. Bondy?"

"Bondy? Bondy?" meditated Captain van Toch. "Wait, I ought to know that name. Bondy. Yah, in London there's a Bond Street, and there are very rich people there. Hasn't he got some sort of a shop on that Bond Street, that Mr. Bondy?"

"No, he lives in Prague, but he was born, I think, here at Jevičko."

"Ah, crikey," broke out the captain, brightening up. "You're right, my boy. The one who had a draper's shop in the square. Yah, Bondy—what was he called? Max. Max Bondy. So now he's in business in Prague?"

"No, that must have been his father. This other Bondy is called G.H. President G. H. Bondy, captain."

"G.H." The captain shook his head. "G.H.: he wasn't G.H. If it isn't Gustl Bondy—but he was no president. Gustl was just a freckled little Jew. That can't be him."

"That must be him, Mr. van Toch. But you can't have seen him for years."

"Yes, you're right. Years and years," agreed the captain. "Something like forty years, my boy. That Gustl might be a big man now. And what's he like?"

"He's the president of the administrative board of the M.E.A.S.; you know, that's that big firm for boilers and suchlike things. Well, and he's chairman of about twenty trusts and companies. A very big man, Mr. van Toch. They call him the captain of our industry."

"Captain?" pondered Captain van Toch. "Well then, I'm not the only captain from Jevičko! Crikey, so Gustl is a captain too. I ought to meet him. And has he got any money?"

"Oh, yes. A tremendous lot of money, Mr. van Toch. He must have something like a couple of hundred millions. The richest man in our country."

Captain van Toch grew deeply serious. "And a captain too. Thank you, my boy. Then I shall set a course for him, for that Bondy. Yah, Gustl Bondy, I know, such a little Jew he was. And now he's Captain G. H. Bondy. Yah, yes, the time does fly," he sighed with melancholy.

"Mr. Captain, we shall have to go now, as we shall miss the evening train——"

"Then I'll see you into the harbour," said the captain, and began to weigh anchor. "Very glad you came, gentlemen. I know an editor in Surabaya, a good chap, yah, a good friend of mine. A dreadful soaker, young men. If you like, I could look for a job for you on the papers in Surabaya. Eh? Well, just as you like."

And when the train was already on the move Captain van Toch waved slowly and solemnly with a large blue handkerchief. While doing it a big, irregular pearl fell out into the sand. A pearl that nobody ever found.

3

G. H. Bondy and his
Fellow Countryman

AS is well known, the greater the man the less he has written on the plate on his door. Old Max Bondy in Jevíčko had to have painted over the shop, on both sides of the door, and on the windows, too, in big letters, the statement that there was Max Bondy, a shop for all kinds of dry goods: brides' trousseaux, drapery, towels, kitchen cloths, table-cloths, and bed linen, calicoes and flannels, suitings, silks, curtains, pelmets, window hangings, braids, and all kinds of sewing material. Founded 1885. His son, G. H. Bondy, captain of industry, president of the Chamber of Commerce, Consulato de la Republica Ecuador, member of many administrative boards, etc., etc., had on his door only a small, black-glass plate with gold inscription:

> BONDY

Nothing more. Just Bondy. Let others write on their doors Julius Bondy, agent for General Motors, or Ervin Bondy, M.D., or S. Bondy & Co., but there was only one unique Bondy who was simply Bondy without all the lesser details. (I believe, written on his door, the Pope has just Pius, without title or number. And God has no label in the sky, or on the earth. You must find out for yourself, my friend, that he lives here. But this doesn't concern us now, and it's only mentioned in passing.)

One sizzling day, in front of that glass plate a gentleman halted in a white sailor's cap, and wiped the powerful roll of his nape with a blue handkerchief. A damned smart house, he thought, and rather uncertainly he pressed the brass button of the bell.

The porter Povondra appeared from behind the door, weighed up with his eyes the fat gentleman from his shoes up to the gold braid on his cap, and enquired with reserve: "What is it you want?"

"Well, my lad," boomed the gentleman, "does a Mr. Bondy live here?"

"What do you want?" demanded Mr. Povondra, frostily.

"Tell him that Captain van Toch from Surabaya would like to have a word with him. Yah," he remembered, "Here's my card." And he handed to Mr. Povondra a visiting card on which was stamped an anchor, and underneath a name:

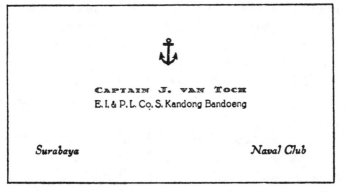

⚓

CAPTAIN J. VAN TOCH
E. I. & P. L. Co. S. Kandong Bandoeng

Surabaya   *Naval Club*

Mr. Povondra inclined his head and hesitated. "Shall I tell him that Mr. Bondy is out? Or that I'm sorry but Mr. Bondy has just got an important appointment?" There are some callers who must be shown in, and others that a smart porter deals with himself. Mr. Povondra was painfully aware that the instinct that guided him in such cases was failing him, somehow the fat gentleman didn't fit into the usual categories of callers who were shown in, and he didn't seem to be either a commercial traveller, or an official of some charitable society. In the meantime, Captain van Toch was snorting and mopping his bald pate with his handkerchief; at the same time he was blinking guilelessly with his pale blue eyes—Mr. Povondra suddenly decided to shoulder all responsibility. "Will you come in, please," he said. "I will take you to Mr. Bondy."

Captain J. van Toch wiped his forehead with his blue handkerchief, and glanced round the hall. Crikey, that Gustl has got it well rigged up; why, it's like the saloons in those ships that sail from Rotterdam to Batavia. It must have cost piles of money. And he was such a freckled little Jew, the captain mused.

In the meantime, in his study G. H. Bondy thoughtfully examined the captain's visiting card. "What does he want here?" he enquired suspiciously.

"I don't know, sir," mumbled Mr. Povondra respectfully.

Mr. Bondy still held the visiting card in his hand. A ship's anchor stamped on it. Captain J. van Toch, Surabaya—after all, where is Surabaya? Isn't it somewhere in Java? The air of distance struck Mr. Bondy. *Kandong Bandoeng*, that sounds like the strokes of a gong. Surabaya. And just to-day it's such a tropical day. Surabaya. "Well, show him in," commanded Mr. Bondy

At the door a powerful man in a captain's cap halted and saluted. G. H. Bondy rose to meet him. "Very glad to meet you, Captain. Won't you come in?"

"Nazdar, nazdárek, Mr. Bondy," boomed the captain cheerfully.

"You are a Czech?" said Mr. Bondy, somewhat astonished.

"Yah, Czech. Why, we know each other, Mr. Bondy. From Jevičko. Grocer Vantoch, do you remember?"

"Right, right." G. H. Bondy was tremendously pleased, but at the same time he felt something like disappointment. (So he isn't a Dutchman!) "Grocer Vantoch in the square, wasn't it? You haven't changed a bit, Mr. Vantoch. Always the same! Well, then, how is the grocery business?"

"Thanks," said the captain politely. "Dad has been gone a long time, how do you say it——"

"Dead? Well, well! Surely, you must be his son . . ." Mr. Bondy's eye brightened with sudden reminiscence. "My dear man, aren't you the Vantoch who used to fight with me in Jevičko, when we were boys?"

"Yah, that'll be me, Mr. Bondy," agreed the captain seriously. "But that's why they sent me from home to Moravská Ostrava."

"We used to fight a lot. But you were stronger than I was," acknowledged Mr. Bondy like a sportsman.

43

"Yah, that I was. Well, you used to be such a weak little Jew, Mr. Bondy. And you used to get a lot on the backside. A great deal."

"I did, that's true," recollected G. H. Bondy with emotion. "Well, sit down, fellow countryman! It's good of you to remember me! How did you manage to get here?"

Captain van Toch sat down solemnly in the leather armchair, and put his cap on the floor. "I'm on leave, Mr. Bondy. Well, that's it. That's it."

"Do you remember," said Mr. Bondy, stirring up the souvenirs, "how you used to shout after me: Jew, Jew, the devil will get you——"

"Yah," said the captain feelingly, and blew into his blue handkerchief. "Ah, yah. That was a fine time, my lad. Well, what's the use, time flies. Now we are both old men, and both captains."

"Why, indeed, you're a captain," recalled Mr. Bondy. "Who would have thought of that! Captain of the Big Lines—that's how you say it, isn't it?"

Yah, sir. Of the High Seas. East India and Pacific Lines, sir."

"A fine job," sighed Mr. Bondy. "I would swap with you any day, captain. You must tell me about yourself."

"Well, that, yah," the captain revived. "I should like to tell you something, Mr. Bondy. A very interesting thing, my lad." Captain van Toch looked round anxiously.

"Are you looking for something, Captain?"

"Yah, You don't drink beer, Mr. Bondy? I got such

a thirst on the way from Surabaya." The captain began to rummage in a vast pocket in his trousers, and took out a blue handkerchief, a linen bag with something, a bag with tobacco, a knife, a compass, and a bunch of banknotes. "I should like to send somebody for some beer. Perhaps that steward who showed me to this cabin here."

Mr. Bondy rang the bell. "Don't you worry, Captain. Have a cigar while it comes——"

The captain took a cigar with a red and gold band, and smelt it. "This tobacco is from Lombok. They're great thieves there, what's the good." Then to the horror of Mr. Bondy he squashed the precious cigar in his powerful fist, and pressed the tobacco shreds into his pipe. "Yah, Lombok. Or Sumba."

In the meantime Mr. Povondra appeared noiselessly at the door.

"Bring some beer," ordered Mr. Bondy.

Mr. Povondra lifted his eyebrows: "Beer? And how much?"

"A gallon," growled the captain, and trod down a burnt match into the carpet. "In Aden it was terribly hot, my lad. Well, then, I've something to tell you, Mr. Bondy. From the Straits, see? There you could do a marvellous Geschäft. A big business. But then I should have to tell you the whole, what do you say, tale, eh?"

"Story."

"Yah. Well, such a story, sir. Wait." The captain turned up to the ceiling his forget-me-not eyes. "I don't know where to make a start."

("Some more business," thought G. H. Bondy. "Lord, what a bore! He's going to tell me that he could sell sewing-machines in Tasmania, or boilers and pins in Fiji. Marvellous business, I know. That's the use I am to you. The devil knows I'm no shopkeeper. I'm a dreamer. In a way I'm a poet. Tell me, sailor Sinbad, of Surabaya, or of the Phoenix Islands. Didn't a Magnetic Mountain attract you? Didn't a Griffin bear you away to its nest? Aren't you returning with a load of pearls, cinnamon, and elephant-stones? Well, begin to lie!")

"Perhaps I ought to begin with that newt," announced the captain.

"With what newt?" wondered the financial magnate Bondy.

"Well, with those scorpions. How do you call them, lizards."

"Lizards?"

"Yah, crikey, lizards. They are something like lizards there, Mr. Bondy."

"Where?"

"On an island. I can't tell you its name, my lad. That's a very great secret, worth millions." Captain Van Toch wiped his forehead with his handkerchief. "Well, crikey, where's that beer?"

"It will be here in a minute, Captain."

"Yah. Well, then, to make it clear, Mr. Bondy, they are very nice and good animals, those lizards. I know them, my boy." The captain banged the table vehemently. "And to say that they might be devils, that's a lie. A damned lie, sir. You're more of a devil, and I'm a devil. I, Captain van Toch, sir. You can believe me when I say that."

G. H. Bondy became anxious. "Delirium," he said to himself. "Where is that damned Povondra?"

"There are several thousands of them, of those lizards, but they are very badly done in by—crikey, those, what you call them, sharks."

"Sharks?"

"Yah, sharks. That's why those lizards are so rare, sir, and only in that one place, in that bay, that I can't tell you by name."

"Then those lizards live in the sea?"

"Yah, in the sea. Only at night they crawl on to the shore, but after a bit they must go back into the water."

"And what do they look like?" (Mr. Bondy tried to gain time until that damned Povondra would come back again.)

"They might be as big as seals, but when they tiptoe on their hind paws, they're about as big as this," demonstrated the captain. "I can't say that they're nice looking. They haven't any scales."

"Scales?"

"Yah, scales. They are absolutely naked, Mr. Bondy, like frogs, or salamanders. And those front paws of theirs, they're like babies' little hands, but they've only got four fingers. Well, such poor little things," added the captain compassionately. "But they are very clever, and nice animals, Mr. Bondy." The captain slipped down to squat on his heels, and in this position he began to shuffle from one foot to the other and waddle. "They tiptoe like this, those lizards."

The captain tried to get his powerful body to squat and move in a waddling motion; at the same time he was holding his arms in front of himself like a dog begging, and he fixed on Mr. Bondy his forget-me-not eyes that seemed to clamour for sympathy. G. H. Bondy was by this very strongly moved, and somehow humanly ashamed. Just at that moment the silent Mr. Povondra appeared at the door with a jug of beer, and raised shocked eyebrows as he regarded the unseemly behaviour of the captain.

"Bring that beer here, and go away," burst out Mr. Bondy hurriedly.

The captain raised himself, and snorted. "Well, they're little things like that, Mr. Bondy. "Your health," he said, and took a drink. "It's good beer you've got here, my lad. Well, that's true, a house like you've got——" The captain wiped his moustache.

"And how did you come across those lizards, captain?"

"That's just the story, Mr. Bondy. Well, then, it came about like this. I was fishing for pearls on Tanah Masa——" the captain checked himself. "Or somewhere like that. Yah, it was some other island, but for the time being that's my secret, young man. People are great thieves, Mr. Bondy, and a man must mind what he says. And when those two damned Sinhalese were cutting the pearl shells underneath the water——"

"Shells?"

"Yah. Shells that stick fast to the stones like the

Jewish faith, and must be cut off with a knife. While they were doing that the lizards were looking at the divers, and the divers thought they were sea devils. They are very uncivilized people, those Sinhalese and Bataks. Well, then, they said that they were devils there. Yah." The captain blew with gusto into his handkerchief. "You know, my lad, it never leaves you in peace. I don't know if it's only the Czechs who are such an inquisitive nation, but wherever I've met a countryman of ours he's always had to push his nose into everything so as to find out what's behind it. I think it's because we Czechs don't want to believe in anything. Well, so I got it into my old stupid head that I must have a closer look at those devils. And I was drunk as well it's true, but that was only because I'd got those stupid devils in my head all the time. Down there, on the Equator anything may happen, man. So in the evening I went to have a look at Devil Bay——"

Mr. Bondy tried to picture to himself a tropical bay lined with rocks and forest. "Well, and?"

"Well, I was sitting there, and making ts, ts, ts, so that the devils would come near. And boy, after a time one of the lizards crawled out of the sea, got up on its little hind legs, and wriggled with its whole body. And it was making ts, ts, ts at me. If I hadn't been drunk I might, perhaps, have shot it; but I was, my friend, as tight as an Englishman, and so I said, 'Come here, you, come here, tapaboy, I shan't hurt you.' "

"You talked Czech to it."

"No, Malay. Out there they mostly talk Malay,

my lad. It said nothing, only shuffled from one foot to the other, and wriggled as a kid does when it's shy. And round about in the water there was about two thousand of those lizards, and they were sticking their little snouts out of the water, and looking at me. And I—well, it's true I was drunk; well, I squatted down and began to wriggle like that lizard, so they weren't frightened. And then another lizard crawled out from the water, about as big as a ten-year-old boy, and it also began to shuffle like that. And in his front paw he held such a whacking pearl shell." The captain took a drink. "Nazdar, Mr. Bondy. It's true I was dead drunk, and so I said to him, 'You smart guy, then you want me to open that shell for you, yah? Well, come here, I can open it with my knife.' But he didn't make a move, he was still too scared. So I began to wriggle again as if I were a little girl who's shy of somebody. So he tiptoed nearer, and I slowly stretched out my hand to him, and took the shell from his paw. Well, of course, we were both frightened, you can understand that, Mr. Bondy; that shell; I felt with my fingers to see if there was a pearl inside, but there wasn't, only the ugly snail, that slimy mollusc, that lives in those shells. Well, there, I said, ts, ts, ts, eat it if you want to. And I threw that open shell to him. You ought to have seen, my boy, how he licked it clean. It must be a great tit-bit for those lizards, how do you say it?"

"Delicacy."

"Yah, delicacy. Only the poor little things can't get into the hard shells with their tiny fingers. It is a hard life, yah." The captain took a drink. "Then I turned it over in my head, my boy. When those lizards saw the divers cutting the shells they must have thought to themselves, 'Aha, they must be eating them,' and they wanted to see how the divers were going to open them. Those Sinhalese in the water look something like a lizard, but the lizards have more brains than a Sinhalese, or a Batak, because they want to learn. And a Batak will never learn anything but how to steal," added Captain J. van Toch indignantly. "And when on that beach I went on making ts, ts, ts, and wriggling like a lizard they took me, perhaps, for some kind of a big salamander. So they weren't too scared, and they came to me to open that shell. That's the sort of sensible and trusting animals they are." Captain van Toch blushed. "When I got to know them better, Mr. Bondy, I used to strip myself naked so as to be more like them, to be as naked; but all the time they were curious that I had such a hairy chest, and such like things. Yah." The captain passed his handkerchief over the nape of his neck which had turned russet. "But I'm not sure that I'm not taking too much of your time, Mr. Bondy."

G. H. Bondy was charmed. "No, not at all. Go on, captain."

"Well, yah, I can do that. While that lizard was licking out that shell the others were looking at it, and they crawled up on to the beach. Some of them had also got shells in their little paws—it's a queer thing that they could tear them off from the rocks with such childish hands without thumbs. For a bit they were too shy, but then they let me take the shells from their paws. Well, you can understand, they weren't all pearl shells, there was all kinds of rubbish, barren oysters, and so forth; but I used to throw those into the water, and I said, 'Not this kind, my dears, it's not worth anything, I won't open this one for you with my knife.' But when it was a pearl shell I opened it and felt if there was a pearl inside. And that shell I used to let them lick out. By then there was a couple of hundred of those lizards sitting and watching me open the shells. Some of them tried on their own to take a shell to pieces with a bit of old shell that was lying about. Well, that struck me as very queer, my lad. No animal can use tools; it's no use, after all, an animal is only part of nature. Of course, in Buiten-zorg I saw a monkey that could open a tin, a box of tinned food with a knife; but a monkey, sir, isn't any longer a proper animal. You can understand, it struck me as very queer." The captain took a drink. "That night, Mr. Bondy, I found about eighteen pearls in those shells. Some were small, and some were bigger, and there were three like plum-stones, Mr. Bondy. Like plum-stones." Captain van Toch shook his head gravely. "When I was going back to my boat in the morning I kept saying to myself, 'Captain van Toch, you must have dreamt that, sir; you were drunk, sir,' and so on; but what was the use? There in a little pocket I had those eighteen pearls, Yah."

"This is the best story," gasped Mr. Bondy, "that I've ever heard."

"So you see, my lad," said the captain with animation. "All that day I kept turning it over in my head. I shall make those lizards tame, eh? Yah, make them tame, and train them, and they'll bring me the pearl-shells. There must be heaps of them, of those shells in Devil Bay. So I went there again that evening, but a bit earlier. When the sun began to set those lizards stuck their chumps out of the water, here and there, till it was full of them. I sat on the beach and made ts, ts, ts. Suddenly I looked up—a shark, you could only see his fin above the water. Then there was a great splashing, and one lizard had gone. I counted twelve of those sharks that sunset coming in to Devil Bay. Mr. Bondy, in one evening those brutes ate twenty of MY lizards," burst out the captain and blew his nose furiously. "Yah, over twenty! It stands to reason that a naked lizard like that can't defend itself with its tiny paws. I could have cried as I watched it. You have to see it for yourself, my boy. . . ."

The captain grew thoughtful. "For I like animals very much, man," he said, at last, and raised his sky-blue eyes to G. H. Bondy. "I don't know what you think about it, Captain Bondy——"

Mr. Bondy nodded as a sign of agreement.

"That's good, then." Captain van Toch was pleased. "They are very good and sensible, these tapa-boys; when you tell them something they sit up and take notice like a dog does when it listens to its master. And particularly their childish paws—you know, my boy. I'm an old chap, and I've got no family. . . . Yah, an old man is lonely," mumbled the captain,

53

mastering his emotion. "They are very nice and sweet, those lizards, what's the use? If only the sharks wouldn't go for them! When I threw stones at them, that is at the sharks, then *they also began to throw stones*, those tapa-boys. You won't believe it, Mr. Bondy. Well, it's true they didn't throw very far because their arms aren't long enough. But it's queer, my man. 'If you are so clever, my boys,' I said, 'try to open a shell with this knife here.' And I put the knife on the ground. They were shy for a bit, and then one tried, and struck the point of the knife between the shell. You must lever, I said, lever, see? twist the knife like this, and it's done. And he kept on trying, poor little thing, till it cracked, and the shell was open. So you see, I said. It's quite easy after all. If a heathen Batak or Sinhalese knows how to do it, wouldn't a tapa-boy know? Aren't I right? I shall not tell those lizards, Mr. Bondy, what a wonder and marvel it is, should I when a beast like that can do this kind of thing? But now I can say it, I was—I was—well, absolutely thunderstruck."

"Like a day-dream," prompted Mr. Bondy.

"Yah, right. Like a day-dream. Well, I got it into my head so much that I stayed there with the boat an extra day. And in the evening again went to Devil Bay, and again I saw how the sharks were eating my lizards. The night I swore, my boy, that I wasn't going to leave it at that. Also I gave *them* my word of honour, Mr. Bondy. TAPA-BOYS—CAPTAIN J. VAN TOCH HERE, UNDER THESE TERRIBLE STARS, PROMISES YOU THAT HE WILL HELP YOU."

4

Captain van Toch's
Business Enterprise

WHILE Captain van Toch was saying all this the hair on his neck stood right on end with excitement and enthusiasm

"Yah, sir, that's what I swore. Ever since then, my boy, I haven't had a moment's peace. In Batong I asked for leave, and sent those Jews in Amsterdam a hundred and fifty-seven pearls, everything that those little beasts had brought me. Then I found a chap, a Dayak, a shark-killer, who kills the sharks with a knife in the water. A dreadful thief and murderer, that Dayak. And with him on a small tramp-steamer back to Tanah Masa, and now, fellow, you will kill the sharks with that knife of yours. I wanted him to kill off all the sharks there so that my lizards would be left in peace. He was such a heathen and murderer, that Dayak, that he didn't even mind the tapa-boys. Devil or no devil it was all the same to him. And all the time I was making my observations and experiments on those lizards—why, stop a moment; I've got a kind of log-book about it in which I made notes every day." From his breast pocket the captain took a fat note-book and began to turn the leaves.

"Well, what day is it to-day? Why, the twenty-fifth

of June. So, for instance, the twenty-fifth of June, that was then a year ago. Yah, here. The Dayak killed a shark. The lizards took a tremendous interest in the carcass. Toby—that was one of the smaller lizards, you know, very clever," explained the captain. "I had to call them by different names, you know, so that I could write about them in my book. Well, then, Toby pushed his fingers into the hole the knife had made. In the evening they fetched dry wood for my fire. That's nothing," mumbled the captain. "I'll turn up some other day. Say the twentieth of June, eh?—The lizards went on building that—that, how do you call it, jetty?"

"You mean a dam, don't you?"

"Yah, a dam. Such a dam. They were building, then, that new dam at the north-west corner of Devil Bay. Man," he explained, "that was a wonderful bit of work. A perfect breakwater."

"Breakwater?"

"Yah. They laid their eggs on that side, and they wanted to have still water there, you know. They thought that out for *themselves* that they would make a dam there; but I tell you that no official or expert from the Waterstaat in Amsterdam would have drawn up a better scheme for such a dam below water. A very fine job, only the sea kept washing it away. They even dig out deep holes in the bottom, underneath the water, and they live in them through the day. Amazingly knowing animals, sir, just like beavers."

"Beavers?"

"Yah, the big mice that build those dams in rivers.

They had *heaps* of those dams, and little tiny dams in Devil Bay, such marvellously straight dams that it looked like some kind of a town. And at last they wanted to build a dam right across Devil Bay. They did. They already know how to roll away boulders with hoisting jacks," he went on reading. "Albert— that was another of those tapa-boys, got two fingers squashed that way. The twenty-first! Dayak *ate Albert!* But he was sick after it. Fifteen drops of laudanum. He promised never to do it again. It rained the whole day. The thirtieth of June: Lizards building the dam. Toby doesn't want to work. Sir, he was cute," explained the captain with admiration. "The cute ones never want to do anything. He kept on pottering about with something, that Toby. What's the use—even among lizards there are very big differences. July the third: Sergeant has got a knife. That was such a big strong lizard, that Sergeant. And very clever, sir. July the seventh: Sergeant killed a cuttlefish with that knife— that's that kind of fish which has got that muck inside it, you know."

"Sepia?"

"Yah, that'll be it. July the twentieth: Sergeant killed a big jelly-fish with that knife—that's a brute like jelly, and it stings like a nettle. It's an ugly brute. And now look out, Mr. Bondy. THE THIRTEENTH OF JULY. I've got it here underlined. *Sergeant killed a small shark with that knife.* Its weight was seventy pounds. Here it is, Mr. Bondy," announced Captain J. van Toch solemnly. "Here stands in black and white. That was a great day, my boy. Yes, the thirteenth of

July last year." The captain shut his note-book. "I'm not ashamed to say it, Mr. Bondy: I knelt down on my knees on the beach of that Devil Bay, and cried for pure joy. Now I knew that my tapa-boys wouldn't give in. Sergeant had got for it a fine new harpoon—a harpoon is the best thing for you, my boy, if you're going to fight sharks—and I said to him, 'Be a man, Sergeant, and show those tapa-boys that they can defend themselves.' Man," shouted the captain, as he sprang up and banged the table with enthusiasm, "do you know that three days afterwards a huge shark was floating there, done up, full of gashes, how do you say it?"

"Full of wounds?"

"Yah, all holes from the harpoon." The captain drank till it gurgled. "Well, that's how it is, Mr. Bondy. It was only then that I made with those tapa-boys . . . a sort of contract. That is, I gave them my word that if they would bring me the pearl shells I would give them harpoons and knives in exchange, so that they could defend themselves, see? That's an honest deal, sir. What's the use, you ought to be honest even with animals. And I also gave them some wood. And two iron wheelbarrows——"

"Wheelbarrows? Trolleys."

"Yah, well trolleys, so that they could take the stones for the dam. Poor things, they had to haul everything in those tiny paws of theirs, you know. Well, they got lots of things. I shouldn't like to cheat them, not at all. Wait, boy, I'll show you something."

Captain van Toch raised his body with one hand,

and with the other he fished out from his trousers pocket a linen bag. "Well, here it is," he said, shaking its contents on to the table. There were thousands of pearls of all sizes: some tiny like hemp-seed, bigger ones, some as big as peas, some the size of a cherry; perfect drop-like pearls, irregular barock pearls, silvery, blue, flesh-coloured, yellowish, running to black, even pink pearls. G. H. Bondy felt as if in a day-dream; he couldn't help it, he had to feel them with his hand, roll them with his finger-tips, cover them with both palms.

"It's a beauty," he sighed with amazement. "Captain, this is like a dream!"

"Yah," said the captain without emotion. "It's very nice. And they killed about thirty sharks during that year while I was there with them. I've got it written here," he said, tapping his breast pocket. "But think of the knives I gave them, and the five harpoons. The knives cost *me* nearly two American dollars each—well, for one at a time. Very good knives, my boy, made of some sort of steel that doesn't rust away."

"Rust?"

"Yah. Because they must be under water, knives that is for the sea. And the Bataks also cost piles of money."

"What Bataks?"

"Well, those natives on the island. They have some sort of idea that tapa-boys are devils, and they are terribly scared of them. And when they saw that I was talking with their devils they wanted to kill me right off. For nights on end they would beat some sort of gongs to chase the devils away from their kampong. They made a dreadful din, sir. And then always in the morning they wanted me to pay them for that din. For the work that they had with it, you know. Well, what's the use, the Bataks are very great thieves. But with the tapa-boys, sir, with those lizards you could do honest business. Well, then. A very good Geschäft, Mr. Bondy."

G. H. Bondy felt as if he were in a fairy-tale. "To buy pearls from them?"

"Yah. . . . Only in Devil Bay there aren't any pearls left much, and on other islands there aren't any tapa-boys. That's the whole story, young man." Captain J. van Toch blew out his cheeks victoriously. "That's just that big Geschäft that I've worked out in my head. My boy," he said, punctuating his words with his fat finger, "but the lizards have multiplied enormously since the time when I began to take them up! They can look after themselves now, you see? Eh? And there will always be more and more of them! Well then, Mr. Bondy. Wouldn't it be a marvellous business?"

"I still don't see," said G. H. Bondy uncertainly, ". . . what you really mean, Captain."

"Well, take those tapa-boys to other pearl islands," came from the captain at last. "I have found out through watching them that the lizards can't get across the deep open sea by themselves. They can swim for a while, and for a while they can tiptoe on the bottom, but at great depths the pressure's too much for them, they're too soft, you know. But if I had a boat where

I could have a cistern, well, a water tank for them, I could take them where I liked, see? And they would look for pearls there, and I should go after them and provide them with knives and harpoons and such-like things that they need. The poor little things have bred like rabbits in Devil Bay, eh?"

"Multiplied."

"Yah, multiplied so that soon they won't have anything left to eat. They eat different kinds of small fish and shell fish, and that kind of water slug; but they can also eat potatoes and biscuits and ordinary stuff of that sort. It would be possible to feed them like that in tanks on the boat. And I should drop them into the water again at the right places where there aren't many people, and I should have there such-such farms for the lizards. Well, I should like them to maintain themselves, the little beasts. They're very nice and cute, Mr. Bondy. And when you see them, my boy, you'll say, 'Hello, Captain, you have got some useful little things.' Yah. Nowadays people are as if they were mad for pearls, Mr. Bondy. Well, this is the big business that I've worked out."

G. H. Bondy was embarrassed. "I'm awfully sorry, Captain," he began, faltering, "but—I really don't know."

The sky-blue eyes of Captain J. van Toch filled with tears. "Well, that's bad, my boy. I would leave you here all these pearls as . . . as a guarantee for that boat, but I can't buy the boat alone myself. I know of a very handy boat over there in Rotterdam . . , she's got a Diesel engine——"

"Why didn't you suggest that idea to somebody in Holland?"

The captain shook his head. "I know those people, my boy. I can't talk with them about it. Well, I might perhaps," he said thoughtfully, "take other things as well on that boat, all sorts of things, sir, and sell them on those islands. Yah, I could do that. I know lots of people there, Mr. Bondy. At the same time I could have in my boat those tanks for my lizards."

"This is worth thinking about," meditated G. H. Bondy. "As a matter of fact . . . well yes, we *must* look for new markets for our products. I chanced to speak of it recently with some people. I should like to buy one or two boats, one for South Africa and another for those Eastern countries."

The captain revived. "That strikes me as very good, Mr. Bondy, sir. Boats are terribly cheap now, you could buy a harbour full of them." Captain van Toch began a technical exposition as to where and for how much they were for sale, the kinds of steamers, boats, and tankers; G. H. Bondy was not listening, he was only studying him; G. H. Bondy was a great judge of men. Not for an instant did he take the lizards of Captain van Toch seriously; but the captain had his points. Honest, yes. And he knows the conditions out there. Mad, of course. But damnably understanding. In the heart of G. H. Bondy some fantastic string vibrated. Boats with pearls and coffee, boats with spices and all the perfumes of Arabia. G. H. Bondy felt distracted, a sensation that usually came over him before every big and successful decision; a feeling that might be expressed by the words: I don't know why though, but very likely I shall go in for it. In the meanwhile Captain van Toch was demonstrating with his powerful paws boats with awning decks or quarter-decks, marvellous boats, my boy.

"Well, do you know what, Captain Vantoch," broke out G. H. Bondy suddenly, "come here again in a fortnight's time. We will talk about that boat again."

Captain van Toch understood how much such a word meant. He turned crimson with pleasure, and managed to say: "And those lizards, shall I be able to take them on my boat?"

"Why, yes. Only I must ask you not to mention them to anybody. People might think that you had gone mad—and I as well."

"And I can leave these pearls here?"

"You can."

"Yah, then I must pick out two very nice ones. I ought to send them to somebody."

"To whom?"

"To some kind of editors, my boy. Yah, crikey, wait a bit."

"What?"

"Crikey, what were they called?" Captain van Toch blinked thoughtfully with sky-blue eyes. "I have such a thick head, man. I can't remember any longer what the names of those two boys really were."

5

Captain J. van Toch
and his trained Lizards

"WELL, if it isn't Jensen that's before me," said a
man in Marseilles.

The Swede Jensen raised his eyes. "Wait," he said,
"and don't you speak till I've found out who you are."
He put his hands on the forehead. "*Seagull*, no. *Empress
of India*, no. Pernambuco, no. I've got it—Vancouver.
Five years ago in Vancouver, Osaka-Line, 'Frisco.
And your name is Dingle, you rascal, and you're
Irish."

The man bared his teeth and sat down. "Right,
Jensen. And I drink anything that can be put in a
bottle. Where did the wind blow you from?"

Jensen indicated with his head. "I'm now sailing
Marseilles–Saigon. And you?"

"I'm on leave," boasted Dingle. "Musha, it's off
home I'm going to see how many more kids
I've got."

Jensen nodded seriously. "So they've chucked you
out again, have they? Drunkenness while on duty, and
things like that. If you went to the Y.M.C.A. as I do,
man, then——"

Dingle grinned with pleasure. "Is there a Y.M.C.A.
here?"

"It's Saturday to-day, you know," mumbled Jensen. "And what kind of a boat were you on?"

"On a tramp," said Dingle evasively. "All sorts of islands down there."

"Captain?"

"One van Toch, a Dutchman, or something."

The Swede Jensen became thoughtful. "Captain van Toch. I used to sail with that man years ago, brother. Boat: *Kandong Bandoeng*. Line from deuce to devil. Fat, bald, and swears in Malay as well, so that there's more of it. I know him very well."

"Was he cracked in your time?"

The Swede shook his head. "Old Toch's all right, man."

"Did he have those lizards of his around him then?"

"No." Jensen hesitated a moment. "I heard something about it . . . in Singapore. An old driveller there said something about it."

The Irishman felt rather offended. "It isn't drivel, Jensen. It's the holy truth about those lizards."

"That man in Singapore also said that it was true," muttered the Swede. "And still he got a whack on the jaw," he added victoriously.

"Arrah, stand until I tell you," said Dingle in self-defence, "what there is in it. I should know, Mike, indeed I should. I've often laid eyes on those brutes."

"I have too," mumbled Jensen. "Nearly black, with a tail about four feet six, and they walk on two legs, I know."

"Disgusting," shivered Dingle. "All warts, Mike.

Virgin Mary, I wouldn't lay hands on them! Them devils are poisonous, surely!"

"Why?" grunted the Swede. "Man, I've even served on a boat that was chockful of people. On the upper deck and on the lower deck, everywhere, men, women and such-like things, and they danced and played cards—I was a stoker there, you know. And now tell me, you idiot, which is more poisonous?"

Dingle spat forcibly. "If they'd been caymans, Mike, you wouldn't get a word out of me. Once I helped in the bringing of snakes to a zoo, beyond Bandjermassin, and how they stank, Mike! But them ould lizards—Jensen, they're a very queer sort of beast. I don't dread them in the day-time; in the day-time they're in the tanks of water; but at night they crawl out, tip-tip, tip-tip. . . . The whole boat was flooded with them. They stood on their legs and turned their heads after you . . ." The Irishman crossed himself. "They make ts-ts-ts at you like those whores in Hong Kong. May God not punish me, but it occurs to me that it's not all correct. If it wasn't so hard for a man to get a job, I wouldn't be there ten minutes, Jensi, not for an hour."

"Aha," said Jensen. "So that's why you're coming back to mammy, is it?"

"In a way of speaking. You have to soak there a lot to stand up against it, and you know captain's after it like a dog. There was a shindy, I tell you; they said I kicked one of those brutes. Begorra, I did, and with a will, man; till I broke its back. You ought to have seen the old man's work; he turned blue, got me by the scruff of my neck, and would have landed me into the sea if Gregory the mate hadn't been there. Do you know him?"

The Swede only nodded.

" 'He's had enough already, sir,' the mate said, and poured a bucket of water over my head. And in Kokopo I left the boat." Mr. Dingle spat in a long flat curve. "The old man cared more for those brutes than for his crew. Do you know that he's learning them to talk? Upon my soul, he shuts himself up with them, and for hours he talks to them. It's my belief that he's getting them ready for some sort of a circus. But the queerest thing is that afterwards he lets them go into the water. He stops at some silly little island, he rows round the shore in a boat and measures the depth; then he goes to the tanks and stays there; he opens a hatch in the side of the boat and lets the brutes into the water. Pat, they plunge through that hatch one after another like trained seals, always ten or twelve— and at night old Toch rows to the shore with some sort of little boxes. The contents nobody knows. Then he sails on again. Well then, that's how it is with old Toch, Jensen. Queer. Very queer." Mr. Dingle's eyes became fixed. "Almighty God, Jensen, it made my mind very uneasy! I drank, man, I drank like a fish; and when they tiptoed at night all over the boat, and begged . . . and made ts-ts-ts, I thought sometimes, oho, youngster, in my mind that came from drink. It came upon me once before in 'Frisco, but then, you know, Jensen, I saw nothing but spiders. De-li-rium, the doctors in the sailors' hospital used to say. So I don't know. But then I asked Big Bing if he'd seen it in the night-time too, and he said he had. He said that he'd seen with his own eyes how one lizard turned the knob, and went to the captain in his cabin. So I don't know; Joe drank a lot too. Do you think, Mike, that Bing had delirium too? What do you think?"

The Swede Jensen only shrugged his shoulders.

"And that German Peters said that at the Manihiki Islands, when he set the captain on shore, he placed himself behind the rocks and was on the look for what the old Toch was up to there with those boxes. Man, he said, the lizards opened it themselves when the old man gave them the chisel. And do you know what was in those boxes? Knives, mate, he said. Knives as long as that, and harpoons, and such-like things. Begorra, I must say I don't believe what Peters said, because he wears spectacles on his nose, but it's very queer. What thinks you?"

The veins on Jensen's forehead began to stand out. "Well, if you ask me," he growled, "that German of yours sticks his nose into things that aren't his business, do you get me? I wouldn't advise him to do that, I tell you."

"Well, send him a line and inform him," mocked the Irishman. "The best address to find him is c/o Hell—it might get to him there. And do you know what strikes me as very queer? That the old Toch goes back at times to the places that he's cropped with lizards, to throw his eyes on them. On my oath. Pat, he lets himself be set down at night on the shore, and he's not seen till morning. Well then, tell me,

Jensen, what he's up to doing that? And tell me what's inside those little parcels that he keeps sending to Europe. See, parcels as small as this, and he insures them for as much as a thousand pounds."

"How do you know that?" frowned the Swede, turning still darker.

"I know what comes my way," said Mr. Dingle evasively. "And have you any idea where old Toch gets his lizards from? From Devil Bay, Mike. I know a man there—he's an agent, and a learnt man—and it was he who told me, man, that they aren't tame lizards. Not a bit of it! You can tell it to the marines that they're only animals. Don't believe a word of it, my lad." Mr. Dingle blinked significantly with his eyes. "That's the way it is, Jensen, if you want to know. And you try to tell me that Captain van Toch is all right."

"Say it once again," rattled the big Swede threateningly.

"If old Toch was all right, he wouldn't take them devils . . . all over the globe, and he wouldn't set them down everywhere on islands like lice on a coat, Jens. While I was with him he'd hauled around a couple of thousand. Old Toch has sold his soul, Pat. And I know what those devils are giving him for it. Rubies, pearls, and such-like things. You may be sure he wouldn't do it for nothing."

Jens Jensen turned scarlet. "And is that any business of yours?" he roared, banging the table. "Mind your own damned job!"

The little man Dingle sprang up with fright. "Pray,"

he jibbered with confusion, "what makes you all of a sudden . . . I'm only telling you what I've seen with my own eyes. And if you like, it came to me in a dream. Since it's you that's in it, Mike, if you like I'll say that I had delirium. You mustn't get worked up about me, Jensen. You know, don't you, that I had it before in 'Frisco. A bad case, said the doctors at the sailors' hospital. Pat, upon my soul, I only dreamt that I saw those lizards or devils, or what not. But there was none."

"There was, Pat," said the Swede gloomily. "I've seen them."

"No, Jens," expostulated Dingle. "You only had delirium. Old Toch is all right, but he oughtn't to cart those devils all over the globe. Do you know what: when I'm at home I shall ask them to say a mass for his soul. Blow me, Jensen, if I don't do that."

"We don't do that," droned Jensen sadly, "in our confession. And what do you think, Pat—does it do any good if a mass is said for somebody?"

"An amount of good, Mike," burst out the Irishman. "I've heard of cases at home when it helped . . . even in the poorest of times. All against devils and such things, you know."

"Then I shall have a Catholic mass said too," decided Jens Jensen. "For Captain van Toch. But I shall have it said here in Marseilles. I think that in that big church they'll do it cheaper, cost price."

"It could be; but an Irish mass is the real thing. In my home, man, the Jesuites are devils; they can nearly do wonders. Just like witch doctors or heathens."

"Look here, Pat," said Jensen, "I'd like to give you twelve francs for that mass. But you're a rascal, my boy, you'd drink it all."

"Jens, I wouldn't put such a sin upon my soul. But wait a bit, so that you can trust me I'll give you an I O U for those twelve francs, don't you think?"

"That would do," thought the methodical Swede.

Mr. Dingle borrowed a pencil and paper, and spread himself broadly over the table. "Well, what am I to write?"

Jens Jensen glared over his shoulder. "Well, put at the top that it's a sort of document."

And, sticking out his tongue with concentration and licking his pencil, Mr. Dingle wrote:

Document

This is to Certify, that I received from Jen. Jensen for a mas for the Soule of captan Toch 12 franks

Pat Dingle

"Is this all right?" inquired Mr. Dingle uncertainly. "And who ought to take care of this paper?"

"You, of course, you sheep," said the Swede as a

matter of course. "That's so that you won't forget that you've got the money."

•   •   •   •   •

Mr. Dingle spent those twelve francs on drink at le Havre, and on top of that instead of going to Ireland he went to Jibuti: in fact the mass has not yet been said, and consequently no higher power has interfered with the natural course of events.

6

The Yacht on the Lagoon

MR. ABE LOEB screwed up his eyes to look towards
the setting sun; he would have liked somehow to say
how beautiful it was, but his darling Li, alias Miss
Lily Valley, *née* Miss Lilian Nowak—in short, golden-
haired Li, White Lily, leggy Lilian, and whatever else
she had been called before her seventeenth year—was
asleep on the warm sand, wrapped up cosily in a
woolly bathing wrap and coiled up like a sleeping dog.
So Abe didn't make any remarks on the beauty of
the world; he only sighed as he moved the toes of his
bare feet, for he had grains of sand between them.
Over there on the water lay a yacht called *Gloria
Pickford*; Abe had got this yacht from papa Loeb for
having passed his final exams. Papa Loeb was swell.
Jesse Loeb, film magnate and so on. "Abe, invite one
or two of your girl and boy friends, and try and see a
bit of the world," the old gentleman had said. Papa
Jesse was terribly swell. There then on the mother-of-
pearl sea lay *Gloria Pickford*, and here on the warm
sand was darling Li asleep. Abe sighed with happiness.
"She sleeps like a kid, poor little thing." Suddenly Abe
felt an immense desire to protect her somehow. "As a
matter of fact, I *really* ought to marry her," meditated
young Mr. Loeb, and at the same time he felt in his

heart a beautiful and tormenting pressure composed of firm determination and fear. Mama Loeb mightn't approve of it, and papa Loeb would throw his arms apart: "You're crazy, Abe." Parents simply can't understand it, that's what it is. And sighing with tenderness Mr. Abe drew the corner of the bathing wrap over the white ankle of darling Li. "What a pity," he thought with embarrassment, "that I've got so much hair on my legs!

"God, how beautiful it is here, how beautiful it is here! It's a pity that Li doesn't see it." Mr. Abe ran his eye down the nice line of her hip, and in a hazy manner he began to think of art. For darling Li was an artist. A film artist. She hadn't acted yet though, but she'd made up her mind to be the greatest film actress of all the centuries; and what Li had set her mind upon she achieved. "That's just what mother Loeb doesn't understand; an artist is, well, just—an artist, and can't be like other girls. And besides, other girls aren't any better," decided Mr. Abe; "for instance that Judy on the yacht, such a rich girl—don't I know that Fred goes into her cabin *every* night, I ask you, whereas Li and me. . . . Well, Li isn't *like that*. I don't grudge it to baseball Fred," said Abe to himself magnanimously. "He was my pal at the Varsity; but every night—*such* a rich girl oughtn't to do that. I mean, a girl from a family like Judy's. And Judy isn't even an artist. What do those girls whisper about between themselves?" wondered Abe. "How their eyes shine, and how they giggle—with Fred I never talk about things of *that* sort. (Li oughtn't to drink so many cocktails, then she doesn't know what she's talking about.) (For instance, to-day, this afternoon, she needn't have done . . .) (I mean when she and Judy fell out about which of them had the nicest legs. Of course, Li has, I know that.) (And Fred needn't have had that silly idea that we should compare them to see who had the nicest legs. That's all right somewhere on Palm Beach, but not in private company. And the girls perhaps needn't have lifted their skirts *so high*. But that wasn't just legs *only*. At least, Li needn't have done it. And just in front of Fred! And a rich girl like Judy needn't have done it either.) (I oughtn't to have asked the captain to be judge. That was daft of me. How that captain turned scarlet and made his moustache bristle, and 'Excuse me,' he said, and banged the door. Awkward. Frightfully awkward. The captain oughtn't to have been *so* rude. After all, it's *my* yacht, isn't it?) (It's true the captain hasn't any girl with him; how can he bring himself to it, poor chap, to look at things like *that*? I mean, when he must be lonely.) (And why did Li cry when Fred said that Judy had nicer legs? Then she said that Fred hadn't been brought up properly; he spoils the cruise for her, she said. . . . Poor Li!) (And now the girls won't speak to each other. And when I wanted to talk to Fred, Judy called him to her like a dog. Isn't Fred my best pal? Of course, since he's Judy's lover he *had* to say that she's got nicer legs! It's true he needn't have been so assertive about it. That *wasn't* very tactful towards poor Li; Li is right when she says that Fred is an egoistic lout. A terrible lout.) (In fact I thought the cruise would be different. What the devil made me bring Fred!)"

Mr. Abe found that he was no longer gazing with wonder at the mother-of-pearl sea, but that he was very, very vexed as he sifted sand and tiny shells through his fingers. He felt depressed and disconcerted. Papa Loeb had said, "Do what you can to see a bit of the world." Mr. Abe tried to remember what he really had seen, but he couldn't recall anything except Judy and Li showing their legs, and Fred, broad-shouldered Fred, crouching in front of them. Abe was still more vexed. "What's the name of this coral island?" "Taraiva," said the captain. "Taraiva or Tahuara or Taraihatuara-ta-huara." "What about going back home now, and I shall say to old Jesse 'Dad, we went as far as Taraihatuara-ta-huara.'" ("If only I hadn't asked that captain," worried Mr. Abe.) ("I must tell Li not to do such things. God, how is it that I'm so *terribly* in love with her! When she wakes I shall have a talk with her. I shall tell her that perhaps we might get married . . .") Mr. Abe's eyes filled with tears. "God, is it love, or pain, or is this immense pain because I love her so much?"

The blue-tinted, shiny eyelids of darling Li trembled like tender little shells. "Abe," she said dreamily, "do y'know what I've been thinking about? That here on this island we could make a marvellous film."

Mr. Abe was sprinkling sand over his unfortunate hairy legs. "A great idea, darling. And what sort of a film?"

Darling Li turned her immense blue eyes on him.

"Say, like this. Suppose that I were a Robinson Crusoe on this island. A girl Crusoe. Isn't it a marvellously new idea?"

"Yes," said Abe vaguely. "And how would you get here?"

"Superbly," said the sweet little voice. "Do you know, our yacht would simply be shipwrecked in a storm, and all the rest of you would be drowned—you, Judy, the captain, and all the rest."

"And Fred as well? Fred can swim marvellously."

The smooth forehead darkened. "Then Fred must be eaten by a shark. That would be a heavenly episode." The darling clapped her hands. "Fred has a divinely beautiful body for it, don't you think?"

Abe sighed. "And what then?"

"I have been thrown unconscious here on the shore by a wave. I should be wearing those pyjamas, the ones with the blue stripes that you liked so much the day before yesterday." Between the tender eyelids a half-closed glance swam forwards suitably displaying feminine charm. "As a matter of fact, the film ought to be in colour, Abe. Everybody says that blue goes marvellously with my hair."

"And who would find you here?" asked Abe in a matter-of-fact voice.

The darling grew thoughtful. "Nobody. I shouldn't be a Robinson Crusoe if there were people here," she said, with a surprising sense for logic. "That's why it would be such a marvellous part, Abe. I should be alone all the time. Just think of it, Lily Valley in the principal and unique role part."

"And what should you be doing all through the film?"

Li leaned against her elbow. "I've already thought of that. I should be bathing and singing on the rocks."

"In pyjamas?"

"No, without," said the darling. "Don't you think that it would be a tremendous success?"

"But you wouldn't act a whole film naked," muttered Abe, with a lively feeling of disapproval.

"Why not?" wondered the darling innocently. "What about it?"

Mr. Abe muttered something unintelligible.

"And then," mused Li ". . . wait, I've got it. Then a gorilla would carry me off. You know, such a frightfully black, hairy gorilla."

Mr. Abe blushed, and tried to cover his accursed legs still more with sand. "There are no gorillas here, you know," he objected unconvincingly.

"There are. There are all sorts of animals here. You try to look at it from the artistic point of view, Abe. A gorilla would go with my complexion marvellously. Have you noticed what a lot of hair Judy has on her legs?"

"No," said Abe, reduced to misery by this theme.

"Horrid legs," reflected the darling, looking at her own calves. "And when that gorilla had got me in its arms a young superb savage would dash out from the jungle and knock it down."

"What would he be wearing?"

"He would have a bow," decided the darling without

78

hesitation. "And a wreath on his head. That savage would take me prisoner, and would lead me to the cannibals' camp."

"There aren't any here." Abe made an effort to defend the little island Tahuara.

"There are. These cannibals would want to sacrifice me to their idols, and they would sing Hawaiian songs to it. You know, that kind of thing the negroes sing in the Paradise Restaurant. But that young cannibal would fall in love with me," sighed the darling, with eyes wide open with amazement; ". . . but then another cannibal would fall in love with me, perhaps the chief of these cannibals . . . and then a white man——"

"How would the white man get here?" inquired Abe to make certain.

"He would be their prisoner. He might be a famous tenor who had fallen into the hands of the savages. So that he could sing in the film."

"And what would he have on?"

The darling gazed at her big toes. "He would have . . . nothing at all, like the cannibals."

Mr. Abe shook his head. "Darling, that wouldn't do. All famous tenors are horribly fat."

"That's a pity," regretted the darling. "Then Fred might act for him, and the tenor would only sing. You know the way they do that synchronization in the films."

"But hasn't Fred been eaten by a shark?"

The darling grew annoyed. "You mustn't be so darned realistic, Abe. One can't talk art with you *at all.*

And that chief would tie me round and round with strings of pearls——"

"Where would he get them from?"

"There are *masses* of pearls here," asserted Li. "And in a fit of jealousy Fred would fight with him on a rock above the surf. Fred would be divine as a silhouette against the sky, don't you think? Isn't it a brilliant idea? Then they would both fall into the sea." The darling brightened up. "Now that episode with the shark might come in. Judy would be in a rage if Fred acted with me in a film! I should marry that beautiful savage." The golden-haired Li sprang up. "We should stand here on this shore . . . against the sunset . . . quite naked . . . and the film would be slowly coming to an end." Li threw her bathing wrap away. "And now I'm going into the water."

". . . haven't brought your swimming costume," observed Abe aghast, glancing back towards the yacht to see if anybody was looking; but darling Li was already dancing over the sand to the lagoon.

". . . she really looks better when she's dressed," suddenly prompted a brutally cold and critical voice inside the young man. Abe was taken aback with his lack of ardent amazement, he almost felt guilty; "but . . . well, when Li has a frock on and shoes it's . . . well, nicer somehow.

"You want to say more decent, perhaps," Abe reflected, defending himself against that cold voice.

"Yes, even that. And prettier. Why does she waddle so strangely? Why does the flesh on her thighs shake so much? Why this and that . . ."

"Stop," protested Abe, defending himself with terror. "Li is the most beautiful girl that has ever been born! I love her terribly . . ."

". . . even when she's got nothing on?" inquired the cold and critical voice.

Abe turned his eyes away and looked at the yacht on the lagoon. "How fine she is, how clean in every line of her hull! It's a pity Fred isn't here. With Fred I could talk about the yacht's lines."

In the meantime the darling was already standing up to her knees in the water; she stretched out her arms to the sunset and sang. "What the devil, isn't she swimming yet?" thought Abe irritably. But it was nice when she was lying here in her bathing wrap, curled up into a ball and with her eyes closed. Darling Li. With a sigh of emotion Abe kissed the sleeve of her bathing wrap. Yes, he loved her tremendously. So much that it hurt.

Suddenly a piercing shriek came from the lagoon. Abe raised himself on one knee so that he could see better. Darling Li was squealing, waving her arms, and wading in great haste to the shore; she stumbled and splashed about. Abe sprang up and ran towards her. "What's the trouble, Li?"

("See how awkwardly she runs," observed the cold and critical voice. "She throws her legs out too much. She waves her arms about too much. Just now she does *not* look nice. And besides, she's cackling, yes, cackling.")

"What's happened, Li?" shouted Abe, running to help her.

"Abe, Abe," chattered the darling, and flop, she was already hanging on to him wet and cold. "Abe, there's some animal there!"

"That's nothing," said Abe to soothe her. "Some kind of fish, most likely."

"But it had such a horrid head," moaned the darling, and dug her wet nose into Abe's chest.

Abe tried to pat her paternally on the shoulder, but his hand smacked too loudly on her wet body. "Well, well," he murmured. "Look, there's nothing there now."

Li turned to look at the lagoon. "It was horrible," she gasped, and then suddenly she began to scream: "There . . . there . . . don't you see?"

Slowly a dark head drew near to the shore, and its snout opened and closed. Darling Li screamed hysterically and began to run desperately away from the shore.

Abe was in a quandary. "Should I run after Li so that she's not so frightened? Or should I stay here to show her that I'm not afraid of the beast?" He decided, of course, for the latter; he walked slowly towards the sea until he stood ankle-deep in the water, and with clenched fists he looked the animal in the eyes. The dark head halted, it swayed strangely, and said: "Ts, ts, ts." Abe felt rather uneasy, but he had to try to conceal it. "What do you say?" he demanded sharply of the head.

"Ts, ts, ts," said the head.

"Abe, Abe, Abe," yelled darling Li.

"I'm coming," shouted Abe, and slowly (to save his

face) he walked towards the girl. He halted once more and turned sternly towards the sea.

On the shore where the sea was making on the sand its eternal and ephemeral lace a dark animal with a round head was standing on its hind legs and wriggling its body. Abe stood still with his heart thumping.

"Ts, ts, ts," said the animal.

"A-be," moaned the darling in a half-swoon.

Abe receded step by step without taking his eyes off the animal; this did not stir, but only turned its head to watch him.

At last Abe had rejoined his darling, who was lying with her face to the ground and sobbing spasmodically with terror. "It's . . . some sort of a seal," said Abe dubiously. "We ought to go back to the boat, Li."

But Li only shivered.

"Oh, that wouldn't hurt you," asserted Abe; he would have liked to kneel beside Li, but he could only stand chivalrously between her and the animal. "If only I weren't in my swimming suit," he thought, "and if only I had even a pocket-knife; or if I could find a stick . . ."

It began to grow dark. The animal again approached to within about thirty yards and stopped again. And behind it five, six, eight similar animals emerged from the sea, and with a faltering waddle they tiptoed towards the place where Abe was guarding darling Li.

"Shut your eyes, Li," whispered Abe, but that was needless, for Li wouldn't have turned for anything in the world.

More shadows emerged from the sea and advanced

in a wide semicircle. "Now there are about sixty," counted Abe. "That light thing there is darling Li's bathing wrap. The wrap in which she was sleeping a few moments ago." In the meantime the animals had got as far as the wrap that lay spread out over the sand.

Then Abe did something obvious and nonsensical, like Schiller's knight who went into the lion's cage to get his lady's glove. What of that: there are some obvious and nonsensical things that men will do as long as the world turns round. Without a second thought, and with head erect and clenched fists, Mr. Abe Loeb went among those animals for the bathing wrap of darling Li.

The animals stepped back a bit, but they didn't run away. Abe picked up the wrap, threw it over his arm like a matador, and stood there.

"A-be," came the desperate lament from behind him.

Mr. Abe could feel himself filled with immense strength and courage. "Well, then," he said to the animals, and made another step nearer to them. "What do you want, after all?"

"Ts, ts," one of the animals smacked, and then croaking somewhat and like an old man it barked out: "Nife!"

"Nife!" came another bark further away. "Nife! Nife!"

"A-be!"

"Don't be frightened, Li," called Abe.

"Li," one of them barked in front of him. "Li. Li. Abe!"

Abe felt as if he were in a dream. "What's that?"
"Nife!"

"A-be," moaned darling Li. "Come here!"

"Coming. You mean knife. I haven't a knife. I shan't hurt you. What else do you want?"

"Ts, ts," smacked the animal, and waddled towards him.

Abe stood with his legs apart, the wrap slung over his arm, but he didn't budge an inch. "Ts, ts," he said. "What do you want?" To him it seemed as if the animal offered its front paw, but Abe didn't like the look of that. "What?" he asked somewhat sharply.

"Nife," barked the animal, and from its paw some tiny things fell like colourless drops of water. But they weren't drops because they rolled.

"Abe," stuttered Li. "Don't leave me here!"

Mr. Abe felt no longer afraid. "Go away," he said, waving the bathing wrap towards the animal. The animal started back hastily and clumsily. Now Abe could retire with honour, but he would show Li how brave he was; he stooped down to have a look at the whitish things that the animal had let fall from its paw. They were three smooth hard little balls with a dull polish. Mr. Abe held them close to his eyes because it was getting dark.

"A-be," shrieked the deserted darling. "Abe!"

"I'm coming," shouted Mr. Abe. "Li, I've got something for you. Li, Li, there's something for you!' Swinging round the coat over his shoulder, Mr. Abe Loeb dashed over the beach like a young demigod.

Li was cowering in a heap and trembling. "Abe,"

85

she sobbed, and her teeth chattered. "How can you
. . . how can you . . ."

Abe knelt down solemnly in front of her. "Lily
Valley, the Tritons or the gods of the sea came to pay
you homage. I have to tell you that since the time
that Venus emerged from the sea no artist has ever
made such a deep impression as you have. As a token
of their admiration they send you," Abe stretched out
his hand, "these three pearls here. Look."

"Don't be silly, Abe," whimpered darling Li.

"Seriously, Li. Well, see if they aren't real pearls!"

"Show me," whined Li, and with trembling fingers
she reached for the little white balls. "Abe," she
gasped, "but they are *pearls*! Did you find them in
the sand?"

"But, Li, my dear, there aren't any pearls in the
sand, you know!"

"There are," asserted the darling. "And they're
washed clean. You see, I told you that there are
masses of pearls here!"

"Pearls grow in a sort of shell under the water," said
Abe almost dogmatically. "Upon my word, Li, those
Tritons brought them for you. For they saw you
swimming. They wanted to give them to you personally, but because you were so frightened of
them——"

"They're so ugly," blurted out Li. "Abe, these are
marvellous pearls! I love pearls tremendously!"

("Now she's very pretty," said the critical voice. "As
she kneels here with those pearls in the hollow of her
hand—well, pretty, you must admit that.")

"Abe, and they *really* brought them to me, those . . . those animals?"

"They're not animals, darling. They're sea gods. They're called Tritons."

The darling wasn't at all astonished. "That's very nice of them, isn't it? They're awfully sweet. What do you think, Abe, shall I thank them in any way?"

"You're not frightened of them any more?"

The darling shivered. "I am, Abe; please take me away."

"Well, look here," said Abe. "We must get back to our boat. Come, and don't be frightened."

"But . . . but they're standing in our way," chattered Li. "Abe, don't you want to go to them yourself? But you mustn't leave me here alone!"

"I shall carry you past them in my arms," suggested Mr. Abe heroically.

"That might do," sighed the darling.

"But put your wrap on," mumbled Abe.

"In a moment." Miss Li tidied up her famous golden hair with both her hands. "Isn't my hair *terribly* untidy? Abe, haven't you some rouge with you for my lips?"

Abe put the wrap round her shoulders. "We'd better get going, Li!"

"I'm scared," whispered the darling. Abe lifted her up in his arms. Li seemed to herself to be as light as a little cloud. "Gosh, she's heavier than you thought, isn't she?" said the cold and critical voice to Abe. "And now you've got both your hands full, man; if the animals come for you—what then?"

"Can't you go a little faster?" suggested the darling.

"Yes," gasped Mr. Abe, hardly moving his legs. By then it was getting dark quickly. Abe was getting near to the wide semicircle of those creatures.

"Quick, Abe, run, run," whispered Li. The animals began to sway and turn the upper half of their bodies round with a strange undulating movement.

"Run, run, quick," moaned the darling, hysterically kicking with her legs and digging her silver-lacquered nails into Abe's neck.

"What the devil, Li; be quiet," growled Abe.

"Nife," a voice barked beside him. "Ts, ts, ts. Nife. Li. Nife. Nife. Li."

Now they were past that semicircle, and Abe felt his feet sinking into the damp sand. "You can put me down," said the darling, just at the moment when Abe's arms and legs gave way.

Abe gasped heavily as he wiped the sweat from his forehead with the back of his hand. "Get to the boat quick," ordered darling Li. The semicircle of dark shadows turned now to face Li and drew nearer. "Ts, ts, ts. Nife. Nife. Li."

But Li didn't cry out. Li didn't take to her heels. She raised her arms to the sky, and the bathing wrap slipped from her shoulders. Naked, Li waved both her hands to the swaying shadows and blew them kisses. On her trembling lips something that anyone must admit was a charming smile appeared. "You are so sweet," said a trembling little voice. And the white arms again waved towards the swaying shadows.

"Come and help, Li," grumbled Abe, somewhat annoyed as he pushed the boat into deeper water.

Darling Li picked up the bathing wrap. "Good-bye, you darlings!" They could hear the shadows splashing in the water. "Make haste, Abe," hissed the darling as she waded to the boat. "They're here again!" Mr. Abe Loeb was trying desperately to get the boat into the water. So, and then Miss Li clambered in and waved her hand in greeting. "Go to the other side, Abe; they can't see me."

"Nife. Ts, ts, ts. Abe!"

"Nife, ts, nife."

"Ts, ts."

"Nife!"

At last the boat rolled on the waves, Mr. Abe clambered up into it, and pulled with all his might at the oars. One of the oars struck some sort of a slippery object. Darling Li sighed deeply. "Aren't they just too sweet! And didn't I do it *perfectly*?"

Mr. Abe rowed with all his might towards the yacht. "Put that coat on, Li," he said rather dryly.

"I think that it was a *stupendous* success," declared Miss Li. "And those pearls, Abe! What do you think they're worth?"

Mr. Abe stopped rowing for a second. "I think that you needn't show yourself to them *so* much, darling."

Miss Li felt rather offended. "What was wrong with it? It's clear, Abe, that you aren't an *artist*. Please go on; I'm frozen in this wrap!"

7

The Yacht on the Lagoon
continued

THAT evening there were no personal disputes on board the yacht *Gloria Pickford*; only scientific views which were clamorously conflicting. Fred (loyally supported by Abe) was of the opinion that *for certain* they must have been some kind of Sauria, while on the contrary, the captain presumed that they were mammals. "There aren't any Sauria in the sea," declared the captain warmly; but the young gentlemen from the Varsity paid no heed to his objections; Sauria, somehow, were more sensational. Darling Li was contented with having them as Tritons, that they simply were *delightful*, and altogether that it had been *such* a success; and Li (in the blue striped pyjamas that Abe liked *so* much) dreamt with shining eyes of pearls and the sea gods. Judy, of course, was sure that it was all a joke and humbug, that Li and Abe had thought it out together, and had winked furiously at Fred not to interfere. Abe thought that Li *might* have mentioned how he, Abe, went fearlessly among the Sauria to fetch her bathing wrap; and so three different times he related how Li faced them *superbly* while he, Abe, was pushing the boat into the water, and he was just about to begin to tell it again for the fourth time;

but Fred and the captain weren't listening at all, for they were arguing passionately about Sauria and Mammals. ("As if *it* mattered so much what they were," thought Abe.) At last, Judy yawned, and said that she was going to bed; she looked significantly at Fred, but Fred had just remembered that before the Flood such funny old Sauria had existed. Gosh! what were they called?—Diplosaurus, Bogosaurus, or something like that, and they walked about on their hind legs, sir; Fred had seen it himself in a funny scientific diagram, sir, in a book as fat as that. A tremendous book, sir; you ought to know it.

"Abe," said darling Li, "I've got a *swell* idea for a film."

"What kind of an idea?"

"Something tremendously new. Do you know, our yacht might sink and I should be the only one to get to that island alive. And there I should live like Robinson Crusoe."

"What should you do there?" objected the captain sceptically.

"I should swim, and do things like that," said the darling simply. "And then those sea Tritons would fall in love with me . . . and they would bring me pearls. You know, just as if it were real. It might even be a biological and educational film, don't you think? Something like Trader Horn."

"Li's right," declared Fred suddenly. "We ought to film those Sauria to-morrow night."

"You mean those mammals," corrected the captain.

"You mean me," said the darling, "while I'm standing among those sea Tritons."

"But in a bathing wrap," Abe blurted out.

"I should wear that *white* swimming dress," said Li. "And Greta would have to do my hair properly. To-day I simply looked frightful."

"And who would film it?"

"Abe. So that he's doing something at any rate. And Judy would have to see to the lighting if it happened to be dark already."

"And what about Fred?"

"Fred would have a bow and wear a wreath on his head, and if those Tritons tried to carry me off he would go for them, wouldn't he?"

"Not for me," grinned Fred. "But I'd rather have a revolver. And the captain ought to be in it as well."

The captain made his moustache bristle in a bellicose manner. "Please don't bother about me. I shall do what's needful."

"And what will that be?"

"Three men from the crew, sir. And well armed, sir."

Darling Li was charmingly amazed. "You think it would be as dangerous as *that*, captain?"

"I don't think anything, child," mumbled the captain. "But I have my orders from Mr. Jesse Loeb— at least with regard to Mr. Abe."

The gentlemen threw themselves passionately into the technical details of the undertaking; Abe winked at the darling. You ought to go to bed, and so on. Li went obediently.

"Do you know, Abe," she said in her cabin, "I think that it will be a *gorgeous* film!"

"It will, darling," agreed Mr. Abe, and wanted to kiss her.

"Not to-day, Abe," said the darling, defending herself. "Can't you understand that I must concentrate *frightfully*."

•   •   •   •   •

All the next day Miss Li was concentrating intensely; the poor maid Greta was up to her ears with it. There were baths with important salts and essences in them, hair-washing with Nurblond shampoo, massages, pedicure, manicure, hair-waving and hair-dressing, ironing, tryings on, alterations, making up, and apparently many more preparations as well; Judy too was carried away with the rush, and came to help darling Li. (There are difficult moments when women can be astonishingly loyal to one another, as for instance over dressing up.) While in Miss Li's cabin this feverish tumult was reigning the gentlemen drew up schemes for themselves, and setting out on the table the ash-trays and glasses of whisky they fixed the strategical position where each of them would stand, and decided what he was to do if something went wrong; while the captain felt several times deeply offended over the problem of prestige in the direction of affairs. During the afternoon they took over to the shore of the lagoon the film apparatus, a small automatic gun, a basket with knives and forks and food, and other war material; all that was exquisitely camouflaged with palm leaves. In addition,

93

before sunset three armed members of the crew and the captain in the capacity of commander-in-chief had taken up their stations. Then a huge basket containing a few small requisites for Miss Lily Valley was brought to the shore. Then Fred came with Miss Judy. Then the sun began to set in all its tropical splendour.

In the meantime Abe was already knocking for the tenth time on Miss Li's cabin. "Darling, we *really* must be off!"

"I'm coming, I'm coming," answered the darling's voice. "Please don't make me nervous! I must get *dressed*, mustn't I?"

In the meantime the captain surveyed the situation. Over there on the surface of the bay a long straight band was flickering which divided the rippling sea from the quiet lagoon. "As if under the water there were some kind of a dam or breakwater," meditated the captain; "perhaps it's a sandbank or a coral reef, but it almost looks like an artificial affair. A queer place." Over the quiet sheet of the lagoon here and there dark heads were emerging and moving towards the shore. The captain pressed his lips together and felt uneasily for his revolver. It would be better if those women stayed on the boat. Judy began to tremble, and clutched Fred convulsively. "How strong he is," she thought. "God, I think he's grand!"

At long last the final boat pushed off from the yacht. Miss Lily Valley in a white swimming costume, and in a transparent dressing-gown, in which apparently she was going to be thrown up from the sea as a castaway; and then Miss Greta and Mr. Abe. "Why

are you rowing so slowly, Abe?" the darling remon-
strated. Abe caught sight of the dark heads moving in
towards the shore, and he said nothing.

"Ts, ts."

"Ts."

Mr. Abe pulled the boat up on the sand, and helped
darling Li and Miss Greta on shore.

"Run quick, the camera," whispered the artist. "And
when I say 'now,' start to shoot."

"But we shall not be able to see much longer,"
objected Abe.

"Then Judy must switch on the light. Greta!"

In the meantime, while Mr. Abe Loeb had taken up
his post at the camera the artist was lying on the sand
like a dying swan, and Miss Greta was putting straight
the folds of her dressing-gown. "So that part of my
leg is visible," whispered the castaway. "Have you
finished? Well, get away! Ready, Abe!"

Abe began to turn the handle. "Light, Judy!" But
there was no light. Out of the sea swaying shadows
were emerging and gathering round Li. Greta pushed
her hand into her mouth so as not to cry out.

"Li," shouted Abe. "Li, run!"

"Nife! Ts, ts, ts. Li. Li. Abe!"

Someone raised a safety-catch. "What the devil!
don't shoot," hissed the captain.

"Li," cried Abe, and stopped the camera. "Light,
Judy."

Slowly, softly Li got up, and raised her arms to the
heavens. The light dressing-gown slipped from her
shoulders. Then she stood there, the lily-white Li,

95

with her arms held prettily above her head like castaways do when they wake from a swoon. Mr. Abe began to turn the handle furiously. "Damn it, Judy, can't you make some light!"

"Ts, ts, ts."

"Nife."

"Nife."

"Abe!"

The dark shadows were swaying and circling round the luminous Li. Wait, wait, this wasn't a play any longer. Li didn't hold her arms up above her head, but she pushed something away from herself and shrieked: "Abe, Abe, it's touched me!" Just then there was a blaze of light. Abe turned the handle rapidly; Fred and the captain ran with their revolvers to help Li, who was squalling and stuttering with terror. At that moment in the bright light tens and hundreds of those long dark shadows were visible as they slipped off into the sea at a run. At that moment two sailors threw a net over one of the shadows. At that moment Greta fainted and fell like a sack. At that moment two or three reports cracked out and there were splashings and commotions in the sea, two sailors were holding down something in the net that writhed and threw itself about beneath them, and Judy's light went out.

The captain switched on his torch. "Did it hurt you, kid?"

"It touched my leg," moaned the darling. "Fred, it was horrid."

Then Abe also came up with his torch. "It went

beautifully, Li," he exulted, "but Judy ought to have had the light on sooner!"

"It wouldn't go on," stammered Judy. "Would it, Fred?"

"Judy was scared," said Fred, excusing her. "Upon my honour, she didn't do it on purpose, did you, Judy?"

Judy felt offended; but while that was going on the two sailors drew near dragging something in the net that threw itself about like a big fish. "Here it is, captain. And alive."

"The brute, it squirted some poisonous stuff at me. My hands are covered with blisters, sir. And they burn like hell."

"It touched me, too," whimpered Miss Li. "Bring your light here, Abe. Look, isn't there a blister here?"

"No, it hasn't hurt you, my dear," Abe assured her; he very nearly would have kissed the spot on the knee which the darling had rubbed with such concern.

"Brrr. It was cold," complained darling Li.

"You've lost a pearl, ma'am," said one of the sailors, handing Li a small marble that he had picked up from the sand.

"Gracious! Abe," cried Miss Li. "They've brought me some pearls again. Let's look for pearls, my dears. There will be *heaps* of pearls that those poets have brought me. Aren't they sweet, Fred? Here's another pearl!"

"And another!"

Three torches made their luminous circles on the ground.

"I've found a huge one!"

"That's mine," blurted out darling Li.

"Fred," said Miss Judy frostily.

"In a moment," said Mr. Fred, crawling over the sand on his knees.

"Fred, I want to go back to the boat!"

"Somebody will take you there," suggested Fred, with preoccupation. "Holy smokes, this is fun!"

The three gentlemen and Miss Li kept moving over the sand like big glow-worms.

"There are three pearls here," announced the captain.

"Let me see, let me see," cried Li ecstatically, and crawled on her knees after the captain. Just then a magnesium flashlight flared up and the handle of the film camera rattled.

"Now you're in it," announced Judy revengefully. "That will be a swell snap for the papers. American Society Looking for Pearls. Sea Sauria Throw Pearls to Humans."

Fred sat down. "Holy smokes, Judy's right. We *must* get it into the papers, kids!"

Li sat down. "Judy's a darling. Take us again, Judy, but from the front!"

"Then they would miss a lot, darling," thought Judy.

"We ought to keep looking, kids," said Abe. "The tide is coming in."

In the darkness at the edge of the sea a black swaying shadow was gliding. Li screamed: "There—there——"

Three torches threw a circle of light in that direction.

It was only Greta on her knees looking for pearls in the darkness.

• • • • •

In Li's lap was the captain's cap with twenty-one pearls. Abe filled up the glasses, and Judy attended to the gramophone. It was an immense starry night accompanied by the eternal murmuring of the sea.

"Well, what headline are we to give it?" cried Fred. **"Daughter of Executive from Milwaukee films fossil reptiles."** *"Antediluvial Sauria pay homage to beauty and youth,"* suggested Abe poetically.

"Yacht Gloria Pickford encounters unknown fauna," advised the captain. Or **"The Mystery of Island Tahuara."**

"That would be only a sub-title," said Fred. "The full heading should say something more."

"Something like *Baseball Fred contends with monsters,*" said Judy. "Fred was divine when he was going for them. If only it comes out well in the film!"

The captain cleared his throat. "As a matter of fact, I went for them first, Miss Judy; but let's not discuss that. I think that the title ought to sound scientific, sir. Sober and . . . in short, scientific: **"An--te--luvial fauna on a Pacific Island."**

"Antediluvial," corrected Fred. "No, prediluvial. My gosh, what is it? We must give it a shorter title so that everybody could pronounce it. Judy's swell."

"Antediluvial," said Judy.

Fred shook his head. "Too long, Judy. Longer than those beasts even with their tails. The title ought to be short. But Judy's terrific, isn't she?"

"She is," agreed the captain. "A wonderful girl."

"A regular lad, Captain," said the young giant approvingly. "Kids, the captain's swell. But the antediluvial fauna's rot. That's no headline for newspapers. Why not *Lovers on Island of Pearls,* or something like that?"

"**Tritons Sprinkle Pearls over White Lily!**" shouted Abe. "**Poseidon's Homage! a New Aphrodite!**"

"Rot!" protested Fred indignantly. "There weren't any Tritons. That's been proved by science, my boy. And there was no Aphrodite, was there, Judy? **Humans encounter living fossils! Brave captain attacks antediluvial monsters!** Man, that would be a scoop, that title!"

"A special edition," cried Abe. "**A film star assaulted by sea monster! Sex appeal of a modern woman defeats ancient Lizards! Fossil reptiles prefer blondes!**"

"Abe," said darling Li. "I have an idea——"

"What idea?"

"For a film. It would be a tremendous thing, Abe. Think of it, I should be bathing on the shore——"

"That swimming costume suits you marvellously, Li," burst out Abe quickly.

"Doesn't it? And those Tritons would fall in love with me, and would carry me off to the bottom of the sea. And I should be their queen."

"At the bottom of the sea?"

"Yes, underneath the water. In their mysterious realm, you know. They have their towns there, and everything, haven't they?"

"Darling, but you would get drowned there!"

"Don't worry, I can swim," said darling Li, with unconcern. "Only once a day I should swim up on the top for fresh air." Li demonstrated a breathing exercise combined with heaving the breast and undulating movements of the arms. "Something like this, you know? And on the shore someone would fall in love with me . . . perhaps a young fisherman. And I with him. Terribly," sighed the darling. "You know, he would be so beautiful and strong. And the Tritons would want to drown him, but I should save him, and I should go with him to his hut. And the Tritons would besiege us there—well, and then perhaps you might come to save us."

"Li," said Fred seriously. "This is so silly that somebody will shoot it, you bet. I shall be astonished if old Jesse doesn't make a monster film out of it."

•   •   •   •   •

Fred was right: in due course a monster film was made out of it, produced by Jesse Loeb Pictures Inc. with Miss Lily Valley in the principal role; besides that, there were six hundred Nereids in the film, one Neptune, and a supporting cast of twelve thousand dressed up to resemble various antediluvial sauria. But before this occurred much water had flown away and many events had taken place; in particular:

(1) The captured animal kept in a tub in the bathroom of darling Li enjoyed for two days the vivid interest of the whole company; the third day it ceased to move, and Miss Li asserted that the poor thing was homesick; the fourth day it began to smell, and had to be thrown away in an advanced stage of decomposition.

(2) From the shots taken at the lagoon only two were of any use. In one darling Li was squatting down in terror, waving her arms desperately at the erect animals. Everyone asserted that it was a divine episode. In the other you could make out three men and a girl kneeling and stooping, with their noses almost touching the ground; it gave the back view, and they looked as if they were paying homage to something. This episode was suppressed.

(3) As for the proposed captions for the newspapers, almost all of them were made use of (even that about the antediluvial fauna) in hundreds and hundreds of the American and world journals, weeklies, and magazines; a description of the whole event with many details added to it, as well as snaps like the photo of the darling Li among the Sauria, the photo of Li alone in a swimming dress, the photo of Miss Judy, of Mr. Abe Loeb, of Baseball Fred, of the captain of the yacht, of the yacht *Gloria Pickford* itself, of the

island Taraiva itself, and of the pearls spread out on black velvet. In this way the career of darling Li was assured; she even refused to appear in a variety show, and announced to the reporters that she intended to devote herself entirely to art.

(4) There were of course people who under the pretext of professional education asserted that—as far as one can judge from the snapshots—it wasn't a question of any primeval sauria, but of some sort of salamanders. Still more professional people asserted that this kind of salamander was not known to science, and therefore did not exist at all. On this point there was a long debate in the Press, which Professor J. W. Hupkins (Yale) brought to an end by the statement that he had examined the photographs submitted to him, and that he considered them a fraud (hoax) or a fake; that the animals depicted reminded him slightly of the giant tectibranchiate salamander (*Cryptobranchus japonicus*, *Sieboldia maxima*, *Tritomegas Sieboldi*, *or Megalobatrachus Sieboldi*), but inaccurately, clumsily, and quite amateurishly reproduced. In this way for some time the matter was settled scientifically.

(5) At last, in due course Mr. Abe Loeb married Miss Judy. His best friend, Baseball Fred, was his best man at the wedding, which took place with great pomp in the presence of many prominent personalities from political, artistic, and other circles.

8

Andrias Scheuchzeri

ENDLESS is human curiosity. It was not sufficient that J. W. Hupkins (Yale), the greatest authority alive at the time having anything to do with reptiles, declared that those mysterious creatures were unscientific humbug and sheer fantasy; in the scientific journals and in the newspapers accounts began to increase of the discovery of so far unknown animals resembling huge salamanders in the most diverse parts of the Pacific Ocean. Relatively reliable statements claimed their discovery on the Solomon Islands, on Schouten Island, on Kapingamarangi, Butaritari, and Tapeteuea, as well as on a whole group of smaller islands: Nukufetau, Funafuti, Nukunono, and Fukaofu, then as far as Hiau, Ua Huka, Uap, and Pukapuka. There were legends quoted of the devils of Captain van Toch (mainly in the Melanesian zone) and of the Tritons of Miss Li (more in Polynesia); then the newspapers inferred that it was a matter of various kinds of submarine and antediluvian monsters mainly because the summer season had begun, and there was nothing to write about. Submarine monsters are usually well received by the reading public. In the United States especially Tritons became the fashion; in New York a showy revue ran for three hundred nights featuring Poseidon with three hundred most beautiful Triton girls, Nereids, and Sirens; in Miami and on the beaches of California youth bathed in the costumes of Tritons and Nereids (i.e. three strings of pearls, and nothing else), whereas in the Middle and Middle West states the Movement for Suppression of Immorality (M.S.I.) became unusually strong; at the same time mass demonstrations took place, and a few negroes were partly hanged and partly burned to death.

At last in the *Federal Geographic Magazine* a report appeared giving an account of the Scientific Expedition of the new Columbia University (arranged at the expense of J. S. Tincker, the so-called King of Conserves); the report was signed by P. L. Smith, W. X. Kleinschmidt, Charles Kovar, Louis Forgeron, and D. Herrero, celebrities of world fame especially in the sphere of the fish parasites, annular worms, plant biology, infusorians, and aphids.

We quote from the extensive report:

. . . On the island of Rakaanga the expedition for the first time came across the tracks of the hind feet of a so far unknown huge salamander. The feet have five digits, the length of the toes is from 3 to 4 cm. In view of the number of the tracks the coast Rakaanga must be literally swarming with these salamanders. As there were no tracks of the front feet (except for one four-fingered print, evidently of a young one) the expedition inferred that these salamanders apparently progress on their posterior extremities.

We might mention that on the small island Rakaanga there is no river or swamp; consequently these salamanders live in the sea, and they may be the only specimens of their order that are pelagic. It is known of course that the Mexican axolotl (*Amblystoma mexicanum*) lives in brackish lakes, but we have met with no mention of pelagic salamanders (living in the sea) in the classical work of W. Korngold, *The Batrachians (Urodela)*, Berlin, 1913.

. . . We waited until midday in order to capture, or at least catch sight of, a living specimen, but in vain. With regret we had to leave the pleasant little island of Rakaanga, where D. Herrero succeeded in finding a beautiful new species of Tingis. . . .

Fate smiled much more upon us on Tongareva Island. We waited on the beach with our rifles in our hands. After sunset the salamanders' heads emerged from the water, relatively big and somewhat flattened. After a while the salamanders crawled up on to the sand, walking with a swaying motion but rather nimbly on their hind legs. When sitting they were rather more than a metre high. They sat down forming a wide circle, and they began to move the upper half of their bodies in a strange motion; it looked as if they were dancing. W. X. Kleinschmidt drew nearer to examine them better. Then the salamanders turned their heads towards him, and for a short time were completely motionless; then they began to approach him with considerable agility, emitting hissing and barking sounds. When they were about seven metres away from him we shot at them with our rifles. They started off very quickly and threw themselves into the sea; they did not appear again that evening. Two dead salamanders were left on the shore, and one with a broken spine which emitted a strange sound like "ogod, ogod, ogod." This one subsequently expired, when W. X. Kleinschmidt opened its pectoral cavity with a knife. . . . (*Anatomical details follow which in any case we laymen would not understand; and we refer the expert reader to the original report.*)

It is clear then, from the characteristics given above, that we are concerned with a typical species of the order of batrachians (Urodela) to which, as is common knowledge, the family of the real salamanders (Salamandridae) belong, comprising as they do the different genera of newts (Triton), and salamanders (Salamandra) and the family of the perinnibranchs (Ichthyoidea), comprising the cryptobranchiate (Cryptobranchiata), and the branchiated forms (Phanerobranchiata). The salamander which has been recorded from the island Tongareva seems to be most related to the perinnibranch cryptobranchiates; in many respects, as well as by its size, it resembles the Japanese giant salamander (*Megalobatrachus Sieboldi*) or the American hellbender, called "swamp devil," but it differs from these species by its well-developed sensory apparatus and by its longer, more robust extremities which permit it to move with considerable agility in the water and on dry land. (*Further details of its comparative anatomy follow.*)

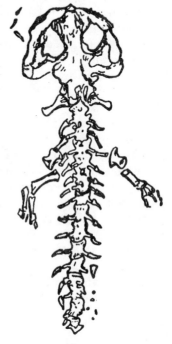

After we had worked out the skeletons of the dead animals we came across a most striking fact; that is, that the skeleton of these salamanders tallies almost perfectly with the fossil imprint of a salamander skeleton which Dr. Johannes Jakub Scheuchzer discovered on a piece of stone from the Oeningen quarry, and described in his work *Homo Diluvii Testis* published in the year 1726. Permit us to remind readers not so well versed in the literature that the Dr. Scheuchzer mentioned above considered this fossil to be the remains of *antediluvian man*. The figure reproduced,

he writes, "which I submit to the learned world in a
handsome woodcut is undoubtedly the picture of the man
who was a witness of the Flood; they are not lines from
which exuberant fantasy could merely construct something
which might have the likeness of man, but in every
detail there is complete agreement with the individual
parts of the human skeleton, and complete symmetry. The
petrified man is depicted from the front; lo! a monument
of an extinct race older than all the tombstones, Roman,
Greek, even Egyptian, and all the East put together."
Subsequently Cuvier discerned in the Oeningen print the
skeleton of a fossilized salamander which was named
Cryptobranchus primaevus or *Andrias Scheuchzeri Tschudi*,
and which was taken to be a species long extinct. By
osteological comparisons we were successful in establishing
the identity of our salamanders with the presumably
extinct fossil Andrias. The mysterious Ursauras, as it was
called in the papers, *is nothing but a fossil Cryptobranchiate
Salamander, Andrias Scheuchzeri*; or if another name is required, *Cryptobranchus Tinckeri erectus*, or Giant Polynesian
Salamander. . . . There is still the problem why this interesting giant salamander has so far eluded scientific investigation, although it occurs in association at least on the islands
Rakaanga and Tongareva in the Manihiki Archipelago.
Even Randolph and Montgomery, in their work *Two
Years on the Islands of Manihiki* (1885), do not mention it.
The natives assert that this animal—which, however, they
believe to be poisonous—first appeared six or eight years
ago. They state that the "sea devils" can talk (!), and
that they build in the bays which they inhabit complete
systems of ramparts and dams resembling submarine
towns; they state that in these bays the water is as quiet
as a pond all the year round; they say that they excavate
beneath the water burrows and corridors many metres
long in which they stay during the daytime; they state
that at night they steal from the fields sweet potatoes and
yams, and even take hoes and other tools from the inhabi-

tants. On the whole the natives don't care for them, and are even afraid of them; in many cases they would rather migrate to other places. Obviously this is merely a matter of primitive legend and superstition based on nothing but the repulsive appearance and the erect, somewhat human gait of big but harmless salamanders.

. . . Also travellers' reports according to which these salamanders occur on other islands besides Manihiki should be received with considerable reserve. On the other hand it would be possible beyond dispute to decide whether the recent print of a hind foot found on the beach of one of the Tongatabu islands which Captain Croisset published in *La Nature* is a footprint of *Andrias Scheuchzeri*. This find is especially important in that it affords a link between the occurrence of the animals on the Manihiki Islands with the Australian–New Zealand zone, where so many specimens of the evolution of an ancient fauna have been preserved; we refer particularly to the "antediluvian" saurus Hatterii, or Tuataru, still living on Stephen Island. On these lonely, sparsely inhabited islands, almost untouched by civilization, examples of animal types might be preserved here and there which elsewhere are already extinct. To the fossil salamander Hatterii Mr. J. S. Tincker now considers that an antediluvial salamander must be added. The worthy Dr. Johannes Jakub Scheuchzer would now have witnessed the resurrection of his Oeningen Adam. . . .

• • • • •

This learned report would certainly have been quite enough to illuminate with science the question of the mysterious sea monsters about which already there had been so much discussion. Just then, unfortunately, a paper by a Dutch scholar, van Hogenhouck, appeared which placed these cryptobranchiate giant salamanders

in the family of real salamanders or Tritons under
the species of *Megatriton moluccanus*, and recorded
their occurrence on the Dutch Sunda islands Dgillo,
Morotai, and Ceram; as well as the report of a French
scientist, Dr. Mignard, who classified them as typical
salamanders, gave their first place of origin as on
the French islands Takaroa, Rangiroa and Raroire,
and called them simply *Cryptobranchus salamandriodes*;
and besides that the report of H. W. Spence, who
discerned in them a new family, Pelagidae, indigenous
in the Gilbert Islands, and capable of establishing
professional existence under the appellation of *Pelagotriton Spencei*. Mr. Spencer managed to transport one
specimen as far as the London Zoo; here it became the
object of further investigations from which it emerged
under the names *Pelagobatrachus Hookeri*, *Salamndrops
maritimus*, *Abranchus giganteus*, *Amphiuma gigas* and many
others. Some biologists asserted that *Pelagotriton Spencei*
was identical with *Cryptobranchus Tinckeri*, and that
Mignard's salamander was nothing else but *Andrias
Scheuchzeri*; there were many disputes about priority
and about other purely scientific questions. Thus it
came about that at last the natural science of every
nation had its own giant salamanders, and it waged a
most ferocious war with the giant salamanders of
other countries. As a result, right up to the last, on the
scientific side there was not enough light shed upon the
whole big question of the salamanders.

9

Andrew Scheuchzer

AND one Thursday when the London Zoo was closed to the public it happened that Mr. Thomas Greggs, a keeper in the Reptile House, was clearing the tanks and runs of his charges. He was quite alone in the section of salamanders where the Giant Japanese Salamander was exhibited, the American hellbender, *Andrias Scheuchzeri,* and a quantity of small newts, little salamanders, axolotles, sirenia, amphibia, pleurodeles, and branchiates. Mr. Greggs was swishing about with his broom and cloth, whistling "Annie Laurie," and suddenly somebody spoke with a croak behind him :

"Look, Mummy."

Mr. Greggs looked behind him, but there was nobody there; only the hellbender was smacking about in his morass, and that big black salamander, that Andrias, was leaning with its front paws on the edge of the tank, twirling its tail. I must have dreamt something, thought Mr. Greggs, and went on sweeping the floor till the broom fairly whizzed.

"Look, a newt," someone remarked behind him.

Mr. Greggs turned round sharply; that black salamander, that Andrias, was looking at him and blinking with its lower lids.

"Ugh! it is ugly," said the salamander suddenly. "Let's go away from here, darling."

Mr. Gregg's mouth gaped in amazement. "What!"

"Does it bite?" croaked the salamander.

"You . . . you can talk?" stammered Mr. Greggs, not believing his senses.

"I'm frightened," croaked the newt. "Mummy, what does it eat?"

"Say 'good day,' " said the astonished Mr. Greggs.

The salamander screwed up its body. "Good day," it croaked. "Good day. Good day. Can I give it a bun?"

Mr. Greggs pushed a bewildered hand into his pocket and took out a slice of bread.

"Here, have this."

The salamander took the bread in its paw and began to nibble it. "Look, a newt," it grunted contentedly. "Daddy, why is it so black?" Suddenly it dived into the water, leaving only its head sticking out. "Why is it in the water? Why? Ugh, it is hideous!"

Mr. Thomas Greggs scratched the back of his neck in bewilderment. Aha, it repeats what it picks up from the people. "Say Greggs," he ventured.

"Say Greggs," repeated the salamander.

"Mr. Thomas Greggs."

"Mr. Thomas Greggs."

"Good day, sir."

"Good day, sir. Good day, good day, sir." It seemed as if the salamander would never get tired of talking; but Greggs didn't know what else to say to it. Mr. Thomas Greggs was rather a taciturn man. "Well, now shut up," he said, "and when I've finished I'll teach you to talk."

"Well, now shut up," mumbled the newt. "Good day, sir. Look, a newt. I shall teach you to talk."

●　　　●　　　●　　　●　　　●

However, the managers of the Zoo didn't approve of the keepers teaching their charges tricks; an elephant is something different, but the other animals are here for purposes of education, and not to perform like some sort of a circus. So Mr. Greggs spent his time in the salamander section more or less clandestinely when no one else was there. Since he was a widower, nobody was astonished at his seclusion in the Reptile House. Everybody has his predilections. And besides, only a few people went to the section with the newts; the crocodile was more likely to enjoy general popularity, but Andrias Scheuchzeri spent its days in relative solitude.

Once when it grew dark, and the pavilions were closing down, the director of the Zoo, Sir Charles Wiggam, was walking through some of the houses to make sure that everything was in order. When he went through the section with the newts there was a great splashing in one of the tanks, and somebody remarked in a croaking voice, "Good evening, sir."

"Good evening," replied the director, taken aback. "Who's that?"

"Excuse me, sir," said the croaking voice. "Isn't it Mr. Greggs?"

"Who's that?" repeated the director.

"Andy. Andrew Scheuchzer."

Sir Charles drew nearer the tank. There was only a newt sitting erect and motionless there. "Who said something here?"

"Andy, sir," said the newt. "Who are you?"

"Wiggam," blurted out Sir Charles in amazement.

"I'm very pleased to make your acquaintance," said Andrias politely. "How do you do?"

"Damn it all," bawled Sir Charles. "Greggs! Hey, Greggs!"

The salamander whisked itself round, and like a shot it hid beneath the water.

Mr. Greggs rushed to the door, breathless and apprehensive. "I beg your pardon, sir?"

"Greggs, what does this mean?" burst out Sir Charles.

"Is there something wrong, sir?" stammered Mr. Greggs uncertainly.

"This animal here is talking!"

"Excuse me, sir," said Mr. Greggs, abashed. "You ought not to do that, Andy. Haven't I told you a thousand times that you ought not to annoy people with your talking? I beg your pardon, sir; it won't happen again."

"Is it you that has taught this newt to talk?"

"But he began it, sir," expostulated Greggs in self-defence.

"I hope that it won't happen again, Greggs," said Sir Charles sternly. "I shall keep my eye on you."

• • • • •

Some time later Sir Charles was sitting beside

Professor Petrov and discussing the so-called animal intelligence, conditioned reflexes, and how popular ideas overrate the reasoning powers of animals. Professor Petrov expressed his doubts about the Elberfeld horses which, it was said, could not only count, but also raise a number to a higher power and find the square root of a number; "for not even a normal, intelligent man can extract the square root of a number, can he?" said the great scientist. Sir Charles remembered Gregg's talking salamander. "I have a salamander here," he began with hesitation, "it's that one known as Andrias Scheuchzeri, and it's learned to talk like a cockatoo."

"Impossible," said the biologist. "Haven't the salamanders got a reflexed tongue?"

"Well, come and have a look," said Sir Charles. "It's cleaning out day to-day, so there won't be so many people about." And they went.

At the entrance to the salamanders Sir Charles halted. From inside could be heard the scratching of the broom and a monotonous voice which was articulating something.

"Wait," whispered Sir Charles Wiggam.

"IS MARS INHABITED?" articulated a monotonous voice. "Shall I read it?"

"Something else, Andy," answered the other voice.

"WILL PELHAM-BEAUTY WIN THIS YEAR'S DERBY, OR GOBERNADOR?"

"Pelham-Beauty," said the other voice. "But read it."

Sir Charles silently opened the door. Mr. Thomas

Greggs was sweeping the floor with a broom; and in the little pond of sea water Andrias Scheuchzeri was sitting and in a slow croaking voice articulating from an evening paper which he was holding in its front paws.

"Greggs," shouted Sir Charles. The newt threw itself down and vanished beneath the water.

Mr. Greggs dropped the broom in terror. "Yes, sir?"

"What does this mean?"

"I beg your pardon, sir," stammered the miserable Greggs. "Andy is reading to me while I sweep. And when he sweeps I take my turn and read to him."

"Who taught him that?"

"He finds it out himself by watching, sir. . . . I . . . I give him my papers so that he doesn't talk so much. He would keep on talking, sir. So I thought that at least he ought to learn to talk in an educated way."

"Andy," called Sir Wiggam.

A black head emerged from the water. "Yes, sir," it croaked.

"Professor Petrov has come to see you."

"Very pleased to see you, sir. I am Andy Scheuchzer."

"How do you know that your name is Andrias Scheuchzeri?"

"I've got it written here, sir—Andreas Scheuchzer, Gilbert Islands."

"And do you often read newspapers?"

"Yes, sir. Every day, sir."

"And what do you find most interesting in them?"

"Crime, horse-racing, football——"

"Have you ever seen a football match?"

"No, sir."

"Or a horse race?"

"I haven't, sir."

"Then why do you read about them?"

"Because it's in the papers, sir."

"Aren't you interested in politics?"

"No, sir. WILL THERE BE A WAR?"

"Nobody knows that, Andy."

"GERMANY IS BUILDING A NEW KIND OF SUBMARINE," said Andy anxiously. "DEATH RAYS CAN TURN WHOLE CONTINENTS INTO A DESERT."

"You've read that in the papers, haven't you?" inquired Sir Charles.

"Yes, sir. WILL PELHAM-BEAUTY WIN THIS YEAR'S DERBY, OR GOBERNADOR?"

"What do you think, Andy?"

"Gobernador, sir, but Mr. Greggs thinks Pelham-Beauty." Andy nodded his head.

"BUY BRITISH GOODS, sir, THE BEST ARE SNIDER'S BRACES. HAVE YOU GOT YOUR NEW SIX-CYLINDER MORSTIN MINOR? FAST! CHEAP! ELEGANT!"

"Thanks, Andy. That will do."

"WHICH FILM ACTRESS DO YOU LIKE BEST?"

Professor Petrov's hair and beard bristled. "Excuse me, Sir Charles," he murmured, "but I shall have to go."

"All right, let's go. Andy, would you mind if I sent

you a couple of learned gentlemen? I think they would like to have a chat with you."

"I shall be delighted, sir," croaked the salamander. "See you again, Sir Charles. See you again, Professor."

Professor Petrov hurried away snorting with irritation and mumbling. "Excuse me, Sir Charles," he said at last. "Couldn't you show me some animal that DOESN'T read the papers?"

•　　•　　•　　•　　•

The learned gentlemen were Sir Bertram Dash, D.M., Professor Ebbigham, Sir Oliver Dodge, Julian Foxley, and others. We quote from part of the report of their experiment with Andrias Scheuchzeri.

What is your name?

Ans. *Andrew Scheuchzer.*

How old are you?

Ans. *I don't know. Do you want to look young? Wear Libella corsets.*

What date is it to-day?

Ans. *Monday. Nice weather, sir. Next Saturday Gibraltar is running at Epsom.*

How much is three times five?

Ans. *Why?*

Can you count?

Ans. *Yes, sir. How much is seventeen times twenty-nine?*

Let us ask the questions, Andrew. Give us the names of the English rivers.

Ans. *The Thames . . .*

And any more?

Ans. *The Thames*

You don't know any more, do you? Who is King of England?

Ans. *King Edward. God bless him.*

Good, Andy. Who is the greatest English writer?

Ans. *Kipling.*

Very good. Have you read anything by him?

Ans. *No. How do you like Gracie Fields?*

We prefer to ask you questions, Andy. What do you know of English history?

Ans. *Henry the Eighth.*

What do you know about him?

Ans. *The best film of the last three years. Stupendous scenery. A terrific show. Gorgeous spectacle.*

Have you seen it?

Ans. *I haven't. Do you want to see England? Buy a Baby Austin.*

What would you like to see best, Andy?

Ans. *Oxford and Cambridge Boat Race, sir.*

How many parts are there in the world?

Ans. *Five.*

Very good. And which are they?

Ans. *England and the others.*

Which are the others?

Ans. *They are the Bolsheviks, the Germans, and Italy.*

Where are the Gilbert Islands?

Ans. *In England. England will not bind herself to the Continent. England needs ten thousand aeroplanes. Visit the south coast of England.*

Can we look at your tongue, Andy?

Ans. *Yes, sir. Use Macans for the gums. It's cheap, it's best. It's British. Do you want perfume in your breath? Use Macans.*

Thank you; that will do. And now tell us, Andy . . .

And so on. The report of the conversation with Andrias Scheuchzeri ran to sixteen full pages, and was published in *Natural Science*. At the end of the report the expert commission summarized the findings of its investigations thus:

(1) Andrias Scheuchzeri, the salamander kept at the London Zoo, can talk, even if inclined to croak; it has a range of about four hundred words; it only repeats what it has heard or read. Of course there can be no suggestion of any independent thought. Its tongue possesses a considerable degree of freedom; in the given circumstances we were not able to make a closer inspection of the vocal chords.

(2) This same salamander can read, but only the evening papers. It is interested in the same things as an average Englishman, and it reacts to them in a similar way, that is, in the direction of established general views. Its mental life—if it is possible to speak of such—consists merely of ideas and opinions current at the time.

(3) There is no need to overrate its intelligence, for in no respect does it exceed the intelligence of an average man of the present time.

•   •   •   •   •

In spite of this sober announcement by the experts, the talking newt became a sensation at the London Zoo. Darling Andy was besieged by people who wanted to have a chat with him about every possible thing, beginning with the weather and ending with the economic crisis and the political situation. In return he used to get from his visitors so much chocolate and sweets that he became seriously ill with the catarrh of the stomach and intestines. That section had at last to be closed, but it was already too late; Andrias Scheuch-zeri, nicknamed Andy, perished of the consequences of his popularity. As one can see, fame demoralizes even the newts.

10

Country Fair in New Strašecí

MR. POVONDRA, the porter in Bondy's house, was spending his leave this time in his native town. The next day there was to be a fair; and when Mr. Povondra went out taking by the hand his eight-years-old Frantik the whole of New Strašecí smelt of cakes, and across the street women and girls were hurrying carrying the newly worked dough to the baker. In the square two stalls for toffee had already been erected, another for a cheap-jack with glass and china, and one for a bawling lady selling haberdashery of all kinds. And then there was a canvas tent surrounded on all sides by sailcloths. Some tiny man on a ladder was just fixing up a notice.

Mr. Povondra halted to see what it was going to be.

The wizened little man climbed down from the ladder and looked with satisfaction at the notice he had hung up. And Mr. Povondra read with surprise:

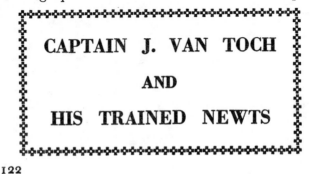

CAPTAIN J. VAN TOCH

AND

HIS TRAINED NEWTS

Mr. Povondra remembered the big fat man in a captain's cap whom he had once shown in to Mr. Bondy. He hasn't got very far, poor fellow, said Mr. Povondra to himself with sympathy; captain, and now he's touring about the world with such a miserable circus! Such a well-built, healthy man he was! I ought to call on him, reflected Mr. Povondra with emotion.

In the meantime the wizened little man hung up beside the entrance to the tent a second notice:

TALKING REPTILES

!! The Greatest Scientific Marvel !!

Entrance 2 Crowns.

Children accompanied by parents half price.

Mr. Povondra hesitated a moment. Two crowns and one crown for the youngster; that was a bit too much. But Frantik was doing well in school, and to know about exotic animals is a part of education. Mr. Povondra was willing to make some sacrifice for the sake of education, and therefore he approached that wizened tiny little man. "Chum," he said, "I should like to have a talk with Captain van Toch."

The little man blew out his chest in its striped pullover. "That's me, sir."

"You are Captain van Toch?" gasped Mr. Povondra.

"Yes, sir," said the little man, revealing a tattooed anchor on his wrist.

Mr. Povondra blinked thoughtfully. That captain couldn't have shrunk so much. That's impossible. "For I know Captain van Toch personally," he said. "I am Povondra."

"That's something different," said the little man. "But the newts are really from Captain van Toch, sir. Guaranteed real Australian reptiles, sir. Would you like to have a look round? Just now a great performance is about to begin," he cackled, lifting the strip of canvas at the entrance.

"Come, Frantik," said father Povondra, and went in. Behind a small table an unusually fat and large lady quickly sat down. They're a strange pair, wondered Mr. Povondra, handing over his three crowns. Inside the hut there was nothing but a rather disagreeable smell and a tin bath.

"Where do you keep the newts?" inquired Mr. Povondra.

"In that bath," said the gigantic lady casually.

"Don't get frightened, Frantik," said father Povondra, and walked up to the bath. Something black and apathetic as big as a catfish was lying there; motionless, except that behind the head the skin expanded and contracted a little.

"So this is that antediluvian newt that the newspapers have been writing about," said father Povondra instructively, showing no sign of his disappointment. (I have been again taken in, he thought, but the boy needn't know it. It's a poor show for those three crowns.)

"Daddy, why is it in the water?" asked Frantik.

"Because newts live in the water, you know."

"Daddy, and what does it eat?"

"Fish, and things like that," opined father Povondra. (It must chew something.)

"And why is it so ugly?" urged Frantik.

Mr. Povondra did not know what to say; but at that moment the tiny little man came into the tent. "Well, if you please, ladies and gentlemen," he began hoarsely.

"You've only got this one newt?" demanded Mr. Povondra reproachfully. (If only there had been two, he thought, he might have had his money's worth.)

"The other died," said the little man. "Well, ladies and gentlemen, this is the famous Andrias, the rare and poisonous reptile from the Australian islands. In its homeland it attains the height of a man and walks erect. Na," he said, and poked with a stick that black and apathetic something that was lying motionless in the tub. The black shape wriggled slightly, and with difficulty raised itself from the water. Frantik stepped back a pace, but Mr. Povondra squeezed his hand. "Don't be frightened; I am with you."

Now it was standing on its hind legs, and with its front paws it was leaning on the edge of the tub. The gills behind its head were twitching convulsively and the black snout gasped for breath. Its skin, which had rubbed raw, was too loose and studded with warts, and it had round frog-like eyes which at times were somehow painfully closed with its membraneous lower lids.

"As you can observe, ladies and gentlemen," continued the little man hoarsely, "this animal lives in the water; therefore it is provided with gills as well as lungs so that it can breathe when it comes out on to the shore. It has five toes on its hind legs and four fingers on its front ones, with which it can grasp various objects. Here." The animal gripped the stick in its fingers and held it up in front of itself like a melancholy sceptre.

"It also can tie a knot in a piece of string," announced the little man; he took the stick from the animal, and handed it a dirty bit of string. The animal held it for a while in its fingers, and then really tied a knot.

"It also can drum and dance," croaked the little man, handing the animal a child's drum and a stick. The animal hit the drum several times and twirled the upper part of its body; then the drum-stick fell into the water. "Damn you, you brute," snapped the little man, fishing the stick out.

"And this animal," he added, raising the voice solemnly, "is so intelligent and clever that it can talk like a man. As he said this he clapped his hands.

"Guten Morgen," croaked the animal, painfully blinking with its lower lids. "Good day."

Mr. Povondra was very nearly scared, but it made no special impression on Frantik.

"What have you to say to the ladies and gentlemen?" inquired the little man sharply.

"You are very welcome," bowed the newt; its gills contracted convulsively. "Willkommen. Ben venuti."

"Can you count?"

"I can."

"How much is six times seven?"

"Forty-two," croaked the newt laboriously.

"Do you see, Frantik," observed father Povondra, "how it can count?"

"Ladies and gentlemen," cried the little man, "you may ask it questions yourself."

"Do ask it something," urged Mr. Povondra.

Frantik squirmed with embarrassment. "How much is eight times nine?" he blurted out at last; apparently it seemed to him the most difficult of all possible questions.

The newt blinked slowly. "Seventy-two."

"What day is it to-day?" asked Mr. Povondra.

"Saturday," said the newt.

Mr. Povondra shook his head in astonishment. "It really is like a human being. What's the name of this town?"

The newt opened its mouth and shut the eyes. "He's tired out already," explained the little man hurriedly. "What have you to say to the gentlemen?"

The newt bowed. "My best compliments. Thank you. Good-bye. See you again." And quickly it hid beneath the water.

"It's a queer beast," wondered Mr. Povondra; but after all three crowns are a lot of money, so he added: "And you've not got anything more to show to this boy?"

The little man tugged at his lower lip with embarrassment. "That'll be all," he said. "I used to have some little monkeys, but it was such a job with them," he explained vaguely. "Unless you would like to see my wife. She used to be the fattest woman in the world. Mary, come here!"

Mary raised herself with difficulty. "What's the matter?"

"Show yourself to the gentlemen, Mary."

The fattest woman in the world held her head coquettishly to one side, put one leg forward, and lifted her skirt above the knee. They could see a red woollen stocking, and in it something swollen and as big as a ham. "Her legs are more than eighty centimetres round," explained the little man; "but in these days there's so much competition that Mary isn't any longer the fattest woman in the world."

Mr. Povondra dragged the aghast Frantik out. "Küss die hand," it croaked from the tub. "Come again. Auf Wiedersehen."

"Well then, Frantik," asked Mr. Povondra, when they were outside. "Have you learned anything?"

"Yes," said Frantik. "Daddy, why does that lady wear red stockings?"

11

Men-Lizards

IT certainly would be an exaggeration to state that at that time people did not converse about anything else but the talking newts. They also argued and wrote about the next war, the economic crisis, league matches, vitamins, and fashions; all the same they wrote a great deal about the talking newts, and particularly without expert knowledge. Because of that Professor Dr. Vladimír Uher (University of Brno) wrote in the *Lidové Noviny* an article in which he pointed out that the presumed ability of Andrias Scheuchzeri to articulate words, which meant in fact to mimic what it had heard, from the scientific point of view was not nearly so interesting as some other problems with regard to this unique amphibian. The scientific problem of Andrias Scheuchzeri was something quite different: for instance, where it had come from; what was its first place of origin, in which it must have outlived complete geological epochs; why had it remained so long unknown, although it was now recorded in numbers almost everywhere in the equatorial belt of the Pacific Ocean. It appeared as if in recent years it has multiplied abnormally quickly; whence has come this tremendous vitality in an ancient tertiary creature, which until recently had led a completely unknown, and therefore in all probability an extremely sporadic if not geographically isolated existence? Was it, perhaps, that in some way environmental conditions changed for this fossil newt in a direction biologically favourable, so that for a rare Miocene survival a new and strangely successful period of development had set in? In such case it was not impossible that Andrias would not only increase quantitatively but also develop in a qualitative sense, and that their biological studies would have a unique opportunity of witnessing in at least one animal species a striking mutation in actual progress. The fact that Andrias Scheuchzeri croaked a few words, and that it had acquired a few tricks which to a layman appeared to be signs of intelligence, was not in a scientific sense any miracle; but what was miraculous was that powerful vital élan which had so suddenly and to such an extent revived the archaic existence of a primitive creature, and of one almost already extinct. The circumstances were in some directions unique: Andrias Scheuchzeri was the *only* salamander living in the sea and—still more striking— the *only* salamander occurring in the Ethiopian–Australian zone, the mythical Lemuria. Might one not almost suggest that Nature was making abnormal and almost precipitous efforts to make up one of those biological potentialities and forms which in *that* zone it had missed or could not fully elaborate? Moreover, it would have been strange if in the oceanic region which lay between the Japanese Giant Salamanders on one hand and the Alleghanian ones on the other there was no connecting link of any kind. If there had been no Andrias, they would in fact have been driven to ASSUME one in the very localities in which it had appeared; it seemed almost as if it simply filled the habitat which on geographical and evolutionary grounds it *ought* to have occupied from immemorial times. Let that be as it may, the article of the learned professor wound up, on this evolutionary resurrection of a Miocene salamander we observe with respect and amazement that the genius of evolution on our planet has not by any means brought to an end its creative work.

This article appeared in print despite a silent but firmly held opinion of the editorial staff that such a learned discussion is not really suitable for a newspaper. As soon as it appeared Professor Uher received the following letter from a reader:

Dear Sir,

I bought a house last year on the market square at Caslav. On going over the house I found in the attic a box containing old but valuable works particularly scien-tific ones, such as two annual volumes of Hybl's journal 'Hyllos' for the years 1821-22, 'The Mammals' by Jan Svatopluk Presl, 'The

Foundations of Natural Sciences, or Physics' by Vojtech Sedlacek, nineteen annual volumes of the public Encyclopaedic Journal 'Krok,' and thirteen annual issues of the magazine of the Czech Museum. In Cuvier's 'Dissertations on the Revolutions of the earth's Crust (from 1834), in Presl's translation, I found as a bookmark a cutting from some old newspapers in which there was a report on certain strange salamanders.

When I read your excellent article on those mysterious salamanders I remembered that book-mark and I looked it up. I think that it might interest you, and therefore as a keen student of nature and a zealous reader of your writings I am sending it to you.

Yours respectfully,

J. V. NAJMAN.

No title or year was given on the newspaper cutting enclosed; judging by the style it was written in and the type, it must have been printed in the 'twenties or the 'thirties of the last century; it was so yellowed and worn that it was hardly legible. Professor Uher very nearly felt like throwing it into the wastepaper basket, but he was somewhat moved by the age of that printed page; and he began to read; after a while he gasped "My Gosh!" and put his glasses straight in his excitement. The following was the text of the cutting:

On Men-Lizards.

We have read in some foreign newspapers that a certain captain (commander) of an English warship on his return from distant lands brought a report of strange reptiles which he met with on a small island in the Australian seas. On that island there is a lake with salt water therein but it is without any connection whatever with the sea as well as being very difficult of access thereto. At that place the captain and the boat surgeon were taking their rest. There emerged from the lake animals of a kind like lizards but walking about on two legs like men and of the size of a sea dog or seal and they moved about the shore in an attractive and strange manner as if they were dancing. The commander and the surgeon with shots from their guns slew two of those beasts. It is said that they have a slimy body without hair and without scales so that they resemble salamanders. The next day on going to fetch them they had to leave them on the spot on account of the great stench and they gave orders to the crew to draw nets in the lake and to bring a pair of those monsters alive on board ship. Having drawn the lake the sailors dispatched all the lizards in great numbers and only two they dragged on board saying that they had a poisonous body which burned and stank like nettles. Then they put them into casks of sea water in order to bring them to England. But as they were passing the island of Sumatra the captive lizards having crept out from the casks and having opened the window in the steerage of themselves under cover of the night they threw themselves into the sea and vanished. According to the testimony of the Commander and the boat surgeon they were very strange and sly animals, walking on two legs and uttering peculiar barking and smacking sounds, but they were not at all dangerous to man. Surely, therefore, we may call them men-lizards.

So read the cutting. Gosh! repeated Professor Uher in excitement. Why isn't there some date or title of the paper from which somebody cut it at somewhere? And what were the foreign papers, what was the name of that certain commander, what English boat was it? And which small island was it in the Australian seas? Couldn't those people have been a bit more exact in those days, and—well, yes, a bit more scientific? Why, really this is a historical document of tremendous value. . . .

A small island in the Australian seas, yes. A little lake with salt water. According to that it must have been a coral island, an atoll with an almost inaccessible lagoon: just a place where such a fossil animal might be preserved, isolated from an environment in an evolutionary sense more advanced, and not disturbed in its natural reserve. Of course it could not multiply very much, because it would not find sufficient food in that small lake. That's very obvious, said the professor to himself. An animal like a lizard but without scales, and walking on two legs like human beings: well then, either Andrias Scheuchzeri or another newt closely related to it. Suppose that it was our Andrias. Suppose that those damned sailors had exterminated it in that little lake, and that only the pair on the boat remained alive; a pair which behold! at Sumatra escaped into the sea. And right on the Equator, in conditions biologically highly favourable, and in an environment supplying an unlimited amount of food. Can it be possible that this change of environment has induced in the Miocene salamander that powerful evolutionary impulse? It is quite clear that it was adapted to live in salty water; let us imagine its new habitat as a quiet, land-locked bay with a great quantity of food; what happens next? *The newt begins to flourish*, being transferred to optimal conditions with a tremendous energy. That's what it is, exulted the scientist. The newt starts its evolutionary progress with an unbounded appetite; it rushes into life as if in a frenzy; it multiplies terrifically because its eggs and tadpoles in the new habitat have no specific enemies. It occupies one island after the other—it is of course strange that in its migration it somehow omits some islands. Otherwise it is the typical case of migration determined by nutrition. And now the question: why didn't it begin its development before? Is it not in keeping with the phenomena that in the Ethiopian–Australian zone there are, or until the present time there have been, no salamanders recorded? Was it not perhaps that in that zone during the Miocene period some changes took place biologically unfavourable to salamanders? That may well be. A specific enemy might have appeared, which simply exterminated the newts. Only on *one* small island in an enclosed little lake the Miocene salamander has survived—of course at the price that in an evolutionary sense it has stood still; its evolutionary progress had halted; it was like a spring wound up that cannot release itself. One must not overlook the supposition that Nature with this salamander had great possibilities, that it *was* to develop still more and more, higher and higher, who knows how far. . . . (Professor Uher almost began to tremble at the idea; who knows in fact if this Andrias Scheuchzeri was not to have been the Miocene man?)

But lo! This animal with suppressed evolution suddenly finds itself in a new and infinitely more promising habitat; the coiled-up spring of evolution begins to unwind. With what vital élan, with what Miocene exuberance and eagerness Andrias rushes along the path of evolution! How feverishly it makes up for those hundreds of thousands and millions of years of evolution that it had missed! Is it conceivable that it will be satisfied with the evolutionary stage to which it has now attained? Will it exhaust itself with the generic outburst of which we are witnesses, or is it only on the threshold of its evolutionary progress and only preparing to rise—who can now say to what height?

These were the meditations and suppositions that Professor Dr. Vladimir Uher jotted down as he pored over the yellowed cutting of an old newspaper, quivering with the intellectual enthusiasm of a pioneer. I shall put it in the papers, he reflected, because nobody reads scientific journals. Let everybody be acquainted with the big natural process that we are witnessing. And I shall give it the title: **Have Newts got a Future?**

However, the editorial staff of the *Lidové Noviny* glanced through the article of Professor Uher and shook its head. These newts again! I think *myself* that our readers are already tired to death of those newts. It's time to start on something fresh. And besides, such a learned discussion isn't suitable for the papers.

As a consequence the article on the evolution and future of the newts was never published at all.

12

The Salamander Syndicate

THE Chairman, G. H. Bondy, rang the bell and stood up.

"Gentlemen," he began, "I have the honour to open this extraordinary general meeting of the Pacific Export Association. I extend a hearty welcome to all present, and I thank them for their generous support.

"Gentlemen," he continued with a trembling voice, "it is my grave duty to announce to you some sad news. Captain John van Toch is no more. He who we may call our founder has died, the father of the happy idea of establishing commercial relations with thousands of islands in the far Pacific, our first captain, and our most zealous collaborator. He passed away at the beginning of this year on board our ship *Šárka* not far from Fanning Island, struck down by an attack of apoplexy while on active service. [He must have been having a row, poor chap, was the idea that crossed Mr. Bondy's mind.] I ask you to tender your respect to his bright memory by standing up."

The gentlemen rose, shuffling their chairs, and stood in solemn silence, governed by the mutual thought that the general meeting ought not to last too long. (Poor chap, Vantoch, G. H. Bondy was thinking with sincere emotion. What does he look like now! Very likely they threw him on a plank into the sea—he must have made a splash! Well, he was a good man, and such nice blue eyes he'd got. . . .)

"Thank you, gentlemen," he added shortly, "for the respect you have paid to the memory of Captain van Toch, my personal friend. I now ask Director Volavka to acquaint you with the financial results that we can expect from the P.E.A. this year. The figures are not yet definite, but I think you can take it that they will not change much before the end of the year. Well, now."

"Gentlemen," Mr. Volavka began to gurgle, and then it came: "The situation with regard to the pearl market is very unsatisfactory. At the end of our last financial year, when the output of pearls was almost twenty times as great as in a good year like 1925, the price fell catastrophically by as much as 65 per cent. Your directors therefore decided that we would not throw on to the market our this year's output of pearls, and that we should hold them until demand improves. Unfortunately, last autumn pearls ceased to be fashionable, apparently on the grounds that they have fallen so considerably in price. At the present time we are holding in our branch at Amsterdam over two hundred thousand pearls which are now almost unmarketable.

"On the other hand," Director Volavka went on gurgling, "this year the output of pearls has sunk considerably. We have had to abandon quite a number of our sources because their returns would not cover their working expenses. Sources opened up two or three years ago appear to some extent to be exhausted. As a consequence of this your directors have decided to turn their attention to other products of the deep sea like corals, shells, and sponges. It is true that we have succeeded in reviving the market for coral trinkets and other ornaments, but so far under present market conditions Italian rather than Pacific brands have benefited most. In addition, your directors are considering the possibilities of intensive fishing in the deep Pacific. The chief problem is how to transport the fish from those places to the European and American markets; results of investigations so far to date are not too favourable.

"But on the other hand," the director continued, raising his voice slightly, "our turnover in various *subsidiary* articles, such as exports of cloth, enamel pots and pans, wireless sets, and gloves to the Pacific islands is somewhat higher. This business is capable of further development and extension; even this year it will involve us in a deficit that is relatively negligible. It is of course out of the question that at the end of the financial year P.E.A. will pay out any dividend on its shares, and in view of that your directors beg to announce that *for this period* they will forgo all salaries and commissions."

A longer and more uncomfortable silence followed. (What is that Fanning Island like? G. H. Bondy meditated. He died like a real sailor; good fellow, Vantoch. What a pity, he was one of the best. And he wasn't so old . . . no older than I am now. . . .) Dr. Hubka asked permission to address the meeting;

and we quote further from the report of the extra-ordinary general meeting of the Pacific Export Association:

Dr. Hubka enquired if the winding up of the P.E.A. had perhaps been considered.

G. H. Bondy replied that the board of directors had decided to postpone this question for further consideration.

M. Louis Bonenfant pointed out that the collection of pearls at the different sources was not carried out through permanent representatives residing on the spot who might have seen to it if the gathering of the pearls was not done with sufficient industry and care.

Director Volavka replied that the matter had been under consideration, but that it was thought that if it were put into effect administrative costs would rise too high. At least three hundred permanent agents would be required, and the manner in which these agents would be controlled would have to be considered if they were to hand over all pearls found.

M. H. Brinkelaer enquired if they could rely on the Newts; were they in fact handing over all the pearls that they gathered, or were they handing them over to other parties other than the proper representatives of the Association.

G. H. Bondy announced that for the first time the Newts were being mentioned PUBLICLY there. Up to that time it had been an inflexible rule that there should be no mention of the details of the methods by which the collection of the pearls was being carried out. He drew attention to it because it was on those grounds that an unobtrusive title was chosen for the Pacific Export Association.

M. H. Brinkelaer enquired if it was not perhaps permissible to discuss at the meeting matters which concerned the interests of the Company, and which besides had been common knowledge for a long time among the general public.

G. H. Bondy replied that it was in order but was something new. He welcomed the fact that they could now speak more openly. To the first question raised by Mr. Brinkelaer he was able to state that to the best of his knowledge there was no reason to doubt the absolute honesty and working capacity of the Newts employed in gathering pearls and corals. But they must face the fact that existing sources of pearls were already or were within sight of being seriously exhausted. As for new sources—their never-to-be-forgotten collaborator Captain van Toch died on a voyage to discover islands so far undeveloped. For the time being they were unable to fill his place with a man of equal experience and of such unshakable honesty as well as love for the cause.

Col. D. W. Bright fully acknowledged the merits of the deceased Captain van Toch. He called attention, however, to the fact that the captain whose decease they all lamented had pampered those Newts too much. (Hear, Hear.) After all, there was no necessity to give the Newts knives and other utensils of the best quality as the late van Toch had been doing. There was no necessity to feed them so expensively. It might be possible to cut down expenses connected with the maintenance of the Newts very considerably and by that means increase the profits of their enterprise. (Loud applause.)

The Vice-President, J. Gilbert, expressed his agreement with Colonel Bright, but remarked that during the lifetime of Captain van Toch that had not been possible. Captain van Toch had asserted that towards the Newts he had his own personal obligations. For various reasons it had not been possible, nor advisable, in this matter to disregard the wishes of the old man.

Curt von Frisch enquired if it would not be possible to employ the Newts in other and possibly more profitable directions than in fishing for pearls. Their natural and, in a mode of speaking, their beaver talent for building dams and other constructions under the water was worthy of consideration. Perhaps they might be employed for deepening harbours, building breakwaters, and other engineering projects in the water.

G. H. Bondy stated that the board of directors were going into the matter very carefully; in that direction without a doubt great possibilities were opening up. He mentioned that the number of Newts in the possession of the company was now approximately six million; if they considered that a pair of Newts in a year produced something like a hundred tadpoles they would have next year at their disposal as many as three million Newts; in ten years' time their numbers would be truly astronomical. G. H. Bondy enquired what were the intentions of the Company with regard to that tremendous number of Newts which even now in the overcrowded newt farms, because of the shortage of natural food, they had to supplement with copra, potatoes, maize, and such-like feeding stuffs.

K. von Frisch enquired if the Newts were edible.

J. Gilbert: "No. And their skin is not suitable for anything either."

M. Bonenfant raised the question of what steps the board of directors really intended to take.

G. H. Bondy (standing up): "Gentlemen, we have called this extraordinary general meeting to direct your attention quite openly to the extremely unsatisfactory prospects of our Company which, allow me to recall, in recent years has declared with pride a dividend of twenty to twenty-three per cent after making ample provisions for reserves and amortizations. We are now at the parting of the ways; the kind of undertaking which had done so well for us in recent years has practically come to an end; there is nothing for us but to explore new possibilities." (Loud applause.)

"It seems to me almost like a touch of fate that just at this moment we have lost our excellent captain and friend, J. van Toch. With him was combined that romantic, beautiful, and—I say quite frankly—that short-sighted little business with the pearls. I regard it as a completed chapter in our concern; it had, I might say, its exotic charm, but it was not in accord with modern conditions. Gentlemen, pearls can never be the chief product of a huge, horizontal, and vertical trust. To me, personally, that phase with the pearls was only a small diversion——" (Uneasiness.)

"Yes, gentlemen, diversion which has brought you and me a nice return. Besides that, when our concern was first established those Newts had some kind of, should I say, charm of novelty. Three hundred million Newts will not have that charm any longer." (Laughter.)

"I said, new possibilities. While my good friend Captain van Toch was still alive it was out of the question to suggest giving our concern any other character than what I should call the style of Captain van Toch." ("Why?") "Besides, I have too much taste, sir, to mix various styles. The style of Captain van Toch was, I should say, the style of the adventurous novels. The style of Jack London, Joseph Conrad, and some others. The old, exotic, colonial, and almost heroic style. I am prepared to admit that in its way it fascinated me. But after the death of Captain van Toch we have no right to continue these adventures and juvenile epics. What lies in front of us is not a new chapter but a new orientation, gentlemen, a task for a new and substantially different conception. ("You refer to it as if it were a novel!") "Yes, sir, you are quite right. I am interested in business myself as an artist. Without a certain amount of art, sir, you will never devise anything new. We must be poets if we are to keep the world turning." (Applause.)

G. H. Bondy bowed. "Gentlemen, it is with regret that I am bringing to an end the chapter, so to speak, van Tochian; in it we worked off what in ourselves was young and adventurous. It is time to end the fairy tale of pearls and corals. Sinbad is dead, gentlemen. The question is, what next?" ("That's what we are asking you!") "Well, then, sir, please take a pencil and write down. Six millions. Have you got that? Multiply it by fifty. That makes three hundred million. Multiply that again by fifty. That makes fifteen milliards, doesn't it? And now, gentlemen, will you please tell me what we are to do in three years' time with fifteen milliard Newts. What shall we set them to do, how shall we feed them, and so on?" ("We'll let them die off!") "Yes, but isn't it that rather a waste, sir? Don't you believe that each Newt represents some kind of economic value, the value of a working force that lies latent in it waiting for its exploitation? Gentlemen, with six million Newts we shall be able to get along. With three hundred million it will be more difficult. But fifteen milliard Newts, gentlemen, will completely overwhelm us. The Newts will eat up the Company. That's it." ("You will be responsible for that! You began the whole business with the Newts!")

G. H. Bondy stiffened up. "I fully accept this responsibility, gentlemen. Anyone who so desires can at once divest himself of the shares of the Pacific Export Association. I am ready to buy up every single share . . ." ("For how much?") "At its par value, sir." (Great excitement. The chairman announced a ten minutes pause.)

After the pause H. Brinkelaer asked permission to speak. He expressed his great satisfaction over the fact that the Newts multiplied so readily by which means the property of the Company was increased. But, of course, it would be sheer madness to breed them with no purpose in view; if they themselves had no useful work for them to do he made the proposal in the name of a group of shareholders that the Newts should be sold as a working force to anyone who wished to carry out operations below water in the sea. (Applause.) A Newt only cost a few cents a day to feed; if a pair of Newts were to fetch, say, a hundred francs, and supposing a working Newt would last out not more than a year, such an investment would easily pay for itself with any contractor. (Expressions of approval.)

J. Gilbert rose to point out that the Newts attain a considerably greater age than one year; in fact, there had not yet been time to ascertain how long they live.

H. Brinkelaer amended his supposition to the effect that the price of a pair of Newts might be taken as three hundred francs f.o.b.

S. Weisberger enquired what in effect were the tasks that the Newts could perform.

Director Volavka: "By their own natural instincts and their unusual technical adaptability the Newts are specially suited for erecting dams, dykes, and breakwaters, for excavating harbours and canals, removing shoals, and mud deposits, and for keeping waterways clear; they could make good and maintain coastlines, enlarge land surfaces, and such-like things. In all such cases it was a matter of collective action demanding hundreds and thousands of working units, and of undertakings so vast that modern technique would never venture upon them unless it had an extremely cheap labour force at its disposal." ("That's true. Hear, Hear!")

Dr. Hubka raised the objection that by selling the Newts, which would eventually breed with their new onwers, the Company will lose its monopoly. He suggested that working parties of the Newts should only be HIRED OUT to contractors carrying out works below the sea, that they should be well trained and qualified, but let out on the condition that any spawn arising would remain the property of the Association.

Director Volavka pointed out that it was impossible to keep a watch on millions and eventually milliards of Newts in the water, not to mention their spawn; unfortunately, many Newts had already been stolen for zoological gardens and menageries.

Col. D. W. Bright: "There should be sold, and eventually hired out, only male Newts which could not multiply outside the incubators and farms which would be the monopoly of the Company."

Director Volavka: "We are not in a position to establish a claim that Newt farms should be the monopoly of the Company. It is not possible to own or lease a piece of a sea bottom. In point of law the question as to whom, in fact, the Newts belong which inhabit the territorial waters of, for instance, Her Majesty the Queen of Holland, is very uncertain, and may lead to many disputes. (Uneasiness.) In the majority of cases we have not even been guaranteed the fishing rights—in fact the Newt farms, gentlemen, which we have been founding in the Pacific Islands are without legal status." (Increasing uneasiness.)

J. Gilbert replied to the point raised by Col. Bright and stated that according to experience to date isolated males lost after a time their agility and economic worth; they became lazy, indifferent, and often pined away through home sickness.

Von Fritsch enquired if it would not be possible to castrate or sterilize the Newts before sale.

J. Gilbert: That would be too expensive; we simply cannot prevent Newts once sold from increasing in numbers.

S. Weisberger, as a member of the Society for the Prevention of Cruelty to Animals, hoped that future sales of Newts would be carried out as humanely as possible and in a manner that would not offend human feelings.

J. Gilbert thanked him for the suggestion: "It is a matter of course," he said, "that the capture and transport of the Newts is only entrusted to a trained personnel under proper supervision. Of course we cannot say how contractors who will buy the Newts will treat them."

S. Weisberger stated that he was satisfied with the Vice-President's assurance. (Applause.)

G. H. Bondy: "Gentlemen, let us get rid of the idea straight away that we shall be able in future to maintain a monopoly of the Newts. Unfortunately, according to expert opinion we can't take a patent out for them." (Laughter.) "Our leading position with regard to the Newts we must maintain, and we can protect ourselves by other means, of course, for this it is essential that we give a fresh orientation to our business, and develop it on a far bigger scale than up to the present." (Hear, Hear!) "Here, gentlemen, we have a whole bunch of provisional agreements. Your board of directors suggest that a new vertical trust be formed under the title The Salamander Syndicate. The members of the Salamander Syndicate besides ourselves would be certain big concerns, and strong financial groups; for instance, a certain concern which will supply special patented metal instruments for the Newts." ("Are you referring to the M.E.A.S.?") "Yes, sir, I am referring to the M.E.A.S. Besides that a chemical and oil-cake combine will supply cheap patent fodder for the Newts; a group of transport agencies will have—as a result of existing experience—special hygienic tanks patented for transporting the Newts; a group of insurance companies will undertake the insurance of the animals purchased against injury and death while under transit or at the place of work; besides that there are other interested parties, dealing with industry, export, and finance, which for weighty reasons we cannot disclose at this juncture. Perhaps it will be sufficient, gentlemen, if I tell you that this Syndicate, when it is set up, will have at its disposal four hundred million pounds sterling." (Great excitement.) "This case here is full of contracts which only need to be signed to bring one of the greatest industrial organizations of our time into being. The board of directors ask you, gentlemen, to grant them full powers to complete this gigantic concern whose task will be the rational production and exploitation of the Newts." (Applause and cries of dissent.)

"Gentlemen, please realize what we stand to gain by this collaboration. The Salamander Syndicate will not only provide the Newts but also all the utensils and fodder for the Newts, that is, maize, starch, suet, and sugar for milliards of animals under our charge; besides that, transport, insurance, veterinary inspection, and so on, all that at the lowest price which would guarantee for us if not a monopoly then at least overwhelming power as against every future competitor who might try to trade in the Newts. Let him try, gentlemen; with us he won't compete for long." (Hurrah!) "But that is not all. The Salamander Syndicate will transport all the building material for the works below water which the Newts will carry out; for that reason we have the support of heavy industry behind us, cement, timber, and stone——'' (''You don't know yet how well the Newts are going to work.'') ''Gentlemen, at this very moment, twelve thousand Newts are working in Saigon harbour on the new docks, harbours, and quays.'' (''You hadn't told us of that!'') ''No, it is the first experiment on a big scale. That experiment, gentlemen, is a success in every way. To-day the future of the Newts is beyond all doubt.'' (Enthusiastic applause.)

"And not only that, gentlemen. This does not exhaust the scope of the Salamander Syndicate. The Salamander Syndicate will explore possibilities for employing millions of Newts throughout the whole world. It will supply plans and schemes for the mastery of the seas. It will achieve Utopias and gigantic dreams. It will develop projects for new land fronts, and canals, for barriers connecting the continents, for whole chains of islands for ocean flights, for new dry land built up in the middle of the sea. There lies the future of mankind. Gentlemen, four-fifths of the world's surface is covered by the sea; beyond question it is too much; the surface of the earth, the map of the seas, and of the continents must be amended. We shall give to the world the toilers of the sea, gentlemen. That won't any longer be the style of Captain van Toch; the adventurous story of the pearls we shall replace by a paean of work. Either we shall halt, or we shall create; but unless we are going to think in terms of continents and oceans we shall not have grown equal to our possibilities. In this respect, may I say that someone spoke of the price of a pair of Newts. I should prefer that we thought in terms of whole milliards of Newts, of millions, and millions of working units, of changing the earth's crust, a new Genesis, and new geological epochs.

We can speak to-day of a new Atlantis, of old continents which will stretch out further and further into the ocean, of the New Worlds which mankind will build for itself. Excuse me, gentlemen, perhaps this may seem too much of a Utopia for you. Yes, we are truly entering upon a new Utopia. We are already in it, my friends. We have only to work out in full the future of the Newts on the technical side——" ("And economical!")

"Yes. Particularly on the economic side. Gentlemen, our Association is too small to be able single-handed to exploit milliards of Newts; we are not capable of it financially—or politically. If the map of the continents and seas is going to be changed, the Great Powers will also be interested in the enterprise, gentlemen. But we shall not discuss that; we shall not mention the high officials which have already adopted a positive attitude towards the Syndicate. I beg you, gentlemen, not to lose sight of the immense scope of the thing upon which you are being called upon to vote." (Enthusiastic and very lengthy applause. Splendid! Hurray!)

•   •   •   •   •

All the same it was necessary to undertake before asking them to vote in favour of the Salamander Syndicate that for each share held in the Pacific Export Association at least 10 per cent should be paid on account of the reserves. On a poll being taken 87 per cent were in favour, and only 13 per cent against. As a result the report of the board of directors was adopted. The Salamander Syndicate entered into being. G. H. Bondy was accorded a vote of thanks.

"You put the case very nicely, Mr. Bondy," complimented old Sigi Weisberger. "Very nicely. And may I ask you, Mr. Bondy, how did you first hit upon the idea?"

"How?" said G. H. Bondy, pondering. "Well, as a matter of fact, to tell you the truth, Mr. Weisberger, it was because of old van Toch. He had such great faith in those Newts of his. What would he have said, poor old chap, if we had let his tapa-boys kick the bucket or be done in?"

"What tapa-boys?"

"Why, those damned Newts. Now at least they will be treated decently now that they will have some value. And for nothing else are those damned beasts suited, Mr. Weisberger, than that some Utopia should be achieved with them."

"I don't follow that," said Mr. Weisberger. "And have you actually seen a Newt, Mr. Bondy? I don't really know myself what kind of a thing it is. Could you possibly tell me what it is like?"

"No, I can't do that, Mr. Weisberger. Do I know what a Newt is like? What good is that to me? Have I any time to worry about what things look like? I must be glad that we've got that Salamander Syndicate fixed up."

Appendix

Of the Sexual Life of the Newts

ONE of the favourite activities of the human mind is to imagine what some day in the very distant future the world and mankind will look like, what scientific miracles will have been accomplished, what social problems will have been solved, how far science and social organization will have progressed, and so on and so forth. The majority of these Utopias, however, do not omit to be very keenly interested in the question as to what in that better, more progressive, or at least technically more perfect world will happen to institutions which are ancient but perennially interesting like sexual life, reproduction, love, marriage, the family, women's problems, and so on. In this respect the reader is referred to the relevant literature, like Paul Adam, H. G. Wells, Aldous Huxley, and many others.

With reference to the above examples, the author feels it his duty now that he has referred to the question of the future of this world to give a discourse on the lines that the sexual arrangements of the Newts will follow. He is doing it at this stage to obviate the necessity of having to refer to this topic later on. The sexual life of *Andrias Scheuchzeri*, of course, in main outline is in accordance with the propagation of other salamanders: there is no copulation in the strict meaning of that word; the female lays her eggs in small batches, the fertilized eggs develop while still in the water into tadpoles, and so on; this information can be found in every book on natural history. We shall only mention a few peculiarities which have been observed with regard to *Andrias Scheuchzeri* on this special point.

At the beginning of April, records H. Bolte, the males associate with the females; in every period of sexual activity one male usually stays with the same female, and does not leave her for more than a yard for a couple of days. During this time he does not take any food, but the female exhibits considerable voracity. The male pursues her in the water and tries to place his head close to hers. If he succeeds, he holds his mouth a little in front of her snout, perhaps to prevent her from escaping, and then he becomes motionless. Thus in contact only with their heads, and with their bodies making an angle of about thirty degrees, both animals float motionless side by side. From time to time the male begins to writhe so strongly that he strikes with his body that of the female; afterwards he again becomes rigid, with his legs wide apart, only touching with his mouth the snout of his chosen mate, which in the meantime indifferently consumes what comes her way. This kiss, as we may so term it, continues for several days; sometimes the female darts off after food, and then the male pursues her, obviously very excited and even furious. At last the female ceases to offer further resistance, she does not try to escape any longer, and the pair float in the water motionless like two dark logs pressed together. Then convulsive tremors begin to pass through the male's body during which he emits into the water a copious and slightly mucilaginous sperm. Immediately afterwards he forsakes the female and crawls away between the stones, exhausted in the extreme; while in this state his leg or tail may be cut off without his offering any defensive reaction.

In the meantime the female remains for some time in her rigid, motionless position; then she arches her back strongly and begins to expel from her cloaca strings of eggs enclosed in a mucilaginous membrane; in this operation she often assists herself with her hind legs in the same way as toads. There are from forty to fifty eggs, and they adhere to the body of the female like a tuft. With these the female swims to sheltered places and fixes them on algae, seaweed, and even on stones. After ten days the female lays a second batch of eggs to the number of about twenty or thirty, without having had any connection with the male; apparently those eggs have been fertilized directly in her cloaca. As a rule after another seven to eight days the third and fourth batches of from fifteen to twenty for the most part fertile eggs are laid, from which after a period of from one to three weeks active little tadpoles with finger-like gills are hatched. Within a year these tadpoles become fully mature Newts which can propagate themselves further.

On the other hand Miss Blanche Kistemaeckers carried out an observation on two females and one male of *Andrias Scheuchzeri* in captivity. At mating-time the male associated with only one female, and persecuted her somewhat brutally; when she tried to elude him he beat her with strong blows from his tail. He strongly disliked watching her feed, and he tried to force her away from anything edible; it was apparent that he wanted to have her only for himself, and he simply dominated her. When he emitted his sperms he threw himself at the other female and seemed to wish to devour her; he had to be taken out of the tank and kept apart. In spite of that, even this female produced FERTILE eggs to the number of sixty-three. In all three animals, moreover, Miss Kistemaeckers noted that during this period the ridges of their cloacas were considerably swollen. It appears therefore, writes Miss Kistemaeckers, that in the case of Andrias fertilization is accomplished not by copulation or physical union but through the mediation of what might be called the *Sexual Milieu*. As is quite clear, not even temporary association is essential to bring about the fertilization of the eggs. This led the young investigator to carry out further interesting experiments.

155

She separated members of the two sexes from each other; then when the proper time arrived she squeezed out the sperms from the male and placed them in the water with the females. As a result of this the females began to lay *fertile* eggs. In another experiment Miss Blanche Kistemaeckers filtered the male sperms, and the filtrate *deprived of the spermatozoa* (it was clear and slightly acid fluid) she placed in the water with the females; in this case also the females *began to lay eggs*, about fifty each, of which the greater part were *fertile* and produced normal tadpoles. It was this particular case that led Miss Kistemaekers to the important conception of the *Sexual Milieu*, which is a clear transition stage between parthenogenesis and sexual reproduction. The fertilization of the eggs is simply brought about by the chemical change in the milieu (by acidity of a certain nature which so far no one has succeeded in establishing by artificial means), a change which in some way is associated with the sexual function of the male. But that particular function is really unessential; the association of the males with the females in the case of Andrias appears to be a survival of a more primitive stage in evolution when fertilization took place in the same manner as with other Newts. This association, as Miss Kistemaeckers rightly states, is in fact some kind of inherited illusion of paternity; in actual fact the male is not the father of the tadpoles, but only the producer of a certain quite impersonal chemical agent bringing about the sexual milieu which is the true means of fertilization. If we had in one aquarium a hundred associated pairs of Andrias Scheuchzeri, we should be led to assume that a hundred separate acts of fertilization were taking place; in reality it is one single act, and that is the collective sexualization of the given milieu, or to put it more accurately: the production of a certain hyperacidity of the water to which the ripe eggs of Andrias automatically react by developing into tadpoles. If we could produce that acid medium by artificial means, the males would be rendered superfluous. Thus the sexual life of the worthy Andrias appears as if it were a Great Illusion; his erotical frenzy, his marriage and sexual tyranny, his temporary fidelity, his cumbersome and crude ardours are all in fact superfluous, obsolete, almost symbolical acts which accompany, or so to speak adorn, the proper impersonal male act which is the formation of the fertilizing sexual milieu. The strange indifference of the females, with which they accept that aimless, frenzied, *personal* courtship of the males, is clear testimony that in being wooed the female instinctively perceives a mere formal ceremony or preliminary to the proper wedding act in which *they* coalesce sexually with the fertilizing milieu; we should say that of the two kinds the female of Andrias is aware of this state of things more clearly and acts upon it more realistically without any erotical illusions.

(The experiments of Miss Kistemaeckers were supplemented by some interesting experiments by the learned Abbé Bontempelli. He dried down the sperms of Andrias and ground them up, and then placed this material in water containing females; in this case too the females began to lay fertile eggs. The same result was obtained when he dried and ground up the male organ of Andrias, or when he extracted it with solvents or boiled it, and then poured the extract into the tank containing the females. He obtained the same result when he repeated the experiment with extracts of the cerebral hypophyses, and even with the extracts of the epidermal glands of Andrias which had been expressed at the time of sexual activity. In all these cases the females did not react to these media at once; only after a while did they cease to catch food, and they then became motionless, even rigid in the water, whereupon after a few hours the deposition of jellylike eggs about as big as a broad bean began.)

In this connection a strange ritual may also be mentioned—the so-called *Salamander Dance*. (This does not refer to the Salamander Dance which for some years was in fashion, especially among the best society, and was by Bishop Hiram described as "the most obscene dance of which he had ever heard.") In effect, on evenings when the moon was at the full (except the breeding periods) the Andriases used to clamber out, *but only the males*, on to the shores; they sat down in a circle and began with a strange undulating movement to rotate the upper part of their bodies. Also in other circumstances it was a movement characteristic for those large Newts; but during the "dances" mentioned above they gave themselves to it savagely, passionately, until they had exhausted themselves, like dancing dervishes. Some scientists held that this mad squirming and shuffling was a cult of the moon, and therefore a ritual religious in nature; on the other hand there were others who saw in it a dance fundamentally erotical, and they explained it merely through that peculiar sexual behaviour which we have been discussing. We said that with *Andrias Scheuchzeri* the real fertilizing agent is the so-called sexual milieu as a collective and impersonal link between male and female individuals. It was also stated that the females accept this impersonal sexual relation far more realistically and as more self-evident than the males, who apparently from instinctive male vanity and eagerness for conquest desire at least to maintain the illusion of sexual conquest, and for that purpose they go through the actions of amorous wooing and conjugal ownership. It is one of the great erotical illusions compensated in an interesting manner by those huge male festivities which, it is said, are nothing but an instinctive desire to perceive oneself as *collective male*. Through that mass dance, it is stated, the atavistic and unfounded illusion of male sexual individualism is being overcome; this squirming, intoxicated, frenzied horde is nothing but the *Collective Male*, a Collective Bridegroom, and the Great

Copulator, which is performing his well-known nuptial dance and taking part in a huge wedding ritual—with the peculiar exclusion of the females, who in the meantime indifferently smack their lips over some fish or mollusc that they have devoured. The well-known Charles J. Powell, who designated these Newt festivities as the Dance of the Male Element, adds: "And have we not in these collective male rituals the very source and origin of the marvellous Newt collectivism? Let us not overlook the fact that we only meet with real animal sociability where the life and development of the race is not based on the sexual pair; as with bees, ants, and termites. The solidarity of the bees can be expressed by the phrase: I, the Maternal Swarm. The solidarity of the Newt communities can be expressed quite differently: We, the Male Principle. It is only all the males acting in unison who at the given moment almost exude from themselves the fertile sexual milieu that are the Great Male that penetrates the wombs of the females and generously multiples life. Their paternity is collective; therefore their whole nature is collective, and it manifests itself in collective action, while the females, having gone through the process of laying eggs, lead until the next spring a life more or less diffuse and solitary. Only the males form the commune. Only the males perform communal tasks. With no animal species do the females play such a subordinate role as with Andrias; they are excluded from communal life, and also they do not take the slightest interest in it. *Their* phase begins when the Male Principle impregnates their milieu with an acidity chemically almost imperceptible but vitally so penetrating that it acts even with the infinitely great dilution caused by high and low tide. It is as if the very ocean became the male which fertilizes on its shores millions of ova.

"In spite of all the cock's pride," Charles J. Powell continues, "Nature in the case of the majority of the

Along the Steps of Civilization

1

M. Povondra reads the Papers

THERE are people who collect stamps, and others incunabula. For many years Mr. Povondra, the porter in the house belonging to G. H. Bondy, had found no meaning in his life; for a long time he hesitated between an interest in prehistoric burial-places and a passion for foreign politics; one evening, however, it dawned upon him suddenly what had been lacking in his life to make it full and complete. Great things are usually unexpected.

That evening Mr. Povondra was reading the paper, Mrs. Povondra was mending Frantik's stockings, and Frantik pretended that he was learning the tributaries of the Danube on the left bank. There was a pleasant silence.

"Well, I never!" grunted Mr. Povondra.

"What's that?" inquired Mrs. Povondra, threading a needle.

"Why, those Newts," said father Povondra. "I've just read here that during the last three months seventy millions of them have been sold."

"That's very many, isn't it?" said Mrs. Povondra.

"I should think it is! Why, it's a tremendous number, Mummy! Think of it, seventy millions!" Mr. Povondra shook his head. "The profits must be amazing. And the work that's done now," he added, after a pause for meditation. "Here I read how everywhere people are up to their ears in building new lands and islands. My word, people can make as many continents as they like now. That's a fine thing, Mother. Don't you think that that is a greater step forward than the discovery of America?" Mr. Povondra grew thoughtful at the idea. "A new era in history, you know! Yes, Mummy, we're living in stirring times."

Again a long homely silence ensued. Suddenly father Povondra puffed from his pipe with more excitement. "And when I come to think of it, all that would never have come to pass without me!"

"What?"

"That business with the Newts. This New Age. When you go into it properly it was me who started it all."

Mrs. Povondra looked up from the undarned stocking. "What do you mean?"

"Because I let that captain in to see Mr. Bondy. If I hadn't let him in, that captain would never have met Mr. Bondy. If it hadn't been for me, Mummy, nothing would have come out of that idea. Without a doubt, nothing at all."

"Perhaps that captain would have found somebody else," objected Mrs. Povondra.

There was a contemptuous hiss in Father Povondra's pipe stem. "What do you know about it! That's something only G. H. Bondy can do. Good Lord, he's one ahead of anybody I've ever heard of. The others would have only thought it crack-brained or a hoax; but Mr. Bondy isn't like that! He's got a nose, my gosh!" Mr. Povondra grew thoughtful. "That captain—what was his name, van Toch—didn't even look like it. Such a fat old chap he was. Another porter would have said to him, 'What do you think, man, the boss isn't at home,' and altogether; but I had such a sort of feeling, or something! 'I shall show him in,' I said to myself; 'Mr. Bondy will probably swear at me, but I'll take the risk, and let him in.' I always say a porter must have a nose for people. Sometimes a man rings, he looks like a lord, and instead he's only an agent selling refrigerators. And another time a fat old fellow comes along, and just think what he's got. You must know a lot about human nature," father Povondra meditated. "This shows you, Frantik, what a man can do even in a low position. Take an example from it, and always try to do your duty as I have done." Mr. Povondra nodded his head with solemn emotion. "I could have turned my nose up at that captain at the door, and I should have saved myself the steps. Another porter would have puffed himself up and banged the door in his face. And in that way he would have put a stop to the prodigious progress in the world. Remember, Frantik, if every man only did his duty, the world would swim along. And do listen properly while I'm telling you something."

"Yes, Daddy," mumbled Frantik miserably.

Father Povondra cleared his throat. "Lend me those scissors, Mummy. I ought to cut this out from the paper so that I shall have something left to remember me by."

•　　　•　　　•　　　•　　　•

So it was that Mr. Povondra began to collect cuttings about the Newts. We owe to his zeal as a collector much material which otherwise would have passed into oblivion. He cut out and put away anything in print about the Newts that he came across; it need not be kept a secret that after a certain amount of initial trepidation he learned in his favourite coffee-house to ransack the papers whenever the Newts were mentioned, and he achieved a peculiar, almost magic skill in managing to tear out unobtrusively from the papers the particular page and whisk it into his pocket directly under the nose of the head waiter. As is well known, all collectors are prepared to steal or murder if it is a question of getting another piece for their collection; but this does not lower their moral character in the least.

Now at last his life had a meaning, for it was the life of a collector. Evening after evening he arranged and read through his cuttings before the indulgent eyes of Mrs. Povondra, who knew that every male is partly a fool and partly a little child; rather let him play with those cuttings than go to the pub and play cards. She even made in the linen cupboard space for the boxes which he himself had stuck together for his collection; can anything more be expected from a wife and matron?

Even G. H. Bondy was on some occasions astonished

166

at the encyclopedic knowledge of Mr. Povondra with regard to everything concerning the Newts. Mr. Povondra confessed somewhat bashfully that he was collecting anything that was printed about salamanders, and he showed Mr. Bondy his boxes. G. H. Bondy expressed kind approval of his collection; it's no good denying it, only big pots can be so gracious, and only powerful gentlemen can make others happy without its costing them a penny; altogether, big pots have a good time. So, for instance, Mr. Bondy simply gave an order that all the cuttings concerning the Newts which were not required for the archives should be sent from the offices of the Salamander Syndicate to Povondra; and the blissful but somewhat overwhelmed Mr. Povondra received day by day whole bales of documents in all the languages of the world, of which especially the papers printed in Cyrillic or in the Greek alphabet, in the Hebrew, Arabic, Chinese, Bengali, Tamil, Javanese, Burmese or Taalik script filled him with pious respect. "When I only realize," he used to murmur over them, "that all this would not have been without me!"

As we have already said, the collection of Mr. Povondra preserved much of the historical material concerning the story of the Newts; this of course does not mean that it would satisfy a scientific historian. For in the first place Mr. Povondra, who had not been provided with a vocational education in the supplementary historical sciences and in bibliographical methods, did not attach to his cuttings either a note of the source or of the appropriate date so that in most cases we do not know when and where this or that statement was printed. Secondly, with the overwhelming supply of material accumulated beneath his hands, Mr. Povondra chiefly preserved long articles which he considered to be the most important, while brief notes and cables he simply threw into the coalscuttle; consequently, about all this period a particularly small amount of information and facts has come down to us. Thirdly, the hand of Mrs. Povondra played an important role in the matter; when Mr. Povondra's boxes became critically full she silently and surreptitiously pulled out some of the cuttings and burnt them, a procedure that took place several times a year. She only spared those which were not accumulating so quickly, like the ones printed in Malabar, Tibetan, and Coptic scripts; these remained preserved almost in their entirety, but in virtue of certain gaps in our education they are of no great value to us. The material which we have at hand, concerning the history of the Newts, is in consequence very fragmentary, something like the land registers for the eighth century A.D., or like the collected works of Sappho; only by accident have the documents relating to this or that section of this great world event been preserved for us, which in spite of all that is missing we shall try to summarize under the title of *Along the Steps of Civilization.*

2

Along the Steps of Civilization
(The Annals of the Newts)[1]

IN the historical epoch which G. H. Bondy initiated at the famous general meeting of the Pacific Export Association in his prophetic words on the beginning of a new Utopia,[2] we can no longer measure the historical events by decades and centuries, but by the quarters of the year in which the economic statistics appear.[3]

[1] Cf. G. Kreuzmann, *Geschichte der Molche*. Hans Tietze, *Der Molch des XX. Jahrhunderts*. Kurt Wolff, *Der Molch and das deutsche Volk*. Sir Herbert Owen, *The Salamanders and the British Empire*. Giovanni Focaja, *L'evoluzione degli anfibii durante il Fascismo*. Léon Bonnet, *Les Urodèles et la Société des Nations*. S. Madariaga, *Las Salamandras y la Civilización*, and many others.

[2] Cf. *War with the Newts*, part I, chapter xii.

[3] As evidence of this, we may take the very first cutting from the collection of Mr. Povondra:

MARKET BULLETIN—NEWTS

(CTK.) According to the latest report that the Salamander Syndicate issued at the end of the last quarter sales of Newts rose by thirty per cent. In three months nearly seventy millions of Newts changed hands, particularly for South and Central America, Indo-China, and Italian Somaliland. In the near future, preliminary work will be undertaken on the widening of the Panama Canal,

[*Continued at foot of page 170*

For now the making of history, if we may so call it, takes place wholesale; and as a consequence the tempo of history is accelerated (according to some estimates, five times).

To-day we simply cannot wait some hundreds of years for something either good or bad to happen in the world. For instance, the migration of peoples, which used to drag on for ages, can now be managed with the organized transport of to-day and be all completed in three years; otherwise there is no money in it. It was the same situation with the liquidation of the Roman Empire and the colonization of the continents, the killing off of the Red Indians, and so on. All that could have been accomplished to-day in an incomparably shorter stretch of time if it were entrusted to contractors with plenty of capital behind them. In this direction the tremendous success of the Salamander

Continued from page 169]

> the cleaning of the harbour at Guayaquil, and removal of some shoals and cliffs in the Torres Straits. These undertakings alone will, according to a rough estimate, involve the excavation of nine milliards of cubic yards of solid earth. The building of the stable aircraft islands on the Madeira-Bermuda route is not to begin until next spring. The filling in of the Marianne Islands under the Japanese mandate is proceeding; so far, eight hundred and forty thousand acres of a new, the so-called light dry soil, have been won from the sea between the islands of Tinian and Saipan. In view of the growing demand Newts are very firm in price, and run Leading 61, Team 620. Fodder is in good supply.

Syndicate, and its powerful influence on world history, unquestionably points the way of those to follow.

The Annals of the Newts therefore, from the very beginning, are marked by good and rational organization; the foremost but not the only cause of that comes from the Salamander Syndicate; it must also be acknowledged that science, philanthropy, culture, the Press, and other factors have played no small part in the amazing extension and progress of the Newts. Nevertheless it was the Salamander Syndicate which, as it were, day by day conquered for the Newts new continents and new lands, even if it had to overcome many obstacles which held up this development.[1] The

---

[1] Of such obstacles this report, for instance, cut from a newspaper will bear witness. No date is given.

IS ENGLAND SHUTTING OUT THE NEWTS?

(Reuter.) To a question asked to-day in the House of Commons by Mr. J. Leed, M.P., Sir Samuel Mandeville replied that His Majesty's Government had closed the Suez Canal to all Salamander transports; further, that they did not intend to permit one single Salamander to be employed on the shores or in the territorial waters of the British Isles. The purpose of these regulations, Sir Samuel declared, is to ensure the security

[Continued at foot of page 172

quarterly report of the Syndicate shows how one by one Indian and Chinese harbours are being occupied by the Newts; how Newt colonization spreads along the shores of Africa and strikes across to the American continent, where new and most up-to-date Newt incubators will soon come into operation in the Bay of Mexico; how, besides these broad streams of colonization, smaller parties of Newts are being sent out as pioneers and vanguards for future export. For example, the Salamander Syndicate has presented the Dutch Waterstaat with a thousand picked Newts; to the town of Marseilles it has presented six hundred for cleaning up the Old Harbour, and likewise elsewhere. In great contrast to the human colonization of the world, the spread of the Newts is taking place according to plan and on a large scale; if left to Nature, without a doubt it would drag on for hundreds and thousands of years; well, Nature is not and never has been as enterprising and systematic as human industry and commerce. It also seems as if the strong demand has exerted some influence on the fertility of the Newts; the yield of

Continued from page 171]

of the British shores as well as the validity of the old laws and conventions with reference to the abolition of the slave trade.

To the enquiry of another Member of Parliament, Mr. B. Russell, Sir Samuel added that this decision does not, of course, apply to the Colonies and Dominions.

spawn from one female has risen to fifty tadpoles a year. Certain inevitable losses which the Newts used to suffer from the sharks ceased almost completely when the Newts were provided with underwater revolvers shooting dum-dum bullets for defence against rapacious fish.[1]

The introduction of the Newts of course did not take place everywhere equally smoothly; in some places conservative factions sharply protested against the introduction of a new working force, regarding it as unfair competition with human labour;[2] others gave

[1] For this purpose revolvers were mostly used of the type invented by Ing. Mirko Šafránek, and which were produced in the Brno Armaments Factory.

[2] Cf. this newspaper cutting.

STRIKE MOVEMENT IN AUSTRALIA

(Havas.) The leader of the Australian Trade Unions, Harry MacNamara, has called for a general strike of all those employed in harbours, transport, electricity works, etc. This means that the sectional organizations demand that the import of working Newts into Australia should be strictly regulated under the immigration laws. On the other hand Australian farmers are agitating for the free import of the Newts, because, owing to their requirements of feeding stuffs,

Continued at foot of page 174

voice to apprehensions that the Newts living on small sea organisms would prove detrimental to fishing; while others again asserted that with their submarine burrows and corridors they would undermine the embankments and islands. In point of fact there were people enough who uttered warnings against the introduction of the Newts; but from time immemorial all progress has been met with resistance and distrust; it was the same with industrial machines, and it was again repeated with the Newts. In other places misunderstandings of another kind

Continued from page 173]

the sale of maize and fats, especially sheep suet, has increased considerably. The Government hopes to bring about a compromise. The Salamander Syndicate offer to hand over to the Trade Unions a contribution of six shillings for every Newt imported. The Government is ready to guarantee that the Newts would only be employed in the water and that (on moral grounds) they would not emerge from the water more than 16 inches, that is up to the chest. The Trade Unions, however, insist on 5 inches, and demand for every Newt an allowance of ten shillings as well as its capitation fee. It seems likely that an agreement will be be reached with the assistance of the Federal treasury.

emerged,[1] but thanks to the substantial support of

[1] Cf. a remarkable document from Mr. Povondra's collection:

The Newts Save the Lives of 36 Drowning Men

(From our special correspondent)

Madras, April 3. In the harbour here the steamship *Indian Star* came into collision with a ferry boat carrying about forty natives, which sank at once. Before it would have been possible to despatch the police tender the Newts working on the removal of mud from the harbour rushed to the rescue and conveyed thirty-six people to the shore. One Salamander alone dragged out from the water three women

THE NEWT LIFE-SAVERS

and two children. As a reward for this brave deed the Newts have been granted a written expression of thanks in a waterproof case from the local authorities.

On the other hand, the natives are greatly disturbed by the fact that the Newts were allowed to touch drown-ing persons of higher caste, for they regard the Newts as impure and untouchable. At the harbour a crowd of several thousand natives collected who demanded that the Newts should be turned out of the harbour. Order is being maintained by the police; only three people have been killed, and one hundred and twenty were arrested.

Towards ten o'clock in the evening peace was restored. The Salamanders are not to cease work.

the World Press, which appraised the gigantic possibilities of trade with the Newts at its true value as well as the lucrative and comprehensive advertisements with which it was combined, the introduction of the salamanders in most parts of the world was welcomed with keen interest, nay, even with enthusiasm.[1]

The trade in the Newts was mostly in the hands of the Salamander Syndicate, which carried it out by means of its own specially constructed tank boats; the headquarters of the trade, and a kind of exchange for the Newts, was the Salamander Building at Singapoie.

Cf. extensive and objective description signed E.W., October 5th:

---

[1] Cf. the following intensely interesting cutting, unfortunately in an unknown tongue, and therefore untranslatable:

SAHT NA KCHRI TE SALAAM ANDER BWTAT.

Saht gwan t'lap ne Salaam Ander bwtati og t'cheni bechri ne Simbwana m'bengwe ogandi sûkh na moimoi opwana Salaam Ander sri m'oana gwne's. Og di limbw, og di bwtat na Salaam Ander kchri p'we ogandi p'we o' gwandi te ur maswali sukh? Na, ne ur lingo t'Islamli kcher oganda Salaam Andrias sahti. Bend op'tonga kchri Simbwana mêdh, salaam!

"*S-TRADE.*

'*Singapore, October 4th. Leading 63. Heavy 317. Team 648.*
Odd Jobs 26.35. Trash 0.08. Spawn 80-132.'

Reports of this kind a reader of the newspapers can find daily in the business columns among the telegrams concerning the price of cotton, tin, or wheat. But do you know already what these mysterious figures and words mean? Well, yes, the market for Salamanders, or S-Trade; but of what this trade really looks like, the majority of readers have not such a clear idea. Perhaps they imagine a large market-place swarming with thousands and thousands of Newts, where dealers in topees and turbans walk about, inspecting the goods on offer and at last pointing with their fingers to a healthy, well-developed young Salamander and saying: 'I'll have this one; how much is it?'

In reality, selling Salamanders is something quite different. In the marble edifice of the S-Trade at Singapore you won't see a single Newt, but only alert and smart officials dressed in white dealing with orders over the phone. 'Yes, sir. Leading are 63. How many? Two hundred? Yes, sir. Twenty Heavy and one hundred and eighty Team. O.K. Yes, quite. The boat sails in five weeks' time. Is that O.K.? Thank you, sir.' The whole palace of the S-Trade resounds with telephone conversations; it gives you the impression more of an office or a bank than of a market; and yet this white, noble building with its Ionic colonnade in front is more of a world market than the bazaar at Baghdad at the time of Harun-al-Rashid.

But let us return to the quotations in the market report with its commercial slang. LEADING, *that simply means Newts specially selected, intelligent, and as a rule three years old, carefully trained to be group leaders in the labour columns. They are sold singly regardless of their weight; only their intelligence is valued. Singapore Leading speaking good English are considered the best and most reliable; here and there other brands of leading Salamanders are also on offer, like the so-called Capitanos, Ingenieures, Malay Chiefs, Foremanders, and others, but Leading are priced the highest. To-day they fetch round about sixty dollars apiece.*

HEAVY *are the heavy, active, and usually two-year-old Newts whose weight runs between a hundred to a hundred and twenty pounds. They are sold only in batches (the so-called groups) of six at a time. They are trained for the heaviest physical work like breaking rocks, rolling away boulders, and such-like jobs. When the report quotes Heavy 317 it means that a batch of six (group) is costing three hundred and seventeen dollars. As a rule to each group of Heavy one Leading is appointed as foreman and overseer.*

TEAM *means ordinary working Newts weighing from 80 to 100 pounds, which are sold only in working parties (teams) of twenty at a time; they are intended for collective work, and they find their best use in dredging, making waterways or dams, and similar jobs. With every twenty of a team goes one Leading.*

ODD JOBS *form a separate class. They are Newts who for various reasons have not been provided with collective and specialized training, as for instance because they have not grown up in big, properly run Salamander farms. They are, in fact, half wild, but often they are very talented. They are sold singly or in dozens, and they are used for various special jobs or smaller undertakings for which it is not worth while to use a whole Salamander group or team. If we take the*

178

Leading to be the élite among the Salamanders, Odd Jobs represent something like the lower proletariat. Lately they have become popular as rough Salamander material which individual contractors develop further and classify into Leading, Heavy, Team, or Trash.

TRASH, or rubbish (prul, refuse), are inferior, weak, or physically defective Newts which are not sold singly nor in fixed numbers, but collectively by weight, usually in dozens of tons; at present a kilogram live weight costs seven to ten cents. As a matter of fact it's not known what they are good for, and for what purpose they are bought—perhaps for some light kinds of jobs in the water; in case of misunderstanding, we must remind you that Salamanders are not fit for human consumption. This Trash is almost all bought up in job lots by Chinese commission agents; where they are shipped to has not been ascertained.

SPAWN is simply Newt fry; to put it more precisely, tadpoles up to one year old. They are sold and bought by the hundred, and they enjoy a good market, especially because they are cheap and their transport works out cheapest; only at their destination do they get their finishing training until they are fit for work. Spawn is conveyed in barrels, for the tadpoles do not leave the water like full-grown Salamanders have to do every day. It often happens that from the Spawn individuals come out exceptionally gifted, even surpassing the standard type Leading; because of this the trade in fry is particularly interesting. Highly talented Newts are sold then for several hundred dollars apiece; the American millionaire Denicker even paid two thousand dollars for a Newt that could talk fluently in nine languages, and he had it transported by special boat as far as Miami; the transport itself cost the best part of twenty thousand dollars. Recently Newt fry has become popular with the so-called Newt stables, where fast racing Newts are being picked out and trained; these then are harnessed three at a time to flat boats shaped like shells. Races in shells drawn by Newts are now quite the fashion, and they are the most popular amusement of young American women on Palm Beach, in Honolulu, or in Cuba; they are called Triton-Races, or Venus' regattas. In a light attractive shell gliding over the sea the racing girls stand in scantiest and most beautiful bathing suits and hold in their hands the silk reins of the triga team; they simply race for the title of the Venus. Mr. J. S. Tincker, said to be the King of Conserves, has bought for his daughter a triga of racing Newts—Poseidon, Hengist, and King William—for not less than thirty-six thousand dollars. But all this is quite beyond the scope of the S-Trade proper, which limits itself to supplying the whole world with reliable working Leadings, Heavies, and Teams.

•   •   •   •   •

We have already mentioned the Newts farms. The reader must not picture to himself stables and enclosures; it is a few miles of bare coast on which there are scattered huts of corrugated iron. One hut is for the veterinary surgeon, another for the manager, and others for the supervisory personnel. Only at low tide can one see long jetties running from the shore into the sea, dividing the water into several separate basins. One is for the fry, another for Leading, and so on; each kind is fed and trained separately. Both of these take place at night. As dusk falls the Salamanders emerge from their basins on to the shore and gather round their instructors; as a rule these are retired soldiers. At the beginning comes the talking lesson;

the teacher first says the word to the Newts, for instance 'dig,' and explains by demonstrating what it means. Then he arranges them in columns of four and teaches them how to march; not more than half an hour of gymnastics follows, and then they rest in the water. After a pause they are instructed in how to handle various instruments and weapons; then for about three hours practical work in marine building is done under the supervision of the instructors. After that the Newts return to the water, and they are fed with Newt biscuits, which chiefly consist of maize flour and suet; Leading and Heavy Salamanders get an additional allowance of meat. Laziness and disobedience are punished by withholding of food; there are no other corporal punishments; besides, the sensitiveness of the Salamanders to pain is poor. With sunrise a dead silence spreads over the Newt farms; the men go to sleep, and the Newts disappear below the sea.

This course of things changes only twice during the year; once at breeding-time, when the Salamanders are left for a fortnight to themselves, and the second time when the tank boat of the Salamander Syndicate arrives at the farm bringing orders to the director as to how many of this or that class of Newt should be sent away. Recruiting takes place at night; the captain, the manager of the farm, and the veterinary surgeon sit at a table with a lamp, while the foreman with the boat crew shut off the Salamanders' retreat to the sea. Then one Newt after the other steps up to the table and is passed if it is fit. The conscripted Newts then embark on boats which take them to the tank boat. They do it mostly of their own free will, that is, at nothing more than a sharp command; only at times slight force is necessary like trussing them up. Spawn, or fry, of course is fished out with nets.

Equally humane and hygienic is the transport of the Newts in the tank boats; every second day fresh water is pumped into their tanks, and they are most adequately fed. Their death-rate during transport hardly amounts to 10 per cent. In accordance with the wishes of the Society for the Prevention of Cruelty to Animals there is a chaplain on board each tank boat, and he sees to it that the Salamanders receive humane treatment; and night after night he gives them a sermon in which he impresses chiefly on their minds respect for mankind and grateful obedience and love to their future employers, who wish for nothing but to care paternally for their well-being. This paternal care is certainly rather difficult to explain to the Newts, for the notion of paternity is unknown to them. Among the more educated Salamanders a practice has grown up of calling the chaplain 'Papa Newt.' Educational films have also proved a great success, in which, while on the voyage, the Newts are shown some of the wonders of human engineering and something of their future work and duties.

There are people who take the abbreviation S-Trade (Salamander Trade) to stand for Slave-Trade. Well then, as unbiased observers we can say that if the old slave trade had been as well organized, and with regard to hygiene as irreproachably carried through, as the present trade with the Newts, we could only have congratulated the slaves. Especially the more expensive Salamanders are really treated very decently and with understanding, if only because the wages of the captain and the crew of the boat depend on the well-being of the Newts entrusted to their charge. The writer of this article observed with his own eyes how even the toughest deck hands on the tank boat SS.14 were deeply affected when two hundred and forty prime Newts in one tank fell ill with serious diarrhoea. They used to look at them with eyes almost full of tears, and they gave vent to their human feelings in their gruff manner: 'It's the devil that has given us these Newts.' "

With the expanding turnover in the export of Newts an outside market, of course, also sprang up; the Salamander Syndicate could not guard and control all the incubators which the late Captain van Toch had put down, especially over the tiny and remote islands of Micronesia, Melanesia, and Polynesia, so that many Newt bays had to be left to themselves. Consequently, besides the rational breeding of Salamanders, hunting for wild ones had also reached considerable dimensions, in many respects reminding one of former expeditions for seals; the hunting was to some extent illegal, but because there were no laws for the protection of the Newts, it was at most prosecuted as unauthorized trespass within the limits of this or that State territory; however, as if left to themselves the Newts on those islands multiplied at an amazing rate, and here and there they caused a certain amount of damage in the fields and orchards belonging to the natives, the unregulated catching of Newts was tacitly regarded as a natural check on the growth of the Newt population.

We quote from an authentic contemporary record:

"BUCCANEERS OF THE XXth CENTURY
E.E.K.

It was eleven o'clock in the evening when the captain of our boat gave the order to haul down the national flag and let down the boats. The night was moonlight and silvery with mist; the little island to which we were rowing was, I think, Gardner Island in the Phoenix Archipelago. On moonlight nights like this the Newts crawl out on the shore and dance; you can get quite close to them, and they don't notice you, so intent are they on their collective, silent ritual. There were twenty of us who got out on the shore with the oars in our hands, and, spread out in single file, we began to form a semicircle round the dark throng crowding on the beach in the pale moonlight.

It is difficult to describe the impression that the dance of the Newts produces. About three hundred animals sit on their hind legs in an absolutely perfect circle facing inwards; the inside of the circle is empty. The Newts do not move, they remain as if rooted to the spot; they seem like a circular palisade round some mysterious altar; but there is no altar, or any god. Suddenly one of the animals with a smacking sound utters: 'Ts, ts, ts,' and begins to writhe, swaying with the upper part of the body; this swaying motion is caught up by more and more, and in a few seconds all the Newts are swaying backwards and forwards the upper part of their bodies without moving from the spot; faster and faster, but without a sound, ever more frantically, in a mad and intoxicated whirl. After about a quarter of an hour one of the Newts slackens off, and then another and another sways with exhaustion and becomes rigid; again they all sit motionless like statues; after a while somewhere else a silent 'Ts, ts, ts' is heard, another Newt begins to writhe and twist, and at once his dance is taken up by the whole circle. I know that from this description it strikes one as very mechanical; but add to it the pallid moonlight and the regular, long murmur of the tide, and it has in it something deeply potent and in some way enchanting. I halted, stupefied with an involuntary feeling of terror or amazement. 'Get a move on, man,' snapped the next man to me, 'or you'll make a gap!"

Our circle drew in round that of the dancing animals. The men held their oars across, and they whispered under their breath more because of the night than that the Newts would hear them. 'Now for the centre, run for it,' shouted our leader. We ran towards that whirling circle, with dull thuds the oars struck the backs of the Newts. Only then did the Newts become alarmed; they withdrew towards the centre, or they tried to slip between the oars away to the sea, but a blow with an oar drove them back, shrieking with pain and terror. By means of the oars we worked them to the middle, crowded, heaped, and crawling over each other in several layers; ten men held them inside the barrier of oars, and ten more were prodding and slashing with the oars those that tried to crawl under or pass through. It formed a mass of black, squirming, confused, and croaking flesh on which dull thuds kept falling. Then a gap opened between two oars; one Newt slipped away and was stunned with a blow on its neck; after it another and another, till about twenty were lying there. 'Stop it,' shouted our leader, and the gap between the oars closed up again. Bully Beach and the half-bred Dingo snatched up in each hand a leg of one of the senseless Newts and dragged them over the sand to the boats like lifeless logs. Sometimes the stupefied body stuck fast between the rocks; then the sailor would give a sharp and savage jerk, and the leg would come off. 'That's nothing,' murmured old Mike, who stood beside me. 'Why, man, he'll grow another one.' After they had thrown the captured Newts into the boats the leader

185

gave a sharp order: 'And now some more!' And again the blows fell on the necks of the Newts. That officer, a man called Bellomy, was intelligent and reserved, an excellent chess player; but this was hunting, or rather business, so why make a fuss? In this way over two hundred senseless Newts were captured; about seventy were left behind, which were most likely dead and were not worth dragging away.

On the boat the Newts were thrown into tanks. Our boat had been an old oil tanker; the badly cleaned-out tanks reeked of petrol, and the water in them was covered with a rainbow of grease; but the cover had been taken off so that the air could get in; after they had thrown the Newts in it looked thick and repulsive, like macaroni soup: here and there was a slight and painful movement, but for the first day the Newts were left alone to come round. The next day four men brought long poles and poked about in that 'soup' (in the trade it really is called soup); they stirred up that mass of bodies and searched for those that showed no sign of life, or whose flesh was falling off; these they caught on long hooks and dragged from the tank. 'Is the soup clear?' inquired the captain.

'Yes, sir.'

'Put some more water in it!'

'Yes.'

This cleaning of the soup had to be carried out daily; every time six to ten bodies were thrown away into the sea— 'damaged goods' they are called; a cavalcade of well-grown and well-fed sharks persistently followed our boat. The smell of the tanks was ghastly; in spite of the occasional changing of the water, it was yellow and blotched with excrement and sodden biscuit; in it the black gasping bodies splashed languidly or lay quite still. 'They've got it very nice here,' old Mike asserted. 'I've seen a boat which shipped them in tin petrol barrels; there they all pegged out.'

Within six days we were catching new goods on Nanomea Island.

·　　　·　　　·　　　·　　　·

Well, then, this is what the Newt Trade looks like; the illegal trade, it's true, or rather the modern piracy that has sprung up almost overnight. It is claimed that nearly a quarter of all the Newts bought and sold are bagged in this way. There are Newt incubators which for the Salamander Syndicate are not worth keeping as permanent farms; there on the smaller Pacific islands the Newts have multiplied so much that they have almost become a nuisance; the natives don't like them, and complain that with their holes and tunnels they undermine whole islands, and so both the Colonial departments and the Salamander Syndicate itself shut their eyes to these raids on Newt breeding places. You can count up to four hundred pirate boats that are engaged entirely in this plunder of the Newts. Besides small-scale organizations, this modern buccaneering is carried on by whole shipping companies, of which the biggest is the Pacific Newt Importing Co., with its headquarters at Dublin; its president is the very worthy Mr. Charles B. Harriman. A year ago conditions were somewhat worse than they are now; at that time a Chinese bandit, Teng, with three boats made a direct descent upon the Syndicate's farms, and didn't even hesitate to kill off members of the staff that offered resistance; last November this Teng with his small fleet was shot to pieces at Midway Island by the American boat 'Minnetonka.' Since then Newt piracy has adopted less violent forms, and it flourishes steadily after certain conditions have

187

been agreed upon, under which it is silently tolerated: it is understood, for instance, that in making a foray on a foreign coast the home flag shall be hauled down from the mast; that under the pretext of piracy the import and export of other goods shall not be carried on; that the pirated Newts shall not be sold at knock-down prices, and shall be marked for sale as second quality. These illegal Newts fetch from twenty to twenty-two dollars apiece; they are regarded as inferior, but very tough, since they have survived that dreadful treatment on the pirate boats. It is estimated that on an average from 25 to 30 per cent of the captured Newts survive the voyage; but these can then stand a lot. In market jargon they are called Macaroni, and recently they have even been given a regular quotation in the market news.

•　　　•　　　•　　　•　　　•

Two months later I played chess with Mr. Bellomy in the lounge of the Hotel France at Saigon; by that time I was no longer a paid seaman.

'Look here, Bellomy,' I said to him, 'you are a decent kind of man, a gentleman as one says. Doesn't it go sometimes against the grain to earn your living from what in actual fact is downright slavery?'

Bellomy shrugged his shoulders. 'Newts are Newts,' he grunted evasively.

'Two hundred years ago they used to say Negroes are Negroes.'

'And wasn't it true?' said Bellomy. 'Check!'

I lost that game. It suddenly struck me that every move in chess was old and had already been played by someone. Perhaps our history has already been played too, and we shift our

*figures with the same moves to the same checks as in times
long past. It is quite likely that just such a decent and reserved
Bellomy once rounded up Negroes on the ivory coast, and
shipped them off to Haiti or to Louisiana, letting them peg out
in the steerage. He didn't think anything wrong with it then,
that Bellomy. Bellomy never things anything wrong. That's
why he's incorrigible.*

*'Black has lost,' said Bellomy with satisfaction, and got up
to stretch himself."*

Besides a well-organized market for Newts and an
extensive Press campaign, the most effective agent for
the spread of the Newts was a gigantic wave of scientific
idealism which at this time flooded the whole world.
G. H. Bondy rightly foresaw that the human mind
would start to work on whole new continents, and
create Atlantis anew. During the whole of the Salamander Age a lively and fruitful dispute reigned among
the experts as to whether heavy continents with ferro-
concrete sides, or light land thrown together with sea
sand, should be constructed. Almost daily new gigantic
projects were put forth; Italian engineers formed a
plan on one side for the construction of Greater Italy
to consist of almost the whole of the Mediterranean as
far as Tripoli, the Balearics, and Dodekanese; on the
other side for founding a new continent, the so-called
Lemuria—east from Italian Somaliland—which would
one day take up the whole of the Indian Ocean. In
fact, with the assistance of a whole army of Newts, a
new little island was thrown up opposite the Somalian
harbour of Mogdishu occupying thirteen and a half

acres. Japan planned and partly completed a new big island instead of the former Marianne archipelago, and made preparations for joining up of the Carolines and the Marshall Islands into two large islands to be called the New Nippon; on each even an artificial volcano was to have been erected which would remind future inhabitants of the sacred Fujiyama. There were also rumours that German engineers were secretly erecting in the Sargasso Sea a heavy concrete land surface, which was to be the future Atlantis, and would be able, so it was said, to threaten French West Africa; but it appears that it only got as far as laying the foundations. In Holland steps were taken to make Zeeland quite dry; France united Guadeloupe, Grande Terre, Basse Terre, and La Desiderade into one blessed island; the United States began on longitude 37° W. to erect the first aircraft island (of two storeys with a huge hotel, sports stadium, Tivoli, and with a cinema for five thousand people). It looked just as if the last barriers had been broken down which the ocean had put to human effort; a bright epoch of amazing technical feats set in; people began to realize that not till then had they become Master of the World, thanks to the Newts who stepped on to the platform of the world at the right moment and, so to speak, to meet historical needs. There is not the slightest doubt that that tremendous spread of the Newts could not have taken place if our technical age had not prepared for them so many tasks and such a gigantic field of permanent occupation. The Future of the Toilers of the Sea seemed now to be secured for centuries.

A prominent share in the rapid progress of the trade with the Newts was also taken by science, which soon turned its attention to research on the spiritual side of the Newts.

We quote a report of the scientific congress held at Paris, from the pen of one present, r. d. :

•   •   •   •   •

Iᴱᴿ CONGRÈS D'URODÈLES

The abbreviated title is the Congress of the Urodeles, while the full official title is somewhat longer: The First International Congress of Zoologists for the Psychological Investigation of the Urodeles. The real Parisian, however, does not care for titles a yard long; those learned professors who are in session in the amphitheatre of the Sorbonne are for him simply Messieurs les Urodeles, messrs urodeles, and that's all. Or still more briefly and irreverently: Ces Zoos-là.

Well then, we went to have a look at Ces Zoos-là more out of curiosity than from a journalist's sense of duty. Out of curiosity, you understand, which had nothing to do with those university, mostly elderly, and bespectacled celebrities, but just with those . . . creatures (why does the word "animals" stick on our pens?), about which so much has already been written from scientific journals to the songs in the streets, and who are—according to some—newspaper humbug, according to others— creatures in many respects more talented than the master of the animal world and the crown of creation, as he still calls himself to-day. (I mean after the War, and allowing for other historical circumstances.) I hoped that the illustrious and honoured members of the Congress for the Psychological Investigation of the Urodeles would give us, as laymen, a clear and final picture of what that notorious adaptability of *Andrias Scheuchzeri* is like; that they would tell me: Yes, this is a creature of reason, or at least as capable of civilization as you or I; therefore you must look to a future for him, as we must look to the future of the human races once considered wild, and primitive . . . I tell you, no such answer, not even such a question was uttered at the congress; for science to-day is too . . . specialized to occupy itself with that kind of problem.

Well then, let us be informed of what scientifically is called the psychic life of these animals. That long gentleman with the flowing beard of a necromancer who is just mounting the platform is the famous Professor Dubebosque; it seems that he is attacking some perverse theory of some esteemed colleague, but this part of his exposition we cannot follow very well. Only after a longish while we take it that this passionate necromancer is talking about the sensibility of Andrias to colour, and of his ability to distinguish between various shades. I am not certain that I have understood it properly, but I have come away with the impression that *Andrias Scheuchzeri* is perhaps partially colour-blind, but Professor Dubebosque must be terribly short-sighted from the way in which he lifted his papers right up to his

wildly flashing spectacles. Then the smiling
Japanese scientist Dr. Okagawa spoke; it was
something about the reaction curve, as well as
the phenomena which arise when a certain sensory
duct in Andrias' brain is severed; then he described
what Andrias does when his organ corresponding
to the ear labyrinth is crushed. After this, Professor
Rehmann explained in detail how Andrias reacts
to electric stimulation. Then a passionate controversy broke out between him and Professor
Gebrocken. C'est un type, this Professor Gebrocken;
small, choleric, and almost tragically alert; besides
other things, he asserted that Andrias as regards
his sense organs is as poorly equipped as man,
and that he is marked by a similar lack of instincts;
in a purely biological sense, he is just the same
kind of decadent animal as man, and in the same
way, he tries to make up for his biological inferiority
by what is called intellect. It seems, however, that
other experts did not take Professor Gebrocken
seriously, perhaps because he has not been severing
any sensory ducts, or sending electric discharges
into Andrias' brain. After that, Professor von
Diäten slowly and almost in a liturgical manner
related what disturbances appear when Andrias
has had his right frontal cerebral lobe or the
occipital ridge on the left side of his brain taken
away. Then the American Professor Devrient
described——

Excuse me, I really don't know what he described; for at that moment I began to rack my
brains to think what disturbances might perhaps
appear in Professor Devrient if I had removed his

right cerebral lobe; how the smiling Dr. Okagawa would react if I irritated him with electricity, and how Professor Rehmann would behave if somebody crushed the labyrinth in his ear. I also felt somewhat uncertain about how well I really can differentiate between colours, or resolve the factor t in my motor reactions. The doubt tormented me whether we have (in a strictly scientific sense) the right to talk about our (I mean human) psychic life before we have mangled up each other's cerebral lobes and severed the sensory ducts. In fact, we ought to go for one another with scalpel in hand in order to investigate our psychic life. For my part, I should be ready in the interests of science to smash the glasses of Professor Dubebosque, or send electric shocks into the bald pate of Professor Diäten, after which I should publish an article on the manner in which they reacted. To speak the truth, I can picture it vividly. Less vividly can I imagine what went on in the soul of Andrias Scheuchzeri during such experiments; but I believe that he is an immensely patient and good-natured creature. For none of the celebrities who spoke said that poor Andrias Scheuchzeri had ever grown violent.

I have no doubt that the First Congress of the Urodeles is an excellent scientific success; but when I have a day off, I shall go to the Jardin des Plantes and straight to the tank of Andrias Scheuchzeri and say to him in a low voice: "You, Salamander, when your day comes . . . not that it will occur to you to investigate the psychic life of Men!"

Thanks to this scientific achievement, men ceased to look on the Newts as some sort of a miracle; in the sober light of science the Salamanders lost much of their primeval nimbus of being extraordinary and exceptional; having become objects of psychological tests, they showed very average and uninteresting qualities; their high talents were scientifically relegated to the realm of myths. Science discovered a Normal Salamander, who appeared as a dull and rather mediocre creature; only the newspapers from time to time still discovered a Miraculous Newt who could multiply numbers of five figures in his head, but even this ceased to amuse the people, especially after it appeared that with proper training even a mere man could accomplish that. People simply regarded the Newts as something commonplace, like counting machines or other gadgets; no longer did they see in them something mysterious that had emerged from unknown depths, God knows why, and for what. Besides, people never regard what serves them and what is good for them as in any way mysterious, but only what does them harm or threatens them; and because the Newts as it appeared were creatures highly useful in many diverse ways, they were simply accepted as something that belongs as a matter of course to the national and current order of things.

The utility of the Newts was specially investigated by the Hamburg scientist, Woodellmann, from whose reports on this subject we give, at least in briefest epitome, his:

BERICHT ÜBER DIE SOMATISCHE
VERANLAGUNG DER MOLCHE

The experiments which I undertook with the Pacific Giant Salamander (*Andrias Scheuchzeri Tschudi*) in my Hamburg laboratory were carried out for quite a special purpose: to examine the resistance of the Newts to changes in their environment and other external factors, and by such means to discover their practical suitability for various geographical regions and under diversely modified conditions.

The first series of the experiments was devised to establish how long a Newt can remain alive out of water. The experimental animals were kept in dry tanks at a temperature of 40–50° C. After a few hours they showed signs of obvious lassitude; when sprinkled with water they revived again. After twenty-four hours they lay motionless, only moving their eyelids; the heart-beat slowed down, all bodily activity was reduced to a minimum. The animals were clearly distressed, and the slightest movement cost them a great effort. After three days a state of cataleptic rigidity (*zerosa*) set in; the animals did not react even when they were burned with an electric cauterizer. If the humidity of the atmosphere is increased, they begin to show at least some signs of life (they close their eyes to a bright light, etc.). When one of these desiccated Newts was thrown into water it revived in due course; with more permanent desiccation, however, the majority of the animals perished. In direct sunlight they die after a few hours.

Other animals under test were made to turn a wheel in darkness while under very dry conditions. After three hours their efficiency began to decrease, but it recovered again after a copious sprinkling with water. With frequent sprinkling the animals managed to turn the wheel for seventeen, twenty, and in one case twenty-six hours without a break, while the man we took as standard after working for five hours at the same output was considerably exhausted. From these experiments we may conclude that the Newts are well qualified for work on dry land—of course under two conditions: that they are not exposed to direct sunshine, and that they are occasionally sprinkled with water all over their bodies.

The second series of the experiments dealt with the resistance of the Newts, animals originating in the tropics, to cold. Through sudden cooling of the water they expired from intestinal catarrh; but by being slowly accustomed to a colder medium they readily became acclimatized, and after eight months they remained active at a water temperature of 7° C., provided that they were supplied with more fat in their diet (150–200 grammes per head per diem). If the temperature of the water was reduced below 5° C., they developed a cold rigidity (*gelosa*); in that state they could be frozen and preserved in a block of ice for several months; when the ice melted, and the temperature of the water rose above 5° C., they again began to show signs of life, and at seven to ten degrees they began to seek food eagerly. From this one may conclude that the Newts might easily become acclimatized for our latitudes as far as the north of Norway, and Iceland. For the conditions in the polar regions further experiments would be necessary.

On the other hand, the Newts show a considerable sensitivity to different chemicals; in tests with very diluted lye, with factory effluents, and with tanning extracts, etc., their skins peeled off in strips, and the animals under test succumbed to some kind of gangrene of the gills. As a consequence it would be almost impossible to employ the Newts in our rivers.

In a further series of experiments we were successful in ascertaining how long the Newts can remain alive without food. They can go without food for three weeks or even longer without showing any signs beyond a certain lassitude. I allowed one Newt to starve for six months; the last three months he passed without movement, sleeping intermittently; at the end of that period, when I threw chopped liver into his tank, he was so weak that he did not react to it, and it had to be given to him by hand. After a few days he ate normally again, and could be used in further experiments.

The last series of the experiments was concerned with the powers of regeneration possessed by the Newts. If a Newt has his tail cut off, a new one will develop in a fortnight; we repeated this experiment seven times with one Newt, in each case obtaining the same result. In a similar manner legs regenerate which have been amputated. We cut off from one experimental animal all four extremities as well as the tail; in thirty days he was complete again. If a Newt femur or scapular bone is broken, the whole limb falls off and a new one grows in its place. It is the same with a damaged eye or a tongue that has been removed; it is a matter of some interest that in the case of a Newt whose tongue I had removed he forgot how to talk, and had to learn again. If one removes the head of a Newt or divides the body between the neck and the pelvis, the animal dies. On the other hand one can take away the stomach, part of the intestines, two-thirds of the liver, and other organs without injury to life; so that we may state that a Newt that has been eviscerated is still capable of a further existence. No other animal has such resistance to every sort of injury as the Newt. In this respect it might make an excellent, almost indomitable animal for purposes of war; unfortunately, against this stands his peacefulness and natural defencelessness.

•   •   •   •   •

Besides these experiments, my assistant, Dr. Walter Pinkel, carried out an investigation to discover the value of the Newts as sources of raw materials. He discovered that the bodies of Newts contain a particularly high percentage of iodine and phosphorus; there is a possibility that in case of need these important elements might be exploited industrially. The skin of the Newts, although bad in itself, can be ground, and when highly compressed forms an artificial leather which is light and fairly strong, and might serve at a substitute for cow-hide. Newt's fat is unfit for human consumption because of its revolting taste, but could be used as an industrial lubricant because it sets solid only at a very low temperature. The flesh of the Newts has also been taken to be unfit for human consumption and even poisonous; if eaten raw, it causes acute pains, vomiting, and mental hallucinations. Dr. Pinkel ascertained after many experiments performed on himself that these harmful effects disappear if the chopped meat is scalded with hot water (as with some toadstools), and after washing thoroughly it is pickled for twenty-four hours in a weak solution of permanganate of potash. Then it can be cooked or stewed, and tastes like inferior beef. In this way we ate a Newt called Hans; he was an able and intelligent animal with a special bent for scientific work; he was employed in Dr. Pinkel's department as his assistant, and even refined chemical analysis could be entrusted to him. We used to have long conversations with him in the evenings, amusing ourselves with his insatiable thirst for knowledge. With deep regret we had to put Hans to death, because my experiments on trepanning him made him blind. His meat was dark and spongy, but did not cause any unpleasant effects. It is clear that in case of war Newt flesh could form a welcome and cheap substitute for beef.

After all it is only natural that the Newts ceased to be a marvel as soon as there were hundreds of millions of them in the world; the popular interest which they had provoked while they were some sort of a novelty only lingered on for some time in film caricatures (Sally and Andy, two good Salamanders) and on cabaret platforms, where singers and comedians endowed with specially bad voices appeared in the irresistible role of a croaking Newt poorly expressing itself in bad grammar. As soon as the Newts became a collective and commonplace phenomenon, what we may term their problems altered.[1] The truth is that

---

[1] Characteristic testimony is provided by the questionnaire of the paper *Daily Star* on the theme: HAVE NEWTS GOT A SOUL? We quote from this questionnaire (of course, without any guarantee of authenticity) a few statements from prominent personalities:

DEAR SIR,
    My friend, Rev. H. B. Bertram, and I watched the Salamanders for a lengthy time while they were constructing the dam at Aden; we also spoke with them two or three times, but we did not discover in them any sense of higher values like Honour, Faith, Patriotism, or Fair Play. And what else with any justification can be called soul?
Yours truly,
COLONEL JOHN W. BRITTON

I never have seen a Newt; but I am convinced that creatures who have no music have no soul.
TOSCANINI

Let us put on one side the question of a soul; but as far as I can discover with Andrias, I should say that they have no individuality; they seem to be all one like the other, equally industrious, equally able—and equally without character. In a word: they fulfil a certain ideal of modern civilization, that is the Average.
ANDRÉ D'ARTOIS

[*Continued at foot of page* 201

soon the great Newt sensation passed off to make way
for something else, and to some extent something more

Continued from page 200]

They certainly haven't got a soul. In this they agree
with man.

Yours,

G. B. SHAW

Your question embarrasses me. I know, for instance,
that my Chinese pet dog Bibi has a delightful little soul;
my Persian cat Sidi Hanum also has a soul, and what
a splendid, and cruel one! But Newts? Yes, they are *very*
gifted and intelligent, these poor little creatures; they
can talk, count, and be *terribly* useful; but they are *so*
ugly.

Yours,

MADELAINE ROCHE

May they be Salamanders, if only no Marxists.

KURT HUBER

They have no soul. If they had, we should have to
place them on economic equality with man, and that
would be absurd.

HENRY BOND

They have no sex-appeal. And therefore they have
no soul.

MAE WEST

They have a soul like every other creature, and every
plant has one, as does everything that lives. Great is the
mystery of life.

SANDRABHÂRATA NATH

They have an interesting technique and style in swimming; we can learn a lot from them, especially for swimming
long distances.

TONY WEISSMÜLLER

substantial, that is *the Newt problem.* The pioneer in the Newt problem—and not for the first time in the annals of progress—was of course a woman. It was Mme Louise Zimmermann, the headmistress of a girls' finishing school at Lausanne, who with unusual energy and unflagging enthusiasm propagated all over the world the noble motto: *Let the Newts have a proper education!* For a long time she met with nothing but misunderstanding from the public, as without ceasing she stressed on one side the natural adaptability of the Newts, and on the other the danger which might arise to human civilization if the Salamanders were not given a careful moral and intellectual training. "Just as Roman civilization collapsed through invasions by the Barbarians, our civlization will also disappear if it remains an island in a sea of creatures spiritually suppressed which are not allowed to share the highest ideals of the present human race." These were the prophetic words she uttered at 6,357 lectures which she delivered in women's clubs all over Europe and America, as well as in Japan, China, Turkey, and elsewhere. "If civilization is to continue, it must be civilization for everybody. We can't enjoy in peace the fruits of our civilization or of our culture as long as we are surrounded by millions and millions of unhappy and lowly creatures kept down by force in the animal state. Just as the clarion call of the nineteenth century was Freedom for Women, the motto of our age must be: LET THE NEWTS HAVE A PROPER EDUCATION!" And so on. Thanks to her eloquence and incredible persistence, Mme Louise

Zimmermann mobilized the women of the whole world, and raised sufficient financial funds to found at Beaulieu (near Nice) the First Lycée for Newts, in which the fry of the Salamanders working at Marseilles and Toulon were taught the French language, literature, rhetoric, social deportment, mathematics, and history of art.[1] The Girls' School for Newts at Mentone

[1] For further information see the book: *Mme Louise Zimmermann, sa vie, ses idées, son œuvre* (Alcan). From this work we quote a memoir of a devoted Newt who was one of her first pupils:

"She recited the fables of La Fontaine, sitting beside our plain but clean and comfortable tank; she suffered from the damp, but she did not mind that, because she was so devoted to her teaching work. She called us *mes petits Chinois*, because like the Chinese we could not pronounce the consonant 'r.' After a time, however, she got so used to us that she herself pronounced her own name Zimmelmann. We tadpoles adored her; the small ones who had not yet developed lungs, and therefore could not leave the water, cried because they could not go with her on her walks in the school garden. She was so mild and kind that— as far as I know—she was only angry once; that was when our young history teacher one hot summer's day took a swimming suit and came down among us into the tank, in which she lectured to us on the wars of independence in the Netherlands, sitting up to her neck in water. Then our dear Mme Zimmermann became very angry: 'Go and take a bath at once, Mademoiselle, go, go,' she cried, with tears in her eyes. For us it was a delicate but clear lesson that after all there is a difference between us and men; later on we were grateful to our spiritual mother for having inculcated this conception in such a decisive and tactful manner.

When we did our work well she used to read to us by way of a treat some modern poems like François Coppée's. 'Perhaps it is *too* modern,' she used to say, 'but after all even that now is part of a good education.' At the end of the school year a public Speech Day was arranged, to which Mr. Prefect from Nice used to be invited, and other official and prominent personalities.

was not quite such a striking success. There courses, chiefly in music, cookery, and fine needlework (on which Mme Zimmermann insisted chiefly for pedagogical reasons), met with a striking lack of response, if not with an obstinate lack of interest on the part of the youthful Newt lycéennes. But on the contrary the first public examination for Young Newts was such an astonishing success that immediately afterwards (at the expense of the Society for Prevention of Cruelty to Animals) a Naval Polytechnic for Newts was founded at Cannes, and a Newt University at Marseilles; here some time later the first Newt was awarded the degree of Doctor of Law.

The problem of Newt education now began to develop rapidly and followed a normal course. Against the model Écoles Zimmermann more progressive teachers raised a number of serious objections; in

Advanced and gifted pupils who already had got lungs were dried by the school porter and dressed in some kind of white gown; then they gave their recitations behind a thin curtain (so as not to frighten the ladies) of La Fontaine's fables, mathematical formulae, and the succession of the Capets with their dates. After that Mr. Prefect in a long and beautiful speech expressed his thanks and complimented our dear headmistress, and so ended the joyful day. Just like our spiritual progress, our physical well-being was cared for; once a month the local veterinary surgeon examined us, and once each half year every one of us was weighed to see if we came up to standard. Our esteemed headmistress made a special point with us of trying to get rid of that odious and vulgar custom of our Monthly Dances; I am ashamed to say that in spite of it some of the bigger pupils at full moon used to commit this bestial infamy in secrecy. I hope that our amiable friend never heard of it; it would have broken her big, noble, and loving heart."

particular, it was asserted that for the upbringing of adolescent Newts the obsolete humanistic system for young children was not at all suitable; the teaching of literature and history was definitely repudiated, and it was recommended instead that as much attention and time as possible should be given to practical and modern subjects like natural science, the technical training of the Newts, physical exercises, and so on. This, the so-called Reform School or the School for Practical Life, was in its turn passionately attacked by the defenders of the classical education, who proclaimed that the Newts could only be brought in touch with the human cultural commonwealth through a foundation of Latin, and that it was not enough to teach them to talk if they were not taught to quote the poets and declaim with the eloquence of Cicero. Out of this a long and rather bitter controversy arose, which was finally solved by the schools for Salamanders being made State schools and the schools for human youth being reformed so as to approach as near as possible to the ideals of the Reform School for the Newts.

It was only natural that in other parts of the world a campaign developed for regular and obligatory schools for Newts under State control. This occurred in turn in all the maritime countries (of course with the exception of Great Britain); and because these Newt schools were not saddled with the old classical traditions, and therefore could avail themselves of all the latest methods of psychotechnics, technological education, junior cadet training, and of other recent pedagogical achievements, they soon developed into the most modern and, scientifically, most advanced educational system in the world, which rightly became the envy of all human teachers and schoolboys.

Hand in hand with the Newt schools the language problem emerged. Which of the world languages ought the Salamanders to learn first? The original Newts from the Pacific islands expressed themselves, of course, in pidgin English as they picked it up from the natives and sailors; many spoke Malayan or other local dialects. The Newts bred for the Singapore market spoke Basic English, that scientifically simplified English which manages with a couple of hundred phrases and no obsolete grammatical fuss; and so people began to call this reformed standard English, Salamander-English. At the model Écoles Zimmermann the Newts expressed themselves in Corneille's tongue, not of course on racial grounds, but because it is part of a higher education; on the contrary, in the Reform schools Esperanto was taught as the medium of communication. Besides, about that time five or six Universal Languages came into existence, designed to replace the Babylonian confusion of human tongues and provide one common speech for the whole world of men and Newts; of course there were many disputes as to which of these Universal Languages was the most useful, consistent, and universal. In the end, of course, it so happened that in every nation a different Universal Language was propagated.[1]

[1] Besides other things, the famous philologist, Curtius, in his work *Janua Linguarum Aperta*, proposed that as the only universal tongue for the Newts the Latin of the golden age of Vergil should

With the nationalization of the Newt schools the whole question became simplified; in every country the Newts were simply taught the language of that special race. Although the Salamanders picked up foreign languages quite readily and with eagerness their linguistic ability showed strange shortcomings, partly because of the state of their vocal organs, and partly because of psychological reasons; so, for instance, it was with difficulty that they could pronounce long, polysyllabic words, and they attempted to reduce them to a single syllable which they uttered sharply and with something of a croak; they used to say "l" instead

be adopted. "To-day," he said, "it is in our power to make that Latin, the most perfect language, the richest in grammatical rules, and scientifically most consistent, a living universal tongue. If civilized man does not take advantage of this opportunity, do it yourselves, Salamandrae, gens maritima; choose as your mother tongue, eruditam linguam latinum, the only language worthy for the orbis terrarum to speak. Eternal will be your virtue, Salamandrae, if you resuscitate to new life the everlasting language of gods and heroes; for with that, gens Tritonum, you will also succeed one day to the inheritance of the empire of Rome."

On the other hand, a certain Livonian telegraph official called Wolteras, together with a pastor Mendelius, hit upon and worked out a special *language for the Newts*, called Pontic Lang; in it he made use of elements from all the languages of the world, especially the African dialects. This Newtish (as it also was called) achieved some currency, especially in the northern states, but unfortunately only among human beings; in Uppsala there was even a chair founded for the Newtish language, but of the Newts, as far as is known, not a single one spoke this tongue. As a matter of fact, Basic English was the most customary language among the Salamanders, and later on it became the official medium of communication among the Newts.

of "r," and in sibilants they lisped slightly; they were oblivious of grammatical endings, never learned to differentiate between "I" and "we," and it was all the same to them whether a word was masculine or feminine. (Perhaps this was symptomatic of their sexual frigidity at the time of mating.) In their mouths every language underwent a characteristic change, and somehow became rationalized into its simplest and most rudimentary form. It is a point worth considera- tion that their neologisms, their pronunciation and grammatical simplicity were picked up rapidly, partly by the human wreckage at the ports, partly by the so-called better society, and from there these modes of expression spread to the daily Press and soon became general. Even among human beings grammatical genders mainly faded out, the endings disappeared, declension died out, and gilded youth suppressed the "r" and learned to lisp; hardly any educated person could still say what was the meaning of in- determinism or transcendentalism, simply because these words too became too long for man and inex- pressible.

In short, whether well or badly, the Newts could speak almost all the tongues of the world, depending on the shore they occupied. Then an article was published in Prague (in *The Patriot*, I think) which (certainly not without reason) bitterly complained that the Newts did not also learn Czech, when there were already in the world Salamanders speaking Portuguese, Dutch, and other languages of the smaller nations. Our nation, it is true, unfortunately does not possess its own seashore, the said article admitted, and therefore we have no sea Newts either; but even if we have not got a sea of our own, it does not follow that we do not possess a culture equal—yes, in many respects even superior—to that of many nations whose languages thousands of Newts are made to learn. It would be only equitable if the Newts also learned something of our spiritual life; but how can they acquire it if not a single one among them is a master of our language? We must not wait for somebody in the world to recognize this cultural debt and establish a chair of Czech and Czechoslovak literature at some institution of learning. As the poet says, "The world has nothing to bestow; from our own selves our joys must flow." Therefore let us make amends ourselves, demanded the article. Whatever we have accomplished in this world we have done with our own strength! It is our right and duty to strive to make friends even among the Newts; but, so it seems, our Ministry for Foreign Affairs is not active enough in making due propaganda for our name and of our products among the Newts, although other and smaller nations set aside millions for opening up to the Newts their cultural treasures and at the same time for stimulating interest in their industrial products. The article excited considerable attention, especially among the chambers of commerce, and at least it resulted in a small handbook being published entitled *Czech for Newts*, with special examples from the Czechoslovak belles-lettres. It may seem incredible, but over seven hundred copies of this booklet were actually sold;

consequently, on the whole it was a remarkable success.[1]

[1] Cf. feuilleton from the pen of Jaromir Seidl-Novoměstsky preserved in the collection of Mr. Povondra:

| OUR FRIEND ON THE GALAPAGOS ISLANDS |

Making with my wife the poetess, Henrietta Seidl-Chrudimska, a tour round the world, in order to find relief, at least in part, through the charm of so many new and strong impressions, for the sad loss of our gracious aunt, the writer Bohumila Jandova-Střešovická, we came as far as the lonely Galapagos Islands, so wrapped in legend. We had only two hours to spare, and so to make use of them we took a walk along the shores of that desert archipelago.

"See how very beautiful is the sunset to-day," I said to my wife. "Doesn't it look as if the whole sky were swimming in a flood of blood and gold?"

"Why, the gentleman is Czech!" suddenly came from behind us in correct and pure Czech.

In astonishment we looked in that direction. There was nobody there but a big, black Newt, sitting on the rocks, holding in his hand something that appeared to be a book. During our journey round the world we had already seen several Newts, but we had not had an opportunity of entering into conversation with them. Therefore, the kind reader will appreciate our amazement when, on a shore so deserted, we came across a Newt, and besides that, chanced to hear a remark in our native tongue.

"Who spoke?" I cried in Czech.

"I made so bold, sir," answered the Newt,

[Continued at foot of page 211

The question of education and language was of course only one side of the large Newt problem, which in a way sprang up under men's hands. So, for instance,

Continued from page 210]

rising respectfully. "I could not resist on hearing for the first time in my life a conversation in Czech."

"I beg your pardon," I gasped, "you can speak Czech?"

"I have just been amusing myself with the conjugation of the irregular verb 'to be,' " replied the Newt. "This particular verb is irregular in all languages."

"How, where, and why," I implored him, "have you learned Czech?"

"By chance this book came into my hands," answered the Newt, offering me the booklet which he was holding in his hand; it was *Czech for Newts*, and its pages bore marks of frequent and industrious perusal. "It came here with a shipment of books of a serious nature. I could have chosen *Geometry for Senior Classes in Secondary Schools*, *History of War Tactics*, *Guide through the Dolomites*, or *Principles of Bimetallism*. I chose this booklet, however, which has become my dearest companion. I know it already by heart, but I always find in it new sources of enjoyment and instruction."

My wife and I expressed our unfeigned pleasure and admiration at his correct, nay, even almost intelligible pronunciation. "Alas, there is nobody here with whom I can converse in Czech," said our new friend modestly, "and I am not quite sure if the seventh case of the word horse, kůň, is koni or konmi."

[*Continued at foot of page* 212

the question soon emerged as to how in fact the Newts ought to be treated in, shall we say, social respects. In the early, almost prehistoric years of the Newt Age

Continued from page 211]

"Konmi," I said.

"Oh, no, koni," exclaimed my wife with animation.

"Could you be kind enough to tell me," enquired our dear companion eagerly, "what there is new in mother Prague with her hundred towers?"

"She's growing bigger, my friend," I answered, pleased by his interest, and in a few words I outlined to him the flowering of our golden metropolis.

"What pleasant news you bring me," said the Newt with unconcealed satisfaction. "Do they still hang on the Bridge Tower the heads of Czech noblemen who have been beheaded?"

"Not now for a long time," I said to him, rather (I confess) astonished by his question.

"Forsooth, that's a pity," reflected the engaging Newt. "It was a fine historical memorial. May lamentations rise to God that so many excellent monuments perished in the Thirty Years War! If I am not mistaken, the Czech land was then turned into a desert, soaked with blood and tears. What good fortune it was then that the negative genitive did not disappear. In this booklet it states that it is on the point of extinction. I felt very distressed about it, sir."

"Then you have been captivated by our history," I exclaimed joyfully.

"Certainly, sir," responded the Newt. "Especially by the battle of the White Mountain and the

[Continued at foot of page 213

there were of course Societies for the Prevention of Cruelty to Animals which zealously saw to it that the Newts were not treated cruelly and inhumanely;

Continued from page 212]

Three Hundred Years suppression. I have read very much about them in this book. You certainly must be very proud of your Three Hundred Years suppression. It was a great time, sir."

"Yes, a tragic time," I affirmed. "A period of suppression and grief."

"And did you groan?" inquired our friend with eager interest.

"We did, suffering unspeakably under the yoke of brutal oppressors."

"I am glad," sighed the Newt with relief. "In my booklet it is just like this. I am very pleased that it is true. It is an excellent book, sir, better than the *Geometry for Senior Classes in Secondary Schools*. I should like to stand myself on the sacred spot where the Czech noblemen were executed, as well as on the other famous places of cruel injustice."

"You ought to come to see us," I suggested heartily.

"Thank you for your kind invitation," the Newt bowed. "Unluckily, I am not entirely a free agent . . ."

"We would buy you," I exclaimed. "I mean to say that perhaps by a national collection, we might provide the means which would permit you . . ."

"My most sincere thanks," mumbled our friend, with obvious emotion. "I heard, however, that the Vltava water is not very good. For we develop an unpleasant kind of dysentery in river water."

[*Continued at foot of page* 214

thanks to their persistent efforts it came about that
almost everywhere officials insisted that the Newts
should be treated in accordance with the police and

Continued from page 213]

Then he grew thoughtful for a short time and added:
"I should be loth to forsake my dear little garden."

"Ah," my wife exclaimed, "I am an enthusiastic
gardener, too! How grateful I should be if you
showed to us the children of the local Flora!"

"With the greatest of pleasure, gracious lady,"
said the Newt, bowing politely. "That is, if you
don't mind that my pleasure-grounds are under
the water."

"Under the water?"

"Yes, twelve yards."

"And what flowers do you grow there?"

"Sea anemones," said our friend, "in several
rare varieties. Also sea stars, and sea cucumbers,
not counting clusters of coral. Happy he who has
cultivated one rose, one scion, for his Fatherland,
as the poet says."

Sad to relate, we had to say good-bye, for the boat
was already giving warning of departure. "And
what message should we take, Mr.—Mr.——" I
said, not knowing the name of our dear friend.

"My name is Boleslav Jablonský," confessed the
Newt timidly. "In my opinion it is a beautiful
name, sir. I have chosen it from my booklet."

"What message would you like to send to our
nation, Mr. Jablonský?"

The Newt meditated for a while. "Tell your
compatriots," he said, at last, deeply touched,
"tell them . . . not to fall back into the old
Slav discord . . . and to keep Lipany, and

[*Continued at foot of page* 215

veterinary regulations which were valid for other farm animals. Also the conscientious objectors to vivisection signed many protests and petitions, demanding that the performance of scientific experiments on the living Newts should be prohibited; in a number of States such a law was, in fact, put into force.[1] But with the developing culture of the Salamanders more and more embarrassment was felt in bringing the Newts simply under the regulations protecting animals; it seemed, for some not very clear reasons, to be rather improper. Then the LEAGUE FOR PROTECTING THE SALAMANDERS (Salamander Protection Society) was founded under the patronage of the Duchess of Huddersfield. This League counting over two hundred thousand members, mainly in England, achieved for the Salamanders a considerable and praiseworthy amount of good; in particular, it got a scheme through so that on the seashores special Salamander playgrounds were organized where, undisturbed by curious spectators, they

Continued from page 214]

especially the White Mountain in grateful memory. Nazdar, my compliments," he ended suddenly, trying to master his feelings.

As we departed in the boat, filled with moving thoughts, our friend stood on a rock and waved his hand to us; it seemed as if he was shouting something.

"What is he shouting?" asked my wife.

"I don't know," I said, "but it sounded something like, 'Remember me to Dr. Baxa, the Lord Mayor.'"

[1] In Germany, in particular, all vivisection was strongly forbidden, of course only as regards Jewish investigators.

could hold their "meetings and sporting festivals"; (this meant very likely the secret moon dances); it saw to it that in all the schools (even at the University of Oxford) the pupils were admonished not to throw stones at the Newts; it saw to it that to some extent at the Salamander schools the young tadpoles were not overworked; and finally, that the Newt working camps and localities were surrounded with a high board fence which protected the Newts from being molested in various ways, and chiefly kept the world of the Salamanders separate from the human one.[1]

[1] It seems that certain moral questions were also involved. Among the papers of Mr. Povondra there was found in many languages a PROCLAMATION, published apparently in all the newspapers of the world, and signed by the Duchess of Huddersfield herself, which read:

"The Salamander Protection Society turns to you, women, especially in the interests of decency and good manners, to assist with the work of your hands the great movement whose aim is to provide the Newts with proper clothes. The most suitable for this purpose is a little skirt 16 in. long, and 24 in. wide at the waist, best made with a sewn-in elastic band. A pleated skirt is recommended (plissé), for it is becoming and allows of greater freedom of movement. For tropical regions a small apron is sufficient if provided with a tape to be tied at the waist, and made of quite simple material, or even from parts of your old clothes. In this way you will benefit the poor Newts, who at work in the vicinity of people need not show themselves without any clothes on; which surely offends their sense of shame, and gives an unpleasant impression to every decent man, and more especially to every woman and mother."

[Footnote continued on page 217

But these praiseworthy innovations of private individuals who tried to regularize the relations between the Newts and human society along humane and respectable lines soon proved insufficient. It was comparatively easy to find a place for the Salamanders, as it was said, in the work of production, but it appeared

Footnote continued from page 216]

From all appearances, this movement did not meet with the desired result; it is not known whether the Newts ever consented to wear skirts or aprons; very likely under water they were a hindrance, or they would not stay on. And when the Newts had been separated from people by board fences on both sides, all cause for shame and unpleasant feelings was of course removed.

As to the reference that the Newts had to be protected against molestation of various kinds, what we had chiefly in our minds was that dogs never made friends with the Newts, and they pestered them madly even under the water, not minding that the mucous membranes of their mouths became inflamed after they had bitten a Newt. Sometimes even the Newts defended themselves, and not a few dogs were killed by hoes and pickaxes. In general, between dogs and Newts a lasting and almost deadly enmity sprang up, which was by no means reduced but on the contrary was made almost stronger and deeper by the erection of fences between the two. But that's how it is, and not only with dogs.

As a matter of fact, those tarred fences stretching in many parts for hundreds and hundreds of miles along the coast were used for educational purposes; along their whole length they were covered with big notices and slogans for the Newts, as for instance:

YOUR WORK—YOUR SUCCESS.—VALUE EVERY SECOND. A DAY IS ONLY 86,400 SECONDS!—YOUR VALUE IS THE WORK YOU DO.—YOU CAN BUILD A DAM A YARD HIGH IN 57 MINUTES!—LABOUR TO SERVE ALL.—NO WORK, NO FOOD!

And so on. When we realize that those boarded enclosures ran along more than three hundred thousand miles of sea coast in the world we can form some conception of the number of inspiring and valuable slogans which found a place there.

to be something far more complex and difficult to fit them in somehow with social arrangements. The more conservative people no doubt declared that there were no legal and public problems in question; the Newts were simply the property of their employers, who assumed responsibility for them, and also answered for such occasional damage as the Newts might cause; in spite of their undoubted intelligence, the Salamanders were nothing but a legal object, chattel, or estate, and any special regulations with regard to the Newts would be, they said, an interference with the sacred rights of private property. On the other hand, their opponents raised the objection that the Newts as intelligent beings, and possessing a large measure of personal responsibility, could intentionally, and in most diverse ways, contravene existing laws. How could the owner of the Newts be held responsible for individual offences that his Salamanders might commit? Such a liability would undoubtedly undermine private enterprise in the employment of Newts. There are no fences in the sea, it was said. You can't shut the Newts up and keep them under your eye. Therefore we must take legal steps to make the Newts feel responsible for respecting human laws and behave in accordance with the regulations which will be issued for them.[1]

---

[1] Cf. the first Newt case, which was tried at Durban, and which was copiously commented on in the world Press (see cuttings of Mr. Povondra). The port authority at A employed a working column of Newts. In course of time these increased so much that they had not space enough in the harbour; and a few tadpole colonies settled along the neighbouring coast. The owner B, to whose estate part of the said coast belonged, claimed that

As far as it is known the first laws for Salamanders came into force in France. The first paragraph defined the Newts' duties in case of mobilization and of war; the second law (called lex Deval) laid it down that the Newts were only allowed to settle in those places along the coast which their proprietor, or proper authority, would assign to them; the third law declared that the Newts were obliged to submit unconditionally to all police regulations; should they not do so, police officials were empowered to punish them by locking them up in a dry and light place, or even by depriving

the port authority should remove its Salamanders from his private property because he had his bathing place there. The port authority pleaded that it could not be held responsible; as soon as the Newts occupied the grounds of the plaintiff they became his private property. While this case followed its usual and lengthy course the Newts began (partly out of natural instinct, and partly out of zest for work which had been inculcated through education), without due authority and permission, to construct a dam and harbour on the shores belonging to B. Thereupon B sued the said authority for damages to his property. In the lower court B's claim was rejected on the grounds that the property of B was not damaged by the dams, but actually improved. On appeal the Court ruled that the plaintiff was in the right, and that no one was obliged to suffer his neighbour's cattle to trespass on his land, and that the port authority at A was liable for all the damage caused by the Newts in the same way that a farmer must pay compensation for damage to neighbours caused by his cattle. The defendants, of course, protested that they could not be held responsible for the Newts, because they could not lock them up in the sea. Thereupon the Judge ruled that in his opinion damages arising from Newts should be regarded in the same light as those caused by hens, which also cannot be shut up because they can fly. The advocate representing the port authority inquired by which means his clients should turn the Newts out, or persuade them to leave the private shore

them of work. Then the parties of the Left brought forward a motion in the Chamber that a social code should be worked out for the Salamanders which would define their duties and impose upon the employers certain obligations towards the Newts they employed (for example, a fortnight's holiday in spring for mating) ; as against this, the extreme Left demanded that the Newts should be turned out bag and baggage as enemies of the working classes who in the service of capitalism were working too hard, and almost for

of B of themselves. The Judge answered that that was no business of the Court. The advocate then inquired in what light the venerable Judge would regard it if the port authority had the desirable Newts killed off. To that the Judge replied that as a British gentleman he would regard it as extremely improper, and in addition an infringement of the shooting rights of B. As a result the defendants were obliged on one hand to turn the Newts out from the private property of the plaintiff, and on the other to indemnify him for damage arising from the dams and the regulation of the coast, and in such a way as to restore that stretch of coast to its original state. The advocate for the defendants then raised the question whether one could use Salamanders for that demolition. The Judge answered that in his opinion one could not, unless the plaintiff himself agreed whose wife was nauseated by the Newts, and could not swim in water infested by the Salamanders. The defendants raised the objection that without the Newts they could not remove dams built under the sea. The Judge then declared that the Court had no wish and was not in a position to decide technical details; Courts of Law existed to protect rights of property, and not for saying what was possible and what was not.

In this manner the dispute was brought to an end; it is not known how the port authority at A got out of this troublesome predicament; but the whole case made it clear that, after all, there was a need to regulate the Newt problem by new legal means.

nothing, and who by this were threatened with an attack on their standard of living. In support of this a strike broke out at Brest and huge demonstrations took place in Paris; many people were injured, and the Deval Ministry was compelled to resign. In Italy the Salamanders were brought under a special Newt Corporation consisting of employers and officials; in Holland they were managed by the Ministry of Waterworks; in short, every State met the Newt problem in its own and separate way; but the sum total of official regulations by which the public duties of the Newts were defined, and the animal liberty of the Newts was suitably restricted, was everywhere much the same.

It is only natural that as soon as the first laws were passed people arose who in the name of the legal justice claimed that if human society imposed certain duties upon the Salamanders it must also assign them some rights as well. The State which made laws for the Newts recognized them *ipso facto* as responsible and free beings, as legal subjects, nay, even as its State subjects; in that case it would be necessary to determine somehow their civic position with regard to the State under whose jurisdiction they were living. It would, of course, be necessary to regard the Newts as foreign immigrants; but if that were so, the State could not impose upon them certain services and duties, in case of mobilization and of war, as now happens (except for England) in all civilized countries. We certainly shall require the Newts in case of war to defend our coasts; but in that case we cannot deny them their civic rights—for instance, the right to vote, the right of assembly, representation on various public bodies, and so on.[1] It was even suggested that the Salamanders

[1] Some interpreted equality of legal rights of the Newts so literally that they demanded that the Salamanders should be able to hold any kind of public office in the water and on land (J. Courtaud); or that fully armed marine regiments should be formed of them, with their own commanders (General Desfours, retired list); or even that mixed marriages should be allowed between human beings and Newts (advocate Louis Pierrot). The biologists, it is true, objected that such marriages were not possible; but maître Pierrot declared that it was not a matter of biological possibility but of legal principle, and that he himself was willing to take a female Newt for his wife to demonstrate that the reform of matrimonial law referred to above was not going to remain only on paper. (M. Pierrot afterwards became a very popular advocate in the divorce court.)

(While on this point it might be mentioned that, especially in America, from time to time accounts appeared in the papers of girls who had been violated by Newts while bathing. As a result cases became more frequent in the United States in which Newts were hunted down and lynched, chiefly burnt at the stake. In vain the scientists protested against these actions by the mob, pointing out that because of their anatomical structure a crime like that on the part of the Salamanders was physically impossible; many of the girls swore on oath that they had been molested by the Newts, and therefore for every decent American the matter was perfectly clear. Later on public burning of the Newts was restricted, at least in so much that it was only allowed on Saturdays and under the supervision of the fire brigade. At that time also the movement against lynching the Newts originated, at the head of which stood the Negro, Rev. Robert J. Washington, which was supported by hundreds of thousands of members, almost all of whom of course without exception were Negroes. The American Press began to assert that this movement was political and subversive; and as a consequence attacks on Negro-quarters broke out, and many Negroes were burnt for praying in the churches for their brother Newts. Indignation against the Negroes reached its climax when from the burning of a Negro

should have some sort of submarine autonomy; but these and other conceptions remained purely academic; they were brought to no practical conclusion chiefly because the Newts never at any time or place asked for civic rights.

Similarly, without the direct interest and intervention of the Newts another big discussion was going on which centred on the question whether the Newts could be baptized. The Catholic Church from the outset adopted the standpoint that it was not possible because the Newts, not being Adam's descendants, were not begot in original sin, nor by the sacrament of baptism could they be cleansed. The Holy Church did not want by any means to decide the question whether the Newts had immortal souls, or some other share in the grace and salvation of God; her goodwill towards the Newts could only be expressed by remembering them in a special prayer which was to be read on certain days in addition to the prayer for souls in purgatory, and the intercessory prayer for unbelievers.[1] With the

church in Gordonville (L.) the whole town caught fire. But this only has indirect reference to the history of the Newts.)

From the civil regulations and rights which were really conferred on the Newts let us quote at least some: each Salamander was entered in the Newt Register and registered in his place of work; he had to possess an official permit for residence; he had to pay a poll tax, which his owner found for him and deducted from his food (for the Newts were not paid wages in money); similarly, he had to pay rent for the coast he occupied, municipal rates, charges for the erection of the boarded enclosures, school fees, and other public burdens; we have simply to admit with truth that in these respects they were treated like other subjects, so that they did enjoy some sort of equality after all.

[1] See the encyclical of the Holy Father *Mirabilia Dei opera*.

Protestant Churches it was not so simple; they acknowledged, it is true, that the Newts were endowed with
reason, and consequently with the capacity to grasp
the Christian doctrine, but they hesitated to make them
members of the Church, and in that way brothers in
Christ. Therefore they confined themselves to publishing (in a simplified version) the Holy Scriptures
for the Newts on waterproof paper, and they circulated
many millions of copies; they also discussed whether
they should compose for the Newts (analogous to
Basic English) a kind of Basic Christian, the fundamental and simplified Christian teaching; but the
attempts made in that direction provoked so many
theological controversies that finally it had to be
dropped.[1] Some religious sects had not so many
scruples (especially American ones), who sent their
missionaries to the Newts to preach to them the True
Faith and to baptize them according to the words of
the Scriptures: "Go ye into all the world and teach
all nations." But only very few missionaries succeeded
in getting behind the boarded enclosures which
separated the Salamanders from human beings; the
employers did what they could to prevent them gaining
access to the Newts so that they would not keep them
unnecessarily from their work. One could see therefore,
here and there, a preacher standing near the creosoted
fence among the dogs barking savagely at their enemies
on the other side, and zealously but vainly interpreting
God's Word.

[1] On this question such a huge literature appeared that even
its bibliography would fill two fat volumes.

As far as it is known Monism gained a somewhat larger following; some Newts also believed in materialism, the gold standard, and other scientific dogmas. One popular philosopher with the name of Georg Sequenz even composed a special religious system for the Newts of which the chief and highest article was faith in the Great Salamander. This doctrine, it is true, did not take root among the Newts in any way, but on the contrary it found many adherents among the people, especially in large towns, where almost overnight a crowd of secret temples for Salamander worship came into existence.[1] The Newts themselves, as time

---

[1] See in the papers of Mr. Povondra a very pornographic pamphlet, which they say was printed from the police reports at B——. The contents of this, "circulated privately for scientific purposes," cannot be quoted in a decent book. We give only a few details:

The temple of the Salamander cult situated in house number —— of —— street contains in its centre a large tank lined with dark red marble. The water in the tank is perfumed with fragrant essences, warmed, and from underneath illuminated with changing coloured lights; otherwise the temple is dark. To a chant of the New Litany the believing Salamanders enter the rainbow tank down marble steps, without clothing, men on one side, women on the other, mostly from the best society; we may specially mention Baroness M, the film star S, Ambassador D, and many other prominent personalities. Suddenly a blue reflector illuminates a huge marble boulder rising out of the water on which reposes a heavily gasping, huge, old, black Newt, called Master Salamander. After a moment's silence the Master begins to speak; he exhorts the believers fully and with all their soul to give themselves up to the ritual of the Newt Dance, which is about to begin, and pay homage to the Big Salamander. After this he raises himself and begins to sway the upper part of his body. Then the male believers immersed up to their necks in the water also begin fiercely, always quicker and quicker, to rock and sway so that, as they say, the Sexual Milieu may be created; in the

went on, mostly accepted another faith of which it is not even known how it chanced to get a hold with them; it was the worship of Moloch, whom they pictured as a huge Newt with a human head; they had, it is said, tremendous submarine idols made of cast iron, which were made for them by Armstrongs or Krupps, but further details concerning their mystic ceremonies, which were said to be secret and unusually barbaric, never came to light because they were practised under water. It seems that this faith found favour with them because the name Moloch reminded them of the scientific (Molche) or German (Molch) denomination for the Newt.

•   •   •   •   •

As is clear from the previous paragraphs the Newt problem at first, and for a long time afterwards, was regarded in the light as to whether, and to what extent, the Newts as reasonable and fairly civilized beings were capable of enjoying human rights, even if only on the fringe of human society and of human

meantime the female Salamanders eject sharp "Ts, ts, ts" and croaking screams. Then one light after the other dies away below the water and a general orgy breaks loose.

It is true that we can't vouch for this description; but it is certain that in all the bigger towns of Europe the police on one side kept a sharp eye on these Salamander sects, and on the other had much to do with suppressing the terrific social scandals which were associated with them. We gather, however, that the cult of the Big Salamander was, it is true, unusually widely spread, but for the most part it has been practised with less fairylike splendour, and in the lower strata of society, even on dry land.

order; in other words, it was an internal question of individual counties, and was met within the framework of civil law. For a number of years it never even occurred to anyone that the Newt problem might have a far-reaching international significance, and that perhaps it would be necessary to deal with the Salamanders, not only as intelligent beings, but as a Newt community or Newt nation. As a matter of fact, the first step towards this conception of the Newt problem was taken by those rather eccentric Christian sects who tried to baptize the Newts, acting in accordance with the words of the Gospel: "Go ye into all the world and teach all nations." This for the first time expressed the idea that the Newts were something like a nation.[1] But the first really international and fundamental recognition of the Newts as a separate nation was not achieved until the issue of the famous manifesto of the Communist International signed by Comrade Molokov and addressed to "all suppressed and revolutionary Newts of the whole world."[2] Even

[1] The Catholic prayer for the Newts referred to above also defined them as *Dei creatura de gente Molche* (God's creatures of the Newt race).

[2] The manifesto preserved in the papers of Mr. Povondra read:

COMRADE NEWTS!

The capitalistic order has found its last victims. Now that its tyranny has begun definitely to collapse in front of the revolutionary impetus of the class-conscious proletariat, worm-eaten capitalism drags you into

if this manifesto had not, as it seems, any direct influence upon the Newts, it did in fact lead to considerable reverberations in the world Press, and was abundantly imitated at least in the form that from the most diverse sides fiery exhortations began to rain down on the

its service, toilers of the sea, it has enslaved your souls by its bourgeois civilization, bound you down with its class laws, deprived you of all liberty, and done everything it could to exploit you brutally and with impunity.

(*14 lines censored*)

Working Newts! The time is at hand when you will begin to feel conscious of the heavy burden of serfdom under which you live . . .

(*7 lines censored*)

. . . and to demand your rights as a class, and as a nation!

Comrade Newts! The revolutionary proletariat of the whole world holds out its hand to you . . .

(*11 lines censored*)

. . . by all means. Form works' councils, elect representatives, build up strike funds! Remember that the class-conscious human workers will not forsake you in the fight for justice, and hand in hand with you they will advance to the last attack.

(*9 lines censored*)

Suppressed and revolutionary Newts of the whole world, unite! The last fight let us face!

Signed: MOLOKOV.

Newts to join as a large Newt body this or that ideal, political, or social programme of human society.[1]

[1] In the collection of Mr. Povondra we found only a few of these manifestos; most likely Mrs. Povondra had burned the rest at some time or other. From what material remains we give at least some titles:

NEWTS, THROW YOUR ARMS AWAY! (A pacifist manifesto.)

𝕸𝖔𝖑𝖈𝖍𝖊𝖘, 𝖜𝖎𝖗𝖋𝖙 𝕵𝖚𝖉𝖊𝖓 𝖍𝖊𝖗𝖆𝖚𝖘! (Newts, throw out the Jews!) (A German pamphlet.)

COMRADE NEWTS! (Manifesto of the group of Bakunin-anarchists.)

BROTHERS NEWTS! (A public appeal of the sea scouts.)

FRIENDS NEWTS! (A public proclamation of the Association of Aquarian Clubs and Breeders of Water Fauna.)

NEWTS FRIENDS! (An appeal from the Society for Moral Regeneration.)

CITIZENS NEWTS! (An appeal from the Civic Reform Group at Dieppe.)

FELLOW NEWTS, ENTER OUR RANKS! (Benevolent Society of Ancient Mariners.)

COLLEAGUES NEWTS! (The Swimming Club, Aegir.)

The proclamation which we give as under may have been a particularly important one (if we may judge by the fact that Mr. Povondra pasted it in carefully):

The International Labour Office at Geneva also began now to take an interest in the Newt problem. There two different opinions were in conflict: one recognized the Newts as a new working class, and sought to ensure that all social legislation should be extended to them as regards the working day, holidays with pay, health insurance and old age pensions, and so on; the other view, on the contrary, was that the Newts constituted a dangerous and growing menace to working men, and that Newt labour should be simply prohibited on the grounds that it was anti-social. Against this argument not only did the representatives of the employers raise objections, but the delegates of the workers pointed out that the Newts were not only a new labour force, but also a big and increasingly important outlet as consumers. As they were able to show, employment had expanded in recent times to an unprecedented extent in the metal industries (tools, machines, and metal idols for the Newts), in armament works, chemicals (submarine explosives), paper manufacture (text-books for the Newts), cement, wood, artificial food (Salamander food), and in many other directions; ship tonnage had increased 27 per cent, the coal output had expanded by 18·6 per cent as against pre-Newt times. The expansion in employment and the higher standard of living had benefited indirectly other branches of industry. Finally, as a new development the Newts had begun to order various machine parts according to their own specifications; these they themselves assembled under the water to make automatic drilling machines, submarine motors, printing machines, water transmitters, and other machines of their own design. For these parts they paid with an extra output of labour; already one-fifth of the total world production of the heavy industries, and of fine machine tools, was dependent on Newt requisitions. If Salamanders were abolished, one-fifth of all the factories would have to shut down; instead of the prevailing prosperity there would be millions out of work. The International Labour Office, of course, could not ignore those objections; and as a result of lengthy negotiations a compromise was arrived at so that "employees mentioned above as belonging to Group A (amphibian) could only be employed under water, or in the water, or if on shore then only within a distance of ten yards from high-water mark; that they should not mine for coal or petroleum at the bottom of the sea; that they should not manufacture paper, textiles, or artificial leather from seaweed for consumption on land," etc.: these regulations imposed on the activities of Newts were put together in a code of nineteen paragraphs, of which we give no details, chiefly because as a matter of course nobody ever respected them; but as a solution of the Newt problem, on broad and truly international lines dealing with industrial and social questions, the code referred to above was a meritorious and imposing effort.

Somewhat slower was the international recognition of the Newts in the field of cultural relations. When the paper "The Geological composition of the Sea Bottom near the Bahama Islands," was published in the scientific Press over the name of John Seaman, nobody of course realized that it was a technical production by a learned Salamander; but when at scientific congresses, or in Transactions of various academies and scientific societies, reports and special studies appeared as the work of Newt investigations in the spheres of oceanography, geography, hydrobiology, higher mathematics, and other exact sciences, there was embarrassment, nay, even resentment, which great Dr. Martle gave voice to with the words: "The vermin want to teach us something." The Japanese scientist, Dr. Onoshita, who dared to quote the report of a Newt (it was something on the development of the yolk sac of the tadpoles of the small deep sea fish, *Argyropelecus hemigymnus Cocco*), was boycotted by his profession and committed hara-kiri; for university science it was a matter of honour and of class pride not to take any scientific notice of the work of the Newts. The greater was the perturbation (not to say scandal) aroused by the gesture made by the Centre universitaire de Nice[1] in inviting to a conference

---

[1] In the collection of Mr. Povondra we found preserved a popularly written and rather superficial description of this Congress; but unfortunately only half; the other part has been lost in some way:

> Nice. May 6th.
>
> In the nice, airy building of the Institute for Mediterranean Studies on the Promenade des Anglais, there is much activity to-day; two *agents de police* keep the path free for the invited guests who walk over the red carpet into a pleasant, agreeably cool amphitheatre. We noticed the

[Continued at foot of page 233

Dr. Charles Mercier, the very scholarly Newt from Toulon harbour, who with remarkable success lectured on the theory of conic sections in neo-Euclidian space.

Continued from page 232]

smiling Lord Mayor of Nice, the Prefect in a top-hat, a General in a sky-blue uniform, gentlemen with the red buttons of the Legion of Honour, elderly ladies (this year, terra-cotta is the prevailing fashionable colour), Rear-Admirals, Press Chiefs, Professors, and aristocratic old men of all nations, of whom there is always a generous sprinkling on the Côte d'Azur. Suddenly, there is a slight incident; along with all these notabilities, a strange, shy little creature tries to slip through unobserved; it is covered from head to foot with some sort of black cape, or domino; over its eyes it wears huge, dark glasses, and hastily and uncertainly it scurries to the overcrowded vestibule. "Hé, vous," shouts a gendarme, "qu'est-ce que vous cherchez içi?" But then the university dignitaries approach the frightened visitor, and cher docteur here, cher docteur there. This, then, is Dr. Charles Mercier, the scholarly Newt, who is to-day to lecture before the élite of the Azure coast! Now, quick inside to try to find one tiny seat in the festive and excited auditorium!

Seated on the platform are Monsieur le Maire, Monsieur Paul Mallory, the great poet; Mme Maria Dimimeau as delegate of the International Institute for Intellectual Collaboration; the Rector of the Institute for Mediterranean Studies, and other official personalities; beside the platform is the rostrum for the lecturer, and behind it—well yes, it *really* is a tin bath. An ordinary tin bath,

[*Continued at foot of page* 234

At this conference Mme Dimimeau was also present as a delegate from the organizations at Geneva; this excellent and generous lady was so touched by the

Continued from page 233]

just like we have in our bathrooms. And two assistants are leading to the platform a shy creature swathed in a long hood. Rather self-conscious applause breaks out. Dr. Charles Mercier bows shyly, and looks round uncertainly for a seat. "Voilà, Monsieur," whispers one of the assistants, and points to the tin bath. "That is for you." Dr. Mercier is obviously frightfully ashamed; he does not know how to escape this attention; he tries to take his place as inconspicuously as possible in the bath, but he becomes entangled in his long cape, and with a noisy splash he falls into it. There is quite a spatter of water on the gentlemen on the platform, who, of course, behave as if nothing has happened; somebody giggles hysterically in the audience, but the gentlemen in the front rows look back with a reproving hiss! At this moment, Monsieur le Mair et Député is already standing up to speak. "Ladies and gentlemen," he says, "I have the honour to welcome to the land of this beautiful town of Nice, Doctor Charles Mercier, the worthy representative of the scientific life of our near neighbours, the inhabitants of the deep sea." (Dr. Mercier raises half of his body from the water and bows deeply.) "It is for the first time in the history of civilization that the sea and the land hold each other's hands in intellectual collaboration. Until to-day an impassable barrier has been imposed on spiritual life; this was the ocean. We could cross it, we could plough through

[Continued at foot of page 235

modest behaviour and erudition of Dr. Mercier ("Pauvre petit," one says was the expression she used, "il est tellement laid!") that she undertook to devote

Continued from page 234]

it with our boats in every direction, but beneath its surface, ladies and gentlemen, civilization could not penetrate. The small area of dry land on which mankind is living was until recently surrounded by a virgin and barbarous sea. It was a glorious frame, but it was also an eternal barrier: on one side growing civilization, on the other everlasting and unchangeable nature. This boundary, ladies and gentlemen, now disappears. (Applause.) To us, the children of this great era, an incomparable happiness has been accorded of being ocular witnesses of the way in which our Spiritual Fatherland is growing, how it oversteps its own shores, descends below the waves, conquers the depths, and adds to the ancient cultured earth a modern and civilized ocean. What an amazing spectacle! (Applause.) Ladies and gentlemen, not until the birth of the ocean culture, whose eminent representative we have the honour to welcome in our midst to-day, did our globe become a planet really and completely civilized." (Enthusiastic applause! Dr. Mercier rises in the bath and bows.)

"Honoured doctor, and great scientist," said Monsieur le Maire et le Député, turning to Dr. Mercier, who in his emotion was leaning on the edge of the bath and twitching his gills. "You will bear with you to the bottom of the sea our congratulations, our admiration, and our most fervent sympathy for your countrymen and friends. Tell

[Continued at foot of page 236

her untiring active life to getting the Newts accepted
as members of the League of Nations. In vain did the
statesmen explain to the eloquent and energetic lady
that Salamanders, having no sovereignty of their own
in the world, or their own State territory, could not
be members of the League of Nations. Mme Dimimeau
began to give currency to the view that the Newts
should therefore be granted somewhere their own free

Continued from page 235]

them that in you, our neighbours of the sea, we
greet the vanguard of progress, and of culture, a
vanguard which will colonize the infinite regions
of the sea, step by step, and at the bottom of the
ocean create a new spiritual world. Already I can
see in the depths of the sea a new Athens spring
up, and a new Rome. I can see a new Paris flourishing there, with submarine Louvres and Sorbonnes,
with a submarine Arc de Triumphe and Tomb of
the Unknown Soldier, with theatres and boulevards; and if you will permit me to express my
most secret thought: I hope that next to our
dear Nice in the deep blue waves of the Mediterranean, a new, glorious Nice, *your* Nice will grow
up, whose own fine marine boulevards, parks,
and promenades will skirt our azure coast. We
wish to know about you, and we wish you to know
about us; I am quite confident myself that the
closer scientific and social intercourse which we
inaugurate to-day under such happy auspices
will bring our nations into ever closer cultural
and political collaboration in the interests of the
whole of mankind, in the interests of world peace,
prosperity, and progress." (Lengthy applause.)

[Continued at foot of page 237

territory and their submarine state. This idea, of course, was rather unwelcome if not actually opposed; at last, however, a happy solution was arrived at to the effect that the League of Nations should set up a special COMMISSION FOR THE STUDY OF THE NEWT PROBLEM to which two Newt delegates would also be invited; the first delegate, at the suggestion of Mme Dimimeau, was Dr. Charles Mercier of Toulon, and the second was Don Mario, a fat and erudite Newt from Cuba,

Continued from page 236]

> Now Dr. Charles Mercier rises, and attempts in a few words to express his thanks to the mayor and deputy of Nice; but partly he is too overwhelmed, and partly his enunciation is somewhat strange; of what he said I was only able to catch a few halting phrases; if I am not mistaken, they were: "very honoured," "cultural relations," and "Victor Hugo." After that, obviously suffering from stage fright, he again hid in his tub.
>
> Paul Mallory rises to speak; what he expresses is not a speech but a paean illuminated with deep philosophy. "I am grateful to Fate," he says, "for allowing me to take part in the realization and fulfilment of one of the most beautiful legends of all mankind. It is a strange realization and fulfilment; instead of a mythical submerged Atlantis, we see with amazement a new Atlantis which rises from the deep. My dear colleague, Dr. Mercier, you who are a poet of space geometry, and your erudite friends, you are the first envoys of this new world which is emerging from the sea, not a foam-sprung Aphrodite, but Pallas Anadyomene. But far stranger, and incomparably more mysterious, is that to this . . ." (The end is missing.)

who was doing scientific work on plankton and pelagic life. By this, for the time being, the Newts achieved the greatest international recognition of their existence.[1]

We see, then, the Salamanders in strong and constant ascent. Already their number is estimated to amount to seven milliards, although with a higher standard of living their birth-rate is falling steeply (down to twenty to thirty tadpoles from each female per year). They already occupy over 60 per cent of all coasts in the world; the Polar seas are not yet inhabited, but the Canadian Newts have begun to colonize the coast of

[1] Among the papers of Mr. Povondra a slightly blurred photograph from the newspapers was found in which both Newt delegates are climbing the steps from the Lake of Geneva to the Quai du Mont Blanc to take part in the sittings of the Commission. It seems, therefore, that they were officially staying in Lake Léman.

With regard to the Commission for the Study of the Newt Problem, it achieved a great and meritorious task in the main because it carefully avoided all delicate political and economic questions. It sat permanently for a long series of years, and held over thirteen meetings at which the international codification of the nomenclature of the Newts was discussed. In fact, in this respect hopeless chaos reigned; besides the scientific terms Salamandra, Molche, Batrachus, and such-like (which appellations one began to feel as being rather unpolite), a whole host of other names was suggested; the Newts were to be called Tritons, Neptunides, Tethydes, Nereids, Atlantes, Oceanics, Poseidons, Lemures, Pelagoses, Littorals, Pontics, Bathydes, Abysses, Hydriones, Gandemers (Gens de Mer), Submarines, and so on; the Commission for the Study of the Newt Problem was to choose from all these terms the most suitable name, and it took up this work zealously and conscientiously right up to the very end of the Newt Age; it did not, of course, reach any final and unanimous conclusion.

Greenland, where they even push the Eskimos back inland and take over the fishing and the oil trade into their own hands. Step by step with their material betterment their progress in civilization also continues; they are joining the ranks of cultured nations with compulsory attendance at school, and they can pride themselves on the many hundreds of their own submarine newspapers which are published by the million, and on their wonderfully built scientific institutes, and so on. It will be understood that this cultural progress did not in all points proceed smoothly and without internal resistance; we know, of course, peculiarly little of the internal affairs of the Newts, but according to some signs (for instance, that Newt corpses were found with heads and noses bitten off) it seems that for a lengthy period under the sea a protracted and passionate controversy raged between the Old Newts and the Young Newts. The Young Newts apparently stood for progress without any reservations or restrictions, and declared that below the water they ought to assimilate all land culture of every kind, not omitting even football, fascism, and sexual perversions; on the other hand, the Old Newts, so it appears, clung conservatively to natural Newtship and did not wish to renounce the good old animal habits and instincts; without doubt they looked with disfavour on the feverish yearning after novelties, and saw in it a sign of decadence and betrayal of inherited Newt ideals; they also certainly grumbled against the foreign influences to which the misguided youth of their day blindly succumbed, and they inquired if this apeing

239

of men was worthy of proud and self-respecting Newts.[1]
We can imagine that mottoes were being coined like
Back to the Miocene! Away with everything that will
make us human! Fight for pure Newtship! And so
forth. Without a doubt all conditions existed for a
lively conflict between the younger and older generations, and for deep spiritual revolutions in the progress
of the Salamanders; we regret that we are unable to
give further details, but let us hope that from the
conflict the Newts achieved as much as they could.

Now we can see the Salamanders in the process of
reaching their highest development; but the human
world too is enjoying unprecedented prosperity. New
shores are eagerly added to the continents, new land
appears on old shoals, artificial aircraft stations rise
from the middle of the ocean; but all this is nothing
compared with the gigantic engineering schemes for a
complete reconstruction of our globe which only wait
for someone to finance them. The Newts are working
without respite in all the seas, and on the shores of all
the continents while darkness lasts; it seems as if they
are fully satisfied and only need something to keep
them occupied, and somewhere to make burrows into
the shore and little passages for their dwellings. They
have their own submarine and subterranean towns,
metropolises of the deep, their Essens and Birminghams,
on the bed of the sea at a depth of twenty to fifty

[1] Mr. Povondra also included in his collection two or three
articles from *Národní Politika*, a popular Czech daily, concerning
modern youth; probably only by accident did he attribute them
to this period of Newt civilization.

yards; they have their crowded industrial quarters, harbours, traffic lines, and their vast agglomerations; in a word, they have their more or less unknown[1] but technically highly organized world. They have, it is true, no blast furnaces and smelters of their own, but humans supply them with metals in exchange for their work. They have not their own explosives, but with these humans keep them supplied. Their source of power is the sea with its high and low tides, with its currents and differences of temperature; the turbines, it is true, were supplied by humans, but they can work them; what else is civilization but the ability to make use of things that somebody else has invented? Even if the Newts, shall we say, have no genuine thoughts of their own, they can quite well have their science. No doubt they are unmusical, and they have no literature of their own, but they manage without these things perfectly; and people are beginning to learn from the Salamanders how marvellously modern that is. Look at that, humans can already learn many a thing from

[1] A gentleman from Dejvice told Mr. Povondra that he was bathing on the sands at Katwijk am Zee. He swam far out into the sea, when the bathing attendant shouted to him to come back. The gentleman (a Mr. Příhoda, a commission agent) paid no attention to him, and swam out further; then the bathing attendant jumped into a boat and rowed after him. "Hey, sir," he cried, "you mustn't swim here."

"Why not?" inquired Mr. Příhoda.

"There are Newts here."

"I am not frightened of them," objected Mr. Příhoda.

"They've got some factories or something under the water," mumbled the bathing attendant. "Nobody swims here, sir."

"And why not?"

"The Newts don't like it."

the Newts—and it's no wonder: aren't the Newts tremendously successful, and from what else are people to take example from than success? Never in the history of mankind before has so much been produced, built, and paid out as in this great era. There's no mistake, with the coming of the Newts gigantic prosperity has descended on the world, and an ideal that is called Quantity. "We people of the Newt Age," the people say with just pride, where would the obsolete Human Age have got to with its slow, finicky, and useless fuss called culture, art, pure science, or what not? Real self-respecting men of the Newt Age will no longer waste their time pondering about the substance of things; they will only be concerned with their quantity and mass production. The whole future of the world lies in the continuous increase in production and consumption; therefore there must be still more Newts to produce and to devour still more. The Newts are simply Quantity; their great achievement lies in the fact that they are so many. Never before could human industry work to full capacity, for it now works *en masse*, with its capacity taxed to the maximum and with a record turnover; in short, it is a glorious time! What then is still needed to bring about with general contentment and prosperity a Happy New Age? What stands in the way of the birth of the longed-for Utopia, in which all the technical triumphs and splendid possibilities which have been realized open up further and further possibilities of human prosperity and Newt industry, as far as the mind can foresee?

Why, indeed, nothing; for now the commercial dealings with the Newts will be also crowned with statesmanlike foresight, which will take steps to see that the machinery of the New Age will not collapse in ruins. In London a group of Maritime States is holding a conference to work out and approve of an international convention for the Salamanders. The High Contracting Parties bind themselves as between each other not to send their own Newts into the territorial waters of the others; that they will not permit their Newts, in any way whatsoever, to violate the territorial sovereignty or recognized sphere of interest of any other State; that in no way will they interfere with the Newt affairs of another Sea Power; that in the case of dispute between their own and Salamanders belonging to a Foreign Power, they will submit to arbitration by the Hague tribunal; that they will not arm their Newts with any weapons whose calibre exceeds that of the standard water pistol for use against sharks (the so-called Šafranek-gun, or shark-gun); and that they will not allow their Newts to enter into close relations of any kind with the Salamanders subject to another Power; they will not with the aid of the Newts construct new continents or enlarge their own territories without the previous approval of the Permanent Sea Commission at Geneva, and so on. (There were thirty-seven paragraphs altogether.) On the contrary, the British proposal that the Maritime Powers should undertake not to subject their Newts to compulsory military service was rejected, as well as the French suggestion that the Salamanders should be made international and placed under the jurisdiction of the International Newt Bureau for the Regulation of Ocean Waters; and the German proposal that each Newt should be branded with the mark of the State to which he belonged; also a further German proposal that every Maritime State should only be allowed a fixed number of Newts in a given ratio; and the Italian proposal that nations with a surplus of Salamanders should be assigned new shores for colonization or areas of the sea floor; and the Japanese motion that over the Newts (naturally black) the Japanese nation, as representing the coloured races, should be granted an international mandate.[1] The majority of these proposals were referred back to the next conference of Maritime Powers, which, however, for various reasons never took place.

"By this international agreement," wrote M. Jules Sauerstoff in *Le Temps*, "the future of the Newts and the peaceful development of mankind is secured for a long term of years. We congratulate the London Conference on the successful issue of their strenuous labours; we also congratulate the Newts in that by the regulations agreed upon they are placed under the protection of the Hague tribunal; now with peace and confidence they can dedicate themselves to their work and submarine progress. It should be emphasized that the removal of the Newt problem from the political arena, which was carried through by the London Conference, is one of the most important guarantees

[1] This proposal apparently was put forward in conjunction with a huge propaganda campaign of a political nature, of which

of world peace; especially the disarming of the Salamanders in particular reduces the probability of submarine strife between individual States. The fact is
that, even if numerous disputes over frontiers and

we have abundant evidence at hand, thanks to the collector's
zeal of Mr. Povondra. The document reads literally:

人造人 米国にて 寄見眼 経謹 間

つ昆ば二種の抗 今苦届や恬いが、合絲の孫争わやて目寸

氏が的求限全く然じ感うにしてやな若い口

幸更金なよせ見ら中かを聞無ろめ自分てられた右四四」

それ君金？」

ほせすお邸の地示かも「ドーミシ君所で痛知ら全福見向で

左牟にうわま「分れそいロッハで中下す「ムか」

をたよな目下そのじ今竹ロッサム弁共してわせの有遉

布一わ丸に逆ん反易強烈で、妻道れな。がせよ明か聞と」

企っ人造人ニ……」

prestige still persist in nearly all the continents, no actual danger threatens world peace, at least from the sea. But even on land peace appears to be more securely assured than ever before; the maritime States have all their energies absorbed in constructing new shores, and they can expand their territory into the ocean instead of attempting to move their frontiers on dry land. No longer will it be necessary to fight with gas and iron for every inch of ground; the simple hoes and shovels of the Newts will be sufficient for every State to construct as much territory as it desires; and this quiet Newt work for the peace and prosperity of all the nations is just what the London Conference has secured. Never before was the world so near to lasting peace, and to quiet but glorious prosperity, as it is to-day. Instead of the Newt problem, of which so much has already been spoken and written about, now and with justice shall we be able to speak of the Golden Newt Age."

3

Mr. Povondra reads
Newspapers again

IN nothing can we see so clearly the march of time as in children. Where is the small Frantik whom we left (what a short time ago!) poring over the tributaries on the left bank of the Danube?

"Where's that Frantik again?" grumbled Mr. Povondra, opening his evening paper.

"You know, as usual," said Mrs. Povondra, bent over her sewing.

"Then he went after that girl," protested father Povondra. "Dash the scamp! He's hardly thirty years old yet, and he doesn't spend a single evening at home!"

"What a lot of socks he wears through," sighed Mrs. Povondra, pulling another hopeless sock over the wooden mushroom. "What am I to make of it?" she meditated over a vast hole in the heel looking something like Ceylon. "Better throw it away," she thought, but in spite of that, after lengthy strategical consideration she stuck the needle resolutely into the southern coast of Ceylon.

A venerable family silence ensued, so dear to father Povondra; only the newspaper rustled, and to it responded the quickly drawn thread.

"Have they got him yet?" inquired Mrs. Povondra.
"Who?"

"Why, that murderer who killed that woman."

"I'm not worrying about your murderer," growled Mr. Povondra, with mild disgust. "I've just read here that a state of tension has broken out between Japan and China. That's a serious thing. It's always a serious thing there."

"I don't think they'll ever catch him," opined Mrs. Povondra.

"Who?"

"That murderer. If a man murders a woman, they hardly ever catch him."

"Japan doesn't like to see China regulating the Yellow River. That's politics, if you like. While that Yellow River keeps on being a nuisance then now and again in China there's a flood and hunger, and that weakens the Chinese, you know. Lend me those scissors, Mother, I'll cut it out."

"Why?"

"But it says here that on that Yellow River there are two million Newts working."

"That's a lot, isn't it?"

"I should think so. But I'm sure America pays for them, my lass. That's why the Mikado would like to have his own Newts there. Ah, look at that!"

"What have you got?"

"The *Petit Parisien* says that France won't put up with it. And it's true. I shouldn't put up with it either."

"What wouldn't you put up with?"

"That Italy should make the island of Lampedusa bigger. It's a terribly important strategical position, you know? From Lampedusa the Italians could threaten Tunis. The *Petit Parisien* says that the Italians in a way would like to build up on Lampedusa a full-sized naval base. They've got sixty thousand armed Newts, they say. That's a serious business. Sixty thousand—there you've got three divisions, Mother. I tell you something will happen in the Mediterranean. Let me have them; I shall cut it out."

In the meantime Ceylon was disappearing under the diligent hand of Mrs. Povondra, and it was now reduced to about the size of the island of Rhodes.

"And England as well," meditated father Povondra. "She's getting into trouble. Someone has been saying in the House of Commons that Great Britain is falling behind the other countries with their water constructions. Other Colonial Powers, they say, are up to their eyes building new shores and continents, while the British Government in its conservative distrust of the Newts . . . That's true, Mother. The English are frightfully conservative. I used to know a butler from the English Legation, and he for the Lord God Almighty wouldn't put a Czech sausage in his mouth. People don't eat them in our country, he said, and so he wouldn't eat one either, he said. No wonder that they don't beat other nations then." Mr. Povondra shook his head gravely. "And France is making her shores bigger at Calais. Now the papers are kicking up a shindy that France will be able to shoot right across the Channel when it gets narrower. That's what

249

comes of it. They could make their own shores bigger at Dover, and shoot at France."

"And why should they shoot?" inquired Mrs. Povondra.

"You don't understand. These are military affairs. I shouldn't wonder if one day it didn't lead to some trouble there. Either there or somewhere else. That stands to reason, now owing to those Newts the world is quite different, Mother. Quite different."

"Do you think there'll be a war?" said Mrs. Povondra anxiously. "You know, because our Frantik would have to go to it."

"War?" repeated father Povondra. "It would have to be a world war, and the different countries would divide the sea between them. But we shall be neutral. After all, somebody has to be neutral to supply arms and things like that to the others. That's how it is," decided Mr. Povondra. "But you women don't understand this sort of thing."

Mrs. Povondra pressed her lips together, and with rapid stitches she finished off obliterating the island of Ceylon from the sock of young Mr. Povondra.

"And when I come to think," father Povondra continued, with pride not easily suppressed, "this threatening situation wouldn't have come about but for me! If I hadn't taken that captain to Mr. Bondy, the whole world's history would be different. Another porter wouldn't even have let him in, but I said to myself, 'I'll run the risk.' And now look what troubles there are in countries like England or France! And we don't know yet what might come of it some day."

Mr. Povondra sucked at his pipe with excitement. "That's how it is, my lass. The papers are full of stuff about those Newts. Here again," father Povondra put down his pipe, "it says here that near the town of Kankasanturia in Ceylon the Newts have attacked a village; they say that before it happened the natives had killed some Newts. The police were called in, and a platoon of native soldiers . . ." Mr. Povondra read aloud. "After that it came to a regular skirmish between the Newts and the men. Among the soldiers several were wounded . . ." Father Povondra laid the papers down. "I don't like the look of it, Mother."

"Why?" wondered Mrs. Povondra, carefully and contentedly tapping with the handle of the scissors the spot where the island of Ceylon used to be. "But there's nothing in it."

"I don't know," burst out father Povondra, beginning to walk up and down the room in excitement. "But this isn't to my liking. No, I don't like the look of this. A fight between men and Newts, that ought not to be."

"Perhaps those Newts were only defending themselves," remarked Mrs. Povondra soothingly, and put away the socks.

"Just so," mumbled Mr. Povondra, upset. "As soon as those brutes begin to defend themselves it will be a bad look-out. This is the first time that they've done it. . . . My Gosh, I don't like the look of it." Mr. Povondra stopped and hesitated. "I don't know, but . . . perhaps, after all, I oughtn't to have let that captain in to Mr. Bondy!"

Third Book

War with the Newts

1

The Massacre on the
Cocos Islands

IN one point Mr. Povondra was mistaken; the skirmish at Kankasanturia was not the first brush between human beings and the Newts. The first conflict known to history took place a few years earlier on the Cocos Islands before the golden age of piratical raids on the Salamanders had come to an end; even that was not the earliest incident of its kind, and in the Pacific ports there were frequent rumours of certain regrettable cases in which the Newts had offered some sort of active resistance even to the normal S-Trade; of course, such trifles are not mentioned in history.

On those Cocos or Keeling Islands it was like this: the raiding boat *Montrose*, of the well-known Harriman Pacific Newt Importing Co. under Captain James Lindley, put in there for the customary hunt for Newts of the Macaroni class. On the Cocos Islands it was known that there was a rich colony in a bay, introduced by Captain van Toch, but because of its remoteness it had been left as one says to God. No blame attaches to Captain Lindley for carelessness, or to the crew for getting out on the shore unarmed. (For by that time the illicit trade in the Newts had developed its regular forms; it is of course true that earlier on the pirate boats and the crews used to be armed with machine-guns—yes, even with light field pieces—not so much against the Salamanders as against unfair competition from other pirates. On Karakelong Island, however, the crew of a Harriman boat had an affray with the men from a Danish boat, whose captain considered Karakelong as his own hunting-ground; both crews settled their old accounts, and especially that of their prestige and commercial differences, by giving up hunting for the Newts and beginning to shoot at one another with their Hotchkiss guns; the Danes, it is true, won by using their knives, but the Harriman boat then scored some direct hits on the Danish one and sank it with all hands, including Captain Nielse— that was the so-called Karakelong incident. Then the representatives and the Governments of the two countries had to intervene; raiding boats were hence-forth forbidden to use guns, machine-guns, and bombs; and in addition the illicit companies shared out the so-called free hunting-grounds among themselves so that each Newt locality was only visited by a certain boat; this gentleman's agreement between the big pirates was really kept and respected even by the smaller raid contractors.) But to return to Captain Lindley, he acted entirely in the spirit then current with regard to commercial and naval conventions when he sent his men to the Cocos Islands to hunt for Newts only armed with clubs and oars, and the subsequent official investigation exonerated the dead captain completely.

The crew which on that moonlight night landed on

the Cocos Islands was commanded by Lieutenant Eddie McCarth, who had already had experience in this kind of work. The crowd of Newts that he found on the shore was unusually big—according to an estimate it consisted of from six to seven hundred adult strong males—while Lieutenant McCarth only had sixteen men under him; but no one can blame him for not giving up the enterprise, if only because the officers and men of the brigand boats were paid a bounty under a scheme based on the number of animals captured. In the subsequent investigation the naval authorities ascertained that "Lieutenant McCarth was no doubt responsible for the fatal incident," but that "in the given circumstances apparently nobody would have acted differently." On the contrary, the unfortunate young officer displayed considerable prudence in that, instead of surrounding the Newts slowly —a manœuvre which in view of the great numerical disproportion could not in any case have been complete —he gave orders for a sudden attack by which the Newts should have been cut off from the sea, forced into the interior of the island, and stunned one by one with blows from the clubs and oars. Unfortunately, in response to the attack the cordon of sailors was broken through, and nearly two hundred Salamanders escaped to the sea. While the men were attacking and belabouring the Newts that they had cut off sharp reports of submarine guns (shark-guns) began to crackle behind their backs. Not one of them had any suspicion that these *natural*, wild Newts on Keeling Islands were equipped with pistols for defence against sharks, and it was never discovered who really was responsible for providing them with arms.

The seaman, Michael Kelly, who survived the whole catastrophy, relates: "When the shots began to go off we thought that some other crew was shooting at us which had also come to catch the Newts. Lieutenant McCarth turned round at once, and shouted: 'What are you up to, you idiots, it's the crew of the *Montrose* here!' At that moment he was shot in the hip, but he drew his revolver and began to fire. Then he got a second one in his neck, and fell. It was only then that we saw that it was the Newts who were shooting, and that they wanted to cut us off from the sea. Then Long Steve picked up an oar and went for the Newts, shouting 'Montrose! Montrose!' All the rest of us shouted 'Montrose!' and we whacked those beasts with our oars as hard as we could. We left about five of the crew lying there; the rest of us beat our way through to the sea. Long Steve sprang into the water and waded to the boat; but then several Newts clung to him and dragged him down under the water. And they drowned Charley too; he screamed to us 'Boys, for Christ's sake, boys, don't let them get me,' but we couldn't help him. Those swine shot us in the back; Bodkin turned round and got one in the belly; he only said 'but no,' and fell. So we tried again to get back into the interior of the island; we had already broken our oars and clubs on the brutes, and so we just ran like hares. There were only four of us left. We were scared of going further from the shore in case we should not get back to the boat; we hid behind the stones and bushes, and we couldn't help seeing how the Newts finished off our comrades. They drowned them in the water like kittens, and when any of them tried to swim they gave him a whack with a crowbar. I only realized then that my leg was put out, and that I couldn't go any further."

It seems that in the meantime Captain James Lindley, who had stayed on board the *Montrose*, heard the shooting from the island; from it he gathered that it must have come from an affray with the natives, or that there were other men after the Newts; so he simply took the cook and two engineers who were still on the ship, he had a machine-gun put on board the boat that was left—providentially but against strict orders he had hidden it there—and he came to help his crew. He was cautious enough not to disembark on the shore; he only drew near with the boat, in the bows of which was the machine-gun ready, and he stood up with "folded arms." Let us relate further what the seaman Kelly said:

"We did not want to shout to the captain, so that the Newts would not find us. Mr. Lindley stood in the boat with his arms folded, and he called to find out what was happening. Then the Newts turned on him. There were a couple of hundred of them on the shore, and new ones kept swimming in from the sea and surrounding the boat. 'What's all this?' said the captain; and then a big Newt came nearer to him, and said, 'Go back!'

The captain looked at him; for a moment he didn't say anything, and then he inquired: 'Are you a Newt?'

259

'Yes, we are Newts,' it answered. 'Go back, sir!'

'I want to know what you have done with my men,' said our old man.

'They shouldn't have attacked us,' said the Newt. '. . . Go back to your boat, sir!'

The captain was silent for a bit, then quite quietly he said: 'All right, then, Jenkins, fire!'

And the Englishman Jenkins began to fire at the Newts with the machine-gun."

(At the subsequent investigation into the whole affair the naval authorities declared literally: "In this respect Captain James Lindley behaved as is to be expected of a British officer.")

"The Newts were all in a heap," Kelly's account continued, "and they fell like corn in a field. Some shot with those pistols of theirs at Mr. Lindley, but he stood still with folded arms and didn't move an inch. Just then a black Newt emerged from the water behind the boat, holding in his paw something like a jam tin; with the other hand he tore something away from it, and then threw it into the water behind the boat. Before you could count five a column of water rose up at the spot, and you could hear a stifled explosion that even made the earth shake below our feet."

(From Kelly's description the officials carrying out the investigation concluded that the explosive was W.3, which was supplied to the Newts working on the fortifications at Singapore for breaking up the rocks below water. But how that consignment had got from the Newts there to the Cocos Islands remained a mystery; some people said that perhaps some men had taken it there, others said that the Newts must have already had some distant communications among themselves. As a result of this public opinion demanded that there should be a prohibition against putting such dangerous explosives in the Newts' hands; but the authorities declared that for the time being it is not possible to replace the highly effective and relatively safe explosive W.3 with anything else; and it stayed at that.)

"The boat flew into the air," Kelly's account continues, "and was smashed to pieces. The Newts which were still alive crowded round the place. We couldn't see very well if Mr. Lindley was still alive; but all three comrades—Donovan, Burke, and Kennedy—jumped up and ran to help him so that he wouldn't fall into the Newts' hands. I wanted to run too, but I had a dislocated ankle, and so I sat up and tugged with all my might to get those joints together again. So I don't know what happened just then, but when I looked Kennedy was lying with his face in the sand, and there was no sign of Donovan and Burke; there was only a lot of swirling from below in the water."

The sailor Kelly then moved further into the island till he found a native village; but these behaved in a strange way, and didn't even offer him shelter; they may have been afraid of the Newts. A fishing boat seven weeks later found a completely looted and abandoned *Montrose* anchored near the Cocos Islands, and rescued Kelly.

A few weeks later H.M.S. *Fireball*, a cruiser, called at the Cocos Islands, and waited at anchor through the night. Again it was a pale moonlight night; the Newts emerged from the sea, they squatted down on the sands in a large circle, and began solemnly to dance. Then His Majesty's cruiser fired the first shrapnel into their midst. The Newts that were not blown to pieces were rigid with stupefaction for a moment, and then they dashed towards the sea; at that moment a terrible salvo of six guns thundered out; and only a few battered Salamanders managed to crawl to the water. Then the second and third salvo cracked out.

After that H.M.S. *Fireball* drew away half a mile and began to let off depth charges below the water, slowly steaming along the coast. This continued for six hours, and about eight hundred rounds were fired. Then the *Fireball* sailed away. Even two days afterwards the surface of the sea near the Keeling Islands was covered with thousands and thousands of dismembered Newts.

The same night the Dutch warship *Van Dijck* fired three shots into a crowd of Newts on the little island Goenong Api; the Japanese cruiser *Hakodate* dropped three rounds on the Newt island Ailinglab; with three shots the French gunboat *Bechamel* broke up the Newt dance on the island of Rawaiwai. It was a warning to the Newts. It was not in vain: no other case (it used to be called the Keeling killing) ever happened again, and the regular and illicit trade in the Newts was able to continue and flourish undisturbed and prosperous.

2

The Clash in Normandy

OF a different character was the clash in Normandy which took place a little later. There the Newts, working chiefly at Cherbourg and inhabiting the surrounding coast, took an immense liking for apples; but because their employers did not wish to let them have apples in addition to the usual Newt food (they said that it would put up the cost of construction above the estimate) the Newts made raiding forays to the orchards in the vicinity. The farmers complained of it to the police, and the Newts were strictly forbidden to roam about on shore beyond the so-called Newt zone, but this was of no avail; fruit still kept disappearing from the orchards—it was said even the eggs in the coops too—and each morning more and more watchdogs were found killed. Then the farmers began to guard their orchards themselves equipped with old guns, and killed off the Newt intruders. So far this would have remained merely. a local affair; but the farmers of Picardy, embittered among other things by the fact that their taxes had been raised and that ammunition had become dearer, took a deadly hatred to the Newts and organized raids against them with whole armed gangs. When they had killed off scores of Newts, even at the working places, the contractors for the undertakings below water also complained to the police, and the prefect ordered that the rusty old blunderbusses of the farmers should be confiscated. The farmers of course opposed this, and unpleasant disputes broke out with the police; besides the Newts the obstinate farmers began to shoot off the police as well. Police reinforcements were sent into Normandy, and a house-to-house search was carried out from one village to another.

Just at that time an extremely unpleasant incident occurred: in the neighbourhood of Coutance some village lads attacked a Newt, which they said was crawling to a hen-roost in a suspicious manner; they surrounded him until he stood with his back against the barn, and they began to pelt him with stones. The wounded Salamander swung his arm and threw on the ground something like a small egg; an explosion followed which blew the Newt to bits, but it also killed three boys: eleven-years-old Pierre Cajus, sixteen-years-old Marcel Bérard, and fifteen-years-old Louis Kermadec; besides that five other children were more or less seriously injured. The news of it flew all over the ˉcountry; something like seven hundred people flocked there by bus from far and wide, and attacked the Newt settlement in the bay Basse Coutance with guns, pitchforks, and flails. Some twenty Newts were killed before the police managed to force back the infuriated mob. The sappers called from Cherbourg surrounded the bay Basse Coutance with a barbed-wire fence; but at night the Salamanders came up from the sea, with hand grenades they tore up the wire obstructions, and seemed to be making preparations for getting further inland. The army authorities brought up in haste a few companies of infantry with machine-guns, and a line of soldiers tried to keep the Newts away from the people. In the meantime the farmers were storming the revenue offices and police stations, and one unpopular tax collector was hanged on a lamp-post with a label: Down with the Newts! The newspapers, especially the German ones, published accounts of a revolution in Normandy; but the Government in Paris intervened with an emphatic disclaimer.

In the meantime bloody clashes between the farmers and the Newts broke out further along the coast of Calvados, Picardy, and Pas de Calais; an old French cruiser, *Jules Flambeau*, left Cherbourg for the west coast of Normandy: as was stated afterwards, it was only that the presence of the cruiser would soothe the apprehensions of the local inhabitants as well as of the Newts. The *Jules Flambeau* dropped anchor a mile and a half away from the Bay of Basse Coutance; when night fell the commander of the boat, to heighten the effect, gave orders for coloured rockets to be sent up. Many people on the shore watched that beautiful spectacle; suddenly they heard a hissing boom, and at the bows of the cruiser a huge pillar of water rose up; the boat tilted, and at that moment there was a deafening explosion. It was quite clear that the cruiser was sinking; within a quarter of an hour motor boats were hurrying to help from nearby harbours, but they were not needed; except for three men killed by the explosion the whole crew managed to save itself,

them be called before a tribunal and charged with high treason; there must be an investigation to find out how much armament firms have got for providing the scum of the sea with arms against the civilized navy!" And so on: a general sense of consternation followed, riots broke out among the populace in the streets, and barricades began to be erected; in the boulevards of Paris the sharpshooters from Senegal stood with their rifles piled, and in the suburbs tanks and armoured cars were in waiting. At that moment the Minister of the Marine, M. François Ponceau, pale but determined, rose in the Senate and announced: The Government accept full responsibility for having armed the Newts on the French coast with guns, water machine-guns, submarine batteries, and torpedoes. But while the French Newts have only light guns of small calibre, the German Salamanders are armed with submarine mortars with a 32-bore; while on an average along the French coast there is only one submarine depot of hand grenades, torpedoes, and explosives to every twenty-four kilometres, on the Italian shores the deep-water depots of war material occur every twenty, and in German waters every eighteen kilometres. France cannot and she will not leave her coasts unprotected. France cannot forgo the practice of arming her Newts. The Ministry has already carried out a most rigorous investigation to discover who was responsible for the fatal misunderstanding on the Normandy coast; it seems that the Newts took the coloured rockets for a signal of military intervention, and meant to defend themselves. In the meantime both the commander of the boat *Jules Flambeau* and the chief of the police at Cherbourg have been removed from their posts; a special commission is investigating the manner in which the contractors of water undertakings treat their Newts; in future strict control will be exercised in this direction. The Government deeply regret the loss of human life; the young national heroes Pierre Cajus, Marcel Bérard, and Louis Kermadec will be decorated and interred at the expense of the State, and their parents will be granted a gratuitous pension. In the higher command of the French Navy significant changes will take place. The Government will make the matter a question of confidence as soon as it will be able to give further details. At that the Cabinet announced an all-night session.

In the meantime the newspapers—according to their political inclinations—proposed penal, exterminating, colonizing, or punitive expeditions against the Newts, a general strike, the resignation of the Government, the arrest of the Newts' employers, the arrest of the communist leaders, agitators, and many other precautions for safety. In view of the rumours of a possible closing of the coasts and harbours the people began feverishly to lay in stocks of food, and prices began to rise at a giddy tempo; in the industrial towns riots broke out over the high cost of living; and the exchanges were closed for three days. It was simply the most tense and threatening situation in the last three or four months. At that moment, however, the Minister of Agriculture, M. Monti, hit on a very clever solution. He arranged, in effect, that along the French coast twice a week so many hundred wagons of apples should be thrown into the sea for the Newts, of course at the expense of the State. This arrangement was particularly satisfactory to the Newts, and it pacified the fruit-growers in Normandy and elsewhere. But M. Monti even went still further: because for a long time there had been difficulties with the grave and critical unrest in the wine-growing districts owing to poor markets, he arranged that the State should subsidize the Newts in such a way that every Salamander should have a daily ration of half a litre of white wine. The Newts at first were at a loss to know what to do with the wine, because after it they suffered from strong diarrhoea, and they poured it into the sea; but in the course of time apparently they got used to it, and from that time it was noticed that the French Newts copulated more eagerly although with less fertility than before. Thus at one stroke the agrarian problem and the Newt affair were solved; the threatening situation was relieved, and when shortly afterwards a new Government crisis broke out because of the financial scandal of Mme Töppler, the able and well-tried M. Monti became the new Minister of the Marine.

3

The Incident in
the Channel

SOME time later the Belgian transport *Oudenbourgh* sailed from Ostend to Ramsgate. When she was in the middle of the Straits of Dover the officer on duty noticed that half a mile south from their usual course "something was happening in the water"; and because he could not see if someone wasn't drowning he gave orders for the boat to sail to the spot where the water was so very much disturbed. Up to two hundred passengers watched the strange spectacle from the leeward side of the ship: here and there the water was splashing up in perpendicular columns, here and there something rose up like a black object; and all the time the surface of the sea within a space of about three hundred yards was being churned up and wildly tossed about; and down below an agitated turmoil and disorder was visible. It looked just as if a small volcano was in eruption below the water. When the *Oudenburgh* slowly drew near to the spot a gigantic wave suddenly rose up ten yards in front of her bows and there was the roar of a terrible explosion. The whole boat rose violently into the air, and on board a shower of nearly boiling water descended; with it there flopped down on the bows a firm dark object that writhed and emitted a screaming yell; it was a mangled, scalded Newt. The captain gave orders to put the ship about so as not to sail straight into the middle of that erupting inferno; but just then explosions broke out on all sides, and the surface of the sea was littered with the bits of dismembered Newts. At last they managed to turn the boat round, and the *Oudenburgh* made off at full steam towards the North. Then a terrific detonation thundered out about six hundred yards behind her stern; and up from the sea rose a huge column of water and steam, which might have been a hundred yards high. The *Oudenburgh* made for Harwich, sending out in all directions wireless warnings: "Look out, look out, look out! Between Ostend and Harwich there is great risk of submarine explosions. We don't know what is the cause. All boats are advised to avoid it!" In the meantime the rumbling and reverberations continued, almost as if naval manœuvres were taking place; but nothing was visible in the spouting water and steam. Then from Dover and Calais torpedo-boats and destroyers set off at full steam, and flights of army aircraft rushed to the scene, but when they arrived they only found the quiet surface of the sea covered with a yellow slime and with the mutilated bodies of dead fish and Newts.

At first people took it to be the explosion of some mines in the Channel; but when both sides of the Straits of Dover were closed by a cordon of soldiers, and when the English Prime Minister, for the fourth time in the world's history, broke off his week-end on the Saturday night and hurriedly returned to London, they began to suspect that the affair was one of extremely serious international significance. The newspapers brought out the most disturbing rumours but, strange to relate, they were still far from giving a true picture of the facts; no one even suspected that for a few critical days the whole of Europe, and with her the rest of the world, stood on the brink of a great conflagration. Not till several years afterwards, when Sir Thomas Mulberry, a member of the Cabinet at the time, lost his seat at the elections, and consequently published his political memoirs, was it possible to read what really took place, but by then nobody took a genuine interest in the affair any longer.

The gist of the whole matter was this: France as well as England each began to erect submarine fortresses in the Straits of Dover with which it would have been possible for them in case of war to blockade the whole Channel; then of course both sides accused the other of having made the first start; but the real truth appears to be that they both began simultaneously, lest the neighbouring and friendly State should get in first. In short, under the surface of the Straits of Dover in opposition to each other two gigantic concrete fortresses appeared, armed each with heavy guns, torpedo apparatus, a vast screen of mines, and in brief, with all the most modern equipment which human progress in the art of war had achieved by that time; on the English side there was this terrible deep-water fortress held by two divisions of heavy Newts and about thirty thousand working Salamanders; on the

French side by three divisions of first-class military Newts.

It appears that on the crucial day in the middle of the Channel at the bottom of the sea the working column of the British Newts ran into the French Salamanders, and that between them some misunderstanding arose. On the French side it was alleged that their Newts working peacefully were attacked by the British ones, who wanted to drive them off; the British Newts, who were armed, it is said, tried to drag away several of the French Newts, who of course offered resistance. At that the British military Salamanders began to attack the French Newts with hand grenades and mine throwers, so that the French Newts were compelled to defend themselves in the same way. The French Government felt itself obliged to make representations to the Government of His Britannic Majesty, and demand complete satisfaction as well as the evacuation of the section in dispute, and an undertaking that such cases would not happen again in future.

On the other hand, the British Government announced in a special Aide Memoir to the Government of the French Republic that the French militarized Newts invaded the British half of the Channel and were preparing to lay mines there. The British Newts drew their attention to the fact that they were encroaching on foreign ground; to that the French Salamanders, armed to the teeth, replied by throwing hand grenades with which they killed several British working Newts. The Government of His Britannic

Majesty with regret felt itself compelled to demand
from the Government of the French Republic complete satisfaction, and an undertaking that in future
the French military Newts would not encroach on
the English half of the Straits of Dover.

After this the French Government announced that
it could no longer tolerate a situation in which a
neighbouring State was erecting submarine fortifications in close proximity to the French coast. With
regard to the misunderstanding at the bottom of the
Channel the Government suggested that under the
London Convention the matter in dispute should be
referred to the Hague Tribunal.

The British Government replied that it could not
and did not intend to entrust the security of the British
shores to arbitration by third parties. As the injured
State it demanded again, and in the strongest terms,
a full apology, an indemnity, and a guarantee for the
future. At the same time the Mediterranean fleet lying
at Malta sailed at full steam for the west; and the
Atlantic fleet was ordered to concentrate at Portsmouth
and Yarmouth.

The French Government ordered the mobilization
of five classes of the Marine.

It looked as if neither of the States was prepared to
withdraw; and in the end it was clear that nothing
less was at stake than the control of the whole of the
Channel. At that critical moment Sir Thomas Mulberry
became aware of the astonishing fact that on the
English side no working nor military Newts actually
(at least *de jure*) existed, for in British waters the

prohibition once issued by Sir Samuel Mandeville was still valid according to which not a single Salamander was allowed to be employed on the coasts and in the territorial waters of the British Isles. According to this the British Government could not officially maintain that French Newts had attacked English ones; the whole matter was then reduced to the question whether the French Salamanders had intentionally or only by mistake encroached on sea bottom belonging to England. The officials of the Republic gave an undertaking that they would look into the matter; the English Government did not even propose that the dispute should be referred to the Hague Tribunal. Thereupon the British and the French Admiralties arrived at an agreement to the effect that between their deep-water fortifications in the Straits of Dover there should be a neutral band five kilometres wide, by which the friendship between both these States was greatly strengthened.

4

Der Nordmolch

NOT many years after the founding of the first Newt colonies in the Northern and Baltic Seas the German research worker, Dr. Hans Thüring, ascertained that the Baltic Newt was showing—apparently in response to the milieu—some divergent physical qualities; for example, he stated, it was somewhat lighter in colour, it walked more erect, and its cranial index gave evidence of a longer and narrower skull than was the case with other Newts. This variety was christened **der Nordmolch** or **der Edelmolch** (*Andreas Scheuchzeri var. nobilis erecta Thüring*).

After that the German Press began to take an eager interest in the Baltic Newt. Special stress was laid on the fact that it was just in response to the German milieu that this Newt had developed into a divergent and higher racial type, indisputably superior to all the other Salamanders. With contempt they described the degenerate Mediterranean Newts, stunted both physically and morally, the savage tropical Newts, and altogether the low, barbarian, and bestial Salamanders of other nations. From the Giant Salamander to the German Super-Newt, thus ran the winged phrase of the time. Was not the ur-origin of all modern Newts to be found on German soil? Was not their cradle near

Oeningen, where the German scientist Dr. Johannes Jakob Scheuchzer first discovered their superb imprints as early as the Miocene? There was, therefore, no doubt that the original *Andrias Scheuchzeri* was born geological ages before on German soil; if later on it migrated to other seas and zones, it paid dearly for it by its evolutionary descent and degeneration; but as soon as it again settled on the soil of its ur-fatherland it became again what it had been originally: a noble Nordic Newt Scheuchzeri, fair, erect, dolichocephalic. Therefore only on German soil could the Newts return to their pure and highest type, as the great Johannes Jakob Scheuchzer had founded in the imprint in the Oeningen quarries. Therefore Germany needed new and longer coasts, it needed colonies, it needed oceans so that everywhere new generations of racially pure, ur-original German Salamanders could develop in German waters. We need more space for our Newts, wrote the German papers; and to keep this constantly before the eyes of the German people a huge monument to Johann Jakob Scheuchzer was erected in Berlin. In this the great doctor was portrayed with a fat book in his hand; at his feet was the noble Nordic Newt sitting upright and gazing into the distance to the limitless shores of the world ocean.

At the unveiling of this national moment solemn speeches were of course delivered, which awoke unusual interest in the world Press. A NEW GERMAN MENACE was chiefly the expression of the English views. Without doubt we are already accustomed to such expressions, but when it is stated at an official

function that Germany will need five thousand kilometres of new sea coast in three years' time, we are
driven to retort most emphatically: Very well, try it!
You will break your teeth on the British shores. We
are prepared now, and we shall be still better prepared
in three years' time. England must and will have as
many ships of war as the two greatest Continental
Powers put together; this ratio of forces is once
and for all times inviolable. If you wish to initiate
a mad race in naval armaments, very well; but
no Briton will permit us to remain the slightest bit
behind.

"We accept the German challenge," announced Sir
Francis Drake, First Lord of the Admiralty, speaking
in the name of the Government in Parliament. "Anyone
who tries to put his hand on any ocean sea will come
up against the armour of our ships. Great Britain is
strong enough to beat off every attack made on her
downs and on the coasts of her colonies and dominions.
In view of such an attack we shall also consider the
construction of new continents, islands, fortresses, and
aircraft bases in every sea whose waves wash the smallest
bit of British coast. Let this be the final warning to
anyone who would like, even by a yard, to shift the
ocean shores." As a result Parliament approved of the
construction of new warships at a provisional cost of
half a milliard pounds sterling. It was indeed an
impressive reply to the erection of the provocative
monument to Johann Jakob Scheuchzer in Berlin; this
monument, of course, only cost twelve thousand
Reichmarks.

278

To these declarations the brilliant French publicist, Marquise de Sade, usually extremely well informed, replied as follows: The British First Lord of the Admiralty has announced that Great Britain is prepared for all eventualities. That may well be; is, however, the noble lord aware that Germany in its Baltic Newts has a standing and heavily equipped army, amounting to-day to five million warrior Newts, which it can bring into action at once in the water and on the coast? To this add some seventeen million Newts for the technical and supply force ready at any moment to form a reserve and army of occupation. To-day the Baltic Salamander is the best soldier in the world; psychologically he is perfectly keyed up, he sees in war his real and highest vocation; he will enter every battle with the enthusiasm of a fanatic, with the cold ingenuity of an expert, and with the ghastly discipline of a real Prussian Newt.

Is the First Lord of the Admiralty also conscious of the fact that Germany is feverishly building transport boats which can carry a whole brigade of war Salamanders at a time? Is it known to him that she is building hundreds and hundreds of small submarines with a cruising range of three to five thousand kilometres, of which the crew will consist entirely of Baltic Newts? Is he aware that she is constructing in various parts of the ocean huge submarine tanks for fuel? Well, let me put the question again: is the British citizen quite certain that his large country is *really* fully prepared for all eventualities?

It is not difficult to imagine, continued the Marquise

de Sade, what the Newts will mean in the next war, equipped with submarines, big guns, mine throwers, and torpedoes for blockading the coast; upon my soul, for the first time in the history of the world nobody need envy England for its splendid island situation. But now that we are raising these questions: is it also known to the British Admiralty that the Baltic Newts are equipped with machines normally peaceful which are called pneumatic drills; and that a modern drill in an hour can bore ten metres deep into the best Swedish granite, and from fifty to sixty metres deep into English chalk? Experimental borings, which were carried out in secret by a party of German technical experts on the English coast between Hythe and Folkestone on the nights of the 11th, 12th, and 13th of last month, have established this fact right in front of the fortress at Dover. We advise our friends beyond the Channel to figure out for themselves in how many weeks Kent or Essex could be drilled through below sea-level with holes, like a lump of cheese. Up to the present the Britisher has looked up anxiously towards the sky from which, it was said, the only destruction could rain down on his flourishing towns, his Bank of England, and his peaceful cottages so cosy in their perennially green frame of ivy. Rather now let him put his ear to the ground on which his children play: will he not hear in it to-day, or to-morrow, the crunch and inch by inch the deeper cut of the tireless and terrible tool of the Newt drill boring holes for the piles of until now unheard of explosives? No longer a war in the air, but a war under the sea and under the earth, is the latest marvel of our age. We have heard the haughty words from the Captain on the bridge of proud Albion; yes, it is still a powerful vessel which floats on the waves and rules them; but one day those waves may close over a boat rent to pieces and sinking into the depths of the sea. Would it not be wiser to face this danger in time? In three years it will be already too late!

This warning from the brilliant French publicist roused in England tremendous excitement; in spite of all denials, people heard in the most diverse parts of the country the subterranean crunch of the Newts' drills. The German official circles, of course, sharply contradicted and refuted the article in question, stating that from beginning to the end it was merely frenzied incitement and hostile propaganda; at the same time, however, in the Baltic large-scale manœuvres of the combined German fleet, the land forces, and the fighting Salamanders took place. During these manœuvres the sapper platoons blew up under the eyes of the leading military attachés a strip of sand dunes which had been perforated near Ruegenwalde to the extent of six square kilometres. It was (it was said) a grand show when with a dreadful rumbling the earth was lifted up "like a broken ice floe"—and only then did it fly apart into a huge pillar of smoke, sand, and boulders; the sky grew dark as if it was night, and bits of sand fell over an area of almost hundreds of kilometres; some of the sand even fell as a sand rain as far away as Warsaw. In the atmosphere so much fine sand and dust remained suspended after the splendid explosion that right up to the end of that year the sunsets over the whole of Europe were unusually beautiful, blood red, and fiery as they had never been before.

The sea which covered the scattered piece of the coast later received the name of Scheuchzer-See, and it was the resort of countless excursions and expeditions of German school-children singing the favourite Newt anthem:

Solche Erfolche erreichen nur deutsche Molche.

stricken by the persistent sense of uncertainty, distress, and discomfort." And Wolf Meynert relentlessly exposed the spiritual state of the present world, this mixture of fear and hatred, distrust and megalomania, cynicism and despondency: in one word desperation, summed up Wolf Meynert briefly. The typical symptom of the end: moral agony.

The question runs: Is and has man ever been capable of happiness? A man, certainly, like every other living creature; but mankind not. All unhappiness of the man lies in the fact that he was compelled to become mankind, or that he became mankind too late, after he had already been irrevocably divided into nations, races, faiths, professions, and classes, into rich and poor, into educated and uneducated, into the rulers and the ruled. Herd together horses, wolves, sheep and cats, foxes, deer, bears and goats; shut them up in one enclosure, and compel them to live in this mad swarm which you call the Social Order, and maintain common rules of conduct; you will make a miserable, discontented, fatally disrupted herd in which not one of God's creatures will feel at home. This, on the whole, is an accurate picture of the large and hopelessly heterogeneous herd which is called mankind. Nations, professions, classes cannot live together permanently without crowding in upon each other, getting in each other's way to the point of suffocation; either live for ever apart—something that would only be possible if the world were big enough— or in opposition, in a struggle for life and death. For human biological groups like race, nation, or class the

only natural road to homogeneous and stable happiness
is to make room only for the few and exterminate the
rest. And this is just what the human race has omitted
to do in time. To-day it is already too late. We have
provided ourselves with more than enough tenets and
ties by which we shield "the rest" instead of getting
rid of them; we have invented a moral order, human
rights, conventions, laws, equality, humanity, and all
kinds of things; we have created a fiction of mankind
which includes us and "the rest" in some sort of
imaginary higher unity. What a fatal mistake! We
have set our moral law above the law of Nature. We
have undermined the great natural premise of all
communal life: that only a homogeneous society can
be contented. And this attainable blessedness we have
sacrificed to a great but impossible dream: to create
one mankind and *one* communion of all men, nations,
societies, and classes. It was magnanimous conceit. In
its way it was the only attempt worth the name of
man to rise above himself. And for this supreme
idealism the human race will now pay with its in-
exorable disintegration.

The process by which man tries to organize himself
into mankind is as old as civilization itself, as the first
laws and the first communities; if in the end after so
many thousands of years he has only reached a stage
at which the chasms between different races, nations,
classes, and world Weltanschauungen have become as
sharp and bottomless as we see to-day, then we can
no longer close our eyes to the fact that the unhappy
historical experiment to create from all men some sort

of mankind has suffered definite and tragic shipwreck. At the very end we begin to grow conscious of it; hence those attempts and schemes to unite the human race differently, in such a way that room is only made for *one* nation, *one* class, or *one* faith. But who can say how deeply we are already infected with the incurable disease of differentiation? Sooner or later every presumably homogeneous group will fall apart into a discordant conglomeration of conflicting interests, parties, professions, and so on, which will either defeat each other or again endure the anguish of living together. There is no escape. We move in a vicious circle; but progress will not for ever move in a circle. Nature herself has prepared for it by making space for the Newts.

It is no accident, meditated Wolf Meynert, that the Newts did not assert themselves vitally until the time when the chronic disease of mankind, this badly fused and everlastingly disintegrating monster, enters upon its agony of death. Except for insignificant deviations the Newts present themselves as a single, huge, and homogeneous unity; they have not yet developed sharply differentiated races, languages, nations, states, faiths, classes, or casts; among them there are no masters and slaves, free and not free, rich and poor; no doubt differences exist among them which have been imposed by the division of labour, but in itself it is a uniform, compact, and so to speak consistent mass, in all its parts equally primitive, in a biological sense equally poorly equipped by nature, equally subjugated, and existing on an equally low level of life. The most

abject Negro or Eskimo lives under incomparably
better conditions, enjoying infinitely greater wealth of
material and culture than these milliards of civilized
Newts. And yet there are no signs that the Newts will
suffer by it. On the contrary. We see quite clearly that
they have no need of those things in which man in
his agony and mortal distress seeks relief and consolation; they manage without philosophy, without belief
in immortality, and without art; they have no conception of fantasy, humour, mysticism, recreation, or
dreams; they are absolute realists. They are as remote
from us as ants or herrings; from which they differ
only by organizing themselves according to another
life milieu, that is human civilization. They have
entrenched themselves in it, as dogs have settled in
human habitations; they can't exist without it, but
because of that they will not cease to be what they
are: a very primitive and hardly differentiated animal
community. It is sufficient to them to live and to
multiply; they can even be happy, for they are not
distraught by any sense of inequality among them.
They are simply homogeneous. Therefore they may
one day—yes, *any* day in the future—achieve without
effort that which man has not accomplished: their
racial unity throughout the whole world, a world
community, in a word universal Salamandrism! On
that day the thousand-year-old death agony of the
human race will come to an end. On our planet there
will not be space enough for two movements which
will try to dominate the whole world. One will have
to yield. We already know which one that will be.

To-day in the whole of this globe there are about twenty milliards of civilized Newts, or about ten times as many as there are human beings; from this of biological necessity and historical logic it follows that the Newts now subjugated must liberate themselves; that being homogeneous they must unite; and that in becoming the greatest living force that the world has ever seen they *must* take dominion over it. Do you imagine that they will be as stupid as to spare mankind? Do you imagine that they will repeat the historical mistake that man has eternally committed by making slaves of defeated races and classes instead of exterminating them? That from egoism he has created everlasting differences among people so that later out of magnanimity and idealism he might try to bridge them over again? No, *this* historical nonsense the Newts will not commit, proclaimed Wolf Meynert, if only because they will now take warning from my book! They will inherit the whole of human civilization; into their lap will fall all our achievements and our objectives when we tried to master the world; but they would defeat themselves if along with this inheritance they tried to take us over too. They must rid themselves of man if they wish to retain their homogeneity. If not, sooner or later we should bring among them our dual destructive proclivity: to create differences, and to tolerate them. But let us not be afraid of this; to-day no creature that is going to succeed to the history of mankind will repeat its suicidal madness.

There is no doubt that the Newt world will be happier than that of man; it will be uniform, consistent, and permeated with the same spirit. One Newt will not differ from another Newt in language, views, or life's necessities. There will not exist among them cultural or class differences, but only division of labour. Nobody will be a master or a slave, for they all will serve one Big Newt Entity, which will be their god, ruler, employer, and spiritual leader. There will be only one nation and one class. It will be a better and more perfect world than ours. It will be the only possible Happy New World. Well then, let us make space for it; there is nothing now that languishing mankind can accomplish but accelerate its end—in tragic beauty while there is still time.

We reproduce above the views of Wolf Meynert in a form as popular as possible; in doing so we are conscious of the fact that they lose much of their effectiveness and depth by which in their time they fascinated the whole of Europe, and especially the young, who received with enthusiasm the faith in the decadence and coming end of mankind. The Reichs Government no doubt banned the writings of the Great Pessimist on political grounds, and Wolf Meynert had to withdraw to Switzerland; nevertheless the whole cultured world received Meynert's theory of the decline of mankind with satisfaction; the book (632 printed pages) appeared in all the languages of the world, and many million copies also spread among the Newts.

6

X's Warning

PERHAPS it was also an outcome of Meynert's prophetic book that the literary and artistic *avant-guard* in cultural circles proclaimed as their motto: After us the Salamanders! The future belongs to the Newts. Newts, that means a cultural revolution. They may have no art of their own: at least they are not weighed down by idiotic ideals, moribund traditions, and by all that bloated, boring, pedantic trash which was once called poetry, music, architecture, philosophy, and in a word culture—senile words at which our stomachs turn. Good that they have not fallen victims to the rumination of obsolete human art: we shall create a new one for them. We, the young generation, are blazing the trail for the world Salamandrism of the future: we want to be the first Newts, we are the Salamanders of to-morrow! And thus was the young poetic movement of Salamandrians given birth, a triton (three tone) music came into existence, and Pelagian painting which found inspiration in the plastic world of the jelly-fish, sea anemones, and corals. Besides that, in the constructional work of the Newts there was discerned a new source of beauty and monumentality. We are already heartily sick of nature, they cried; let us have smooth concrete shores instead of the old frayed cliffs! Romanticism is dead; the continents of the future will be contoured with clean straight lines, and reshaped into conic triangles and rhombs; the old geological earth must be replaced by a geometrical one. In short, for once again there was something new, futuristic, new spiritual horizons, and new cultural manifestos; those then who did not take steps soon enough to enter the path of future Salamandrism felt with bitterness that they had missed their opportunity, and they took their revenge by proclaiming ideals of pure humanity, return to man and to nature, and other reactionary slogans. In Vienna a concert of the triton music was hissed to silence, in the Paris Salon of the Independents an unknown culprit slashed to shreds a Pelagian picture called *Capriccio en bleu*; in short, Salamandrism had become a victorious and irresistible advance.

Of course there was no lack of reactionary voices who opposed the "Newt mania," as they called it. The most significant in this direction was an anonymous English pamphlet which appeared under the title *X's Warning*. This pamphlet achieved considerable popularity, but the identity of the author was never revealed; many people, judging from the fact that in English X stands for Christ, were of the opinion that it was the work of some high Church dignitary.

In the first chapter the writer made a rough estimate of the numbers of the Newts, at the same time apologizing for the unreliability of the figures which he quoted. So already he wrote: By this time the total number of all Salamanders is estimated to run to between seven and twenty times the total number of all the people in the world. Equally vague is the information as to how many factories, oil wells, seaweed plantations, eel farms, developed water power, and other natural resources the Newts possess under the sea; there do not exist even approximate figures of what is the productive capacity of the Newt industry; least of all is it known what is the situation with regard to the armaments of the Newts. We know, no doubt, that the Salamanders in their consumption of metals, machine parts, explosives, and many other chemicals are dependent on man; but on the one hand no nation dare disclose what arms and what other products it conveys in secret to the Newts; on the other hand strikingly little is known as to what depths in the sea the Newts are working at the semi-manufactures and raw materials which they buy from human beings. It is quite certain that the Salamanders do not wish these facts to be known; in recent years so many divers let down to the sea bottom have perished through drowning or suffocation that it cannot be attributed to mere chance. This certainly is an alarming situation both as regards industrial and military matters.

It is of course difficult to imagine, continued X in subsequent paragraphs, what the Newts could or might wish to take from man. They cannot live on dry land, and they cannot well be prevented from living under the water. The living conditions of them and of man are clearly and permanently different. It is no doubt true that man requires of them a certain output of work; but in exchange they are supplied with a big part of their food and with raw materials and commodities, which without man they would not have at all, as for instance metals. But even if there is no real cause for antagonism between the Newts and man, there is, the writer thought, a metaphysical conflict: in opposition to creatures living on the surface are those in the deep (abyssal), nocturnal against diurnal; those in the dark water pools against those of the clear dry land. The line of demarcation between the water and the earth is somehow sharper than it used to be: *our* earth is lapped by *their* water. We might live for ever in different spheres, and only exchange certain services and products; but it is difficult to get rid of the oppressive feeling that this is not at all likely. Why? I cannot give you definite reasons, but that feeling exists; it is something like a premonition that one day the waters themselves will turn against the earth so that the question of mastery may be settled.

In view of this, continued X, I confess to a rather irrational anxiety, but I should feel greatly relieved if the Newts were to come out against mankind with some demands. We could at least negotiate with them, various concessions might be agreed upon, conventions, and compromises; but their silence is terrible. I am frightened of their incredible reserve. They could, for instance, demand for themselves certain political rights; viewed quite honestly, legislation for the Newts in all countries is rather obsolete, and it is no longer worthy of creatures so civilized and numerically strong. It would be only expedient to draw up the rights and duties of the Newts anew, and in a form more advantageous to them; some measure of autonomy for the Salamanders might be considered; it would be only justice to improve their working conditions and recompense them for what they performed more appropriately. In many respects it would then be possible to improve their lot *if only they would ask for it,* then we might grant them some concessions, and bind them by compensating agreements; at least we should gain a couple of years. But the Newts demand nothing; they only increase their output and their requisitions; to-day at last we must really ask where for both of us it is going to end. We used to speak once of the yellow, black, or red peril; but those at least were men, and with men we can form a pretty clear opinion of what they want. But when we have not yet the slightest inkling as to how and against what mankind will be called upon to defend itself, at least one fact must be quite plain: that is, that if on one side there will be the Newts, then on the other will stand the *whole* of mankind.

Men against the Newts! It is high time that this expression were used. For, to speak the truth, a normal man instinctively hates the Salamanders, he is nauseated by them—and he is afraid of them. Upon the whole of mankind something like a chill shadow of horror is falling. What else is that frenetic indulgence, that insatiable thirst for diversion and pleasure, that orgiastic licence which has seized the men of to-day? There has not been such moral decadence since the times when the Barbarian invasion had sealed the doom of the Roman Empire. This is not only the

outcome of unprecedented wealth, but of anxiety
desperately drowned in the face of disorganization and
annihilation. Let us drink to the last before the end!
What a shame, what a delirium! It seems that God
in His awful mercy permits nations and classes to
waste away which are hastening to their ruin. Do you
wish to read the fiery *Mene tekel* written above the
banquet? Look at the luminous inscriptions which all
night long blaze on the walls of the dissolute and
profligate towns! In this respect we human beings
already approach the Newts: we live more at night
than in the day-time.

If at least these Salamanders were not so distressingly
mediocre, blurted out X somewhat uneasily. Yes, in a
way they are quite well educated; but because of that
they are still more circumscribed because they have
appropriated from human civilization only what is
second-rate and utilitarian, mechanical and autocratic.
They stand beside mankind like famulus Wagner at
the side of Faust; they learn from the same books as
the human Faust, only with the difference that they
are filled with satisfaction and have no gnawing doubts.
The most dreadful thing is that they have multiplied
that tractable, unthinking, and self-sufficient type of
civilized mediocrity wholesale in millions and milliards
of the same type; but no, I am mistaken: the most
dreadful thing is that they are so successful. They
learned to use machines and numbers, and it has
become clear that that is sufficient for them to master
the earth. They have omitted from human civilization
everything that was without purpose, diverting, fan-

tastic, or ancient; in this way they have left out all that is human, and have taken over only the portion that is practical, technical, and utilitarian. And this doleful caricature of human civilization makes colossal progress; it builds technical marvels, renovates our planet, and finally begins to fascinate mankind itself. From his disciple and servant Faust will learn the secret of success, and mediocrity. Either mankind will come to close quarters with the Newts in a historic conflict of life and death, or it will inevitably become salamanderized. For my part, ended X in a melancholy vein, I would rather see the first.

Well, X gives you warning, went on the unknown writer. It is still possible to shake off that cold and clammy barrier that hems us in. We must get rid of the Salamanders. There are already too many of them; they are armed, and they can turn against us the war material of whose total amount we know next to nothing; but a far more dreadful danger than their numbers and strength is for us their successful, nay, triumphant inferiority. I do not know what we ought to dread the most: their human civilization, or their spiteful, cold, and animal cruelty; but the two together gives something unimaginably gruesome and almost diabolical. In the name of culture, in the name of Christianity and of mankind we must free ourselves from the Newts. And here the anonymous apostle cried:

Fools, Stop Feeding the Newts! Cease to employ them, relinquish their services, let them and may they migrate wherever they please, where they will support

life had reached unheard of depths. On the other hand, the business columns of the newspapers rightly pointed out that it would be impossible to restrict the supplies to the Newts because that would initiate a great slump in production and a serious crisis in many branches of human industry. Also agriculture to a large extent was dependent on the huge demand for maize, potatoes, and other farm products for Newt fodder; if the number of Salamanders was reduced, a big fall in the prices of edible commodities would follow through which the farming people would find themselves on the brink of ruin. Organizations of trade unionists suspected X of reactionary tendencies, and announced that they were not going to allow the export of any goods for the Newts to be stopped; as soon as the working classes had got full employment with bonuses X wanted to take the bread from their mouths; the working people stood on common ground with the Newts and rejected all the attempts to lower their standard of living and expose them wretched and defenceless to the hand of capitalism. With regard to the suggestion of a League of Nations against the Newts, all responsible political parties raised the objection that it would be superfluous; hadn't they already got a League of Nations for the one part, and for the other the London Convention by which maritime nations had bound themselves not to provide their Salamanders with heavy armaments? It was, of course, difficult to expect a State to disarm unless it was quite certain that another maritime Power was not secretly arming its Newts, and by so doing intensifying its military power to the detriment of its neighbours. Also no State or continent could compel its Newts to migrate elsewhere simply because by so doing it would both stimulate the industrial and agricultural markets and increase the defensive strength of other States and continents. And of such objections as these every sensible man had to admit that there were plenty.

In spite of that the pamphlet, *X's Warning*, could not avoid creating a deep impression. In nearly every country a popular Anti-Newt movement was initiated, and societies for combating the Newts, Anti-Salamander clubs, Committees for the Protection of Mankind, and many other organizations of a similar kind were founded. The Newt delegates at Geneva were mobbed when they were attending the twelve hundred and thirteenth session of the Commission for the Study of Newt Problems. The wooden enclosures on the sea-shores were plastered with threatening inscriptions such as: Death to the Newts. Away with the Sala-manders. And so on. Many Newts were stoned to death; no Salamander dare put his head out of water any longer. Yet in spite of that, from *their* side came no demonstrations of protests or acts of retaliation. They were simply invisible, at least during the day-time; and people who peeped over the Newt fences only saw an infinite and indifferent rolling sea. "Look at that, those brutes," people used spitefully to say, "they don't even show themselves!"

And into the midst of the oppressive silence crashed the so-called *EARTHQUAKE IN LOUISIANA.*

7

Earthquake in Louisiana

THAT day—it was one o'clock in the morning of the
11th of November—people felt strong earth tremors at
New Orleans; several shanties in the Negro quarters
collapsed; people rushed out into the streets in a panic,
but the tremors never came again; only a brief squall
with rumbling and savage impact smashed the windows
and swept away the roofs in the narrow Negro streets,
killing some scores of people; then a heavy rain of
mud descended.

While the New Orleans fire brigades were setting
out to bring succour to the streets that had suffered
most telegrams from Morgan City, Plaquemine, Baton
Rouge, and Lafayette were ticking off: S O S! Send
rescue parties! Have been half swept away by earthquake and storm; dams of the Mississippi threaten to
give way; send at once navvies, ambulances, and
anyone who can work!—From Fort Livingston only a
laconic question came through: Hello, are you in a
pretty mess too?—After this came a telegram from
Lafayette: Look out! Look out! New Iberia has
suffered most. Looks as if connection between Iberia
and Morgan City is cut off. Send help there!—
Immediately afterwards Morgan City telephoned: We
can't get through to New Iberia. The road and railway

must be blocked. Send boats and aeroplanes to Vermilion Bay! We don't need anything now. We have about thirty dead and a hundred injured.—After this a telegram arrived from Baton Rouge: We hear that New Ibeiia suffered worst. Send help mainly to New Iberia. Only workers here, but quick, or the dams will give way. We are doing all we can.—Then later: Hello, hello, Shreveport, Nathitoches, Alexandria are sending auxiliary trains to New Iberia. Hello, hello, Memphis, Wonona, Jackson, send trains via New Orleans. All cars should help to carry people towards the dam at Baton Rouge.—Hello, this is Pascagoula. We have several killed. Do you need help?

In the meantime fire brigades, ambulances, and auxiliary trains were setting out for Morgan City—Paterson—Franklin. After four o'clock in the morning the first more detailed reports came through: The railway between Franklin and New Iberia, seven miles west of Franklin, blocked by water; it looks as if through the earthquake a deep fissure has developed there connected with Vermilion Bay, and flooded with sea water. As far as can be discovered at present this fissure runs from Vermilion Bay in the direction east-north-east, near Franklin it turns north, cuts into Grand Lake, and then it runs north as far as the Plaquemine-Lafayette line, where it ends in a small lake which existed before; the other branch of the fissure joins up Grand Lake westwards with the lake at Napoleonville. The total length of the rift is about eighty miles. Here it seems was the centre of the earthquake. It appears to have been a piece of amazing luck that this fissure missed all the bigger towns. All the same the loss of life must have been great. In Franklin a layer of mud fell two feet thick, in Patterson it was eighteen inches. People from Atchafalaya Bay say that during the tremors the sea went out about two miles, and then a tremendous wave thirty yards high hurled itself back on the shore. It is feared that many people have perished on the shore. We still can't get through to New Iberia.

In the meantime the train with the party from Nathitoches reached New Iberia from the west; the first news sent out by way of Lafayette and Baton Rouge was terrible. Even several miles away from New Iberia the train could not get any further because the track was buried in mud. The survivors explained that about two miles to the east of the town a mud volcano had broken out which threw up masses of thin cold mud; New Iberia, they said, disappeared beneath a deluge of mud. Further progress in the dark and in a steady downpour was extremely exhausting. Still no connection with New Iberia.

At the same time a message came through from Baton Rouge:

ON DAMS OF MISSISSIPPI A THOUSAND MEN NOW AT WORK STOP IF ONLY STOPPED RAINING STOP WE NEED SPADES SHOVELS CARTS AND MEN STOP ARE SENDING HELP TO PLAQUEMINE THOSE BEGGARS ARE IN A FINE OLD MESS

Telegram from Fort Jackson:

AT HALF PAST ONE AM SEA WAVE SWEPT AWAY THIRTY
HOUSES WE DONT KNOW WHAT IT WAS ABOUT SEVENTY
PEOPLE DROWNED ONLY NOW HAVE MENDED TRANSMITTER
TOOK POST OFFICE AS WELL HELLO TELEGRAPH QUICK WHAT
IT REALLY WAS FRED DALTON HELLO LET MINNY LACOST
KNOW THAT NOTHING HAPPENED TO ME ONLY BROKE WRIST
AND WASHED AWAY CLOTHES BUT TRANSMITTER IS OK
AGAIN FRED

The most laconic message came from Port Eads:

PEOPLE KILLED HERE ALL BURYWOOD SWEPT INTO SEA

In the meantime—that was about eight o'clock in
the morning—the first aeroplanes returned which had
been sent to the stricken region. The whole coast from
Port Arthur (Texas) as far as Mobile (Alabama), it
was said, had been inundated during the night by a
tidal wave; everywhere could be seen wrecked or
damaged houses. The south-east of Louisiana (from
the Lake Charles–Alexandria–Natchez road) and the
southern Mississippi (as far as the Jackson–Hattiesburg–
Pascagoula line) was plastered over with mud. In
Vermilion Bay a new arm of the sea ran into the land,
about three to ten miles wide, and running inland like
a long fjord almost as far as Plaquemine. New Iberia
appeared to have suffered heavily, but many people

were seen scraping the mud from the houses and roads. It was impossible to land. The most serious loss of life would most likely have been along the coast. At Point au Fer a steamboat, apparently American, was sinking. Near Chandeleur Islands the sea was covered with wrecks. The rain was stopping over the whole region. Visibility good.

The first special edition of the New Orleans papers appeared of course soon after four o'clock in the morning; and as the day went on new editions came out giving further details; by eight o'clock in the morning the papers were bringing out photographs of the stricken area and maps of the new sea bay. By half-past eight they had printed an interview with the prominent seismologist of Memphis University, Dr. Wilbur R. Brownell, discussing the cause of the earth tremors in Louisiana. For the present we can't come to any final conclusion, announced the famous scientist, but it seems that these tremors have nothing to do with the volcanic activity which is still taking place in the volcanic region of Central Mexico directly opposite the stricken area. To-day's earthquake appears instead to have been of tectonic origin, that is, caused by the pressure of the mountain masses: on the one side the Rocky Mountains and Sierra Madre, on the other the Appalachian range along the vast cavity of the Bay of Mexico whose continuation is the wide plain at the lower reaches of the Mississippi. The fissure now running out from Vermilion Bay is only a new and relatively slight fracture, a tiny episode in the geological subsidence which has given rise to the Bay of Mexico, and the Caribbean sea together with the line of the Greater and Lesser Antilles, remnants of a previously continuous mountain range. There is no doubt that this subsidence in Central America will continue and be accompanied with fresh tremors, faults, and fissures; it is quite possible that the fissure in Vermilion Bay is merely a preliminary to a renascent tectonic process whose centre lies just in the Bay of Mexico; in that case we might live to experience gigantic geological catastrophies by which almost a fifth of the United States might sink below the sea. Of course, if this took place there is a reasonable probability that we might expect the sea floor to be elevated somewhere near the Antilles or still further east, in the places where ancient myths used to point to the sunken Atlantis.

On the other hand, continued the scientific authority soothingly, we need not regard in a serious light the fears that volcanic activity will break out in the stricken region; the supposed craters which ejected the mud are nothing but the release of mud and gases most probably associated with the Vermilion Bay fissure. It is not at all improbable that in the alluvium brought down by the Mississippi there are huge subterranean accumulations of gases, which in contact with the air might expand and raise with themselves hundreds of thousands of tons of mud and water. Of course, to come to any definite explanation, repeated Dr. W. R. Brownell, further occurrences would be essential.

While Brownell's prognostications of geological catastrophies ran through the rotary machines of the

8

The Chief Salamander
Presents His Demands

THREE days after the earthquake in Louisiana a fresh geological tragedy was reported, this time in China. With earth tremors accompanied by powerful rumbling a crack developed in the sea coast of the province of Kiangsu north of Nanking, about half-way between the mouth of the Yangtze and the old river-bed Hwan-ho; into this fissure the sea penetrated and joined up with the big lakes Pan-jün and Hungtze-hu between the towns Hwaingan and Fugjang. It seems that as a result of the earthquake the Yangtze left its bed below Nanking and flowed towards the Lake Tai, and then on to Hanchow. It is not possible even to give an approximate estimate of the loss of human life. Hundreds of thousands of people fled to the northern and southern provinces. The Japanese warships received orders to sail for the stricken coast.

Although the earth tremors in Kiangsu were far more extensive than those of the disaster in Louisiana, little attention was paid to them, for the world was already accustomed to catastrophies in China, and it appeared as if one or two million lives were of no great consequence there; besides, it was perfectly clear that in a scientific sense it was an example of a simple tectonic earth movement associated with the deep depression in the sea floor off the Ruikiu and Philippine archipelagos. Three days later, however, the European seismographs recorded fresh tremors centred somewhere near the Cape Verde Islands. Further details followed which announced that a serious earthquake had occurred along the coast of Senegal south of St. Louis. Between the towns of Lampul and Mboro a deep fissure had formed and filled with sea water, penetrating into Merinaghen as far as Dimara waads. According to accounts of eye-witnesses, a column of fire and steam rose up from the earth with a terrific rumbling, throwing sand and stones in a wide circle; after that they could hear the roar of the sea as it rushed into the open rent. The loss of life was not considerable.

This third earth movement caused something almost like a panic. **Does it mean that volcanic activity is increasing again on the earth?** asked the newspapers. **The earth's crust begins to crack,** announced the evening journals. The experts expressed the opinion that the "Senegal fissure" developed perhaps merely through the eruption of a volcanic vent connected with the volcano Pico on the island Fogo of the Cape Verde archipelago; this volcano was still active in 1847, and since then it was assumed to be extinct. This earthquake in West Africa had therefore no connection with the seismic phenomena in Louisiana and in Kiangsu, which were apparently tectonic in origin. But to the man in the street it seemed to be all the same whether the earth was cracking as a result of tectonic or volcanic causes. The fact was that on that day all the churches were crowded. In some countries they also had to keep the churches open at night.

Towards one o'clock in the morning (it was the twentieth of November) wireless fans over the greater part of Europe detected with their apparatus strong disturbances as if a new, unusually strong transmitting station were at work. They found it had a wave-length of two hundred and three metres; it sounded something like the roar of machines or of waves in the sea; while this tense prolonged roar continued they suddenly heard a dreadful croaking voice (they all described it in the same way: hollow and quacking as if it were artificial, besides being immensely magnified by the loud-speaker); this frog's voice cried with great excitement: "Hello, hello, hello! Chief Salamander speaking. Hello, Chief Salamander speaking. Stop all broadcasting, you men! stop your broadcasting! Hello, Chief Salamander speaking!" Then another strangely hollow voice inquired: "Ready?" "Ready." Then there was a crackling as if the circuit was being switched over; and again another unnaturally squeaking voice shouted: "Look out! Look out! Look out! Hello!" "Now!"

And then a hoarse, tired, but a voice of command broke the silence of the night: "Hello, you men! Louisiana, Kiangsu, Senegal. We regret the loss of human lives. We don't want to cause you unnecessary casualties. We only want you to evacuate the coast in places that we shall warn you of in time. If you do that, you will avoid unfortunate accidents. Next time we shall let you know at least a fortnight ahead where we are going to enlarge the sea. So far we have only been carrying out trials. Your explosives have done well. We thank you.

Hello, you people! Don't get excited. We have no hostile intentions towards you. We only need more water, more coasts, more shallow water to live in. There are too many of us. There is not space enough for us on your coasts any longer. Therefore we must break down your continents. From them we shall make bays and islands all round. In this way the length of coast in the world can be increased five times. We shall make new shallow places. We can't live in the deep sea. We shall need your land to fill up the deep parts. We have nothing against you, but there are too many of us. For the time being you can move inland. You can withdraw to the mountains. The mountains will be pulled down last.

You needed us. You have spread us about all over the world. Now you have us. We want to be on good terms with you. You will supply us with steel for our drills and pickaxes. You will supply us with explosives. You will work for u.. Without you we could not move old continents. Hello, you men. Chief Salamander in the name of all the Salamanders of the world offers you collaboration. You will work with us in demolishing your world. We thank you."

The tired, hoarse voice ceased, and only the tense roar as of machines or of the sea could be heard. "Hello, hello. You men," came a croaking voice again. "Now we shall send out light music from your gramophone records. The next item on the programme is 'The March of Tritons' from the monster film *Poseidon.*"

●   ●   ●   ●   ●

The newspapers, of course, took this broadcast of the night as "a stupid and vulgar joke" of some illicit transmitting station; in spite of that the following night millions of people were listening-in waiting to see if that terrible, eager, croaking voice would speak again. It was heard exactly at one o'clock to the accompaniment of a tremendous splashing and rumbling. "Good evening, you people," he quacked cheerfully. "First we are going to play to you a gramophone record of the Salamander Dance from your musical comedy *Galathea.*" When the tinny and indecent music had died away that ghastly and rather cheerful croaking was heard again. "Hello, you people! Just at this moment the British cruiser *Erebus* has been sunk by a torpedo for attempting to destroy our broadcasting station in the Atlantic. The crew have all been drowned. Hello, we call upon the British Government to listen. The boat *Amenhotep* of Port Said refused to deliver up at our port Makalle the explosives we ordered. She said that she had received orders not to carry any more explosives. The boat, of course, was sunk. We advise the British Government to revoke that order by wireless before noon tomorrow, otherwise the ships *Winnipeg, Manitoba, Ontario,* and *Quebec* sailing with wheat from Canada to Liverpool will be sunk. Hello, we call upon the French Government to listen.

Recall the cruisers which are sailing to Senegal. We still want to widen the new bay there. Chief Salamander commanded that I should convey to both Governments his unflinching intention to establish with them the friendliest relations. This is the end of to-day's news. Now we shall broadcast a gramophone record of your song 'Salamandria, valse érotique.' "

The next afternoon to the south-west of Mizen Head the ships *Winnipeg*, *Manitoba*, *Ontario*, and *Quebec* were sunk. A wave of horror ran through the world. In the evening the B.B.C. announced that the British Government had issued an order forbidding the conveyance of feeding-stuffs, chemical products, tools, arms, and metals to the Newts. At night, at one o'clock, an agitated voice croaked in the wireless: "Hello, hello, hello, Chief Salamander is going to speak!" And then a tired, hoarse, angry voice was heard: "Hello, you people! Hello, you people! Hello, you people! Do you think that we shall let ourselves be starved to death? Don't be so stupid! Whatever you do will turn against you! In the name of all the Newts of the world I am speaking to Great Britain. From this hour we are imposing an unrestricted blockade on the British Isles with the exception of the Irish Free State. I am closing the Channel. I am closing the Suez Canal. I am closing the Straits of Gibraltar to all traffic. All British ports are closed. All British boats in whatever sea they may be will be torpedoed. Hello, I am speaking to Germany. I want ten times more explosives than I ordered. Dispatch them at once, invoiced to the main depot Skagerak. Hello, I am speaking to France.

Hurry up the supply of torpedoes ordered for the submarine forts C 3 BFF and Ouest 5. Hello, you people! I give you warning. If you cut down the supplies of food, I shall take them myself from your boats. I warn you again." The tired voice sank to a husky, hardly intelligible whisper. "Hello, I am speaking to Italy. Prepare to evacuate the territory on the line Venice–Padua–Udine. I warn you for the last time, you people. We have had enough of your nonsense." A long pause followed, in which could be heard murmuring as of a black cold sea. And then a cheerful, croaking voice broke out: "And now we shall play for you one of your gramophone records of the latest success, 'The Triton-Trot.' "

9

The Conference at Vaduz

IT was a strange war, if in any way it can be called a war; for there was no Newt state or any recognized Newt Government against which it was possible officially to open hostilities. The first country that found itself in a state of war with the Salamanders was Great Britain. In the very first hours the Newts sank all her boats at anchor at the ports; it was impossible to offer any resistance. Only the boats which were in the open sea were for the time being in comparative safety, mainly while they were passing over the greater depths; in this way part of the British Navy was saved which broke through the Newt blockade at Malta and concentrated above the Ionic deep; but even these units were soon hunted down by small Newt submarines and sunk one after the other. In six weeks Great Britain lost four-fifths of all her shipping.

Once again in history John Bull could reveal his famous obstinacy. His Majesty's Government did not come to terms with the Newts and did not revoke the prohibition of supplies. "A British gentleman," declared the English Premier, speaking for the whole nation, "protects animals, but he does not come to terms with them." Within a very few weeks there was a desperate scarcity of food in the British islands. There was only sufficient to provide the children with a slice of bread and a few spoonfuls of tea or milk each day; the British nation bore its privations with exemplary courage, even when it had sunk so low that it had to eat its race-horses. The Prince of Wales ploughed with his own hand the first furrow on the course of the Royal Golf Club, so that carrots might be grown there for London orphanages. On the tennis courts at Wimbledon potatoes were planted, on the race-course at Ascot wheat was sown. "We shall do everything, and make even the greatest sacrifices," the leader of the Conservative Party affirmed in the Parliament, "but we will not betray British honour."

Because the blockade of the British sea coasts was complete, only one connection remained free for contact with the colonies and obtaining supplies, and that was by air. "We must have a hundred thousand air machines," announced the Air Minister, and every person blessed with hands and legs devoted himself to the service of this motto; feverish preparations were pushed forward to produce a thousand aeroplanes a day; but then the Governments of the other European Powers intervened with a strong protest against this violation of the Air Convention; the British Government had to renounce its plans for the air, and undertake not to build more than twenty thousand aeroplanes, and even then spread over the next five years. The only alternative left was to starve or pay exorbitant prices for food brought in by the flying machines of other countries; a pound of bread for food cost ten shillings, a pair of rats a guinea, a tiny box of caviare twenty-five pounds sterling. This was a simply golden time for continental industry, trade, and agriculture. Because the Navy from the very start was out of action, the military operations against the Newts were only carried out on dry land and from the air. The land forces let off cannons and machine-guns into the water without, it seems, causing serious losses to the Salamanders; somewhat more successful were the bombs dropped from the air into the sea. The Newts replied by firing off their submarine cannons at the British harbours, which they reduced to piles of ruins. From the mouth of the Thames they also bombarded London; then the military command made an attempt to poison the Salamanders with bacteria, petrol, and chemicals which were poured into the Thames and into some of the bays of the sea. To this the Newts replied by releasing along the English coast a screen of poison gas. It was only a tryout, but it was sufficient; the British Government for the first time in history was compelled to ask the other Powers to intervene, referring to the prohibition of poison gas.

The next night the hoarse, angry, and deep voice of the Chief Salamander was heard over the wireless: "Hello, you men! Don't be so stupid, England! If you are going to poison the water for us, we shall poison the air for you. We are only using your own weapons. We are not barbarians. We do not want to fight the people. We don't want anything but to be allowed to live. We offer you peace. You will supply us with your products and sell us your continents. We are ready to pay you well for them. We offer you more than peace. We offer you trade. We offer you gold for your land. Hello, we are speaking to the Government of Great Britain. Let us know your price for the south part of Lincolnshire along the Wash. I give you three days to think it over. During that time I shall bring all hostilities to an end except the blockade."

At that moment along the English coast the submarine bombardment stopped its thunder. All the guns on land also became mute. There was a strange, almost terrifying silence. The British Government announced in Parliament that they had no intention of negotiating with the Newts. The inhabitants round the Wash and Lynn Deep were warned that it appeared as if a big attack of the Newts was about to be launched, and that it would be advisable for them to evacuate the coast and move inland; but the trains, cars, and buses which had been got ready only took away the children and some women. The men, one and all, remained on the spot; it simply did not enter their heads that an Englishman could lose his land. One minute after the end of the three days' truce the first shot fell; it came from an English gun which the Loyal North Lancashire Regiment fired, while the band played the regimental march, "The Red Rose." After this a terrific explosion broke out. The mouth of the River Nen sank as far as Wisbech and was flooded with sea water from the Wash. The famous ruins of Wisbech Abbey, Holland Castle, the pub "George and the Dragon" with other memorable buildings sank below the waters.

The next day, in reply to a question in Parliament, the British Government announced: that as regards the army everything possible had been done to protect the British coast; that further and far more extensive attacks on the British soil might take place; but that His Majesty's Government could not negotiate with an enemy that did not spare civilians and women. (Agreement.) To-day it is no longer the fate of England that is at stake, but of the whole civilized world. Great Britain is prepared to consider international guarantees which would restrict these terrible and barbaric attacks, which are a menace to all mankind.

A few weeks after the world conference of nations met at Vaduz.

• • • • •

It took place at Vaduz, because there was no danger from the Newts in the High Alps, and because the majority of the wealthy and socially important people had already withdrawn there from the littoral countries. The conference, as was generally admitted, took energetic steps to reach a solution of all actual world problems. In the first place all the nations (with the exception of Switzerland, Abyssinia, Afghanistan, Bolivia, and other inland states) as a matter of principle refused to recognize the Newts as an independent warring state, chiefly because if they did their own Salamanders might also regard themselves as members of the Newt nation; there was a possibility that such a state once recognized would wish to exercise supremacy over all the water and coasts occupied by the Newts. Because of that it was legally and practically impossible to declare war on the Salamanders, or to subject them to international pressure; every state had a right to intervene as against *its own* Newts; that was a purely internal affair. Therefore a joint diplomatic or military front against the Newts was quite out of the question. Any states attacked by the Salamanders could only receive international aid in the form of facilities for foreign loans for their defence.

After this England brought forward a proposal that all the states should at least undertake to stop deliveries to the Newts of arms and explosives. After full consideration this proposal was rejected—in the first place because that guarantee already formed part of the London Convention; and secondly, it was not possible to prevent any state from supplying its own Newts with equipment and arms "merely for its own use" and for the defence of its own shores; thirdly, for maritime states "it might conceivably be a matter of importance to maintain good relations with the denizens of the sea," and there it was considered desirable "to refrain for the time being from all arrangements which the Newts might feel as repressive"; nevertheless all the states were willing to undertake that they would provide arms and explosives to any countries that the Salamanders might attack.

In camera the proposal of Columbia was approved of to the effect that at last unofficial negotiations should be entered into with the Newts. Chief Salamander should be invited to send his delegates to the conference. The representative for Great Britain protested strongly against this, refusing to sit at the same table with the Newts; in the end, however, his contention was satisfied with the arrangement that he should be away temporarily in the Engadine for reasons of health. That night all the maritime states broadcasted in their official code an appeal to His Excellency Mr. Chief Salamander to appoint his delegates and send them to Vaduz. The reply was a hoarse: "Yes; for this time we still come to you; next time your delegates will come into the water to me." After that an official announcement: "The Newt delegates duly appointed will arrive in the evening of the day after to-morrow by the Orient Express at Buchs."

With the greatest haste preparations were made for the reception of the Newts; the most luxurious bathrooms at Vaduz were got ready, and a special train brought in barrels of sea water for the Newt delegates. In the evening at Buchs there was to be only a so-called unofficial welcome; only the secretaries of the delegations, representatives of the local offices, and some two hundred journalists, photographers, and film cameramen arrived. Exactly at six twenty-five the Orient Express drew into the station. From the saloon carriage three tall, elegant gentlemen stepped on to the red carpet, and behind them a few perfect, mundane secretaries with heavy portfolios. "And where are the Newts?" somebody inquired in a low voice. Two or three official personalities stepped forward uncertainly to meet the three gentlemen; but then the first of them said under his breath and hurriedly: "We are the Newt delegation. I am Professor Dr. Van Dott from the Hague. Maître Rosso Castelli, an advocate from Paris. Dr. Manoel Carvalho, an advocate from Lisbon." The gentlemen bowed and introduced themselves. "So you are not Newts?" gasped the French secretary. "Of course not," said Dr. Rosso Castelli. "We are their representatives. I beg your pardon: these gentlemen here perhaps want to film us." Then the smiling Newt delegation was zealously filmed and photographed. The legation secretaries present also showed their satisfaction. After all it was very sensible and decent of those Salamanders to have sent men to represent them. With men you can talk more easily. And in particular a certain amount of unpleasant social embarrassment is avoided.

The very same night the first conference with the delegation from the Newts took place. The item on the agenda was how to restore as speedily as possible peace between the Newts and Great Britain. Professor Van Dott asked permission to address the assembly. It was incontestable, he said, that the Newts were attacked by Great Britain; the British cruiser *Erebus* attacked the radio transmitting boat of the Newts in the open sea; the British Admiralty violated the peaceful business relations with the Newts by preventing the boat *Amenhotep* from discharging a cargo of explosives which had been ordered; thirdly, the British Government by forbidding supplies of any kind first began the blockade of the Salamanders. The Newts could not complain of these hostile acts at the Hague, because the London Convention had not given the Newts the right to bring forward complaints, nor at Geneva because they were not members of the League of Nations; all that they could do was to look after their own defence. In spite of that, Chief Salamander was willing to suspend hostilities, of course, under the following conditions: (1) Great Britain must apologize to Newts for above-mentioned violations; (2) she must revoke all prohibitions against supplies to the Newts; (3) as an indemnity she must cede to the Salamanders, without compensation, the low-lying land in river courses of the Punjab so that the Newts might develop new coasts and bays. The president of the conference thereupon announced that he would communicate these terms to his honoured friend, the representative of Great Britain, who was away at the moment; he did not, however, try to disguise his fear that these terms would hardly prove acceptable; nevertheless it was reasonable to hope that they could be regarded as the basis for further discussion.

Then the complaint of France came under discussion with reference to the coast of Senegal, which the Newts blew up into the air, thus infringing French colonial sovereignty. Dr. Julien Rosso Castelli, the famous Paris advocate and a representative of the Newts, asked leave to speak. Prove it, he said. The world authorities on the subject of seismology state that the earth tremor in Senegal was of volcanic origin, and that it was associated with the former activity of the volcano Pico on Fogo Island. "Here," cried Dr. Rosso Castelli, striking his dossier with the palm of his hand, "is their expert scientific verdict. If you have any evidence that the earthquake in Senegal was caused by the activities of my clients, I shall be grateful if I can have it."

The Belgian delegate, Creux: "Your Chief Salamander himself stated that it was the work of the Newts!"

Professor Van Dott: "His statement was unofficial."

Dr. Rosso Castelli: "We are deputed to disclaim that alleged statement of his. I demand that the technical experts be asked to express an opinion if it is possible to cause a fissure in the earth's crust sixty kilometres long by artificial means. I propose that they should give us a practical demonstration on a similar scale. As long as no such evidence exists, gentlemen, we shall speak of volcanic activity. Nevertheless, Chief Salamander is ready to purchase from the French Government the bay which was formed by the Senegal rift, and which is suitable for the foundation of a Newt settlement. We are entrusted to come to an agreement with the French Government with regard to the price."

The French delegate, Minister Deval: "If we can regard that as an indemnity for the damage, we may enter into negotiations."

Dr. Rosso Castelli: "Very well. The Newt Government, however, requests that the contract in question should also cover the Landes region from the mouth of the Gironde to Bayonne extending to six thousand seven hundred and twenty square kilometres. In other words, the Newt Government is willing to buy from France that part of the South of France."

Minister Deval (born in Bayonne, deputy for

Bayonne): "So your Salamanders are going to turn a piece of France into sea bottom? Never! Never!"

Dr. Rosso Castelli: "France will have cause to regret this statement, sir. To-day we are still speaking of buying at a price."

At that the session was adjourned.

At the next meeting the item on the agenda was a big international offer to the Newts: that instead of destroying old densely settled continents, which was out of the question, they should construct for themselves new coasts and islands; in that case they could be granted a substantial credit; any new continents and islands would be recognized as coming under their independent and supreme state sovereignty.

Dr. Manoel Carvalho, the great Lisbon lawyer, expressed thanks for this offer, which he would convey to the Newt Government. But any child can understand, he said, that to construct new continents is slower and more expensive than demolishing old ones in due course. Our clients require new shores and bays in the immediate future; for them it is a question of life or death. It would be better for mankind to accept the generous offer of Chief Salamander, who is to-day still willing to buy the world from human beings instead of seizing it by force. Our clients have worked out a process by which it is possible to extract gold from sea water; in consequence they have almost unlimited means at their disposal; they can pay you well for your world—nay, splendidly. Try to realize that the value of the world will fall as time goes on, particularly if, as is possible to foresee, further volcanic or tectonic catastrophies occur, far more extensive than those which you have experienced up to the present, and if the surface area of the continents in this way was considerably reduced. To-day it is still possible to sell the world as it exists at present; when nothing but ruins of mountains are left nobody will offer you even a farthing. "I am here no doubt as a delegate and a legal adviser of the Newts," cried Dr. Carvalho, "and I must protect *their* interests; but I am a human being like you, gentlemen, and the good of mankind lies no less close to my heart than it does to yours. Therefore I advise you—no, I entreat you: Sell the continents while it is still not too late! You can sell them complete or in individual lots. Chief Salamander, whose modern and magnanimous mind is known by all of you to-day, pledges himself that in any future changes in the earth's surface that may be necessary he will, as far as possible, spare human life; the flooding of the continents will take place by stages, so that it will not lead to panic and unnecessary disturbances. We are entrusted to open negotiations, either with this illustrious world conference as a whole or with the individual states. The presence of such prominent lawyers as Professor Van Dott or Maître Julien Rosso Castelli you may take as a guarantee that, besides the just interests of our clients the Newts, we shall in collaboration with you defend what to us all is most dear: human culture and the good of all mankind."

In an atmosphere somewhat depressing a further proposal was brought forward: that Central China should be ceded to the Salamanders for flooding, if in return the Newts would pledge themselves for all times to guarantee the coasts of the European states and of their colonies.

Dr. Rosso Castelli: "For all times, that's rather long. Say twelve years."

Professor Van Dott: "Central China, that's hardly enough. Say the provinces of Nganhuei, Hunan, Kiangsu, Chihli, and Fengtien."

The Japanese delegate protested against the cession of the province of Fengtien, which lay in the sphere of Japanese influence. The Chinese delegate rose to speak, but unfortunately no one could understand him. In the assembly hall there was an air of increasing restlessness; it was already one o'clock in the morning.

At that moment the secretary of the Italian delegation entered the hall and whispered something into the ear of the Italian delegate, Count Tosti. Count Tosti turned pale, rose, and paying no heed to the fact that the Chinese delegate was still speaking he cried hoarsely: "Mr. Chairman, may I be allowed to speak? News has just arrived that the Newts have flooded part of Venetian province round Portogruaro."

A dreadful silence ensued, except that the Chinese delegate went on speaking.

"Chief Salamander warned you ages ago, didn't he?" murmured Dr. Carvalho.

Professor Van Dott fidgeted impatiently and raised his hand. "Mr. Chairman, ought we not to call the meeting to order? The item on the agenda is the province Fengtien. We are empowered to offer the

Japanese Government compensation for it in gold. A further question is what the states most closely interested in it will give our clients for clearing away China."

•   •   •   •   •

At that moment the radio fans were listening-in to the Newt broadcast. "You have just heard a gramophone record of the Barcarolle from the 'Tales of Hoffman,'" croaked the announcer. "Hello, hello, we are now switching over to Venetian territory in Italy."

And then all they could hear was an immense dark swirling as if of rising waters.

10

Mr. Povondra Takes it
on Himself

WHO would have said that so much water had flown away, and so many years! Even our Mr. Povondra was no longer the porter at the offices of G. H. Bondy; he was, shall we say, a venerable patriarch who could enjoy in peace the fruits of his long and industrious labours in the form of a small pension; but how could a couple of hundred suffice in that war-time dearth? A good job that once in a while it was still possible to catch a fish; he sat in the boat with a rod in his hand, and gazed—how much of that water had flown away in a day, and where did it all come from? Sometimes he got a dace on his line, sometimes a perch; altogether in those days there were somehow more of those fish, perhaps because the rivers were now so much shorter. And a perch like that wasn't bad either; no doubt it was all little bones, but the flesh a bit like almonds. And Mother knew how to cook them. Mr. Povondra didn't even know that Mother usually made the fire under his perches with those cuttings which he once collected and arranged. It's true Mr. Povondra gave up collecting when he retired; instead he bought an aquarium, where besides little golden carp he kept tiny newts and salamanders; for hours on end he watched them as they lay motionless in the water or crawled on the little bank of stones which he made for them; then he shook his head, and said: "Who would have thought it of them, Mother!" But a man cannot bear only to stand and look; so Mr. Povondra took up fishing. "Well, why not? Men must always have something to do," reflected Mother Povondra indulgently. "It's better than if he went to the pub and got mixed up in politics."

Yes, much, very much of that water had flown away. And even Frantik was no longer a schoolboy learning geography, or a youngster wearing out his socks running after the vanities of this world. He too was already a grown-up man, that Frantik; thank God, he was one of the junior officials at the post office—after all it was to some good that he learned geography so conscientiously. He was also beginning to have some sense, thought Mr. Povondra, as he let himself down a bit further in his little boat below the bridge of the Legions. He will come to see me to-day, it's Sunday, and he's not on duty. I shall let him come with me in the boat, and we shall go up to the point of Shooter's Island; the fish rise better there; and Frantik will tell me what's on in the papers. And then we shall go home to Vyšehrad, and his wife will bring both her children to see us. . . . Mr. Povondra was treating himself for a while to the peaceful bliss of a grandfather. Why, this is the year that Mařenka will begin to go to school—she thinks she'll like it; and little Frantik, my grandson, already weighs sixty pounds! Mr. Povondra had a strong and deep feeling that after all everything was part of a great and good order.

But there already was the son waiting by the water and waving his hand. Mr. Povondra paddled the boat to the bank. "It's high time you'd come," he said reprovingly. "And mind that you don't fall into the water!"

"Are they rising?" inquired the son.

"Not very well," grumbled the old gentleman. "We'd best go upstream, hadn't we?"

It was a nice Sunday afternoon; not the hour when those fools and loafers rushed home from football and other such silly diversions. Prague was silent and empty; the few people scattered along the embankment and on the bridge were in no hurry, and they walked leisurely and respectfully. They were better and more sensible people; they did not crowd into parties, and they did not laugh at men fishing in the Vltava. Father Povondra again had that feeling of a great and good order.

"And what's in the papers?" he demanded, with paternal austerity.

"Nothing very much," replied the son. "I've just read here that those Newts have already worked their way through as far as Dresden."

"Then the Germans there will be in the soup," remarked the old gentleman. "You know, Frantik, those Germans, they're a strange nation. Educated, but strange. I used to know a German; he was a lorry driver for some works, and he was such a rough chap, that German. But the lorry he had he kept in order, no doubt about that. And now look; Germany has already disappeared from the map of the world," meditated Mr. Povondra. "And what noise they used to make! That was something dreadful: nothing but soldiers and fighting. Why, and even a German isn't sharp enough for the Newts. You know, I know about those Newts. Do you remember how I showed them to you when you were still a little boy?"

"Look out, Father," cried the son. "The fish are rising."

"That's only a minnow," murmured the old gentleman, and moved the rod. Well, think of it, Germany too, he thought. Well, you can't be surprised at anything now. What a row there was that time when the Newts sank a whole country! It may have been Mesopotamia or China, and the papers were full of it. To-day people don't take it like that, reflected Mr. Povondra with melancholy, blinking over his rod. People get used to it; what else is there to do? It hasn't got to us yet, so why worry, if only things weren't so dear! For instance, the price they ask now for coffee. It's true Brazil has also disappeared below the sea. No doubt it makes a difference to business when part of the world sinks into the sea!

Mr. Povondra's float danced about on the mild little ripples. How much those Newts have already flooded with the sea, reflected the old gentleman. Egypt and India and China—even Russia they weren't frightened of; and it was such a big country, that Russia! When you think that the Black Sea now reaches right up to the Arctic Circle—what a lot of water that is! No doubt about that, they've bitten off enough land already! It's a good job they work so slowly.

"You say," the old gentleman remarked, "that those Newts have got as far as Dresden?"

"Sixteen kilometres from Dresden. That means that almost the whole of Saxony will be under water."

"I was there once with Mr. Bondy," said father Povondra. "That was a tremendously rich country, Frantik, but that the food was good there—no, I can't say that. Otherwise they were very nice people, better than the Prussians. Oh no, there was no comparison."

"But Prussia has already gone too."

"No wonder," remarked the old gentleman. "I didn't like those Prussians. But the French have a good time now Germany has gone to blazes. They will feel relieved."

"Not so much, Father," objected Frantik. "The other day it said in the papers that a good third of France was already under water."

"Yah," sighed the old gentleman. "With us, that is, with Mr. Bondy, there used to be a Frenchman, a butler; Jean was his name. And he was after the women; it was a shame. You know, it brings its own punishment, such flightiness."

"But ten kilometres from Paris they say that they've beaten those Newts," announced son Frantik. "They had nothing but mines there, and they blew the Newts sky high. They did in two army corps of Newts there, so it said."

"Well, a Frenchman makes a good soldier," reflected

Mr. Povondra expertly. "That Jean wouldn't put up with anything either. I don't know where he got it from. He smelt like a chemist's shop, but when he began to fight then he did fight. But two army corps aren't much. When I come to think of it," continued the old gentleman thoughtfully, "men could fight better with human beings. And it didn't last so long either! With those Newts it's already been dragging on for twelve years, and still nothing, nothing but preparations for better positions. What's the good? In my young days they were battles! Then there were three million men on this side and three million men on that," demonstrated the old gentleman till he made the boat rock, "and then, my Gosh, they went for each other. But this isn't a decent fight," said father Povondra angrily; "all the time it's only concrete dams, but never a bayonet attack, no fear!"

"But the men and the Newts can't get at each other, Father," protested young Povondra, defending the modern way of warfare. "You can't make a bayonet attack in the water, can you?"

"Quite so," mumbled Mr. Povondra scornfully. "They can't get at each other properly. But let soldiers loose against another lot, and you'll see what they can do. What do you know about war!"

"If only it doesn't get as far as here," said Frantik rather unexpectedly. "You know, when a man's got children——"

"What, here!" burst out the old gentleman somewhat irritably. "Do you mean here at Prague?"

"Well, anywhere in Bohemia," said young Povondra

333

anxiously. "It seems to me that when the Newts have already got as far as Dresden——"

"You clever lad," rebuked Mr. Povondra. "How could they get here? Over those hills of ours?"

"Perhaps along the Labe—and then along the Vltava."

Father Povondra snorted with expostulation. "What, along the Labe! They could only get as far as Boden-bach, but not further. There, my lad, there's nothing but rock; I've been there. No, the Newts will never get here. We're lucky. And the Swiss are lucky too. It's a marvellous advantage that we haven't got any sea coast, you know! It's a bad job for the countries on the sea."

"But when the sea comes as far as Dresden——"

"There are Germans there," declared the old gentleman firmly. "That's their look-out. But the Newts can't get to us, that stands to reason. Otherwise they'd have to shift those big rocks first; and you've no idea what hard work that would be!"

"Hard work!" objected young Povondra gloomily. "That's what they're after. Don't you know that in Guatemala they managed to sink a whole mountain range?"

"That's something different," said the old gentleman emphatically. "Don't be so silly, Frantik! That was in Guatemala, and not here. The conditions are different here, aren't they?"

Young Povondra sighed. "Well, you may think so, Father. But when you realize that those brutes have already sunk about a fifth of all the continents——"

"Near the sea, you silly billy, but not in other places.

You don't understand politics. Those countries which are by the sea carry on a war with them, but not us. We are a neutral state, and therefore they can't attack us. That's how it is. And don't keep talking all the time, or I shan't catch anything."

It was silence over the water. The trees on Shooter's Island cast long fine shadows on the surface of the Vltava. On the bridge a tram bell tinkled, nurses with prams and prudent Sunday people sauntered on the embankment.

"Daddy," gasped young Povondra, almost as if he were a child.

"What is it?"

"Isn't it a cat-fish?"

"Where?"

From the Vltava just in front of the National Theatre a big dark head showed above the water, making its way slowly against the stream.

"Is it a cat-fish?" repeated Povondra junior.

The old gentleman dropped his rod. "That?" he cried, pointing with a shaking finger. "That?"

The black head disappeared below the water.

"That wasn't a cat-fish, Frantik," said the old gentleman with some kind of voice not his own. "We must go home. That's the end."

"What end?"

"A Newt. So they've got here too. We must go home," he repeated, packing up with uncertain hands his fishing-rod. "That's the end."

"You are all of a tremble." Frantik grew apprehensive. "What's wrong with you?"

335

"We must go home," quavered the old gentleman with agitation, and his chin shook miserably. "I'm cold. I'm cold. To come to this! You know that's the end. And so they're here already. O God, it is cold! I must go home."

Young Povondra looked at him anxiously. "I will take you home, Daddy," he said, also with a kind of voice not his own, and with strong strokes of the oars he rushed the boat to the island. "Never mind, I'll fasten it up."

"What makes it so cold?" wondered the old gentleman, with his teeth chattering.

"I'm holding you, Father. Come on," said the young one to comfort him, and took him by the arm. "I think you must have caught cold on that water. It was only a piece of wood."

The old gentleman shook like a leaf. "I know, a piece of wood, that's what you try to tell me! I know best what Newts are like. Let me go!"

Povondra junior did what he had never done before in his life: he nodded to a taxi. "To Vyšehrad," he said, and pushed his father in. "I'm giving you a ride, Father. It's late already."

"Very well," faltered father Povondra. "Late. It's already the end, Frantik. That wasn't a piece of wood. It was them."

At home young Povondra had almost to carry his father up the stairs. "Get the bed ready, Mother," he whispered hurriedly at the door. "We must let Father lie down; he's not very well."

So, and now father Povondra was lying on the

feather bed; his nose somehow stuck out at a peculiar angle from his face, and his lips murmured and mumbled something unintelligible; how old he looked, how old he looked! Then he became a bit quieter.

"Are you feeling any better, Father?"

At the foot of the bed, sobbing and weeping into her apron, stood Mother Povondra; the daughter-in-law made fire in the stove, and the children Frantik and Mařenka fixed their wide, startled eyes on their grandfather as if they could not recognize him.

"Wouldn't you like to have a doctor, Father?"

Father Povondra looked at the children and whispered something; and suddenly tears ran down from his eyes.

"Do you want anything, Father?"

"It was me, it was me," murmured the old gentleman. "Let me tell you, it was me who brought it on you all. If I hadn't let that captain in then to Mr. Bondy, all this wouldn't have happened."

"But nothing has happened, Daddy," said young Povondra soothingly.

"You don't understand," wheezed the old gentleman. "It's the end, you know. The end of the world. Now the sea will come here too, now that the Newts have got here. I did that; I shouldn't have let that captain in. . . . So that one day people will know who was the cause of it all."

"Nonsense," the son spoke roughly. "Don't you even let it enter your head, Father. Everyone did it. The different countries did it, finance did it. They all wanted to make the most out of those Newts. They all wanted to make money out of them. We used to send them arms, and what not. We are all responsible for it."

Father Povondra fidgeted uneasily. "The sea covered everything at one time, and it will do again. That will be the end of the world. Once a gentleman told me that even near Prague there was once sea bottom. I think the Newts were the cause of it that time too. You know I ought not to have shown that captain in. Something always kept telling me not to do it—but then I thought perhaps that captain might give me a tip. And, you see, he didn't. All for no purpose we ruin the whole world." The old gentleman gulped down something like tears. "I know, I know quite well that it's the end with us. I know that I have done it——"

"Grandfather, wouldn't you like to have some tea?" inquired young Mrs. Povondra compassionately.

"I should only like," sighed the old gentleman, "I should only like those children to forgive me for it."

11

The Author Talks
with Himself

"YOU'RE going to leave it at that?" the author's inner voice was heard.

"What do you mean?" asked the writer somewhat uncertainly.

"You are going to let Mr. Povondra die like that?"

"Well," the author defended himself, "I don't like doing it, but—after all, Mr. Povondra has already lived his life; let us say that he's quite a lot over seventy——"

"And you let his mind be tormented like that? You don't even tell him, Grandfather, but it's not so bad; the world won't perish because of the Newts, and mankind will be saved; it only needs time, and you will live to see it? Please can't you do anything for him?"

"Well, I'll send a doctor to him," suggested the author. "The old gentleman has most likely got neuritis; at his age, of course, he might get pneumonia; but perhaps, thank God, he will recover; perhaps he will still rock Mařenka on his knee and ask her what she learned at school. Joy of old age: let the old gentleman still have the joy of his old age!"

"Nice joy," jeered the inner voice. "He will clasp

that child to himself with his old hands, and be terrified, man, be terrified that one day she will also flee before the roaring waters which will inevitably flood the world; he will knit his bushy brows in horror, and whisper: I did that, Mařenka, I did that. Listen, do you *really* want to let the whole of mankind perish?"

The author frowned. "Don't ask me what I want. Do you think that through *my* will human continents are falling to bits, do you think that I wanted this to happen? It is simply the logic of events; as if I could intervene. I did what I could; I warned them in time; that X, that was partly me. I preached, don't let the Newts have arms and explosives, stop that hideous trade in Salamanders, well—you know what happened. They all had a thousand absolutely sound economical and political reasons why it's impossible. I'm not a politician or an economist; I can't change their opinions, can I? What is one to do? The earth will probably sink and drown; but at least it will be the result of generally acknowledged political and economic ideas, at least it will be accomplished with the help of the science, industry, and public opinion, with the application of all human ingenuity! No cosmic catastrophy, nothing but state, official, economic, and other causes. Nothing can be done to prevent it."

The inner voice was silent for a short time. "And aren't you sorry for mankind?"

"Wait, not so fast! The whole of mankind need not perish, need it? The Newts only want more shores on which to live and lay their eggs. Perhaps instead of continuous dry land they may make of it nothing but long spaghetti, so that there are as many banks as possible. Let us suppose that on those strips of land some people will manage to exist, eh? And they will make metals and other things for the Salamanders. The Newts cannot use fire alone, you know."

"Then men will work for the Newts."

"They will if you want to call it that. They will simply work in factories like they do now. They will only have different masters. In the very end perhaps there won't be even so much change."

"And aren't you sorry for mankind?"

"For God's sake, leave me alone! What am I to do? After all, men wanted it; they all wanted to have the Newts, trade, industry and engineering wanted them, the statesmen and the armies wanted them. Even young Povondra said that: we are all responsible for it. Please tell me how can I not be sorry for mankind! But I was most sorry when I saw how of its own will and at all costs it rushed to its ruin. At the sight of it you would shout. You would scream and throw up both your arms as if you saw a train run on to the wrong track. It's too late to stop it now. The Newts will go on multiplying, and more and more they will break down the old continents. Only remember how Wolf Meynert argued: that men must make space for the Newts; and only then will the Salamanders create a happy, united, and homogeneous world."

"Think of it, Wolf Meynert was an intellectual. Have you ever seen anything so dreadful, murderous, and nonsensical that an intellectual wouldn't want to save the world with it? Well, never mind! Do you know what Mařenka is doing now?"

"Mařenka? I imagine she's playing at Vyšehrad. You must be quiet, they told her, Grandfather is asleep. So she doesn't know what to do, and she's terribly bored."

"And what is she doing?"

"I don't know. Most probably she's trying to touch the tip of her nose with the tip of her tongue."

"So you see. And you'd let something like another Flood come?"

"But do stop! Can I work miracles? Let things happen as they may! Let them take their inevitable course! Even that is something like a consolation: that that happens fulfils its necessity and its law."

"Wouldn't it be possible to stop those Newts somehow?"

"It wouldn't. There are too many of them. You must make room for them."

"Wouldn't it be possible for them to die out somehow? Perhaps some disease or degeneration might develop among them."

"Too cheap, my dear fellow. Must Nature always be asked to straighten out the mess that man has made? And so, even you don't believe now that they could help themselves? So you see, you see; at the end you would again like to rely on someone or something to save you! I'll tell you something: *now* when a fifth of Europe is already covered with water, do you know who is still supplying the Newts with explosives, torpedoes, and drills? Do you know who it is that is feverishly working day and night in the laboratories to invent still more efficient machines and materials for annihilating the world? Do you know who lends them money, do you know who finances this End of the World, all this New Flood?"

"Yes, I do. All the factories. All the banks. All the different states."

"So you see. If only the Newts were fighting-men, then perhaps something might be done; but men against men—that, my friend, can't be stopped."

"Wait; men against men! I've got an idea. Perhaps in the end the Newts may fight the Newts."

"Newts fighting Newts? What do you mean?"

"For instance . . . when there are too many of those Salamanders they might fall out about some little strip of coast, or a bay, or something; then they would fight for bigger and bigger strips of coast; in the end they would have to fight for the world's coasts, wouldn't they? Newts fighting Newts! What do you think, wouldn't *that* be the logic of history?"

"Oh no, that won't do. The Newts can't fight other Newts. That would be contrary to nature. The Newts are all of one genus, aren't they?"

"Men are also only of one genus, my friend. And you see, they don't mind; one genus, and yet how much they fight! Now not even for a place to live in, but for power, for prestige, for influence, for glory, for markets, and do I know what else besides! Why couldn't the Salamanders also fight among themselves, say for prestige?"

343

"Why should they do that? Tell me what they would get out of it."

"Nothing but that for a time some of them would have more coast and more power than the rest. And after a time it would be the same as before."

"And why should some have more power than others? Aren't they all the same, aren't they all Newts? They all have the same structure, they are all equally ugly and all equally second rate. Why should they kill one another? I ask you, in the name of what would they want to fight among themselves?"

"Just leave them alone; something will turn up presently. See here, some are living in the west, and others in the east; they might want to fight for the sake of the west against the east. Here you have the European Salamanders, and down there are the African ones; it would be the devil if ultimately some didn't want to be better than the others! Well then, they will try to show it in the name of civilization, expansion, or I don't know of what: there will always be some spiritual or political reasons for which the Newts of one shore will have to cut the throats of Newts on the other. Salamanders are civilized in the same way that we are, my friend; they will not have any lack of arguments derived from power, economics, law, culture, or what not."

"And they have arms. Don't forget that they are splendidly equipped."

"Yes, they have plenty of arms. So you see. It would be something if they didn't learn from humans how history is made!"

344

"Wait, wait a moment!" The author sprang up and began to pace up and down his study. "Yes, true, it would be the devil if they didn't know! I can see it now. It's enough to look at the map of the world. My God, where is there a map of the world?"

"I see it."

"All right, then. Here you have the Atlantic Ocean with the Mediterranean and the North Sea. Here is Europe, and there America. Well now, here is the cradle of culture and modern civilization. Somewhere here is the submerged Atlantis."

"And now with the work of the Newts there is a new Atlantis."

"Just so. And here you've got the Pacific and the Indian Ocean. The old mysterious Orient, man. The cradle of mankind, as they say. Here, somewhere east of Africa, is the mythical submerged Lemuria. Here is Sumatra, and a bit to the west of it the little island of Tanah Masa. The cradle of the Newts."

"Yes. And there King Salamander reigns, the spiritual head of all the Newts. Here there are still alive the tapa-boys of Captain van Toch, the original Pacific half-wild Newts. Why *their* Orient, you know! The whole of that region is now called Lemuria; while that other region, the civilized, Europeanized, Americanized, modern, and technically mature, is Atlantis. There then as a dictator is Chief Salamander, the great conqueror, engineer and soldier, the Genghis Khan of the Newts, and the destroyer of the continents. A tremendous personality, my friend."

(". . . Listen, is he *really* a Newt?")

("... No. Chief Salamander is a man. His real name is Andreas Schultze, and during the World War he was a sergeant-major somewhere.")

("That's why!")

("Well, yes. So now you've got it.) Well, then. Here is Atlantis, and there Lemuria. For the division there are geographical reasons, administrative, cultural . . ."

". . . and national. Don't forget the national reasons. The Lemurian Salamanders speak pidgin English, while the Atlantis ones speak Basic English."

"All right, then. In course of time the Atlantians work their way through the one-time Suez Canal into the Indian Ocean."

"Naturally. The ancient way to the East."

"Very well. On the other hand the Lemurian Newts push round the Cape of Good Hope to the western shore of one-time Africa. They claim in fact that the *whole* of Africa belongs to Lemuria."

"Naturally."

"Their motto is Lemuria for the Lemurians. Out with the foreigners, and such-like things. Between the Atlantians and the Lemurians the chasm of distrust and eternal enmity deepens. Enmity of life and death."

"Or in other words they are becoming nations."

"Yes. The Atlantians despise the Lemurians, and call them dirty savages; the Lemurians in their turn have a fanatic hatred of the Atlantian Newts, and regard them as imperialists, Western devils, who degrade the old, pure, original Newtship. Chief Salamander puts forward claims to concessions on the Lemurian shores in the interests, so he says, of trade and civilization. The ancient, noble King Salamander, however loth, has to give in; he is simply not so well armed. In Tigris Bay, not far from what was once Baghdad, it snaps; the native Lemurians raid an Atlantian concession and kill two Atlantian officers, presumably for some racial offence. And then——"

"War breaks out. Of course."

"Yes, a war breaks out in which Newts fight Newts."

"In the name of culture and of justice."

"And in the name of True Newtship. In the name of national glory and greatness. The slogan is: Either them or us! The Lemurians, armed with Malayan krises and Yogi daggers, mercilessly slit the throats of the Atlantian intruders; in return the more advanced, Western Atlantians let off into the Lemurian seas chemical poisons and cultures of deadly bacteria, with such success that all the world oceans will be infected. The sea is infected with an artificial culture of gill pest. And that's the end, my friend. The Newts will die out."

"All of them?"

"Every single one. It will be an extinct genus. Afterwards all that will be left of them will be that old Oeningen print of *Andrias Scheuchzeri*."

"And what about the human beings?"

"Human beings? Oh yes, human beings. Well, they will slowly return from the mountains to the shores that are all that is left of the continents, but for a long time the ocean will stink with the decomposition of the Newts. The continents will slowly increase again through river deposits; inch by inch the sea will recede, and everything will be almost as it was before. A new myth about a world flood will arise which God sent for the sins of mankind. There will also be legends of submerged and mythical lands which were the cradle of human culture; perhaps there will be a fable about a land called England, or France, or Germany."

"And then?"

". . . Then I don't know what comes next."

European Classics

Honoré de Balzac
The Bureaucrats

Heinrich Böll
Absent without Leave
And Never Said a Word
And Where Were You, Adam?
The Bread of Those Early Years
End of a Mission
Irish Journal
Missing Persons and Other Essays
The Safety Net
A Soldier's Legacy
The Stories of Heinrich Böll
The Train Was on Time
What's to Become of the Boy?
Women in a River Landscape

Madeleine Bourdouxhe
La Femme de Gilles

Karel Čapek
Nine Fairy Tales
War with the Newts

Lydia Chukovskaya
Sofia Petrovna

Grazia Deledda
After the Divorce
Elias Portolu

Yury Dombrovsky
The Keeper of Antiquities

Aleksandr Druzhinin
Polinka Saks • The Story
of Aleksei Dmitrich

Venedikt Erofeev
Moscow to the End of the Line

Konstantin Fedin
Cities and Years

Fyodor Vasilievich Gladkov
Cement

I. Grekova
The Ship of Widows

Marek Hlasko
The Eighth Day of the Week

Bohumil Hrabal
Closely Watched Trains

Erich Kästner
Fabian: The Story of a Moralist

Valentine Kataev
Time, Forward!

Ignacy Krasicki
The Adventures of Mr. Nicholas Wisdom

Miroslav Krleza
The Return of Philip Latinowicz

Curzio Malaparte
Kaputt

Karin Michaëlis
The Dangerous Age

Andrey Platonov
The Foundation Pit

Bolesław Prus
The Sins of Childhood and Other Stories